# Unforgiven

## GRAEME SLY

 Book Publishing.com

Editing, design, typesetting and publishing by UK Book Publishing

www.ukbookpublishing.com

ISBN: 978-1-916572-92-8

# Unforgiven

# Chapter 1

## 20TH MARCH 1941 – THE BATTLE OF KEREN

Captain Angus MacMillan, leader of the Scottish Highland Second Light Infantry Division, slumped in a dusty bunker surveying the remnants of his command. He was an intimidating figure to encounter on the battlefield. The meagre army rations had depleted any excess weight, but powerful, broad shoulders and a chiselled torso remained. The muscles on his biceps and forearms bulged under his uniform; his trousers were tailored to accommodate his brawny thighs. His close-set, dark eyes were difficult to fathom, and a cultivated, thick-set beard hid his stubby chin. It was possibly his prodigious aura and a degree of common sense that deterred anyone from drawing comparisons between his facial features and that of the lowly pig.

As instructed by General William Prat the previous night, the Fifth Indian Infantry Battalion were to keep the Italians engaged and potentially push them back along the top of Mount Sanchil. A simultaneous attack would be led by MacMillan. His brigade would launch a dawn raid along Pinnacle Peak – a raised elevation on the floor of the gorge where the enemy had advanced and dug themselves in.

1

The element of surprise worked in their favour. They overran the occupied, entrenched opposition in less than thirty minutes. However, as daylight strengthened, the highlanders were exposed and vulnerable to attack from the Italian troops commanding the summits of Sanchil Peak. The initial engagement resulted in substantial casualties, and they were forced to withdraw.

The Italians turned their attention to the stranded and exposed Scottish troops below, who could neither advance nor retreat. For the remainder of the eternal day, the sniper above steadily picked them off. Had it not been for the Royal Air Force (RAF) flyby in the late afternoon, the entire company would have been lost. The string of eight British aircraft attacked the mountain top, allowing the few remaining survivors of MacMillan's unit to retreat to safety.

Unfazed by the destruction it illuminated along its path, the sun crept beyond the towering granite summits of Mount Sandchil – light began to fade. The oppressive heat abated. During the day, the sun's rays reflected off the jagged, rocky walls into the stricken gorge turning it into an inferno. There was little wind disturbing the valley, yet the air was thick with dust from the relentless aerial bombardment from the RAF planes intent on annihilation with their combined, successive deliveries. The pilots of the Vickers Wellington aircrafts had little time to survey and appreciate the unusual scenery; every nerve was tensed. They prepared for manoeuvres to evade the full barrage of high calibre, enemy anti-aircraft fire from units peppered along the adjacent peaks.

In addition to the overabundant casualties of war, the calamitous pounding virtually rid the area of all signs of vegetation and life. All that remained was a scattering of pinkish-grey baobab trees that haphazardly towered over everything. Sturdy, smooth trunks and branches stretched heavenward like beseeching arms: immovable sentries from another world pleading for the ruination to stop. For thousands of years, they forced their roots into the parched earth, soaking up what little moisture there was. During their stupendous growth, they had witnessed the rise and fall of civilisations. Their most recent exposure to man-made hostility appeared to leave them unscathed and unchanged.

Unabating Howitzer and Ordnance mortars complemented the aerial assault. Wave after wave of Allied Forces and Indian Infantry Divisions attacked and counter-attacked during the day in bloody conflicts losing the ground they initially gained, leaving the dead and wounded littering the scarred landscape. By occupying the high ground on the western slopes as well as the entire mountain ranges of Zeban and Falestoh to the east, the Italian opposition seemed to have an impenetrable defence. There was little evidence of the enemy showing any signs of attrition, yet what seemed like an unending wave of fresh reinforcements, eventually dried up.

Mussolini's troops were repelled from Italian Somaliland, Ethiopia, and Sudan. They were now fighting to retain control of Eritrea and the Red Sea. Despite their preceding defeats, the resistance in Keren dragged on for eight long weeks. By blowing up the Dongolaas Gorge and blocking the road and rail link to the city, they thwarted any hopes of enemy advancement, resulting in a daily Groundhog Day 'cat and mouse' scenario.

Although Captain MacMillan had advanced little through the ranks of command, he proved his worth as a leader of men. His inability to adhere to instruction without question was his downfall. Yet in the heat of battle and in the face of danger, he maintained the mental fortitude to be calm and focused. His men respected him. He was a man of few words and when he spoke, people listened. He reviewed his exhausted comrades and reflected on his devotion to balancing the scales of justice: the decisions that led him to this current position.

He was only eight years old when he had lost his entire family apart from his Uncle William. Everyone he ever loved was taken from him during the German Zeppelin air raid on 2nd April 1916 in Edinburgh – the last time the world was at war. What Angus remembered about that day was crouching in a doorway with his fingers in his ears, terrified. Uncle William sat beside him doing the same.

The family had gathered in the basement function room of the McAndrews Ale House to celebrate his father's birthday. Angus's mother, father and two older sisters were there along with his aunt, uncle and their three sons. While the rest of the family were enjoying the free-flowing local ale, he and his Uncle William left the pub to collect their food order from the new Munroe Butcher and Pie shop two streets away. Munroe's beef pies had been an instant success with the locals, and that night, the freshly baked delicacies were eagerly awaited by the family back at the pub.

As they reached the bakery, the first of the deployed bombs landed directly on the pub. The eight family members along with the landlord and his wife were instantly killed in the explosion as the three-storey building collapsed. There was no warning: the Zeppelin cruised silently above, releasing a steady trail of bombs snaking their way to the unsuspecting homes and buildings below. After the first explosion, detonations were repeated at regular intervals as the craft glided through the sky towards the centre of Edinburgh, leaving a wake of destruction, smoke, and ruin.

The bombardment seemed infinite. It was, however, over in less than forty minutes. Given the severity of the damage that was inflicted during the raid, it was surprising that the casualties only amounted to 26. It was little consolation to Angus given his personal loss. He never saw his family again. He recalled the emptiness inside his young chest as he viewed the row of coffins at the family funeral.

One of the things Angus recalled missing the most, was the simple home comfort of sitting in the metal bath in front of the fire, having his back scrubbed by his mother. His sisters would be nearby chatting while they darned or sewed. The injustice thrust upon him at such an early age became the motivation behind his desire to make a difference.

It was a tragic and difficult time for both Angus and his Uncle William. William ran a successful farm adjacent to the large sheep estate where Angus had grown up. Notwithstanding his own traumatic circumstances, William took on the role of raising his nephew as well as running both family estates. William was never outwardly emotional in front of Angus, but it was not uncommon to hear his uncle crying in his bedroom late into the night. For Angus, tears never flowed. Perhaps, if they had, they would have washed away his pain, isolation, and loneliness.

Angus would inherit the family land when he turned eighteen. As well as developing through his statutory education, Angus was taught how to care for the accounts, land, animals, and estate duties in preparation for his inheritance. He proved to be shrewd and proficient at balancing the ledgers. The mental challenges kept his mind from dwelling on the darkness of his senseless loss. Angus matured with speed and was justifiably proud of his growing physical strength: the result of his labour on both farms.

When the day came and the title deeds were signed over, Angus asked his uncle to remain in charge of the estate and to be paid an equal share of the net profits. His grief, carried with him for over a decade, changed. It morphed into a desire for retribution; a need to fight injustice.

At nineteen he joined the police force. But two years of dealing with petty crime and ridding the streets of the disorderly, left him unfulfilled. Driven by a desire to do more, he enlisted in the army. After completing his training, his attachment was sent to South Africa and during the final two years, he fought alongside Allied forces in the south and up into East Africa. He now found himself stationed in Eritrea.

He dismissed his reflections and shifted his attention back to the four remaining members of his unit, waiting for their next instruction. He drained the remaining swallow of water from his canteen and wiped the droplets from his beard with the back of his hand. Of his remaining troops, there were three Privates: MacDonald, Andrews and Walker, and his close friend, Lieutenant Robert Hunter. Robert and Angus had fought side-by-side ever since they were stationed in South Africa.

"That was a hell of a day, Bob," Angus finally said.

Robert nodded gravely but did not reply. He was plagued with macabre images burned into his memory. One, a terrified young soldier cowering behind a rock not large enough to provide adequate sanctuary. Robert watched the puff of dust from his tunic as the bullet had struck him in the centre of his chest.

Grotesque scenes of dead and dying comrades consumed him. He felt powerless as they resigned themselves to their fate. He shook his head and punched his fist down into his lap to prevent it from shaking.

"It was a bloody suicide mission! That bastard, Prat, might as well have shot those poor buggers himself. We almost lost the entire unit." He stared into the nothingness, voicing what all of them were thinking.

Angus empathised with his friend's anger but said, "That's war, my friend. None of it makes sense. The general was counting on the Indian Fifth Brigade to take the summit. They failed. We were sitting ducks. I will be having words with the pompous prick. We followed our orders…" The captain broke off as he, too, became overwhelmed by his recollections.

Angus lifted his chin. "There's something I want to run by you." He paused to gather his thoughts then continued, "Last night at the briefing with Prat, we received some new intel. According to the RAF, the dagos have moved a munition store outside the walls of the city into an old Mission about four clicks north-east of where we were this morning." He removed his blade from its sheath and began tracing the outline of the gorge in the sand at the base of the bunker.

Robert's brow furrowed. He was slightly confused. "The RAF? Can't they blow the thing up instead of just looking at it?"

"Unfortunately, it's not that simple for a couple of reasons. Firstly, to ensure an accurate hit, they would have to fly low into the gorge between the mountains. The anti-aircraft guns line the peaks either side and they will be easy pickings." Angus continued with his drawing in the sand. "Secondly, the entire Mission, including the roof, is apparently constructed from solid stone. Even a direct hit would have little impact. I've seen an aerial photo of it. Odd looking place – looks like a giant crucifix."

Robert tried to imagine the odd-shaped building – surely it could not be that inaccessible and impenetrable?

Angus went on, "Surveillance over the last 48 hours has confirmed much activity, and judging by the volume of what the Italians have been packing into it, it must have an extensive underground storage area. It's probably why they chose it in the first place." He wiped his blade along his trousers to remove the dirt. "It would be more effective to detonate from within. I want to blow it up. We did a good job of ousting the Italians this morning and that area is clear, for the moment – perfect time for a raiding party – but tonight is our only chance." Angus looked down at his completed sketch in the sand with the location of the cross-shaped building, and shoved his blade into it.

He paused, looked at his friend, smiled broadly and concluded, "Plus, Prat knows nothing about the idea. They plan another suicide mission tomorrow. In my opinion, if they were to launch a massive attack on it during the day, the Italians would simply divert their defence to ensure their valuable ammunition remains intact. It seems they have an endless supply of buggers waiting to take the place of the next man to fall."

Angus stood. He looked at each of his remaining men. "A stealth mission will attract less attention and will therefore have a greater chance of success. By sunup tomorrow, they would have already reoccupied Pinnacle Peak. That's how this back-and-forth shit storm has gone for the last eight weeks. Prat's intended attack has little-to-no chance of success." His unblinking eyes stared into the bland expanse of land surrounding them. "We owe it to our boys. Our losses today should count towards something more significant in this God-forsaken war."

Robert said nothing but contemplated the magnitude of what he had just heard.

Angus did not wait for a response from Lieutenant Hunter. He felt sure he could count on his friend's support. He turned to his men, raised his voice, and said, "Andrews! I want you three to supervise the collection of our fallen men. Return to the barracks and present this note to General Prat. I have requested sufficient re-enforcements to assist in retrieving the bodies commencing twenty hundred hours."

He held the note in his outstretched hand before continuing, "It's full moon tonight, so take care. You'll tell the general I'll be waiting for you at Pinnacle Peak." He lowered his voice. "The lieutenant and I will not be meeting you there because we are going to blow the hell out of the Italian munition store. Obviously, don't mention that bit to Prat!" Angus thrust the note into the soldier's hand.

"Sir! Yes, sir!" Andrews tucked the note into his pocket, retrieved his rifle and set off for the barracks with the other two in tow. There was no questioning of the order.

Robert shuffled uncomfortably with a mixture of emotions. Sabotaging the mission appealed to him but there were two major issues. "The shit will hit the fan if the collection of our men is not supervised by either of us. Whether we successfully blow the munition hold or not, if it's unsanctioned, Prat will have our guts for garters. You know what he's like. He's a stickler for discipline."

"I understand your reservations," Angus replied, "but we only have a narrow window of opportunity to deliver a killer blow. I need you with me on this one."

He shifted his focus back to the proposed clandestine operation. "Although there's steady activity during the day, filling and decanting their arsenal, surveillance has reported little activity at night. For the last two days, there have only been a couple of guards on duty with a change of shift around midnight. You and I can take them out, enter the Mission, set explosives on a timer and clear out before it goes off. What do you think?"

Robert was six foot six inches tall and, physically, the two of them could not look more different. Angus resembled a human equivalent of a brick privy: not overly tall, but solid and immovable. Robert, on the other hand, looked like he could be uprooted by a brisk breeze, especially after his recent involuntary weight loss from inadequate nourishment.

Despite his frame and apparent lack of muscle, though, Robert was surprisingly strong. Long legs supported his lean torso with a loping gate as he walked. Cropped blond hair provided a stark contrast against his skin darkened by exposure to the fierce African sun. A previous altercation on the field of battle had left his prominent nose slightly crooked, but it did not distract from his striking blue eyes and proud jaw.

He placed his hand on top of Angus's helmet as if placating a wayward child and said, "Angus, my friend, you know full well my dumb ass would follow you straight into hell if you asked me to, but if we are going to do it, it's got to be done right. We don't have a whole heap of time and there's a lot to organise."

Angus faced his friend and said, "That's why I need you, Bob. Look, if we fail to get our act together in time, we can drop the whole thing, but let's give it a go." He retrieved a notebook and pen from his breast pocket and began to outline his plan.

# Chapter 2

## BISRAT MISSION

For a fabrication that dated back to 1361, it was surprisingly well preserved. The Mission building, constructed from local granite harvested from the gorge, was rough but sturdy. Although exposed to the elements and manmade folly over hundreds of years, it remained unaffected and at peace. Its design reflected the spiritually significant number seven: symbolic of intuition, inner wisdom, and divine perfection.

If viewed from above, Bisrat was fashioned in the shape of a giant cross; the single-storey length stretched precisely one hundred metres long from north to south. It was seventy metres at its widest – east to west. Seven semi-circular concrete domes, each twenty metres in diameter, dominated the external roof in a symmetrical fashion; five running along the length of the stipes and one on either side completing the patibulum. Seven square equidistant windows were set into the thick walls along its length.

The north and south entrances were accessed through cedarwood double doors. Both were positioned below a circular window of the same width. Each set of doors was engraved with a lampstand bearing seven lit candles. To the east, a solid square tower crowned with a large brass bell stretched above the main building. Identical to the engravings on the doors, lampstands and candles were sculpted into each wall.

The brilliant, whitewashed walls of both structures basked in sunlight during the day. At night, they seemed to emit a radiated glow. Perhaps it was the contrast of the white walls against the dullness of the surrounding landscape that gave it the aura of a luminary.

Shortly before 6 pm, as Angus and Robert studiously planned the Mission's demise, another RAF attack was taking place along the shadowy peaks on the summit. With the sun now set and the moon in no hurry to take its place, the pilots wisely followed the directives and increased their altitude to avoid contact with the unlit mountain tops. The deployment of bombs was relatively ineffective at hitting targets with precision. It was, however, a clear message to the Italians of their relentless intent.

A few weeks earlier, the Vickers Wellington bomber had undergone radical engineering upgrades that escalated their payload from two and a half tonnes to four. It also enabled a solo pilot to fly the aircraft, deploy bombs and operate the landing gear from the cockpit. This was their first night raid utilising the enhanced aircraft with a solo occupant rather than the standard crew of six. However, the increased weight made the crafts slightly less responsive to the controls.

The last plane ignored the sanctuary of the high skies, broke formation and flew low through the centre of the gorge. Twenty-one-year-old Ronan Styles was an exceptionally talented pilot, with an ego to match. His commanding officer referred to him as that 'baby-faced pain in the ass' behind his back.

His boyish good looks made him seem significantly younger than he was, but there was no denying his talents in the cockpit. He always had to be first; always had to be the best. As frustrating as it was for his peers, he generally was. Although the youngest of the eight pilots, he would have led tonight's invasion, but his commanding officer had rescinded the privilege in view of Ronan's latest arrogant stunt: an unauthorised low fly-by of the control tower.

The plane was in complete darkness. The roar of its engine echoed off the cliffs as it sped in search of its target. Previously, he and his crew had successfully led twelve daylight raids along the crest of the mountain ranges, deploying bombs and destroying targets, but he had never flown this route. In poor light, it was utter madness.

Before take-off, the pilots of the Wellington bombers were given clear instruction to maintain an altitude of two thousand metres above their target and five hundred metres above the highest mountain peak. They were informed of the infantries' plans to attack and destroy the Bisrat Mission in the morning. Regardless of this, the zealous pilot now weaved his aircraft through the blackened valley in search of the Italian munition hold.

The Hotchkiss anti-aircraft defences along the ridge blindly released their thirteen-millimetre slugs at two hundred and fifty rounds per second into the dark skies above. The growl of the engines could be heard, and the destructive effects of the explosions could be seen, but the planes were invisible. They raced overhead untroubled. Even the deviant craft roaring through the gorge at low altitude went unnoticed.

Ronan, the fighter ace, had taken an imprudent risk in flying at such a low altitude in the gorge between the mountains. His bravado failed to counteract the fact that he felt very much alone and vulnerable. A wave of uneasiness swept over him as he viewed the speed with which the barely-lit, uneven ground raced to meet him. He contemplated increasing his elevation for his own survival but at that same moment, he caught a glimpse of the faint glow of the Mission rising out of the darkness. His target was in range. He steadied his resolve, maintained his position, and prepared to deploy the bombs.

The inky walls of the gorge narrowed towards the Mission, embracing it like the arms of the grim reaper. The young pilot failed to appreciate how quickly the bottleneck was closing in on his vast wingspan. Milliseconds before he swept over the crucifix structure, he deployed his destructive cargo. Distracted by the momentary jolt caused by the first detonation, he almost flew directly into a gigantic tree that stretched up out of the shadows. With his heart in his mouth, he banked left and heaved at the controls to gain altitude.

The outstretched branches brushed the belly of the craft. Instinctively looking down at his near escape, he sighted a soldier clinging awkwardly to the tree. His distraction was short-lived; the aircraft shuddered violently. Beads of sweat appeared at his temples. His knuckles turned white as he gripped the yoke.

The two Bristol Pegasus piston engines screamed as more than a thousand horsepower strained to force the reluctant, laden ship to alter its course. Only half of the payload had been deployed. The retained weight disabled his ascent. The left wing struck against the granite rockface at more than three hundred and fifty kilometres per hour. Like tissue paper it ripped off, leaving the unbalanced projectile cartwheeling towards the ground.

The severed cockpit sent the pilot and half a tonne of twisted metal twenty metres into the air. It descended in a perfect parabola and intercepted with a secondary detonation of explosives and fuel. The fireball could be seen from thirty kilometres away and the energy release from the impact created an earth tremor that could be felt by the armed forces on the valley floor. Fragments of debris and shrapnel slammed into the wall of the city and showered the nearby buildings and streets: the last foolish act of the young pilot.

Francesco Messe – code name 'Il Lepardo' (the leopard) – returned to the sanctuary of the Keren barracks in the city. His average build and Caucasian features were unremarkable. However, the steady gaze of his pale green eyes gave the impression he could see into your soul. His persona was identical to the creature after which he had been named: quiet, solitary, and deadly.

Already prized for his extensive list of kills dispatched with emotionless efficiency, today's achievements would elevate him to legendary status. Earlier in the day, in the baking confines of his rocky recess on the mountain, he had slaughtered twenty-eight members of Angus MacMillan's command. They were the enemy. He picked them off one by one: clean kills requiring only a single bullet for each. He was devoid of the human emotions of remorse, contempt, or fear. His coldness was immoral.

The only emotion he ever displayed was the affection he expelled on his bolt-action Carcano M91 sniper rifle with its four-power Ordnance Optic telescope. He treated it with the utmost respect.

It was religiously disassembled, and every component meticulously cleaned; the scope sighted to ensure its precision and accuracy.

Having passed the threshold of one hundred kills, today's achievements gave him no sense of fulfilment. He was the best at what he did. The exposed troops below were merely target practice, requiring slight adjustments for wind, altitude, and distance. Every shot was a triumph.

As he crept over the rough terrain in the dark, he became aware of the sound of an approaching aircraft. He felt untroubled. He was well versed in the result of bombs deployed incessantly whilst on the mountain sheltered in his stony caves. He was only a few minutes away from the city; travelling through the last shallow basin of the gorge. Harm was beyond him.

He stopped to assess his position. The silence of the gorge was ravaged with the uproar of aircraft engines. The sound echoed off the valley walls; a distinct amplification of the boom and roar of something travelling at high speed, becoming louder by the second.

For the first time in his life, he felt uncertain. Uncertainty turned to fear as his suspicions were confirmed: the approaching plane was intent on attack. He held his beloved rifle in his right hand and sprinted towards the city walls. The distance to the city gates was too great; he realised he would not make it. Ahead and to his left, he spotted a vast baobab tree looming out of the darkness. He changed direction towards it.

Francesco's most memorable kills involved considerable degrees of difficulty. When processing the complex calculations required to hit the intended targets, he was always in control. As he raced towards the odd-shaped tree, he was anything but. His fears were bolstered and confirmed as the bombs were deployed. The intense night sky was illuminated with each blast. The ground shook beneath his feet as the explosions raced towards him.

At the base of the tree, he tripped and went sprawling into the gravel: his helmet and rifle lost in the process. He blinked and looked up at the tree in disbelief. A large opening was visible in the trunk with a shrine in its recesses. Framed by flower petals and candles was a stone tablet with the image of a woman holding a new-born baby. A halo surrounded the woman's head as she lovingly gazed at the infant in her arms. Time to appreciate the bizarre spectacle did not exist. A religious aura prevented him from climbing in. It was the *Madonna of the Baobab*; a holy shrine respected and worshipped by local tribes for hundreds of years.

Unlike the typically smooth-skinned baobab, this tree was pitted and scarred with lacerations and holes, possibly from ancient attacks of less reverent foe. After retrieving his helmet and rifle he grappled with the gashes in the trunk to haul himself up. The aeroplane was almost upon him. He squeezed into a narrow gap between two large branches. The plane shot overhead, grazing the canopy of the tree. A bomb exploded. Intolerable light, suffocating pressure and unbearable heat bombarded his senses. His world was then engulfed in the deepest of darkness.

Robert Hunter succeeded in securing a handful of the items Angus listed. The British munition holds were running low: desperately in need of reinforcement from the delayed supply convoys heading up from the south. He managed to scavenge two kilograms of C4 and two detonators. Angus, on the other hand, obtained spare magazines and rounds for their Webley pistols and Enfield rifles and four phosphorus grenades.

The sun had set as Angus returned to the meeting point. He was pleased with himself but realised Robert was less so. Robert placed the explosive blocks and detonators at Angus's feet, shook his head and said, "Christ knows how we are holding the Diegos off. We're just about out of everything!"

The plastic explosives were in two identical brick-shaped rectangles covered in black greaseproof paper. The deadly putty emitted a slight bituminous odour, more from the binding adhesives than from the explosive elements of the compound it contained.

The aluminium pencil detonators were so named for their size and resemblance to the writing implement. When deployed, one end of the hollow tube containing the detonator was inserted into the plastic explosive. The other end housed a cupric chloride phial. Once crushed, the corrosive chloride activated the timer mechanism to release the spring-loaded detonation charge. The two devices were coloured orange and had the informative label 'TEN MINUTES' written in white lettering. That was the *estimated* fuse time before ignition. The temperamental manual mechanisms were affected by temperature and humidity. If initiated in hot and dry conditions, the device could go off in as little as eight minutes. A cool, damp atmosphere could extend the duration to as much as twelve minutes. The four-minute window of uncertainty was disconcerting to Angus, especially since there was no back-up plan or spare detonators – just one pencil detonator to each pack of C4.

His thoughts were interrupted by the sound of approaching aircraft. They both looked at each other and their watches simultaneously in disbelief. "That must be our RAF boys! They never attack this late!" Bob declared in surprise. The shock in his voice was clear.

The shapes of the planes were difficult to determine as they flew high above the mountain range. "Look!" Angus pointed to the air...

From the light of the first detonations, Angus had a fleeting glimpse of the last plane veering off, heading in their direction. Moments later, it surged overhead, flying low and swirling the dust around them.

They stood in silence, trying to blink away the dust. They relied on their ears to calculate what was coming next. The dwindling din was replaced by several rapid explosions emanating from the valley. A brief silence filled the air before a thunderous boom resounded off the cliffs, shaking the ground beneath them.

"Jesus! He must have done it!" Robert could barely contain his excitement. He was visibly relieved. Their night raid was no longer needed. Angus felt slightly deflated. He had mentally prepared himself for the task. He turned to his friend.

"Let's not break out the cigars just yet, Bob. If the mission has been blown, surveillance will send a runner with intel to confirm it. Until then, let's head to the canteen and see if we can rustle up some grub." He turned and walked away.

Robert remained still. He gazed in the direction of the explosion. "That was a hell of a bang though," Robert said confidently. With a breath of satisfaction, he caught up with Angus and headed back to base.

The camp consisted of two rows of equidistant, peak-shaped tents each providing accommodation for four inhabitants. Behind them, there were two larger tents, twenty-four metres square and of the same design, material, and colour. War council meetings generally took place in one of these two larger dwellings. This was the last meeting place before the failed dawn raid with Captain Angus MacMillan, General William Prat, and Brigadier Thomas Reas of the Fifth Indian Infantry Brigade in attendance.

Each canvas construction could be easily erected or disassembled in a hurry. The canteen looked identical to the other tents in the row except one side of the wall was tied back to reveal a handful of folding tables and chairs randomly placed.

To the rear, a seldom used single plate gas burner sat on a small, battered wooden supply crate. Cold rations were heartily devoured before returning to the field.

Angus and Robert were the only souls sitting at one of the tables. Their culinary delights consisted of a can of Bully Beef and a shared can of peach halves washed down with a dissolved Oxo cube in a tin mug of hot water. Regardless, they consumed it with relish after the energy-sapping day. They tipped their heads back to drain the dregs from their mugs. The tent flap was pulled back.

An anxious, red-faced soldier, gasping for breath, stumbled towards them. "I must speak with General Prat immediately!" he managed to wheeze, trying to regain composure.

Angus slammed his mug on the table. "What is it, Corporal? I am Captain MacMillan of the Scottish Light Infantry," Angus stated in a commanding, militant tone.

The corporal stood to attention and saluted. "Intel from surveillance on the Italian munition hold, sir. I was sent to find General Prat and report of the attack, sir." The soldier's breathing began to stabilise.

"Well?" Angus growled menacingly. "What happened? Spit it out, boy!"

The corporal appeared rattled by Angus's enormous physique and disgruntled manner. He hesitated a few moments in his predicament before responding, "It's about the plane, sir… One of our RAF planes. Sir… You see, he bombed the Mission but crashed, sir. Huge explosion! He's dead, sir!"

Angus stood and stepped forward. His eyes looked at the soldier with apprehension. "The large explosion we heard earlier… Was that the plane going down?" His confrontational manner no longer evident; he scratched his chin.

The corporal responded in a more resolute manner, "Yes, sir!"

Robert interjected, "And what about the Mission?"

The corporal's attention diverted to him. "Two direct hits on the munition hold before the crash. One bomb took out the church tower. The other hit the south entrance of the main building, sir. It took out the doors and window. Little damage to the rest of the building, sir." The soldier stopped talking, his tangible anguish at the leaked report was obvious.

Angus approached the young soldier and stood before him. "Very good, young man." He patted him on his shoulder, displaying his appreciation. He pointed to the other side of the tent. "You will find the General in the other large tent in that direction."

The young corporal saluted again, nodded his appreciation, and spun on his heels. His momentary discomfort gone. Angus approached Robert, looked him in the eye and said with a grin, "Well now, me ol' pal. It looks like we're still on then!"

Robert slumped back into his chair, let out a heavy sigh and a barely audible "oh shit".

# Chapter 3

## THE MISSION'S DEMISE

Before Angus MacMillan and Robert Hunter left the canteen, General William Prat entered. "Ah, MacMillan!" he said, purposefully avoiding the title *Captain* to elevate his own stature. "A word if you please."

Angus shot up from his chair: more an act of aggression than a sign of respect. Bob reached for Angus's forearm hoping to remind his friend that restraint would be wiser.

"General," he flatly replied. His raw nerves tightened at the sight of the man to blame for the extensive casualties his unit had suffered earlier that day.

"It was an unfortunate turn of events today; you lost your entire command or at least the lion's share." Prat delivered the statement matter-of-factly and stared at MacMillan with cold, unemotional eyes. It would not take a genius to work out MacMillan's disposition or the reasons for it.

Angus simmered. "Permission to speak freely, sir?"

Prat's mouth twitched. "No, MacMillan, you may not speak freely. It would seem from your demeanour that now would be the worst possible time for you to speak freely, if at all!" He composed himself and continued, "May I remind you, MacMillan, I am the General. YOU answer to ME! I am quite certain that if the Fifth Brigade had succeeded as planned, your division would still be with us." Spittle sprayed from his lips and his eyes narrowed. "We would all be sitting in here congratulating one another for the jolly good spanking we gave the Italians."

Prat straightened his jacket. "It is war, Captain! War! You will honour *your* losses and collect them with proper dignity and decorum. And the next time you consider sending a bloody messenger instead of standing before me in person, I shall make it my solemn bloody oath to have you posted to the most god-forsaken, rat-infested latrine I can find!"

Angus said nothing. He was simmering. He forced his clenched fists, which were ready to strike, behind him.

"Is that clear?!" The general bellowed at MacMillan again. His eyes bulged; veins protruded from his neck.

Angus eventually replied, "Yes, sir." It took all his resolve to not lash out.

Prat turned briskly and marched out of the canteen. Angus ran his hands through his hair. He let out a heavy sigh as he sunk down into his chair. Robert stood motionless. The disbelief of how close Angus had got to striking the general and ending his career, stunned him. He silently eased himself into his own chair. He looked over at his friend and saw his pain. Rob was tempted to say something light-hearted to placate the atmosphere. Angus's eyes confirmed it was too soon for humour. Instead, he said, "Come on, let's go get some air."

At eight o'clock, Captain MacMillan assembled his remaining troops and reinforcements. They prepared to move out. He was still seething inside after his run in with Prat. Lieutenant Robert Hunter knew his friend well enough to know what he was thinking.

Without mentioning the matter again, Angus packed the C4, detonators, ammunition, and the phosphorous grenades into his backpack. Robert knew his friend would not dismiss the attack on the mission. If anything, the earlier interaction would make him more determined to go through with it.

The weather had changed in the last hour. The warm and dry northerly wind had given way to a cooler westerly breeze. It brought with it wisps of cloud: silver streaks drifting inland across the moonlit sky. The cloud cover became more intense and began to diffuse the glow of the full moon on its sluggish ascent. Although it was unusual weather for the time of year, the lower temperature was a welcome respite from the stifling heat the troops were accustomed to. More importantly, the reduced visibility would make the retrieval of their less fortunate men less perilous.

It took them an hour to reach Pinnacle Peak – the site of the earlier bloodbath. The plan for retrieval involved four sets of stretcher bearers. One or two bodies would be carried each time back through the gorge into the safe zone. Once there, they would be ferried by jeep back to base camp.

As the first lot of bearers returned with their morbid loads, Angus watched with a heavy heart. He knew each of these soldiers by name. Seeing their lifeless remains being tossed about and hauled off, filled him with regret and sorrow.

He shook himself to shift the grip of his intense grief and beckoned Lieutenant Hunter. Robert crouched as he covered the short distance over the rocky rubble and sidled up to Angus, fully expecting what would happen next. "I'm going on up to the Mission to take a look. You stay here and supervise. Make sure everyone gets back safely. I don't want anyone left behind. I will rendezvous with you back at base." His tone changed as he continued, "If you run into Prat, give him a kick in the nuts from me." He then grinned at his friend. "If he wants to know where I am, tell him I'm finishing off a final recce of the area to make sure we haven't left anything."

Robert squatted next to Angus, resting his rifle on his lap. He sighed and turned to Angus. "You are a stubborn old ox, aren't you?" He shook his head and sighed again. "You know I can't let you go alone, right?"

Angus crouched alongside his friend. "It was selfish of me to ask you to get involved in the first place and I don't expect you to come with me. Let's be honest, you weren't exactly keen on the idea from the start. I bulldozed you into the whole thing." Angus stared at the ground. "Just buy me some time when you get back, that's all I ask."

Robert rose to his feet and hoisted his rifle on to his shoulder. "You asked me, Angus, because you knew it would be damn near impossible to do it on your own. I'm going with you. I suggest we stop jabbering like a pair of monkeys and get on with it." He patted his companion reassuringly on his back.

Angus wasted no further time. He hailed Private Andrews who stood to attention. Angus gave his orders: "Good work, soldier. See to it we get everyone back to barracks. Lieutenant Hunter and I will do a sweep of the area and meet you back at base."

Andrews saluted, looked at his superior and gave a knowing smile before returning to the work at hand.

They headed off in silence keeping to the far left of the uneven ground where the rugged landscape offered deeper shadows in the ravine basin. The further up the gorge they advanced, it became increasingly apparent to them that the towering rock on either side was drawing ever nearer. The basin floor narrowed too and became more inclined. The air carried with it intermittent wafts of burned wood, fuel, and rubber.

Angus stopped and sniffed the air. His eyes probed the dimly lit terrain for any signs of movement. "Look sharp, Bob. We're getting close. Move out!"

As they rounded the next rise, they caught their first glimpse of the holy Mission. It was still two hundred metres away, but they could see the faint outline. Tendrils of smoke drifting away on the breeze. Cautiously, they advanced for a closer look.

The mountains on either side ended with a series of undulations giving way to a flat, open savannah plain. With half the distance to go, they tucked themselves behind a granite boulder large enough to conceal them. Details of the building's architecture were now more distinct. The pale walls contrasted with the desolate wasteland in which it had been constructed. Its tower had been reduced to a mound of rubble. The wreckage of an aeroplane smouldered. Apart from that, the only noteworthy feature between the Mission building and the city walls some five hundred metres away, was the anomaly of a giant baobab tree.

This mighty feat of nature stood slightly west of the mission – inconsequential as far as their sabotage was concerned, but a remarkable tree. Most of its features were subdued by the diffused moonlight. But even from such a distance, its girth was remarkable. Angus estimated that fifteen men linking arms could not encompass its circumference. He shifted his gaze back to the target. They detected movement around the south entrance.

Bob concealed himself further behind their safehold. "It's teeming with soldiers," he whispered.

"Stay here, I'm going to take a closer look."

Angus left his rifle and backpack, crawled around the rock, and edged his way forward. He was still armed with his pistol and blade. Every so often, he paused to scan his surroundings. The rocky wall of the gorge was sufficiently lit to reveal a raised platform. Angus hauled himself up to the vantage point for a clearer view of the Mission.

It took him a while to realise what else was going on. Apart from the guards, there were another two civilians working on the cavity left by the destroyed doors. Both men wore the traditional white Arabic kandura robes and shemagh head coverings. Angus guessed they were local carpenters enlisted to carry out emergency repairs. He briefly observed the activity before retreating from his position.

Angus returned to Robert. "It's not *teeming with soldiers*, Bob," he said. "There are two locals sealing off the south entrance and two keeping watch. Nothing going on apart from that. If we take out the guards, I can't see the other two putting up much of a fight."

An hour earlier, the Mission's structure and contents had been carefully inspected by senior Italian officers. Having found their ammunition unaffected by the air raid and the structure to be sound, only two guards were left to patrol the entrance with orders for the doorway to be sealed. Access to their stockpile was unaffected. The Italians normally entered the building through the main north entrance facing the city. Naively, they did not anticipate further attempts of sabotage.

Angus and Robert prepared their attack whilst sheltering behind the granite rock. Bob sat close as Angus whispered the modus operandi: "I had hoped to leave several charges throughout the hold, but we don't have that luxury. We'll have to leave the C4 as one charge. We can't risk a misfire. These detonators can be a bit hit and miss and with changing weather conditions, they could still go off anytime between eight and twelve minutes. We can be in and out in less than five."

Angus peered around the rock then continued, "It is likely their stockpile will be in storage underground. I will need to set the charge down there. Hopefully, I'll find more crates of Italian explosives. Even if there aren't, we can still cause a lot of damage. It's unlikely that the cases of ammunition and mortars will explode but, if we can generate sufficient heat, everything in that building will be rendered useless."

He breathed in deeply. "The brass cartridges will melt or at least distort. The cordite, when it's hot enough, will let off gas and add to the blaze. You wouldn't find a single soldier, regardless of which side he's fighting for, prepared to use ammunition that had somehow survived an inferno. The C4 needs to be positioned below to cause maximum damage and we place the four grenades above the hold on the main floor. They are a cocktail of phosphorous and benzene. Once the casing is compromised by the blast, the phosphorous will ignite as soon as it is exposed to oxygen. In turn, the benzene will burn and produce immense heat."

Robert hissed his whisper: "I know how phosphorous grenades work, Angus. I want to know what your plan is for getting in and more importantly getting OUT!?"

Angus checked his Webley pistol to make sure it was fully loaded and returned it to its holster. "I'm going to cross over to the eastern side of the gorge. When I'm in position we advance together and take out the two guards simultaneously. Stealth mode – no gun shot to announce our presence." He unsheathed his knife and pretended to slit his own throat from one ear to the other.

"We leave our rifles here: pick them up on the way back. Check your pistol is loaded and you have sufficient ammo. Take your knife. The Webley is for emergency only."

He scrambled to his feet and crossed the gorge towards the eastern side. There were fewer shadows to shield his movements. Progress was painfully slow as he made his way back up to be level with Robert on the opposite side.

Bob had to marvel at the way Angus moved. Despite his enormous size, he was silent and only briefly visible between recesses. Angus felt his nerves tighten as he drew level with Robert. Now they had to advance in unison without the luxury of direct communication.

Angus carried the backpack containing the explosives and two grenades. Bob had the other two but, in his haste, he left them both on top of the boulder they had used for cover. There was no way he could go back for them now.

"Fuck it," he muttered under his breath.

The walls of the gorge petered out leaving them exposed with minimal shelter. The slope flattened out, opened, and extended towards the city. The guards briefly paused to stare out into the night in the direction of the British and Allied forces before turning and slowly walking back. As the two sentries passed the labourers, they checked their progress before continuing their repetitive patrol.

Over the last stretch Robert and Angus inched along the ground on their stomachs trying not to stir up dust. Eventually, Angus was within spitting distance of the apex of the guards' turn. He remained flat against the ground, sheltered only by sparce shrubbery. His senses focussed on the ever-approaching crunch of gravel under heavy boots.

As the guard drew level with him, there was a pause. Angus held his breath. His heart raced as the stillness drew out for an eternity. He expected to hear a shout of alarm, or worse: have a bayonet thrust into his back. Nothing happened. He heard the unmistakable sound of a match being struck. As he raised his head, his target was facing the Mission with his rifle casually slung over his shoulder. He cupped his hand around the match to shield it from the wind, as he lit a cigarette.

Angus pounced with his drawn knife. The eight-inch blade drove into the soft flesh below the jawbone of the soldier, severing the carotid artery and forcing him off his feet. The cutting edge forged its way into the base of the brain. Angus twisted the handle sharply, killing him instantly.

The sound of the two bodies thumping into the earth alerted the two workers. They rose to their feet, wide-eyed and jabbering in alarm. The second guard turned, raised his rifle, and ran in the direction of the commotion. Robert wasted no time in getting to his feet. His long strides in time with the guards' steps quickly reeled in his quarry. His left hand covered the soldier's mouth while the blade in the right slit his throat. Blood and wind gurgled out of the gaping wound as the soldier twitched involuntarily and sank face down in the dirt.

Having neutralised their targets, Angus retrieved his backpack. He advanced with intent towards the entrance of the Mission where the terrified labourers were huddled together. Robert held his bloodied knife level in his right hand and gave a dismissive gesture to the workers with his left. A translator was unnecessary. The workers glanced at each other, shuffled a few steps sideways then turned and fled back towards the city.

Angus applauded, "Nice work."

He scaled the upper opening of the door cavity not yet sealed by the interrupted repairs. He shone his torch into the spacious sacred room. If there had once been any holy relics governing the interior, they were long gone. There were two dark sycamore crosses built into the walls large enough to crucify a fully grown man. They matched the solid floor. No pews, altar or pulpit adorned the space. Instead, packed rows of wooden boxes furnished the interior. Amongst them were half a dozen crates too large to fit through the basement entrance.

Angus used his blade to open one to check the contents. Inside there were four smaller wooden boxes labelled *Lanciafiamme Spalleggiato Modello* 35 symmetrically packed and surrounded by a raffia-like packing material. The writing meant nothing to him but when he opened one of the internal containers he stopped and stared in awe. An impish grin spread across his face. Each carton contained a flame thrower complete with two full twelve-litre tanks of flammable liquid and compressed propellant gas.

Excitement quickened his pulse as he realised that another six crates contained the same load. *No need to worry about a better location for the C4*, he thought as he placed the plastic explosives at the base of the crates. He removed his pliers from his belt and crimped the tails of the pencil detonators to activate them: hopefully to detonate in a predictable ten-minute window!

He checked his watch, removed the two phosphorous grenades, and placed them on top of the same crate before running back to the south entrance to retrieve Robert's grenades.

"We hit the jackpot, Bob," Angus whispered as he stuck his head out of the entrance. "Crates of bloody flame throwers: dozens of them! Tanks full of pressurised gas and fuel. Ka-fuckin'-boom! Hand me your grenades. I've set the detonators." He stretched his hands out towards Robert in expectation.

Pistol drawn, Robert had been keeping watch over the gorge and surrounding area. He lowered his head and shifted uncomfortably as he turned to face Angus. He was unable to look him in the eye.

"Sorry, mate… I left them back in the gorge." His words sounded pathetic, and he prepared himself for a deserved reprimand. Angus simply looked at him, shook his head and disappeared back into the hold.

Angus shone his torch through the hatch which exposed a large room slightly smaller than the one above. A set of ancient steps led to the lower munitions hold. The air became thicker the further he went down: heavily scented with raw timber, plastic, and some sort of fuel.

He inspected the wooden beams above and noticed the once pristine sycamore was riddled with a mass of tiny holes. Over the centuries, borers had feasted. The weakened ceiling was unlikely to withstand the primary explosion or the mayhem to follow. He grunted with satisfaction before returning to the ground floor.

Francesco *il lepardo* lay draped over a branch in the tree like a lazy cat. He gradually awoke to a world of pain and confusion. His arms and legs dangled motionlessly as he struggled to fill his lungs with air. Everything hurt. His head was twisted to one side, and he barely had the strength to lift it. Staring down at his smouldering right arm in confusion, he blinked to clear his vision.

Blood dripped at regular intervals from raw flesh. He raised his right hand but only his thumb and trigger finger remained. The sleeve of his grigio verde tunic was smoking. Somehow, he hauled himself up to straddle the branch fighting waves of vertigo and nausea. Both eardrums were perforated from the explosion. Blood trickled down his neck and drenched his collar.

High-pitched ringing coupled with a hollow rushing sound filled his head. Over and over, he looked in disbelief from one hand to the other, palm up, palm down. His left hand was unharmed. Each wave of pain was accompanied by dizziness. Involuntary bowel convulsions expelled acidic bile. Movement sapped his strength. He rested his head against the branch, closed his eyes and breathed deeply.

When the nausea passed, he returned to an upright position. He clicked the fingers of his left hand next to both ears but heard nothing. He tried to speak but his voice was inaudible – just the hollow rush of air and incessant whistling. He swayed, trying to remember who he was, where he was and why he was in such dreadful pain. *Why am I in a tree?* He was unable to string logical thoughts together.

Shaking his head did not help. In fact, it made him want to vomit again. He flexed each leg in turn – both seemed to be working. When he steadied himself and looked down at his right leg, though, the fabric of his breeches had been blown off. It hung in tatters, revealing scorched flesh. At that instant the pain from his burned leg hit him with full force. He cried out in unmitigated agony. Severe cramps caused him to puke again.

He looked down further to the base of the tree. A large bowl-shaped crater from the bomb smoked innocently. A movement in his peripheral vision caught his attention. Slowly, he turned his head. A rifle was swinging casually in the slight breeze. Its strap had hooked over a small branch just below him. He squinted, trying to make sense of the spectacle. It was like being in a dream, except the pain was all too real.

He recognised the rifle as his own. He stared at it in the dim moonlight and began to regain his memory. Looking away from the weapon, he took in his surroundings beyond the realms of the tree.

Behind him were the walls of the city. He recalled hurtling towards it. *There was a plane*, he thought. *I climbed the tree to escape the plane…* Looking heavenward, he saw nothing in the dull clouds. He noticed a smouldering wreck close to the city perimeter but had no idea what it was. He looked ahead of him at the Mission building. It too was smoking slightly but remained intact.

With his outstretched hand he reached for the rifle. He cried out in pain then relief, as he retrieved it. Cradling it, he turned his prized possession over and over.

Ironically, the weapon that had ended the lives of so many, brought his memory back to life. Flashbacks from the day invaded his mind – the images of soldiers through the crosshairs of his scope as he pulled the trigger. He remembered his name, his job and his purpose. *I am Francesco Messe. I am a sniper...*

He closed each eye in turn to make sure both functioned as they should. They did. He inspected his right hand again and tried flexing his trigger finger – that too, worked.

Francesco's obvious challenge was how to get out of the tree. The distance to the ground was too high for him to jump. Besides, he was in too much pain to move. His mind wrestled with his predicament. He had to try and formulate some sort of escape...

Angus checked his watch. Three minutes had passed since setting the detonators. It was time to go... He left the confines of the building and clambered out into the fresher, cool air. Robert's short wait had felt substantially longer. He was blatantly restless and jumpy. Angus laid a conciliatory hand on his shoulder and said, "All set, mate. Let's get the fuck outta here."

They needed to distance themselves from the impending explosion. Running as cautiously as possible, they fled back down the gorge.

An Italian reconnoitre had discovered the two British rifles and grenades. They were discussing their find as Angus and Robert came into view. Robert's long strides had outpaced Angus, but as he saw the band of Italians he stopped. Angus kept on running...

One of the soldiers was holding a phosphorus grenade. He caught sight of the two approaching British soldiers and drew his hand back in preparation to throw it at them… Angus drew his pistol and fired.

The bullet struck the soldier's elbow before he could release the missile. The impact forced his hand downwards and the grenade exploded at his feet, engulfing him and his three comrades in a ball of fire and intense white light.

Francesco was still contemplating his dilemma when he saw the fireball erupt. Instinct took over and he lifted his rifle. He sighted two British enemies preparing to flee. He set his sights on the taller of the two and loaded his rifle using his left hand to pump the bolt action. He calculated the distance and windspeed as he had done countless times before. He aimed for the base of the soldier's helmet and fired. The bullet struck low and right in the upper thigh.

The rifle scope had been knocked out of sync. It was the only plausible reason – he never missed! He adjusted the correction screws to rectify elevation and side tracking. Despite the intense pain, he reloaded and fired at the second soldier who was crouched over the first. The bullet struck his target below the shoulder. It was not his finest shooting, but under the circumstances, a phenomenal achievement.

As the two British soldiers retrieved their rifles by the light of the burning bodies, Robert collapsed. A bullet tore through his right thigh. Neither of them heard the gunshot: only the thud as brass struck cloth with a puff of dust. He dropped like a ripe fig. Angus tried to drag him to cover: Robert used his good leg to help propel his body along the ground. They were both vulnerable out in the open. Angus was hit next. The impact of the bullet launched him forward; he landed heavily, face-down on the rough ground next to Bob.

Initially, the graze on his cheek and nose was the only pain Angus felt. The projectile had entered his back below the shoulder blade, deflected off a rib and emerged above the collar bone. When he moved his right arm, the shoulder rasped against damaged tissue. Exposed nerves sent a paralysing spasm down his arm. He closed his eyes, faced the sky and cried out in pain.

Robert managed to prop himself up against a rock. He looked down at his blood-soaked trouser leg in disbelief. Angus used his blade to cut away the material to reveal the damage. The bullet appeared to have missed the bone, but the exit wound was producing a pulsating discharge of blood.

"It's too painful to move," Robert whispered through gritted teeth.

Angus knew Bob would bleed to death if the flow was not abated. He removed his belt and wrapped it above the injury and tightened it amid cries of pain. The oozing discharge slowed to a light trickle.

Angus used the cloth remnants as a pad for his own injury. He placed the wad under his tunic to soak up his own blood. He hooked his good arm around Robert's waist and lifted him to his feet. Gingerly, he slung his rifle over his injured shoulder. They attempted to move… Each step was excruciating, and progress was painfully slow.

Angus's thoughts turned back to the explosives he had set. He glanced at his watch. Nine minutes had passed. As he opened his mouth to speak, the C4 detonated.

The energy released from the initial blast was contained within the sturdy Mission structure. However, the consecutive explosions that followed, reduced the Mission to rubble. Surging shock waves propelled debris and shrapnel down the gorge. The force propelled Angus and Robert through the air before dumping them painfully in the dirt.

The impetus carried across to the large baobab, solving Francesco's dilemma of how to get down. He had no time to brace. The blast catapulted him headfirst from his safehold, snapping his neck on impact. He was killed instantly. The tree suffered further abrasions but remained stoic and unmoveable, as did the holy Madonna shrine within.

The two British soldiers lay motionless under a thick coating of dust. Angus stirred and pushed himself up. He placed a hand on his companion who groaned in response. They both coughed copiously, ridding their mouth and lungs of dust as they struggled to their feet.

Agony engulfed Angus. He was losing far too much blood. Its warmth soaked his back and chest, clinging to his tunic and seeped into his trousers. A shard of metal shrapnel from the blast had lodged itself in his lower back above his hip. He left it there.

Its removal would result in further blood loss. Their only hope was to make it back to the safe zone. Bob's make-shift ligature was working and he had no further injuries from the blast.

Angus contemplated his options. It would be quicker to make it back to safety on his own, but he could not leave his friend. His only option was to carry Bob the rest of the way.

Amid cries of protest and pain, Angus struggled to his feet, stooped and slung his gangly friend over his left shoulder. He quickened his actions. The extra exertion increased his blood pressure. His blood loss did the same...

They ditched their rifles and helmets. Robert's head lolled from side to side against his friend's back. They managed to pass Pinnacle Peak and advanced a further five hundred metres before Angus felt lightheaded. His legs became heavy and burned like fire. His burden doubled in weight, forcing them both to the floor.

They sat back-to-back trying to summon the resolve and strength to continue. Angus reached for Robert's arm, patting it reassuringly. "Well, we did it, Bob."

"We sure did. Thanks for carrying me. There is no way I could return the favour with your fat arse."

Angus laughed but the raking pain was so intense, he stopped instantly and sat very still. In the silence that followed, his thoughts turned to his wife Molly. He touched his left breast pocket that contained the brief letter she had given him before he left for Africa. He did not have the strength to remove it. He did not need to – the message was etched in his heart and his mind: 'Keep your head down, your feet dry and come home. I love you – Molly.'

His throat tightened. His eyes filled with tears as a multitude of memories flashed before him: each one vivid. Angus never cried. Even the loss of his entire family at the age of eight, the birth of his daughter or any other emotionally significant event in his life did not result in tears. The sensation was a little frightening. Subconsciously, he knew he was going to die. He sighed, closed his eyes, and indulged in his most precious of memories. He smiled to himself with a nod before reliving the next. With some, he allowed the details to linger: to be fully explored and relived...

The first time he met Elspeth MacGregor – his Molly. It was his last day on the beat as a police officer in Edinburgh. On patrol at midday on the outskirts of the city, he heard a scream. "Stop him! He's stolen my bag!" a clear, sharp message released from a healthy pair of female lungs from somewhere around the corner.

Angus heard the approaching steps of someone clearly in a hurry. They were about to turn the corner in front of him. He stretched out his arm with a clenched fist and braced for imminent contact. The young fifteen-year-old scamp, clutching the bag under his arm, shot round the corner straight into the outstretched barricade.

The thief's head collided with the brawny bicep halting his advancement. His galloping legs lifted his scrawny frame into the air. He fell to the ground in an ungainly tangle, unconscious. Angus retrieved the scattered contents of the bag which included some coins of little value, a silk handkerchief, and a glass bottle of perfume.

He removed the cap and sniffed the rose and lavender scent. As he replaced the cap, a short, outraged, young lady with rosy cheeks and a shock of auburn hair appeared. She was holding her skirt knee high as she turned the corner and ran straight into Angus's arms. He enfolded her to prevent them both from sprawling onto the pavement.

She recognised the uniform of her saviour, and for a breathless heartbeat, buried her face in his chest. She breathed in the scent of musk and sandalwood before breaking herself away to gather her dignity. She placed her hands on her hips and took large gulps of air into her burning lungs. After blowing an unruly strand of hair off her face, she kicked the little thief in the ribs.

Before the impromptu embrace ended, Angus smelt the fragrance from the bottle on the girl's neck. It smelt finer on her skin. Elspeth thrust out her tiny hand, grasped his and shook it vigorously with surprising strength. The adrenaline was clearly pumping through her feisty veins. "Thank you, officer! Thank you so terribly much! I would never have caught that little bastard if it wasn't for you."

"Just doing my duty, Miss. Glad to be of service." He responded professionally but pondered her strong Glaswegian accent. It made her pretty little mouth produce words that sounded more like a growl than coherent speech! Regardless, in that moment, she was beautiful to him and perfect in every way.

Elspeth retrieved her bag and the contents. Angus watched her every move, intrigued. He recalled that there was nothing of monetary value in the bag. For her, the principle of theft of her belongings outweighed the value of the property itself.

She took a step backwards and introduced herself as Elspeth MacGregor with a twinkle in her eye. Angus looked at her directly, cleared his throat and responded, "Angus MacMillan."

He recalled thinking what an awful name to give a beautiful girl. *Elspeth* made him think of a middle-aged aunty with bad breath and a mole on her chin.

A painful cough shot through his chest like a dagger and brought him back to reality. He turned his head towards Robert. "I'm feeling a bit worse for wear, my friend..." Robert grunted sleepily but did not reply. Angus allowed himself the indulgence of slipping back into the warm embrace of his memories.

Elspeth had only been in Edinburgh a week before her encounter with Angus. With her father's blessing, she had exercised her independence by moving away from Glasgow. She had worked at her father's tailor shop. The family business would be handed down to her older brother Michael, so she decided to choose a different path. She longed for adventure... Her father secured a two-bedroomed flat for her in the city. It was Elspeth's first day at work when her bag was snatched.

At her interview, her bright eyes, buxom stature and larger than life aura agreed with the owner of the Munroe Butcher and Pie Shop. She was employed immediately as the *sole front of house coordinator* – that's how she proudly described her role.

It was the same pie shop that Angus and his Uncle William had visited on the day of the bombing. The day he lost his family. He had avoided it ever since, and in fact, never ate pies of any description, but the redhead with obvious fire in her soul moved him deeply in a way he could not explain. He had to see her again.

Before Elspeth returned to her place of employment, she repeated, "Thank you again, sir. I'm late for work. It's my first day actually, but if you're ever hungry, pop in for a visit. I'll rustle up some grub for ya." Her face was a picture when she smiled.

Angus hated the pie shop. Painted in its black and red, it looked more like a barber shop than a bakery. The colours made him think of death. More to the point, the death of his family.

It took all his resolve to go there the next day. After handing in his police uniform, he was a week away from starting his training as a combatant. He chose to don his best attire: pressed black trousers, white shirt, and double-breasted black jacket. He looked confident but it was an outward mask for the demons he wrestled within.

As he approached the threshold of the bakery, the blood drained from his face, and he collapsed onto the hard floor. As he regained consciousness, his head was cradled in Elspeth's lap. The familiar scent of rose and lavender soothed his mind as she gently rocked him. He was now fully conscious and aware of her stroking his cheek. Elspeth hummed a gentle tune. He remained inert, absorbing the smell of her perfume and the sound of her voice.

He met Elspeth later after she had finished work at a respectable distance from the pie shop. Their first date was an evening walk around Edinburgh Castle. She teased him about fainting and claimed that it was her magnificent smile that caused it. He teased her about her name and told her he would call her *Molly* instead.

Angus opened his eyes and scanned the now tranquil gorge. The mountain tops were silhouetted against the grey, slow-moving cloud. Shivers twitched his spent body as the urge to sleep weighed heavily upon him. He shook his head, contemplating the future he had planned for himself and his family…

On their last reprieve from their duties on the front line, Angus and Robert had travelled to Southern Rhodesia to view farmland that had come up for auction. They were both so taken with the opportunity, they invested in adjacent properties with the view to relocating their families at the end of the war. It all seemed pointless now...

Once powerful, broad shoulders sagged uncontrollably, completely sapped of strength. Bone-weary limbs anchored him down – standing no longer an option. He closed his eyes and allowed the Stygian darkness to enfold him and succumbed to the inevitable, final peace.

# Chapter 4

## 22 SEPTEMBER 1941 – PRETORIA, SOUTH AFRICA

Purposeful footsteps approached with the occasional clatter of plates on a wheeled trolley rousing Robert Hunter from his fitful slumber. The crisp morning air had the familiar undertones of fresh paint and antiseptic. He kept his eyes closed a few moments longer recollecting from memory the layout of the room – twelve recovery beds and their occupants laid out in the new military wing of the South African Pretoria Hospital. The main building was constructed nine years ago but the volume of wounded it now processed demanded rapid and extensive expansion.

Six months had dragged by with varying degrees of suffering and three consecutive surgeries to repair the bullet wound in his right leg. He had no recollection of the initial, botched surgery. It was hastily performed under war zone conditions in Keren, but it was successful enough to retain enough blood to keep him alive. He was flown to South Africa and transported to his current location for further treatment. He remembered nothing of the journey. An emergency trip to theatre on arrival saved his leg from amputation. Infected tissue and fragments of rotten cloth were removed, allowing the damaged flesh vessels and tendons to heal.

Internal bleeding from an offshoot of the femoral artery warranted another invasion. The third and final incisions were to remove a fragment of bone revealed by post-operative X-rays. Pain had receded from its original torturous self to a less gruesome series of aches, twinges, and irritation. On the bright side, he had kept his leg!

He guessed by the arrival of the heavier than average footsteps, that nurse Malaika was on duty this morning. He blinked as his eyes adjusted to the brilliant white walls of the ward. The bleached expanse of a tightly fitting uniform struggling to contain the nurse's fuller figure filled his view. She was the friendliest and caring out of all the staff with an abundance of energy and warmth.

As she approached, an abstract thought occurred to Robert. It was generally Malaika that gave him a bed bath. She performed the act of kindness with such tenderness. It seemed to take longer in delivery than the same service performed on any other patient. He smiled inwardly. Perhaps he was just imagining it.

Malaika's eyes focused on his. "I've got you an extra helping of oatmeal porridge this morning, lovie. Make sure you eat it up, see?" she instructed with a thick Afrikaans accent. Her wide smile enhanced her plump cheeks and bright eyes.

With a groan, he pulled himself up into a sitting position and the attentive angel fluffed his pillows. Two fellow bed-ridden occupants were already sitting up. They looked at Robert and then each other. Knowing smiles and gestures of smooching an invisible lover were performed as Malaika tended her patient. She saw Robert's line of sight, turned, and quelled the teasing duo with a quick, uncharacteristic scowl, reducing them to chastised children.

Her focus returned to her charge. "Doctor says a walk outside for up to an hour today, see? The fresh air will do you good but take it nice and slow and don't overdo it. You don't want me to be cross with you now, do you, lovie?"

Robert nodded. "Thank you, nurse. I will be sure to carry out your orders and the doctor's too."

She beamed again and completed her rounds. Her smile remained but she did not linger at any other bedside quite so long. Finally, she exited with her trolley relieved of its wares. She disappeared along the corridor, humming a tune.

"That chick wants to ride you like a steam train, Englishman. Woo hoo! Oh Robert! Take me, Robert!" Henrick delivered his words theatrically. He spoke with a guttural Afrikaans accent complete with rolling 'r's. He mimicked the motion of a cowboy on horseback negotiating rough terrain, waving an imaginary hat above his head.

Henrick was an enormous South African-born soldier. His head was predominately covered in bandages. He had lost his left eye and was recovering from third degree burns to his face and chest. He never complained of his pain; he deflected it through an endless torrent of insults, jokes, and verbal abuse to those around him. Words exited his mouth before his thoughts processed them. More often than not, he spouted nonsense, resorting to barrels of laughter when corrected or challenged, regardless of his obvious physical discomfort.

"A steam train does not ride you, you pillock! You ride it!" came the correction from the double amputee, Edward. He spoke using the Queen's English. Having lost both legs on the battlefield, he was left somewhere between denial, despair, and action; his absent limbs left him with the ongoing existence of phantom pain.

Today, however, he seemed to be on form. "Anyway, Bob could barely spread his buggered leg to ride a sixpence, let alone straddle the steamy expanse of our dear voluptuous nursie."

All three laughed and their attention turned to their breakfast. Robert always looked forward to the morning banter. He spooned a generous portion of porridge into his mouth. His mind searched for a joke involving an Englishman, a Scotsman, and a South African walking into a pub, but none came to mind.

The interaction helped steer his mind away from the horrors that kept him awake at night and the thoughts that darkened his days. Often, he would wake screaming incoherently in a pool of sweat, only to find escape after sedation. His two new friends never joked about his nocturnal episodes nor questioned him about their origin. They faced their own night terrors and unsettled sleep. Their light-hearted conversation was a respected tonic to them all. An unspoken code between them kept it that way.

After shaving, Robert wrapped his dressing gown over his hospital-issue pyjamas, put on his slippers and picked up his recently acquired walking cane. It had an arched handle shaped from the same piece of wood as its body.

"Someone's in a hurry! Off to give Malaika a seeing to?" Henrick smirked. He never missed an opportunity.

Robert straightened his gown, turned to Henrick, and tartly replied, "No. Actually your mother asked me to meet her in the car park." He grinned and winked at Edward.

"Shit, you must be desperate. She has a beard and hairy legs." Henrick wheezed, slapping his thigh. Again, laughter from the three of them. The other nine bed-ridden souls were either asleep or lost in their own thoughts, unresponsive to the early morning interaction.

The military wing was on the third floor. Robert rode the lift to the ground level. As the door opened, he was met with the sweet pungent scent of fresh blossom. It hung in the air despite the aroma of wax and paraffin from the polished concrete floor. He walked past reception with its empty waiting area, through the large double-doored entrance and out into the crisp morning air.

It was his first time out of the hospital in six months. The scenery gave him an exhilarating sense of freedom. Passers-by seemed oblivious to the beauty. They were absorbed in their own thoughts; walking purposefully to reach their destinations. Before him, an immaculately manicured lawn was split by a contrasting pathway that accentuated the green of the freshly mowed grass.

The promenade met with a generous sidewalk which framed a wide road lined with multi-national cars waiting for their owners. But, the most spectacular feature were the giant jacaranda trees with their abundant flowers in full bloom. They were planted at regular intervals on either side of the long street. Raising his eyes heavenward, he saw an unblemished, iridescent blue sky. He closed his eyes, breathing in the sweet perfume. It was the most alive he had felt for a considerable time. His moment of tranquillity ended abruptly.

"Lieutenant Hunter!"

Robert's eyes shot open. He had not been addressed with that title for many months. The voice was far too familiar and filled him with a sense of dread. He reluctantly lowered his gaze to turn and face the senior officer whom he had not seen since the night they sabotaged the Mission. The night Angus lost his life.

During his recovery, Robert had followed the news religiously. He discovered that after the destruction of the munition hold, a British patrol had found Angus and himself sitting back-to-back in the gorge. They were just a kilometre away from base camp. Robbed of artillery and weapons, the Italians were defenceless to counter the pressing attacks of the British and Allied forces and they were finally driven out of Keren. On the seventh of April, they surrendered at Masawa on the Red Sea and just under ten thousand enemy soldiers were taken prisoner. During the months that followed, Lieutenant Hunter heard nothing relating to the military's decision on their unauthorised sabotage led by Captain Angus MacMillan.

General William Prat now stood before Robert Hunter wearing his flawless officer's uniform. His face displayed his trademark stern expression, and he held a brown dossier under his arm. Robert saluted the general, leaning heavily on his walking stick. No salute was offered in return. The general retrieved the file from under his arm and aggressively presented Robert with a set of documents. He spoke curtly at a volume louder than necessary.

"Medical discharge papers. Count yourself bloody lucky, Lieutenant. Your release means you will still be entitled to your war pension." He stopped abruptly and narrowed his eyes. "If it had been up to me alone, I would have seen to it that you and that bloody buffoon MacMillan were stripped of your ranks and in receipt of a Dishonourable Discharge!" His left eye twitched spontaneously. "As it happens, the powers-that-be have chosen to overlook your insubordination. It is my sincere hope this is the last time I have the misfortune of being in your company. Soldiers that have no respect for authority are a cancer I can do without in my ranks!"

Without any further interaction, he about-turned and strutted back to his military escort vehicle. Robert felt weak and light-headed. He limped over to a nearby bench and collapsed onto it. His shaking hands cradled his head. His body convulsed uncontrollably with each sob that followed and tears ran in rivulets from his closed eyes. The loss of his closest friend still weighed heavily on him. They had become inseparable throughout the time they fought together.

He had written to Molly twice whilst in hospital but she did not reply. The first letter offered his deepest condolences for her loss and what a privilege it was to have served with her husband. A month later, he wrote with a greater sense of urgency regarding their purchased land in Southern Rhodesia. The last letter was sent more than two months ago. There was still no response from her.

After the death of Augus's Uncle William, he had inherited the farm. He was the only remaining heir and family member. Angus was heavily involved in various skirmishes in Southern Africa at the time and instructed his family solicitor to sell the property. During two weeks of respite, Angus and Robert travelled north from South Africa into Southern Rhodesia on the advice of a young pilot they had befriended. He was a graduate from the Southern Rhodesian Air Training Group: an initiative set up by the Empire Air Training Scheme. Its aim was to school British pilots in the art of aerial combat at various training locations throughout Southern Rhodesia.

The pilot spoke of the country with unreserved high regard: a land of unimaginable beauty and endless opportunity. He talked of wide open spaces, plains teeming with wild animals and a countryside of rich, untapped mineral wealth. Angus and Robert made the decision to see it for themselves.

During their two-week visit, both found themselves in awe. They invested in adjacent farmland in Insiza on the outskirts of Bulawayo. Angus used the funds from the sale of his Uncle William's estate to finance the purchase, and Robert halved his land in Scotland to release funds to do the same.

Their military duties meant that both farms had to be overseen by Robert's brother, Malcolm. Once the war ended and their military ties were severed, the plan was to relocate their families to Southern Rhodesia: a new chapter in their lives and a fresh start. Angus wrote to his wife to inform her of their plans for a new life and the opportunities that lay ahead.

He heard nothing from Molly. Robert had considerable resistance from his wife, too. It seemed preposterous to her to leave behind everything familiar and secure to take up a new life in a land they knew nothing about. Both Angus and Robert believed that when both their wives saw Southern Rhodesia with their own eyes, they would fall in love with the destination, just as they had done.

The two farms had become theirs respectively, nearly nine months ago. As arranged, Malcolm Hunter oversaw both properties on their behalf. However, they each needed full-time management. The unprecedented stay in hospital meant Robert was anxious to get back to Southern Rhodesia. His recovery had put everything on hold.

There were also issues with the bank. Following Angus's death, the MacMillan bank accounts in Southern Rhodesia had been frozen, pending legal documents that Molly MacMillan needed to sign and return. In the interim, and without Molly responding to his letters, Robert was covering the expenses for both farms out of his own pocket. He had no choice in the matter. He owed Angus his life. But it did not make his home life any easier.

With the outpouring of his pent-up grief finally vented, he regained his composure. He sat back on the bench feeling cathartic and focussed his mind to assess his situation constructively. The nagging worry or uncertainty had disappeared; he held his medical discharge papers.

The loss of his dear friend remained raw. Their exciting future with its farming venture had lost some of its sparkle but it was still a fantastic opportunity for him and his family. He just had to make them see it that way. He desperately needed to talk to Molly MacMillan...

# Chapter 5

## 23 SEPTEMBER 1941 — LOCHLUICHART MACMILLAN FARM— EDINBURGH, SCOTLAND

Light drizzle had fallen incessantly for the last seven days. By day, the pregnant grey sky barely seemed to move on the cool northerly breeze. It delivered persistent, soaking rain. By night, the thick cloud cover concealed the moon and stars, accentuating the darkness. Elspeth MacMillan felt the chill in the air. Perhaps it was a foretaste of the cold winter to follow, or maybe it simply reflected her exhaustion. She had spent yet another day labouring and tending to the needs of her farm in the absence of her late husband. She checked her watch. It was only 4:30 pm.

Elspeth had been prematurely widowed; left as a single parent to her eight-year-old daughter, Mary. These two labels had been thrust upon her at such a young age. Assessing her life was like seeing it through someone else's eyes: sad and dull. Responsibility weighed heavily on her shoulders. She struggled with so many elements of her existence. However, well-meaning concern from others regarding her welfare was always answered with, "I'm fine."

She sat slumped in her usual armchair, in front of the fire. She stared at the hypnotic embers: their occasional crackle and spit the only sound in the room. Her black feline companion, Sylvester, content after scrounging sufficient sustenance and affection, sprawled out in his pride of place: on the rug in front of the hearth. He had positioned himself close enough to the fire to absorb maximum heat, but far enough away to prevent combustion.

Whilst Angus was alive, she read newspapers daily to follow the progress of the war: scanning for an insight into how her husband was faring so far away from home in South Africa. Her mind tried to imagine him crouching in a trench or active on the battlefield. She took an unprecedented interest in political developments and why Italy had chosen to invade East Africa in the first place. To her, it seemed nothing more than an attempt to lift the spirits of the country out of the depression following the previous global war.

The League of Nations was a powerless institution, incapable of swerving the war. Even the imposed sanctions on Italy had little impact on the impending confrontation. Great Britain continued to supply the Italians with coal. Oil exports continued from France and the USA: two vital commodities that fuelled their invasions. It made no sense at all.

Since Angus's death and funeral, however, she had lost complete interest. During the last few days, her mood matched the weather: cold and bitter. Her evenings in front of the fire, previously a time for respite, were shorter and without reflection. She found herself retreating to bed earlier, longing for sleep to escape from her mental and emotional state. Little Mary knew her mother was struggling. She was never sent to bed this early. Elspeth had not even kissed her daughter goodnight. She reflected... that was not going to be a pattern. Earlier, Elspeth had snapped at Mary for hugging Sylvester too tight. That had been their last verbal interaction for the day.

Mary was her ray of sunshine and hope. When she went down for the night, Molly was reminded of how lonely she was. Angus had been away from them for most of their child's life. The knowledge that he would eventually come home gave her hope. It reduced her isolation to a shelved longing and allowed her to retain the thought that their separation was temporary.

She respected the reasons why her husband felt so strongly about fighting injustice. His entire family had been stolen from him when he was a mere child. Every time they were briefly united between training and his deployment, they were blissfully happy. The long-term future was bright. Being alone was a temporary hardship she was determined and content to endure.

Five months ago, nearly four weeks after Angus had died on the battlefield, a solemn military officer in uniform knocked on Elspeth's door to deliver the news. During the days that followed, Elspeth felt numb. She watched the world go by through someone else's eyes; unable to process the destruction of all their hopes, plans and dreams. There was little time to grieve because the farm demanded all her time and attention.

Then came the delivery of Angus's personal effects. Elspeth had to sign for his wedding ring, uniform, and a pair of his socks that she had darned. A government issue envelope contained the blood-stained note that she had written to him:

'Keep your head down, keep your feet dry and come home. I love you. Molly.'

In the last two years he had been away, she had barely heard from Angus. He had not even bothered to attend his Uncle William's funeral. Apparently, as she was led to believe by his solicitor Arthur Conway, Angus had instructed Uncle William's estate to be sold. Without warning, most of the funds were transferred to Southern Rhodesia for Angus to buy farmland. Had he lost his mind?

So, he was too busy to contact his own wife and daughter but had sufficient time on his hands to shop for land in Southern Rhodesia. He did not even have the bloody decency to contact her!

Now that Angus had died, the entire mess was left squarely in her lap. There were phone calls from the solicitor, demanding she urgently sign documents. There were two unopened letters from a Lieutenant Robert Hunter. Who was *he*? She had not been in any hurry to sign anything and had no interest in reading the letters. She stubbornly decided to let the world wait until she was ready.

Today, Annie, Elspeth's helper, gave her a garbled message about a telephone call from a Malcolm Hunter. She had employed Annie to watch over Mary whilst she was tending to the farm. Malcolm had left a contact telephone number for a remote post office in Umtali, Southern Rhodesia. *Who the hell was Malcom Hunter?*

Notwithstanding her fatigue, she sighed and decided to address the pile of letters that sat on the side table next to her. Starting with the oldest correspondence first, she opened the first letter received from Robert Hunter. It read:

Dear Mrs MacMillan

I am Lieutenant Robert Hunter of the Scottish Highland Second Light Infantry Division and I served with your husband, Captain Angus MacMillan. I want to convey to you my deepest sympathy for your loss. Although I have never had the privilege of meeting you, Angus and I became close friends over the years. He often spoke of his beloved 'Molly' with the greatest of affection.

Your husband was a good man, a good leader, and a good friend. He was passionate about fighting for what he believed in. Sadly, it was that passion that took him from us prematurely. I was with Angus the night he passed. It was Angus who carried me despite being mortally wounded. In fact, if it had not been for his strength, I too would not be here today.

Although I do not recall much of the detail regarding my transfer, I was flown to South Africa where I am currently situated. I have had several operations trying to repair a bullet wound to my leg and it has taken time for me to be able to write to you. I have been unsuccessful in my endeavours to reach you by telephone, which is why I am writing to you.

I hope to be able to speak with you if you will allow me to do so. I want to convey to you how terribly sorry I am for your loss. If there is anything I can do to assist you, in any capacity in the future, please do not hesitate to call on me.

Yours sincerely

Robert Hunter

Elspeth finished reading and dropped the letter and her hands into her lap. Tears were unknowingly flowing; her cheeks were wet from the steady flow. She sniffed loudly and Sylvester shot her a disapproving glance before settling back down in front of the fire.

She thought about the content of the letter. Robert Hunter wrote eloquently enough but under the circumstances had probably penned what anyone else would do in that situation. Angus had confided in him about *his Molly*, had he? She was touched but reverted to her original thought: *well, he bloody well could have called or written!*

She picked up the second letter from the lieutenant.

Dear Mrs MacMillan

I do hope this letter finds you well. Once again, I am sorry for the loss of your husband. I hope my first letter reached you. I have tried contacting you by phone several times but have been unsuccessful.

There are some matters that need to be discussed regarding land Angus acquired in Southern Rhodesia: matters that require urgent attention from yourself since he is no longer with us. I will try and be as succinct as possible.

Some time back, Angus and I were given a rare opportunity to spend two weeks away from the front line. My brother Malcolm arranged for us to visit Southern Rhodesia to view farmland. Angus dearly wanted you to be with him on that trip. He stressed about the logistical impossibility of making it happen and he was worried about your and Mary's safety.

During the journey, Angus tried, on several occasions, to contact you by phone when he could but there was never a reply. After viewing the farms on auction, we were both hypnotised with the area and the opportunity. We invested in a farming area called Insiza near Bulawayo. Angus wrote to his lawyer and included a letter addressed to you.

He instructed his lawyer to transfer funds to secure the purchase. I think I recall Angus saying he could finance it from the sale of his uncle's estate that he'd inherited. Malcolm, who currently resides in Southern Rhodesia, agreed to watch over our investment until we were free from our military service.

In view of Angus's death, the account held with the Reserve Bank of Southern Rhodesia has been frozen, pending receipt of transfer of deed and ownership. There is legal paperwork that needs to be submitted for you to retain your asset. I would be happy to discuss with you any plans you may have for the land in question, and I am happy to look after it for you in the interim period. However, the legal documents are urgent.

I can be reached at the Pretoria Hospital in South Africa. I have written the address, ward number and direct telephone number on the back of the envelope in the hope you contact me.

Yours sincerely,

Robert Hunter

Molly sat contemplating the content of the second letter. Angus had tried to contact her. *When?* She contemplated her daily routine. During the day, she was always out on the farm, rarely in the house. She took Mary with her regardless of what she was doing. If Angus had phoned during the day, obviously they had missed each other. Every day was a blur of chores. It was only in the last two months that Annie had been employed to support her. Perhaps he *had* tried to ring her!

She read the letter again. Apparently, a letter addressed to her was sent to Arthur Conway. She certainly had not received anything of the sort. Perhaps it was in the envelope she received from the lawyer enclosed with the 'important' documents she was supposed to sign.

She reached for the third envelope and opened it. It was quite thick. It contained mostly legal documents with an 'x' marked where she was required to put her signature. Several documents were duplicated. There were three identical sets. She tried to make sense of the legal jargon, but the language was unfamiliar, and it confused her.

There were three further sets related to signing power of attorney over to Arthur Conway himself. To her it suggested if she did, she would have nothing further to do with the land or the bank account. All she could think about was, *Where the hell is the letter from Angus?*

She cried again through sheer frustration, uncertainty, and loneliness. She took a deep breath and regained her composure. She reached out for the phone handset and placed her finger in the dial... The number she dialled was embedded in her mind. The familiar ring tone sounded in her ear as she called her parents' tailor shop. Moments later, her father answered the phone. Elspeth began the conversation with, "Hello Dad. I'm in trouble and I really need your help."

# Chapter 6

## MACGREGOR RESIDENCE, GLASGOW

It took David MacGregor two and a half hours to drive the fifty-plus miles from Elspeth's farm back to his home in Glasgow. The initial journey to see her took less than half that. There was little traffic on the way back at that time of night, but the dense fog had made progress painfully slow. His mind was working overtime the entire way. It was 9:30pm by the time he arrived home.

Earlier, as he was shutting up his tailor shop for the day, he had received the call from Elspeth. He had been concerned about her – given what she had been through. He understood her desire for independence, but he knew in his heart, it would not be long before she either asked for help or admitted defeat.

He promptly raced to her aid. On arrival, he found her in an emotional quandary and completely confused. He sat and carefully read through the correspondence which was lying haphazardly on the table. He got to his feet and hugged his daughter reassuringly before returning home.

On entering the front door of his house, he kissed his anxious wife on the cheek and headed straight to his study. From the serious look on his face and the urgency in his step, she knew not to ask questions until he was ready to talk. As he sat behind his mahogany desk, he picked up the phone and dialled Mathew Baker, the senior partner of the Baker Montague and Forbes Law Firm.

He emerged from his study a little after midnight and found his wife in the lounge pretending to be engrossed in her knitting. He stood in the doorway, leaning on the frame, removed his spectacles and rubbed his eyes. "I don't want you to panic about what I'm about to tell you, but I need you to listen to me and do exactly as I say."

Veronica looked grave. She did her best to keep the panic out of her voice. "What is it, David?"

He took a deep breath and sighed. "It's Elspeth. She's in a world of trouble. Her lawyer is after her land and money. I need you to get Michael to my office by 7am tomorrow and Hamish here by nine."

Veronica felt the tears well in her eyes. Her voice quivered. "Oh David, what are we going to do?"

"I assure you I will explain everything in due course." Determination returned to his face. "When you contact Michael and Hamish, remain calm. You don't need to tell them what it is about. I have a plan, and everything will be ok."

He turned, went back to his office, and shut the door. The study was the second largest room in the house. It housed his extravagant, polished desk and high-backed leather chair. There were two, humbler, reception chairs. Deep-red velvet drapes covered the single window. Adorning the main wall opposite the desk, was a large tapestry of the Battle of Falkirk: the characters, and horses colourfully frozen in time. Below the tapestry stood a large black iron safe.

The phone rang...

"Hello. Thank you for getting back to me so promptly. What do you have for me on Conway?" The conversation was brief but informative.

When the call terminated, he reclined in his chair with his hands behind his head contemplating the information he had received. He stood and paced the room. It helped him to think. In front of the safe, he paused, piecing together his plan of action.

Both Veronica and Michael had access to the safe, yet within the safe itself, a smaller strong box sat welded to the rear of the floor. Only David knew its contents and only he possessed the key. He shifted stacks of neatly bound bank notes and files to open it.

Inside, there were four coloured folders: pink, brown, red, and black. He spent an hour paging through the brown file – rearranging documents and photos into envelopes before labelling and returning them to their appointed place. Finally, he locked the strongbox and the safe, and went to bed.

Michael MacGregor rang the bell to his parents' home at exactly 7:00am. Immediately, the door was opened by his mother. As requested by her husband, she displayed no sign of angst or worry. She embraced her son. "Your father is waiting for you in his study."

Michael was tall and lean. His thick, jet-black hair was meticulously combed into a side parting. The crisp white shirt contrasted with the pin-striped suit and playful paisley silk tie. He was classically handsome and exceptionally well-groomed. Having reinvented the art of perambulation, his movements were more of a glide than a walk. Outwardly, he appeared calm. Inwardly, his heart was racing as he tried to think of the reason for the early-morning summons.

He opened the office door and stood before the desk as he had done many times as a boy. The man seated opposite sported a pair of round spectacles which framed his fathomless eyes. His moustache was fashioned to a point at either end, which detracted from his expressionless mouth. Not for the first time, Michael wondered how they could possibly share the same genes.

"Good morning, Father," he said.

"Take a seat, Michael." David got up from his chair, walked to the door and locked it. Michael gulped. Whatever was about to follow was unquestionably serious. He seated himself in one of the *guest* chairs.

David got straight to the point. "Your sister is in trouble, and we are going to help her."

Michael sat forward. "Elspeth? Really? What is it?"

"I need you to pay attention and remain calm because we don't have the luxury of time." He paused to gather his thoughts then continued. "Angus MacMillan, Elspeth's deceased husband, nominated their family lawyer Arthur Conway to handle the purchase of farmland in Southern Rhodesia. Your sister is due to inherit that land." He raised his head higher and looked directly into his son's eyes. "That lawyer of theirs is evidently up to something. From the documents he has asked Elspeth to sign, it looks like he is trying to keep the land for himself. That also applies to the frozen capital in the Reserve Bank Account."

Michael relaxed back in his chair, a little relieved. Fortunately, the meeting was about his sister and not him. He tried to maintain his poker face.

David continued, "Last night, I managed to get hold of Robert Hunter. He fought alongside Angus and they bought adjacent land near Bulawayo with the intention of farming together. Robert is currently recovering in Pretoria Hospital. When I spoke with him, he confirmed my suspicions. Conway has apparently been dealing directly with the bank to access the capital."

Michael's confusion clouded his mind, and he was still concerned about the locked door. "It all sounds very devious and untoward, but what does that have to do with me exactly?"

A brief respite followed as Veronica knocked on the door. David huffed and unlocked it. Displaying an awkward smile, she brought in a tray of coffee. Unable to hear the conversation in the study from the other side of the solid door, she had interrupted, hoping to find out what it was all about. After a stern look from David, she retreated. Once again, David locked the door.

As Michael sat sipping his coffee with a raised pinkie, David carried on. "It's quite apparent to me that the lawyer, Arthur Conway, is manipulating the system to get his hands on the property in Rhodesia. I need to retrieve files from his office… and that's why you are going to seduce him."

Michael choked and spat out his mouthful. His face turned white with a mixture of horror and disbelief. Coffee dripped off his smoothly shaved chin onto his lap. He shot upright, smashing his cup and saucer on the floor in the process. Immediately, he sat down again feeling overwhelmed and light-headed.

David did not flinch. "Pull yourself together, Michael," he said calmly and walked over to the safe.

Michael's eyes almost protruded from their sockets. "Father?! Whatever do you think of me? Why would you even consider speaking to me that way? I don't understand! I have done nothing to deserve such supposition from you!"

He wanted to run from the room but remembered the locked door. From where he sat, his legs were like jelly, unable to make a break for freedom before a nervous collapse. The safe was opened and David returned to sit behind his desk. He removed the key for the strongbox from the chain around his neck and threw it towards his son. It landed at his feet.

"Open the strong box, Michael."

With trembling hands, he picked up the key as instructed and fumbled with the lock. Michael stared into the hallowed box that he was never privy to before. He peered curiously inside, slightly underwhelmed. All it contained were four coloured files: pink, brown, red and black.

"Bring the brown file. Put the others back," David demanded.

After placing the file before his father, Michael re-seated himself on the edge of his chair. He sat bolt upright, eyes fixed on the floor. His pulse rate quickened. It thumped in his ears. He could barely keep up with his thoughts.

David took a deep breath and addressed his son with a more compassionate, fatherly tone. "You see, my boy... I love you dearly, but your conduct has given me grave concerns. My business and investments will be handed over to you one day. The same family business that has been successful and has continued to flourish for three generations. It is my wish that it will continue to do so under your management. It will then be your duty to pass it on to your son in the same way."

Michael looked up sharply at the last statement.

David continued, "I am at least grateful that you have been discreet and have protected the family name, but I have known about your... *activities* for some time. They are well documented.

In the interests of continuing the family business, you will marry and produce a son, even if you must be gazing into another man's arse when you do the necessary."

Michael gasped for air on hearing the blunt statement from his father. He fought to regain composure, but when he opened his mouth to speak, no words came out. Instead, he looked back down at the unopened brown file.

David softened Michael for his revelations. "I admire how hard you have worked. Frankly, I am proud of how talented you are and how good you are with our male customers. I mean, how much you have learned about tailoring and customer service," he clarified. "You take pride in your work. I'm quite certain that with my guidance, you will ensure the business will continue to be a success, but I also have my concerns and they are justified."

He sat back, observing his son with a blank expression. In the back of his mind, he was conscious of the fact that Michael's dressmaking abilities had already surpassed his own.

Michael wrestled with the mixture of emotions sweeping through him. There were several things he wanted to say or felt obliged to say. In defeat, he sagged into his chair and asked, "How much do you know? How long have you known?"

David sat forward and opened the file. "I know enough. I've had you followed, photographed and investigated over the last four years. I know who you have been involved with and how long you remained with them." His expression remained nonchalant. "I know the... er... *type* you are attracted to and what you do when you are together. I am aware of twelve liaisons during that time. Perhaps there have been more, but twelve for definite."

Michael stared at his father in disbelief.

David continued, "Only a couple have lasted for, should we say, an extended period? Your current bedfellow is on the cusp of a new record for you!"

"Really? And who might that be?" Michael sat back and folded his arms indignantly, testing the mettle of the intel.

"The son of *Johnson MacAvity Locksmiths*. What's their motto again? Ah, yes... 'We keep your front door safe and your back door safer'. Is that it? Or something along those lines... Anyway, Oscar Henry, as he likes to be addressed, is their oldest son: locksmith by day; star studded theatre performer by night."

The colour drained from Michael's complexion.

"You have been together for the past year, have you not? At least that is what YOU believe, but you are sadly mistaken."

Confusion etched Michael's brow.

David removed an envelope from the brown file and slid it across the desk towards his son. Michael saw the name *Oscar Henry MacAvity* written on it. The envelope was not sealed. He pulled out a set of photographs. On the back of each picture, a date and time was recorded. As he flipped through the images, Oscar Henry was captured in multiple locations in various stages of dress or undress. There was a diverse array of male companions with him. Michael was all too familiar with some of the locations. Several shots had been captured through shutters or half opened doors or curtains, all with the subjects in compromising positions.

Michael replaced the photos. David could sense the pain and upset Michael felt below his stony-faced persona.

David continued: "I had MacAvity followed. At first, I wanted to get a measure of the man, but it didn't take long before it became evident that he was being less than honest with you. We had to get sufficient proof to help you avert a scandal. We needed the upper hand and leverage: something to fight back with."

"Wow! You did all that just for me? Thank you!" Michael retorted bitterly. "Now let me out of this god-forsaken room!" He stood and waved his hands theatrically.

David patiently sympathised. "Sit down, son. I don't blame you for being incensed but in time you will realise that I have been trying my best to protect you, us, and our business interests."

Michael was beyond tolerant. "Business interests! What bloody business interests? You run a tailor shop, not Scotland fucking Yard!"

"Watch your tone, young man," David hissed through clenched teeth, losing patience. "Yes, *we* run a tailor shop and a very successful one at that. However, we have extensive investments beyond that that you are unaware of. About ten years ago, I started acquiring vacant land. It seemed like a good idea at the time: hold onto the sites long enough and the value simply increases. I have also built up quite a portfolio of developed properties."

Michael listened with complete disinterest while David continued. "Most I acquired, have more than doubled in value. In addition, I have trading accounts on the stock exchange. Two, I manage myself and several others are being managed by our law firm. When you are ready, I will teach you how to handle them yourself; when to buy and sell and so forth." Michael's attention was captured. "I have made more net profit in one month trading on the stock exchange than our shop makes in a year. You've always had a good head for numbers. However, I have held back from including you because of certain decisions you have made; coupled with the lifestyle you lead… Anyway, that is a discussion for another time. My immediate concern is getting your sister out of this mess."

David slid a second envelope over to his son.

"These are the documented relationships you have had over the last four years. I'm not interested in discussing the ins and outs of your private life further. I am grateful at least that you have shown discretion. If your actions were public knowledge, it would ruin you and us. I'm not going to force my personal viewpoints on you." He walked towards the window, away from his son. "Perhaps, one day the world will be different: more liberal, and sympathetic to your persuasion." He turned, looked straight at Michael again and added, "But right now it isn't. It would be in your best interests to be shrewd and *completely beyond reproach*."

Michael flipped the envelope open but did not remove the contents. His father observed his face as he did so. "For you to take over the business one day, as I intend, I insist that you marry and produce a son. It will also mean your preferences are obscured. Liaisons or relationships with other men, MUST be with explicit caution. If you refuse to marry and produce an heir, I'm afraid I cannot hand the business over to you and we will have to end our association."

Michael removed the contents of the envelope and flicked through the images, recognising the men he had been photographed with. He recalled the times he had shared with them. The last photograph was a picture of an unfamiliar man, smiling: a wide, cheeky grin adorning his handsome face. Mid-thirties, he guessed; just the *type* Michael was attracted to, but he had never met him. *Enchanting*, he thought.

"Who is this?" Michael asked with sparked interest.

"Arthur Conway. Elspeth's solicitor."

He looked at his father with renewed interest. "The one you want me to seduce?"

"Yes. Well, not exactly... I need you to get him alone and to slip this into his drink." David slid over a small clear plastic bag containing a teaspoon of fine white powder.

Michael was puzzled. "What is it?"

"It's a knockout drug – chloral hydrate. Half of the powder in there is enough to incapacitate a man for at least eight hours. Once he's under, I want him photographed explicitly. When he sees the pictures, I think he will be more inclined to do the right thing." A sly smile briefly creased David's otherwise expressionless face.

Hastily, he added, "I don't expect you to *actually do* anything with him or to him, you understand. I just want pictures – images that could end his career."

"I'll do it." Michael needed no further persuasion.

It was David's turn to be surprised. "What, just like that?"

"If it will help Elspeth, yes."

David had expected more resistance. He had a niggling concern about his son being so keen to be involved in seducing a corrupt lawyer, but it was the only plan he had.

"Do we know anything about Arthur Conway?" continued Michael.

"Last night I made a call to Mathew Baker, the senior partner at the law firm. Apparently, Conway used to work for them. There were two main issues with him according to Mathew. Firstly, his sexual persuasion leaned towards younger men, and he wasn't terribly discreet about it. It threatened to embarrass the firm and he was officially warned. He attempted to be more discreet with his liaisons. Then they discovered he had set up shelf companies. He was syphoning extortionate amounts of money from the firm and their clients right from under their noses."

David returned to his chair. "When they confronted him with proof, they threatened to have him barred unless he returned the embezzled funds. He presented them with a banker's cheque for over fifty thousand pounds. He was fired of course and headed to Edinburgh where he opened his current practice. Angus's father and uncle were, unfortunately, two of Conway's clients. They presumed he was trustworthy."

David leant back in his chair, folded his arms, and regarded his son. Michael stood. He paced back and forth across the length of the room in front of the desk. He stopped and turned to his father. "I take it this all has to be done fairly soon?"

David sat forward, placing his hands on his desk, "Yes, we leave for Edinburgh in forty-eight hours. You, me, Hamish and your good friend, Oscar Henry MacAvity."

"Uncle Hamish too?" Michael smirked. "Hired muscle, I take it?"

David nodded.

"What do you need Oscar Henry for?"

"While you keep Mr Conway occupied, Oscar and I will break into Conway's office. There must be further proof of what he's doing. I want to make sure your sister is ok. When you are dealing with the likes of Arthur Conway, you must be a step ahead. I need solid evidence when I confront him."

"And what makes you think MacAvity will do anything of the sort?"

David gave his son a genuine smile. He noticed Michael had chosen to drop the *Oscar Henry* in favour of the more formal *MacAvity*.

"That, my boy, I'm going to leave to you. There are enough damaging photographs in that envelope to destroy the MacAvity business and ruin Oscar Henry for good. After what he has been doing, he owes you the favour. I will rely on your powers of persuasion." He paused to allow his son to further contemplate Oscar Henry's conduct. "He doesn't really have an option in my opinion… Besides, he's a locksmith and has the necessary skills to get into the office and perhaps even a safe." David paused again and sniggered. "One day, once this has all passed, I will sit with a decent dram of single malt and chuckle at the irony of the name *OH MacAvity*."

Still laughing to himself, David got up from his chair and unlocked the door.

Michael retrieved the envelope with the photos of his former lover and stood before his father. "Regarding the other matter… I'm afraid I'm going to need time to consider my options. You are asking a lot if you expect me to marry for the sole purpose of producing a son to carry on the family name and business. I don't particularly want to walk away from the company and start out on my own. It's just a lot to absorb. I need time to think."

David held up his hands and nodded in acknowledgement. He was quite aware that it was a great deal for his son to digest. "Take some time, yes. Just don't take too long. Let me know when you are ready to discuss the matter."

Before leaving the study, Michael turned with an afterthought and asked, "Just as a matter of interest, what exactly are the other files about? What is in the pink file?"

David locked the strongbox, then the main safe door before replying. "I think we both know you made your decision between *pink* and *brown* quite some time ago. Leave it at that."

Hamish MacGregor was three years younger than David. His broad shoulders and powerful arms gave him the thick-set stature of a wrestler. At six foot two and solid as a rock, he overshadowed David in build and height. Although Hamish had a healthy respect for life, his military service and combat training had taught him how to efficiently dispatch an enemy with a variety of weapons, including his bare hands. It was something he excelled at. Sleep did not come easily for him. When he closed his eyes, he saw the faces of those he had terminated and the way it had been achieved.

Following his military service, Hamish never instigated a fight. If called upon to defend himself, he could do so with ruthless efficiency. As a result, the world around him trod carefully. Up until a year ago, his special skills were trivial. However, after leaving the *Dock Yard Tavern*, his favourite drinking establishment, he was ambushed by four thugs.

They simultaneously attacked from both sides. From the left, a six-inch blade slammed into his shoulder. From the right, he was bludgeoned with a heavy baton...

Moments later, Hamish stood, breathing evenly, over the corpses of his attackers. The man wielding the knife had both deep brachial arteries severed under the armpit before the blade and handle was forced through the sphincter into the lower intestines.

The assailant brandishing the plank had his kneecaps shattered with the same weapon. His skull was crushed, leaving scatterings of its custard-like contents on the pavement. The two others were comparatively intact: apart from having their throats ripped out.

There were no witnesses. Hamish piled the bodies onto a horse-drawn cart and covered them with a tarpaulin. He took the carcasses to Becky's Butchery on the outskirts of the city. Becky and Hamish had been together for many years. She knew of his physical strength and abilities but never felt threatened or in danger in his presence. He cared deeply for her: protected her, as she did him.

That night, they kept the mincer going as they disposed of the bodies. The bones were chopped and given as treats to Hamish's two Alsatians. The offal was fed to their very grateful pigs. They worked through the night and when morning broke, the grisly task was complete: all evidence disposed of. Hamish had enough time to clean and dress his own wounds before heading back to the docks to report for work.

When he arrived, the foreman called him into the main office. He informed Hamish that there was no longer a position for him despite him covering the work of three men on a single shift.

It transpired that the entire ambush had been orchestrated by his new boss. Bitter at losing a poker game to Hamish the night before, he had ordered the attack. A good, solid beating was called for in his opinion. He presumed it had not gone to plan when his brother and three accomplices failed to report for duty that morning. He had no evidence though and had been unable to contact any of them. But he knew Hamish had something to do with their disappearance.

"I'm going to have to let you go, Hamish" was all he offered by way of an explanation.

Hamish displayed indifference. "That's a real shame, I was just beginning to like it here."

"Are you not surprised you are being let go?" quizzed the foreman, bewildered by his lack of emotion.

"No, not at all. There's always plenty of work around and plenty of people to take my place. It usually happens with badly managed businesses and foremen that pass the time thinking of little else than their next poker game."

The foreman's eyes narrowed. "Careful, Hamish. I don't care for your tone."

"Oh, there's no hard feelings, mate. I will be on my way then."

Hamish turned at the doorway and couldn't resist adding, "Why don't you pop across to my Becky's butchery? I'll ask her to put aside a few pounds of prime mince. She just got a large shipment in. Don't wait too long though, it's already selling like hot cakes!"

Hamish left without looking back.

Following this, he worked as a supervisor in his brother's warehouse managing the fabric stock. The hours and pay were better and life settled into a predictable routine. That was up until Veronica, his sister-in-law, asked him to meet David at 9am sharp, the next day.

Hamish arrived at the MacMillan household promptly, as requested, and was shown directly into the study. His brother offered him one of the chairs in front of his desk. David wasted no time. "I have asked you here today, because Elspeth is in trouble."

Hamish looked up at his brother. "I'm sorry to hear that. She's a lovely gal. I would hate for anything bad to happen to her."

"Thank you and yes, she is. Unfortunately, there is a lawyer trying to scam her land and money."

Hamish's eyes narrowed. "Do you want me to pay him a visit and break some bones?" He cracked his knuckles.

David shook his head and added, "I don't think it will come to that. But this is what we plan to do..."

# Chapter 7

## 26 SEPTEMBER 1941 – THE GOLDEN THISTLE COURTYARD HOTEL EDINBURGH

Without its usual elaborate external lighting, the Golden Thistle Courtyard Hotel towered hauntingly above the sedate streets that made up its perimeter. Obviously, the start of the war meant the thirty plus beams illuminating the exterior of her grand stone architecture be extinguished until the threat of aerial invasion ceased. It would have been a bright flame attracting the unwanted attention from the deadly aerial moths.

The northeast-facing entrance on Castle Terrace enjoyed the exuberant view of the Saturday farmers' market. Beyond this, lay the historic majesty of the twelfth century Edinburgh Castle.

The stairs of the less regal, rear entrance on Grindlay Street led to a spacious reception area with two doorways leading to public houses located either side. Facing the entrance, a painting hung above double wooden doors of a lone, kilted piper serenading an autumnal valley. The doors opened to a maroon carpeted staircase which led to the well-appointed bedrooms on the floors beyond. All curtains throughout the hotel were drawn to diffuse the light from within. While avoiding attention from the sky, it still enticed customers with well stocked ales and spirits behind closed doors.

The last time the world was at war, public houses were restricted, and attendance discouraged. Alcohol was deemed to be a greater enemy than the German threat. Excessive consumption was frowned upon as it impaired the workforce in the munition factories. This time, however, pubs were viewed as essential for boosting the morale of soldiers and civilians alike. Even though alcohol was heavily taxed, if you could afford it, you were welcome to drink.

The Thistle wholeheartedly agreed with that concept. A left turn through the rear entrance took you into *The Jolly Jester*: a lavishly furnished, upper-class bar and dining area with a high ceiling. Oxblood leather Chesterfield chairs arranged in sets of two and four framed square polished tables. These were neatly positioned around the perimeter of the marbled floor area. A sizeable maroon and gold Persian rug covered the wooden dance floor. It mirrored the colours of the damask patterned curtains concealing the floor to ceiling windows. Periodic brass wall lamps offered mood lighting and were fixed into pale yellow walls.

The generous dark oak bar sported a marble top to match the floor. Highly polished kegerators and tap towers stood proud of the surface ready to dispense beer and ale on demand. Matching bar stools with circular maroon leather cushions sat neatly in front of the brass footrail. Newcomers to the venue would often be momentarily awestruck on entering the opulent room.

Opposite the Jolly Jester, the working-class *Cock and Bull* pub challenged for custom. The atmosphere was jovial and friendly, becoming rowdier as the night progressed and the drinks flowed. In comparison to its posh neighbour, it was modestly furnished. A low ceiling, open fire, exposed brickwork and beams accentuated its rather humble interior. The warm atmosphere and rustic charm meant it was always, by far, the most attended out of the two establishments. The Thistle had succeeded in creating a *honey trap* catering for a mixture of classes.

Michael MacGregor re-entered the Jolly Jester shortly before 7pm. He carried a black bag up to the bar and placed it in front of Barton, the waiter. He stood looking at Michael with a knowing smile, polishing a glass with the towel normally draped over his shoulder.

Barton had been a lucky find. He was in his third year of studies for his Batchelor of Science chemistry degree at Edinburgh University. His heart was devoted to the Glasgow theatre scene where he spent as much of his free time as possible. Michael had met him at one of Oscar Henry's elaborate afterparties, but had no idea he worked behind the bar at the Golden Thistle.

He had a hazy recollection of Barton leading the last partying stragglers whilst they huddled around the piano, drinking champagne. They were singing their own rendition of Julie Garland's *Over the Rainbow*. Michael and Barton had, on more than one occasion, shared a few drinks and giggles.

Having checked into the hotel earlier in the afternoon, Michael had booked two adjacent bedrooms on the first floor. The plan was to get Conway up to Michael's room, drug and photograph him. Bumping into Barton made the enterprise significantly easier. After inspecting the bedrooms and preparing for the night ahead, Michael returned to the bar where he would intercept his target. He recognised Barton immediately.

As their conversation progressed, Michael learned that Barton had been the recipient of Conway's *attention* just over a year ago. Without going into explicit details, he explained he was enticed by Conway with the promise of free-flowing champagne and canapés in a private suite. That night, he was sexually assaulted. The injuries kept him off work and out of university for two weeks.

Since that fateful night, Barton discovered that Conway had a reputation for inflicting injuries of a sexual nature on younger men. He knew of several who had suffered a similar fate, but nothing was ever reported to the police for fear of scandal or prosecution.

Michael divulged enough of his plan to solicit Barton's help to entice Conway upstairs. He produced a bottle of Gordon's Gin from his bag and handed it to the bar tender. "This is filled with mineral water. Use it for my drinks. Make sure Conway gets large shots of the real stuff."

He ordered a gin and tonic and sat at the edge of the bar with a clear view of the doorway and waited...

It had not been difficult for David MacGregor to work out Arthur Conway's schedule. Regardless of what took place in a business sense during the week, Conway religiously made an appearance at The Golden Thistle Hotel on a Friday evening. He would then move off into the city to feed his sexual appetite or return home, alone. Conway's Law Practice was located on the seventh floor of Fountainbridge Quay on Lower Gilmore Place, opposite the Union Canal. The west-facing office windows overlooked his four-bedroomed apartment in Fountainbridge Court. The Thistle Hotel was a fifteen-minute walk and given his predictable schedule, it was the perfect location for the trap.

David, Hamish, and Oscar Henry MacAvity waited at the Ten Sisters Alehouse on Fountainbridge Road. It was positioned on the route Conway would take to the Thistle. David would have preferred to stake out the entrance to Conway's apartment and office. There was little cover for the three of them nearby, so the pub en route seemed to be the best alternative.

Once they caught sight of him, David and Oscar Henry would double back to Conway's office, break in and search it. Hamish would follow Conway to the Thistle and head straight up to the bedrooms on the first floor to await Michael's signal.

Arthur Conway left his office at 6pm, briefly returning home to freshen up before heading to his favourite watering hole. He changed into a fresh white shirt, shaved, and splashed on cologne. A taupe gaberdine overcoat covered his pin-striped double-breasted suit to keep out the evening chill. Admiring his own reflection, he decided he was ready.

Driven by ambition and a determination to succeed, Arthur successfully put himself through law school. It was an incredible achievement given his upbringing. He was now in a position of power and his practice was financially successful. He took pleasure in fleecing the inferior, all artfully delivered under the guise of benevolent, judicious legality. He considered himself to be without weakness, but in truth, his sexual debauchery had landed him in serious trouble with his previous employers in Glasgow.

At the time, being fired for sexual misconduct and embezzlement was a setback, but it turned out to be a blessing in disguise. It pushed him in the direction of starting his own practice in Edinburgh. Ironically, it was also the stepping stone which created the opportunity to extort money from the man he hated the most: his biological father.

Arthur's mother was only nineteen when she conceived him behind the pub kitchen where she worked. The seed of the lustful drunk was well and truly sewn that night and Arthur was the result of their fumbling union. It was bound to happen eventually. Despite him being a wealthy landowner and family man, Arthur's mother allowed him to visit her regularly at her home in exchange for enough money to keep her in food and clothing. She had married in haste to a young man, George Conway, shortly before he left to enlist. He never returned and was still missing in action. When Arthur was born, her suitor insisted that Arthur take the surname of the missing husband to *avoid a scandal*.

As Arthur grew up, he was told his father had died in the war. The regular visitor had to be addressed as *Sir* and Arthur was to show him the utmost respect and be grateful for any gifts. After falling pregnant for a second time, the mother died giving birth. Arthur was taken into care. The biological father made regular contributions to the foster home to ensure a basic education for the child but did not visit him once. Arthur was never adopted. At the age of fourteen he landed his first job as a labourer. A year later, he was able to afford his own humble abode. He worked seven days a week and studied at night.

Arthur struggled to keep up with his university tuition fees. At times he maintained two or three jobs, working all the hours God sent. He persevered. In his last year of law school, he was highlighted as a promising new candidate and became sponsored by the Baker Montague and Forbes Law Firm. The sponsorship freed up his time to concentrate on his studies. On successful completion of his exams, he continued to work for the firm for four years until he was fired.

Conway often reflected on his past as he walked. He was incredibly proud of what he had achieved and congratulated himself on his success. He thought about his future and contemplated the necessary journey to get there. He was completely engrossed in his thoughts. As he walked past the Ten Sisters Alehouse, he was oblivious to the three sets of eyes watching him intently through the window. He was also unaware of the person leaving the pub and following him at a discreet distance.

Conway recalled the day his father had walked into his practice. He had aged considerably since the last time they had seen each other. The old fool wanted to somehow make amends for the years of neglect. Now that Arthur was self-reliant and successful, it seemed his father had a measure of respect for him. He asked Conway to take on the legal work of his estate, manage acquisitions and accounts. Arthur's first reaction was to throw him out of his office, but it occurred to him it was also an opportunity to solicit money from the cretin.

During the years that followed, that is precisely what he did. Every bill he raised, was overcharged. He raised dummy invoices; his father never questioned them; he paid them all. This continued up to his untimely death. Ironically, he was celebrating his birthday in the same pub where he met Arthur's mother. The building was bombed during a zeppelin air raid and his entire family were killed apart from the eldest son Angus and his Uncle William...

The day he learned of this news; Conway laughed until tears ran down his cheeks. The irony was priceless. Having regained his composure, he contemplated the sudden loss of revenue. As it turned out, there was no need for concern. Uncle William took over the running of the estate until Angus came of age. William struggled when it came to financial matters, so the overcharging continued. Even when the estate was transferred into Angus's name on his eighteenth birthday, he made a small fortune from the inflated legal costs and invoicing.

Conway believed the estate was rightfully his: he was the eldest child. But he had no way of proving his birthright. When William passed away, Angus inherited that land too. Arthur, again, made a sizeable profit through creative accounting. When Angus instructed Arthur's law firm to handle the affairs of acquiring the land in Sothern Rhodesia, he spotted a golden opportunity. Not only was he given free rein to control all legal matters while Angus was fighting in East Africa, but the buffoon also went and got himself killed!

With skilful negotiations, he could engineer a means of taking ownership of the prime land, the foreign bank accounts, the lot. The only small obstacle was Elspeth MacMillan, Angus's poor little widow left all alone and defenceless... *She'll be a pushover...* That was his final thought as he stepped into the rear entrance of the Golden Thistle Courtyard Hotel, smiling to himself.

Michael MacGregor was halfway through his drink when Conway entered the Jolly Jester. He stood in the doorway surveying the layout of the pub and the handful of men in business suits engrossed in conversation towards the rear of the room. The air hang heavily, filled and scented with cigar smoke. No one paid Conway the slightest bit of attention. He looked towards the bar and saw a well-dressed young man reading the paper and Barton intently polishing the bar counter. He walked up to the bar and ordered a gin and tonic.

Michael casually looked up from his paper and said to Conway, "Ah! Clearly a man of culture and taste. Gin and tonic, and not the usual scotch drinker. I think we are a dying breed, I'd say."

Conway looked slightly suspicious. "And you are?"

"I'm so sorry, how rude of me. Roger Brown. Not usually up in this neck of the woods. Just passing through on business." Michael held out his hand to shake Conway's. Conway took it, shook his hand and sat down. Barton presented the drink and retreated to the other side of the bar.

Michael took a large swig of his drink and glanced back at the paper. "I do wish this wretched war would end. It's playing havoc with international trade. No action yet from Hitler's 'Operation Sealion' but it can't be long before he invades Britain. It could be years before we are out of this mess. I didn't catch your name, sir?"

"Arthur Conway. What is it you do, Mr Brown?"

"Make as much money, as quickly as possible, to leave plenty of time for fun and games, of course!" Michael threw back his head and laughed. Conway did not.

"I do beg your pardon, Mr Conway. I am a trader in cloth and fabric, but I have been known to dabble in other commodities from time to time. Human trafficking, arms, and ammunition

– you know how it is." Michael smiled wickedly at Conway over the rim of his glass. "I must apologise. It's just that I'm in rather good spirits." He winked and lowered his voice. "I clinched a deal today that will keep me in wine and song for several months. A remarkable achievement given the current financial climate; I'm sure you will agree. Let me buy you a drink, Mr Conway. I'm afraid I don't know anyone in town, and I'm blown if I will celebrate on my own."

Conway did not accept the invitation straight away. "You said you made enough money to 'keep you in wine and song' for months. The expression is 'wine, women and song' is it not?"

Michael stopped smiling and looked a little sheepish. He leant over to Conway and whispered in his ear, "Wine and song are simply a must, but as for women, *that* I can do without." He allowed his lips to gently brush Conway's cheek before returning to his seat.

The corners of Conway's mouth twitched. "I will have a gin and tonic and please, call me Arthur."

Michael ordered a round and moved closer to Conway. "Tell me about yourself. What is it you do exactly? No... Wait... I would like to guess. I'm pretty good at this!" He stood up and examined Conway from top to bottom. "Hmm, a handsome man with exquisite attention to detail regarding his appearance. A man of power and means... I thought politician, but you don't have the grey complexion and sunken eyes due to stress and worry. I'm guessing you are involved in finance, possibly a banker but high up?" He sat down again looking expectantly at Conway like a puppy waiting for a pat on the head.

"I'm actually in law and have my own practice." Conway downed his drink, unaccustomed to such scrutiny. Michael noticed the empty glass and ordered another round. Conway was beginning to feel like *Roger Brown* might save him a trip into the city to quench his appetite…

After another round of drinks, Michael was on good form and had Conway laughing at a joke about a priest and a choirboy, "… and the priest says, 'see you next Sunday for another blessing'!" They both laughed and returned to their drinks.

It was around nine when Michael leant into Conway and whispered, "It's getting a little crowded in here. Would you care to join me in my room upstairs?" He didn't wait for a response. "I say, barman, another two large gin and tonics please and charge them to my room. Come on, Arthur." Michael linked arms with Conway, winked at Barton and headed for the first floor. Conway didn't resist. He was feeling a little lightheaded but excited about what was to follow. He looked forward to subduing this young buck.

The suite Michael had chosen was decorated with a Chinese theme. The king size bed was lower to the floor than usual but stretched wide enough to comfortably accommodate several occupants. The pale-yellow bed covers were complemented by plush golden pillows and matching bed throw. The headboard was an intricate design of carved flowers in four symmetrical repeated squares across its width.

Above the side tables and reading lamps were two rectangular black metal frames featuring Chinese cut-metal, floral designs which contrasted with the sunflower-coloured walls. The maroon carpet matched the drawn curtains and the soft leather sofa below the window. Opposite the bed and adjacent to the bathroom entrance, a mirror hung above a modest wooden desk and chair. It was framed on either side by white storage cupboards.

A room divider, featuring a Chinese dragon embossed in gold, was placed at an angle sheltering the bathroom entrance from view and partially blocking the windows and curtains. The Thistle was the only hotel in the whole of Scotland to have a telephone in a selection of its suites. The black Bakelite phone sat next to a small Emerson radio on the desk.

Michael led the way into the room and placed the drinks on the desk. Conway headed straight for the bathroom and closed the door. Michael wasted no time in retrieving some white powder from his inside jacket pocket and emptied its contents into one of the glasses. He stirred it vigorously with his index finger and watched it dissolve. By the time Conway returned, Michael had removed his shoes, jacket and tie and was tuning the radio in search of some music. The radio crackled as he turned the dial until Glenn Miller's *In the Mood* filled the room. Michael handed Conway the spiked drink and said, "Oh I love this piece of music! Dance with me!"

Conway rejected the offer: "I don't dance."

Michael threw his arms in the air with abandon. "Ok, you drink, I'll dance!"

Conway slouched on the bed and took a large swig of his gin. Michael glided and swayed across the floor, occasionally turning to Conway to smile suggestively over the rim of his glass. He drained his tonic and removed his shirt to reveal a hairless chest. Conway preferred his conquests to be smooth: the younger the better.

As he watched Michael lustfully, he removed his shoes and jacket and undid his tie, before downing his drink. Michael danced into the bathroom, out of sight and stood in front of the mirror composing himself. He had no idea how long the drug would take to work. He congratulated himself on his exceptional acting ability in the character of *Roger Brown*. He had never done anything like this before but found the entire experience thrilling. He was completely sober, having consumed just water and tonic thanks to Barton's sleight of hand behind the bar.

He undressed, leaving only his underpants on, and returned to the room. Conway was on his back, sprawled like a star fish: out cold. Michael marvelled at how quickly the drug had worked. He checked Conway's pulse. Satisfied he was still alive, he immediately stripped off the rest of Arthur's clothing and thumped twice on the bedroom wall. That was the signal Hamish was waiting for.

Hamish entered and uttered an involuntary "Jesus!" as he opened the door. He nearly dropped the camera as he half retreated into the hallway before gingerly re-entering. Conway was completely naked with his backside facing the door. He appeared to be kneeling reverently in front of the bed; his torso and outstretched arms draped across the bed, like he was offering some sort of holy supplication.

Michael was also completely naked. "Come on, Hamish, you've seen a naked man's arse before, haven't you?"

"Not by choice, no. I don't get the appeal personally."

Michael retrieved a black zip-up bag from the cupboard and removed a masquerade mask, strips of silk, lube and an English cucumber of above average length and girth. "Props," he said, turning to Hamish as if he needed some sort of explanation. "I would suggest the best place to photograph from would be behind the room divider. It's supposed to look like the pictures were taken in secret rather than a professional photo shoot."

"I think I'm going to need a stiff drink after this," Hamish grumbled as he followed his directive and got himself in position. "What the hell are you doing?!" he asked as he caught sight of Michael massaging his own penis.

"It's got to look authentic, right? A soft cock won't cut the mustard!"

Hamish just shook his head. "Let's just get this over with."

For the next fifteen minutes, the masked Michael manipulated himself and Conway into several positions while Hamish snapped away with varying degrees of nausea. Conway had a tattoo on his left calf. A pair of interwoven male sex symbols that featured prominently in the pictures.

"And finally," Michael announced, whilst lubricating the first half of the cucumber, with a cheeky smile, "this one's for Barton."

David MacGregor had, over the years, dabbled in some irregular dealings; at least, he had paid someone to deal with them for him. He was completely out of his comfort zone as he and Oscar Henry surveyed the lobby of Fountainbridge Quay. There were no security guards at the entrance of the building. The doors leading to the first floors were open. David's discomfort for *breaking and entering*, intensified when he observed Oscar Henry through the corner of his eye.

Along with the tools of the locksmith trade tucked away in his bag, he had also brought along a change of clothes. Everything he adorned from head to toe was black including Italian leather gloves. David, in comparison, was dressed in his usual business dress: suit, waistcoat and tie; the same he wore every day. Oscar became aware of David's scrutiny. His discomfort increased when Oscar scrutinized him disdainfully.

They crossed the empty street, entered the lobby through the glass doors and headed up the stairs to the first floor. Conway's office was on the seventh floor. They managed to arrive unhindered and in good time, but they could progress no further. A large locked door prevented them from accessing the landing. David stepped aside to let Oscar deal with the obstacle.

He removed a torch from his bag and examined the lock. A few twists and turns using his lock-picking tools, caused the lock to disengage with a loud click. The door opened onto the landing shared by *Conway Solicitors* and *Quay Estate Agents*. The signs for both businesses were identical in size, colour, font and design: scripted in gold leaf and outlined in black.

Conway's door had a flanged rim lock located below a crude, but sturdy, Adlake switch lock. It took Oscar Henry less than three minutes to open both. David was impressed with his prowess. He wondered how many homes had been broken into in the past by the same set of skills.

Once inside, a modest reception area led through to what was obviously Conway's office with a large leather-topped mahogany pedestal desk: the main feature in the room. An equally regal, high-backed leather chair was the *master's throne*. Two chairs offered visitors' seating in front of the desk. The office was not as grand as other lawyers' offices in David's experience, but what concerned him the most was the lack of space to conceal a safe. There were three identical grey filing cabinets loaded with documents in a systematic order. None of them were locked.

They left the office lights off and searched the interior using Oscar Henry's torch. There was nothing in the cabinets relating to Angus. They searched for 'A' and 'M' for MacMillan. David sat down in one of the visitors' chairs and contemplated his folly. He assumed Conway would have a safe or a confidential area for his sensitive documents. It occurred to him it could be in Conway's home. There was certainly nothing untoward in the office and no space to hide anything.

Whilst David contemplated, scratching his chin, Oscar examined the exquisite mahogany desk with his torch. He ran his hands over the leather inlay, occasionally applying pressure. He tried the drawers. None were locked and contained nothing of significance. He sat back on Conway's chair, looking under the desk. He disappeared under it then emerged a few seconds later holding the light in his mouth. Feeling the top and bottom of the desktop at the same time, he lay under the desk like a mechanic examining the underbelly of a faulty car.

He tapped the desk with his knuckles; listened to the sound of the wood and leather. He shone the torch along the seams of the pedestals. David heard him scratching around then, "Aha!" followed by two dull clicks. Oscar surfaced with an obvious sense of satisfaction. He pulled at the large face of the desk. It opened to reveal a hidden drawer. David shot out of his chair and grabbed the torch.

A Walther PPK handgun was the first item they saw. Next to that, were two identical black leather folders. There was an assortment of loose papers, bank statements and transfer receipts. He removed the handgun and placed it in Oscar's carry bag.

There was an open envelope with a letter addressed to Elspeth MacMillan. He also removed this and tucked it into his breast pocket. The first leather folder was the jackpot. He removed each document and photographed them in turn. There were copies of title deeds for *Hillside Ranch* and a map of the southwest of Southern Rhodesia.

The area was called *Insiza* and the boundary lines for the ranch were marked out: 4000 hectares. David was completely unaware that the land was so vast; over 15 square miles of virgin farmland. He knew nothing about farming but could appreciate the size and scope of what Angus had envisioned. He realised why Conway was so keen to get his hands on it. As he paged through the documents, he made note of the bank accounts opened in the name of Hillside Ranch and Angus MacMillan with the Reserve Bank. He also took photographic copies of the correspondence between Conway, the banks, and a law firm in Southern Rhodesia: all of it...

He opened the second leather folder and froze. It seemed Conway was a trophy hunter. The contents could put him behind bars for a very long time, perhaps for life. His *handiwork* was documented in black and white. There were images of battered young men and the wounds that had been inflicted on them. David's stomach churned. He considered the danger he had placed his son in. The contents of the file in his hand meant setting Conway up in the room at the Thistle Hotel had been entirely unnecessary. He didn't know of the file's existence until now. How could he?

An overwhelming urge to retrieve his son took hold of him. He tapped Oscar Henry on the shoulder and gestured it was time to leave. David had all the photographic evidence required. A second thought occurred to him: he would take both folders and examine them with Mathew Baker, his lawyer.

He put the files in his bag, tapping his breast pocket to ensure Elspeth's letter was safe. Recalling the graphic images as he carried his find down the stairs and out of the building, made his palms sweat and stomach churn. The contents of the hidden drawer added a dimension to Conway's character which perturbed David.

# Chapter 8

David and Hamish MacGregor were followed into Arthur Conway's reception area by Mathew Baker, David's lawyer. Having seen the contents of the folders, David asked Mathew to drive to Edinburgh urgently for a meeting. The pretty blonde receptionist in her black tailored business suit sporting a knee-length skirt stood and greeted the trio. She observed them with a welcoming smile. David returned the smile and offered his hand: "Good morning. Liam Lafferty. I have a meeting with Mr Conway." His broad Glaswegian accent did not remotely sound Irish, but she brushed it aside: not her place to question.

"Mr Conway, I'm certain, will be along shortly. He hasn't arrived yet." His lateness was out of character. She puzzled over the cause of his delay. Usually, he was in the office at 8am and would have been supping his second black coffee by now. "Please take a seat." Hamish followed etiquette and retrieved a third chair from Conway's office so all could be seated. They refused coffee and waited. David had a large briefcase which he kept close beside his chair.

The first thing Arthur Conway saw the previous morning when he opened his eyes was a blurred image of a Chinese dragon on some sort of room divider. He had no idea where he was: alone and naked in a strange room. His head was pounding and when he moved, the discomfort in and around his rear, was intense. He showered, dressed, and descended gingerly to the lobby. He was familiar with the layout of the Thistle Courtyard Hotel reception area and began to get flashbacks of last night's events. He recalled the dark-haired young man he had drinks with. He had a hazy recollection of retiring to his room but could not remember anything after that.

The reception desk was manned by the concierge. As Conway walked over, he remembered his name: Bobby: an odd-looking fellow who resembled a retired boxer; completely out of place in his red, black, and gold uniform.

Bobby looked up from his ledger. "Good day to you, Mr Conway. Do you need help with your bag sir?"

"Um no. I don't have a bag." Conway shifted his feet. He suddenly felt uncomfortable.

Bobby smiled reassuringly: professionally adept with such situations. "Right you are, sir. Anything else I can help you with this morning?"

"No..." Conway turned to walk away then changed his mind. "Actually, yes. The man staying in the first room on the first floor... has he checked out?"

"I'll check for you, sir. You mean room 101, first floor?"

"If that's the first room on the first floor then yes."

"Do you remember his name, sir?"

Through a foggy recollection of flashbacks, Conway replied, "Erm, Brown...Roger Brown."

Bobby scanned through the list of names in the hotel ledger. "I'm sorry, sir. There is no record of Mr Roger Brown being in that room, sir. A Mr Dover booked rooms 101 and 103, next door, on the same night, but he's gone, sir."

"Mr Dover booked both rooms and has checked out?" Conway's brow furrowed.

"Let me look again. Ah, yes! Mr Ben Dover checked out last night, in fact. Around 10pm. Odd sort of time to check out, if you ask me, but yes, he's gone."

"Are there contact details where I can reach him?" He strained to decipher the inverted entries in the ledger to glean any information. It wasn't necessary.

Bobby scribbled the number and name of the company listed and handed it to Conway. As Conway's head cleared and focussed on the details, he felt his temper start to rise. The company name listed was *Uranus Tool Hire*. By the expression on Bobby's face, he understood the association of names at the same time Arthur did.

There was a pregnant pause. Conway wanted to explode with fury but disappear at the same time. Bobby did his best to keep a straight face and be businesslike. To ease the awkward silence, he pulled a cloth out of his pocket and began polishing the spotless reception counter. "Will that be all, Mr Conway?"

There was no reply. The last thing Bobby saw was Conway marching stiffly out the exit. For the rest of the day Bobby laughed, shaking his head and repeating: *Roger Brown... Ben Dover... Uranus Tool Hire...*

Arthur walked with a limp to the rear entrance of the hotel to the Jolly Jester and demanded to see Barton the bartender.

Apparently, he was on leave for three weeks. He had no other leads and started the long, slow walk back to his apartment. With every step he vowed to find the man who had humiliated him. Nobody made a fool out of Arthur Conway. As he walked, he quashed the feeling of utter foolishness with rage and a lust for revenge.

After an uncomfortable and restless night, he awoke and checked his watch. He had overslept. In moderate discomfort, he dressed as quickly as he could and headed for his practice. It was nearly twenty past nine before he stepped out of the elevator in front of his office. His receptionist displayed concern for his white face and pained demeanour, but just smiled. She gestured, drawing attention to the waiting visitors.

David MacGregor stood up as Conway entered the reception area.

"I'm terribly sorry for keeping you waiting," he apologised, trying to disguise the physical pain. "Please come through." Conway had ignored the other two visitors until all three were in his office and he was standing behind his desk.

At that moment, he recognised Mathew Baker, the senior partner that had finally fired him. His eyes shifted from Mathew to Hamish to David, trying to make the connection but he failed to do so. After what he had been through at the Thistle Hotel, he suspected there had to be some sort of relevance. But what was it? He suddenly felt rather exposed.

He repositioned himself behind his desk, fumbling with the secret drawer locks.

David produced the Walther PPK handgun taken from Conway's desk. "I think you had better take a seat, Mr Conway." He opened his hidden drawer and stared in disbelief at the empty recess. Slowly, he shut the drawer and sank into his chair.

David sat forward and commenced the meeting. "Mr Conway, I would like to be very clear with you from the start. I am here to attend to matters of the utmost importance. I intend to see them through with you to their conclusion in a manner becoming of gentlemen."

Conway replied with a humourless smile, "Breaking and entering and pointing my gun at me... is that your way of conducting business in a *manner becoming of gentlemen?*"

"Judging by the contents of your files, you are in no position to lecture me on matters of morality."

Conway ignored the comment. "I take it you had something to do with that little charade at the Thistle?"

"We will come to that in time, Mr Conway. I am David MacGregor, Elspeth's father. I believe you are familiar with her. The widow of Angus MacMillan?"

Conway blinked slowly and nodded.

"It seems there are some 'irregularities', shall we say. From what I can gather and what has been confirmed by my lawyer, Mathew Baker – I'm sure you will remember him – you are attempting to take ownership of my daughter's land. You have embezzled a sum of ten thousand pounds from the Reserve Bank of Southern Rhodesia which holds accounts still in the name of Angus MacMillan, you have plans underway to access further capital." David paused, preparing for the impending confrontation.

He continued, "That is not going to happen. Mr Baker is here to ensure the correct procedures are followed. Do you understand?"

Conway crossed his arms. "And if I don't follow them?"

"Then, unfortunately, you will force my hand to take more drastic measures to ensure your cooperation." David took a brown envelope from his briefcase and tossed it across Conway's desk to him.

Conway opened it and paged through the photographs taken by Hamish. The pictures were designed to look as if they had been taken from behind a screen. There was no doubt it was Arthur Conway in the photos: his face and distinctive tattoo featured prominently. The other man's identity was carefully hidden behind a masquerade mask. He paused, squinting at one picture for longer before recognising the object responsible for his current state of discomfort. A half-buried, English cucumber.

David interrupted his thought process. "You may keep those. I have plenty of copies. A set is currently in Mr Baker's possession. Another is ready to be handed over to Scotland Yard. I'm afraid those photos, in the wrong hands, will destroy your career."

Conway placed his elbows on his desk, balancing his chin on his fists.

David continued, "The content of your desk was quite a revelation. I hoped to find a paper trail of what you had been up to with my daughter's land and finances, but your photograph collection has left me speechless. They alone will put you behind bars for a considerable time, perhaps for life. Do you not agree?"

Conway did not have any alternative and he knew it. His brain usually worked through problem solving rapidly but there was no apparent escape from this predicament. His pulse raced. He had to co-operate. "Say I do what you ask… you guarantee my *property* will be returned and those ridiculous photos from The Thistle will just disappear?"

David nodded. "I have intervened in this manner simply to ensure justice is done."

"You seem oblivious to certain facts, Mr MacGregor. If you believed in any form of justice, that land should rightfully be mine."

David looked bewildered. "And how do you come by that conclusion?"

"Angus's father is also my father: except I am his eldest son."

David, Hamish and Mathew exchanged puzzled glances. Conway launched into the tale of his childhood: the death of his mother; him being brought up in an orphanage; his fight to get through law school and eventually taking on his father as a client.

"That is quite a story, it truly is. However, it does not give you the right to embezzle funds and steal from my daughter. I cannot and will not let that happen!" David bellowed the last statement, pointing Conway's gun at him. His hand shook. He took a deep breath and regained his composure. He nodded his head towards his lawyer.

Mathew Baker stepped forward and presented a file to Conway. "I have taken the liberty of preparing the correct documentation. You will notice this includes the following: Title deeds for Hillside Ranch in the name of Elspeth MacMillan; bank account documentation for the reserve bank of Southern Rhodesia and transfer of accounts into her name and authorisation for the immediate release of funds to pay existing running costs and debts. These are to be administrated by her nominated representative, Malcom Hunter. I'm sure you are aware of where you need to sign." He barely paused for breath. "There's just one other thing. The ten thousand pounds sterling you helped yourself to during the land acquisition... You will need to return that amount today, in cash, Mr Conway."

"This is a bloody outrage!" Conway shot to his feet and hammered both clenched fists into his desktop. Hamish shot across the room, grabbed Conway by the back of his neck and slammed his head into the desk. Conway's right cheek impacted with force; he blacked out momentarily. As he regained consciousness, he felt an enormous pressure threatening to crush his skull. Hamish had not relinquished his grip and his bearlike paw pressed down with all the power he possessed; Arthur's legs buckled beneath him.

"That's enough, Hamish," David said calmly. Hamish withdrew; Conway collapsed and slid to the floor below the desk. "Kindly assist Mr Conway back into his chair."

Hamish grabbed Conway by the lapels of his suit and thrust him effortlessly into his seat. Conway removed a handkerchief from his lapel pocket and held it to his cheek to stem the blood flow. The wide-eyed, white-faced secretary stood at the entrance of the office wringing her hands, uncertain as what to do.

David looked at her and politely asked, "I believe Mr Conway could do with ice. Could you be a dear and fetch him some and possibly a towel too?"

She nodded, turned and darted from the office on her urgent errand. Hamish hovered ominously behind Conway. David gestured for him to return to his seat.

A moment later, the secretary reappeared with some ice wrapped in a white kitchen towel and handed it to her boss.

David smiled at her reassuringly. "That will be all, thank you. Leave us, please."

She left as instructed and closed the door behind her.

Conway gathered the file Mathew Baker had left on his desk, carefully avoiding the smear of his own blood streaked across the surface. With his left hand, he held the ice to his injury. With his right, he flitted through the pages, scribbling his signature where necessary. Once completed, he closed the file and pushed it in Mathew's direction. He threw the pen on the desk.

As Mathew checked the documents, David turned back to Conway. "There's just the small matter of the ten thousand pounds, Arthur. May I call you Arthur?" He didn't wait for an answer. "It's probably best to write a cashier's cheque out to Hamish MacGregor. In view of the large sum, I suppose you will need to ring your bank to authorise the release of funds. I'm sure you would like the transaction to go as smoothly as possible for Hamish. He doesn't have as much patience as I do. I am sure you have already worked that out for yourself…"

The agony he was feeling in his face meant Conway had temporarily forgotten about the pain in his backside. He shifted uncomfortably before retrieving a cheque book from his jacket pocket. He reached for the discarded pen on his desk. Once he had committed the words to paper, he flung the cheque across the desk to where David sat. "I don't need to ring the bank. There will be no issue withdrawing the funds."

David handed the cheque to Hamish. He left without a word, carrying David's empty briefcase. Mathew, the lawyer, nodded to David; apparently satisfied the paperwork was in order. Conway nursed his cheek, periodically repositioning the ice against the swelling.

David closed his eyes and rolled his shoulders to release his tension. As he opened his eyes again, they fixed on Conway. "So, what shall we talk about while we wait for Hamish to return?"

Conway was visibly seething. "You will not get away with this."

"Come now, Arthur, I think we both know that is not true now, don't we? Mr Baker will proceed with what's necessary from here. He will also retain a set of those photographs." He patted the folder. "Should you attempt to block or disrupt the process in any way, they will be released to the appropriate authorities. I am undecided with what to do with the pictures we found in the folder in your desk. I feel I will be obstructing the course of justice by NOT handing them in."

"Those photographs are MY property!" Conway felt desperate.

"Perhaps they are. They are also evidence of what you have done and what you are. You are a sick man, Mr Conway. Very sick, indeed. There are the victims to think of. Surely, they deserve justice..." His attention turned towards his lawyer. "What are your thoughts, Mr Baker?"

Mathew shook his head and sighed. "There's all manner of moral, ethical, and legal issues to consider. I would suggest, until we have finalised our affairs and are certain of a trouble-free outcome, we keep the folder in a safe place. It will give us time to contemplate our next move. Our immediate priority is the MacMillan land and finances."

David nodded. He could remember some of the photos quite vividly. They all sat in silence mulling over their individual thoughts. Mathew Baker had never been in a meeting quite like this one. He felt squeamish at the sight of blood. He had never witnessed such violence; especially a man's head rammed into a desk before. However, having seen those photos, Conway obviously deserved it.

Conway contemplated fleeing the office, but his injuries left him in no state for sudden movement. They had him well and truly over a barrel and he could do nothing about it; at least not immediately.

"Magda! Bring me aspirin!" he bellowed.

The obedient receptionist left the office and returned shortly with a tray and four cups of coffee. She handed two tablets and one of the cups to Conway then left in silence. Conway swigged the pills down with a sip, grimacing as he scalded his throat. The others left their drinks on the tray, untouched. Hamish reappeared a short time later and handed the briefcase to David. "It's all there."

Mathew and David stood and followed Hamish out of the office. David turned and addressed Conway for, what he hoped, was the last time: "I cannot say it has been a pleasure meeting you. It is my sincere hope that I never see you again." He turned and all three walked, unchallenged, from the building.

It was early afternoon by the time David, Hamish, Michael, and Oscar Henry left Elspeth to head back to Glasgow. They stayed long enough to fill her in on the events of the last few days and what had been set in motion. Mary and her Uncle Michael had a special bond. So she stamped her feet in a tantrum and ran off to her room crying when Michael had to put her down to leave. After a tearful embrace with her father, Elspeth watched the car disappear down the drive.

It had rained earlier but the sky had cleared to a brilliant blue. The air smelt fresh and clean after the downpour. A faint breeze carried the scent of her blooming calla lilies mixed with wafts of lavender from her herb garden. She felt a sense of calm as she returned to her kitchen. Yeasty aromas of fresh bread baking in the oven greeted her as she entered. She selected one of the green apples from the bowl decorating the kitchen table and bit into its juicy flesh before seating herself to read her letter.

The envelope had been opened. Inside was a folded sheet of paper and several photographs. She placed the pictures on the table and focussed her attention on the familiar handwriting:

My Dearest Molly,

I feel like it has been a lifetime since we have seen each other. Although I have thought of you every day, there has been little time to write from the front line. Time has been quite a blur. The daily engagements and advancement are draining beyond belief. Nights are restless and we are almost permanently in a state of hunger and exhaustion. It is what I signed up for and I feel I am making a positive contribution.

How is our little girl? Probably not so little now. We will be chasing the boys away from Mary before we know it! I look forward to holding you both. I cannot say how long this war will go on for, but our progress in South Africa has so far been steady.

Robert Hunter and I recently had a rare opportunity to take two weeks' leave before being relocated. There was no way I could get back to see you and Mary in Scotland during that time. The usual flights from South Africa and Nairobi to England have all been redirected to ferry troops and vital supplies for the push into East Africa. I did try ringing you several times during my leave whenever I could, but the phone was never answered. I've sent telegrams through Arthur Conway our Solicitor;

I hope you have received them all. I have been so worried that something has happened to you.

Robert was contacted by his brother Malcolm who is currently mining for gold in Southern Rhodesia. He mentioned there was prime farmland due to be auctioned and invited us to attend. He had successfully bid previously on land in the Eastern Highlands, apparently an area full of mountains and forests rich in minerals. He seems incredibly pleased with what he has acquired and was heading to the southwest of the country for another auction. There were a few established farming ranches owned by gold miners that recently went bust and there was potential to purchase prime farmland well below market value. He invited us to join him in Bulawayo to view the land in question, so we did.

We flew into Pretoria and caught a train to Bulawayo, Southern Rhodesia. I'm so glad we did. Malcolm was incredibly helpful. He showed Robert and I around. We had a chance to view the properties and land ahead of the auction on horseback. I ached for days after spending so many hours in the saddle. I bet the horse did as well!

What we saw was worth the journey and the discomfort. The land is breath-taking, Molly. I fell in love with one particular property: HILLSIDE RANCH. 4000 hectares of the most beautiful scenery I have ever seen. 15 square miles!

According to Malcolm, the owner of the farm found gold deposits near the eastern boundary. The mine was registered as 'Red Herring Gold Mine', ironically. Initially, the rich deposits yielded good profits, but it seems the gold just ran out. They exhausted their capital searching for traces of fresh gold reserves and neglected their cattle ranch in the process. The owner of Hillside also dragged 2 of his neighbours into the investment but in the end, they all lost everything. They had 2 consecutive droughts which added to their downfall and the underground water supplies ran dry. Their cattle starved and their crops failed. Their lands were eventually forfeited as a result.

Malcolm is keen to further explore the old gold mine itself and has employed one of the top geologists in the country to assist him. He is not really interested in the rest of the land or in farming. He already has a productive mine and seems truly gripped by the fever for the yellow metal!

The photos I've sent don't do the place justice. There are open fields for grazing cattle and a stream that runs through the southwest section of the property during the rainy season. It has underground water too and windmills supplying water to the northern fields. There is an old farmhouse. It is a bit run down and has been unoccupied for quite some time, but I have spotted another potential site for a homestead with breath-taking views over the fields sloping down towards the stream. There may even be potential to build a small dam in front of the house to stock with trout and pump water up from the stream in the rainy season to fill it.

According to Malcolm, a bunch of farmers were hoping for the land to be subdivided and sold off in smaller lots. If they had clubbed their money together, they could have purchased the land outright and then subdivided it but none of them trusted each other with their capital. The costs of subdivision are expensive. They would have had to wait until the bank arranged for the subdivisions if unsold as one lot. There was no one, they knew of, that would bid on the entire area.

It went to auction, and I bid at the reserve price. There were no other bidders, and no one had any idea who I was or that I even planned to bid! My bid was accepted, and I paid a deposit to secure the purchase. I had 48 hours to arrange the balance. I telegrammed Conway and he arranged for the money to be transferred. I was able to cover the purchase from the sale of Uncle William's estate. It was ridiculously expensive for the transfer to be done so quickly but in doing so, we have secured for ourselves an incredible opportunity, Molly – the land is now ours! I cannot tell you how excited I am about the prospects. I wish you had been with me, and I am sorry that you are hearing this news through a letter, but I have had no success in getting through to you.

Robert Hunter also secured some land next to our ranch. He wasn't so lucky and had a bidding war with two other farmers. He ended up paying the same amount as I did but for just over half the land. He does, however, have a newly built farmhouse that is quite special.

Malcolm Hunter has been kind enough to assist Robert and I in administering the farms temporarily whilst we return to the front line. It is a project I sincerely look forward to and I'm sure, once you have seen the place with your own eyes, you will fall in love with it just like I have. I have given Malcolm permission to explore the old gold mine as he is helping us considerably while we are otherwise engaged. It is important for us to talk as soon as we can regarding the ranch and our future.

It is a lot to take in and I didn't want to do it by letter, but under the circumstances, I had no other choice. Once the war is over, I will bring you and Mary out to Southern Rhodesia to see our new investment. It will be necessary to sell off most of our land in Scotland. We will keep 3 or 4 acres and the house but get rid of the rest.

The Irishman, Fitzgerald, who owns the farm next to ours, will be happy to buy what we are willing to sell. He has been after it since before my father died. We can use the funds to build our future home at Hillside and to get the ranch up and running to full capacity. It is ideal for farming cattle and there is a chronic shortage of beef right now, largely due to the war. When the war is over, I can't see a reason why the demand for prime beef won't increase.

There is so much we need to talk about, and I can't wait to see you. Please try not to feel apprehensive about our exciting new opportunity. Rhodesia has a raw beauty that is difficult to put into words. The climate is pleasant all year round because the country is close to the equator. Summers are hot and wet. The winters can be cold, but they are generally dry. Nothing like the Scottish winters, prolonged rainy seasons, and snow. With the land fully paid for and capital to develop it, I look forward to turning our piece of paradise into a successful enterprise with you and Mary by my side.

Please give Mary a big kiss from me and I look forward to holding you soon.

I love you.

Angus

Elspeth re-read the letter, trying to grasp the full magnitude of the life-changing content. Tears flowed down her cheeks and dripped onto her apron. The letter renewed her sense of loss and longing for her husband. Mary must have sensed her discomfort and came in carrying a handful of wildflowers picked from the meadow; her tears and tantrum at Uncle Michael's departure, already a distant memory. She hugged and kissed her mother and skipped off to her room.

Elspeth tried to put her emotions aside to contemplate what to do about the land she now owned in Southern Rhodesia. Yes, it might have been a fantastic opportunity for her and Angus to develop together, but Angus was gone. Surely a widowed mother could not face such a challenge on her own and drag her young daughter to the other side of the world to fulfil her dead husband's dream? Alone, away from her family and in a foreign land running a ranch where she would not know a single soul, seemed a preposterous idea. There was certainly nothing she could do, for the time being, with a global war raging. She would need to contact Robert and Malcolm Hunter to discuss management of the ranch for the time being. Mary was her main priority, and she had her hands full running her own estate. But a part of her wished she could at least see Hillside Ranch.

She had left the relative security of her father's tailor shop in Edinburgh driven by a sense of adventure. Since marrying Angus and becoming a mother, then a widow, she had considerable responsibility and no time for adventure of any description. She flicked through the collection of photographs Angus had sent with remote detachment before returning them and the letter to the envelope. Right now, Mary came first so she brushed her thoughts aside and began preparing her daughter's dinner.

# Chapter 9

## 30TH SEPTEMBER 1941 – PRETORIA HOSPITAL

It was the usual break-of-dawn start to the day with breakfast served at six, before the nurses attended to their duties: changing bed linen and administering their care. Today, Robert Hunter welcomed the early start. He had been discharged from the hospital and was to be collected by military personnel to escort him to the airport. He had arranged a seat on a cargo plane heading north and would eventually be reunited with his wife and family in Scotland.

It was the first time he had worn his officer's uniform since being injured. He looked and felt significantly smarter than when dressed in his hospital issue pyjamas. The wound to his leg was healing well but he walked with a limp and required a cane. His few worldly possessions were packed in his canvas army-issue pack. He was ready to go.

Nurse Malaika breezed into the recovery wing and made a beeline for Robert. As he turned to face her, she engulfed him with a hearty hug, pressing her ample bosom against him. She smacked a kiss on his cheek. Robert's height did not put her off; she simply pulled him lower to reach. "Ah, Robert, my lovie. We are all going to miss you! Don't you look handsome in your uniform? My, what a picture you are! Doesn't he look handsome, boys?" She directed the question to the peanut gallery consisting of Henrick and Edward: the longest standing patients of whom Robert had become quite fond of during his stay.

"Ya, nurse. Robert is terribly handsome! Isn't he, Edward?" Henrick announced in his thick Afrikaans accent. He nodded vigorously with a grin.

"So handsome..." Edward confirmed with a wink in a dreamy tone. He formed a heart shape with his hands.

Robert disengaged from his bear hug and gave his critics a two's up gesture. He looked directly at his warden. "Nurse Malaika, I would like to thank you and your staff for taking such good care of me during my stay here."

"Don't forget the bed baths, Robert." Edward chipped in helpfully.

"How could he forget the bed baths?" Henrick added. He applied an imaginary lather of soap to his groin.

Nurse Malaika looked at them with contempt. She turned back to Robert with an exuberant smile. "Oh, Robert: an officer and a gentleman. You are most welcome, lovie. If you weren't married, I would have slung you over my shoulder and carried you home with me!" She gave him another farewell squeeze and went on her way.

"That woman has a big heart," Robert said, slinging his pack over his shoulder.

"Ya! And a big arse too!" Henrick again, lowering the tone and laughing at his own joke. His facial burns were healing, and the bandages had been replaced with a black eye patch which covered the empty socket. It made the huge, scarred Afrikaner look like a pirate.

"It's so unlike you, Henrick, to have your mind in the gutter." Edward, the double amputee, lamented judgementally, shifting in his new wheelchair. He wheeled over to Robert and extended his hand. "Nice knowing you, Robert. Having you around has made this place almost bearable."

"Listen, if either of you are ever in Southern Rhodesia, look me up. I will be farming in Insiza, near Bulawayo: *Cedar Tree Hollow*. You are both welcome to come and visit." He walked over to Henrick, who was sitting up in his bed and shook his hand.

"All the best, Rob. Take it easy on that leg." Henrick had a powerful grip which threatened to crush Robert's hand.

They said their goodbyes. Robert was nearly out the door when Henrick called, "Hey, Robert! What do you call a rottweiler with no legs?"

Robert stopped. He did not turn around. Edward rolled his eyes. "Christ, Henrick, I'm right here! It's far too early to be the brunt of your jokes." He shook his head and pushed himself back to his bed.

Robert smiled and shook his head. "No idea, Henk."

"Anything you like! It can't catch you!" More bellows of laughter from Henrick, slapping his thigh.

At that moment Malaika came rushing in. "Oh, good, you're still here, Robert. There's a phone call for you."

"I really should be on my way. I have a plane to catch."

"She said it was urgent."

He turned towards her. "Who is it?"

"A Mrs MacMillan from Scotland."

Robert followed her through into the nurse's office to take the call. "Hello. Mrs MacMillan? Robert Hunter here."

"Hello, Robert. Please call me Elspeth… or Molly. Angus used to call me Molly."

"I'm terribly sorry for your loss, Molly. Angus was a good man and a good friend of mine."

"Yes, he was. Thank you." Silence followed.

Robert broke it. "Unfortunately, I don't have a great deal of time. I'm due to fly out, shortly. I'm returning to Scotland."

Elspeth found her voice. "I just wanted to thank you for your letters and to let you know we have resolved the legal issues regarding Hillside Ranch. My father will be in touch with Malcolm to fill him in on the details. I will wire a transfer to cover the amount you have outlaid on my behalf."

"I'm pleased to hear it. I should be back in Scotland in four or five days. Once I'm home, I will give you a call. Perhaps we could meet up to discuss this further."

"Thank you, Robert. I hope you have a safe flight home."

# 3RD OCTOBER 1941 — CRAWLEY CONCESSION GOLF MINE, PENHALONGA, SOUTHERN RHODESIA

Malcolm Hunter sat at his desk studying the latest assay results for the samples recently taken from the face of the second level drives. The first level ran one hundred and eighty metres north to south, twenty metres below the surface. The second level mirrored the first, thirty metres deeper. The lower drives tracked a reef richer than the one above averaging around 27 grams of gold per tonne of ore.

He was so accustomed to the constant clamour of the ball mill he barely noticed it. The crusher looked like an oversized, mechanical cotton reel. As it rotated, its inner liners lifted fist-sized, metal balls that pulverised the two-inch ore chip feed, sending muddy tails and precious gold to the reduction plant for extraction. A happy mine was a noisy mine. Silence meant breakdown, loss of production and profit.

The basic two-roomed building was uncluttered and simply furnished. The front meeting room could accommodate eight people on its mismatched chairs surrounding a central metal camping table. Malcolm's smaller back office had almost all the essentials: desk, chair, filing cabinets, two small windows and a wall rack laden with neat rows of headlamps, battery packs and belts. Two pairs of wellies stood below the rack, both well used. Malcolm liked to keep a spare pair. Inevitably, boots would end up wet on a trip underground. The only essential the office desperately lacked, was a telephone.

Industrial expansion, economic growth and the increasing population meant Southern Rhodesia had several projects underway to install phone poles and cables on the national grid. But the remote Eastern Highlands mining district was not a priority. The closest phone was over an hour away in Umtali. He tried to keep his trips into town minimal, but by the end of each week, there was usually a need to travel over the Christmas Pass Mountain range to get supplies for the mine. That was when Malcolm would make his necessary calls.

There was no safe in the office. Malcolm felt it would be the most obvious place to look. Several mines in the area had been targeted recently. Two successful robberies had left the owners in dire straits and on the brink of bankruptcy. Malcolm had personally built his iron safe into the lounge floor of his cottage prior to employing a single soul. He was the only one aware of its existence. The steel cubic metre recess was set in a concrete casing over a foot thick. It was hidden beneath a wooden trapdoor covered by a large rug. Malcolm always kept the only key to the safe on his person.

Several things made Crawley Concession Gold Mine unique. Malcolm was the sole owner of the surrounding claims. He was not in a syndicate and as such he answered to no one. The machinery was regularly maintained. The underground hydraulic drilling rigs, skips, hoists, conveyor belts, jaw crusher, ball mill and reduction plant equipment were all in good working order. The rich reef and the efficient operation kept the mine profitable, and all trading accounts were in good standing.

To the untrained eye, the mine itself was an unwanted scar on the landscape. By mining standards, the entire operation was as neat and organised as it could be. Waste rock from underground blasting and lashing was used to manufacture the outbuildings: the main two-roomed office, the large workshop, hoists and pump houses, the cyanide and chemical storage building, reduction plant and compound.

When the builders were not involved in erecting structures on the mine itself, they worked on the new residential quarters which Malcolm had designed for himself. He was in no hurry for it to be finished. He lived alone and his current humble dwelling suited him just fine. The efficient running of the mine took priority.

Malcolm realised that productivity was heavily influenced by the happiness and wellbeing of his workers. He paid a reasonable wage to attract the best labourers and built a mining settlement complete with a clinic and school. Where the rest of the farming and mining community struggled with a shortage of manpower, Crawley Concession prospered.

Water was pumped and filtered from underground drives into seven large header tanks. Four were set on raised platforms adjacent to the plant: a gravity fed supply used in the reduction process. Two tanks provided water to the compound, and one fed the office and Malcolm's residence. It was a slick and streamlined operation.

After his father's death, when Malcolm was 14, Malcolm left the family farm in Scotland to seek his fortune. He never returned. As a child, he was fascinated by the mining of precious metals so he travelled by train to join the Bontddu Gold Mining Company in North Wales. From his very first pay packet, he put aside as much of his earnings as he could to buy shares in the company. After 22 years, Malcolm had worked his way up to the position of Assistant Manager. In 1938, aged 36, he sold his substantial shares and travelled to Southern Rhodesia to explore, first hand, its abundant precious metals.

The history of the Eastern Highlands region fascinated him with its rich tapestry of exploration and trading going back to the early 1400s. The local tribes traded gold through Portuguese East Africa before the Portuguese themselves mined the area the following century. The region was named Penhalonga: 'Penha' meaning *mountain* and 'longa' meaning *long*.

History books were full of colourful tales of ill-fated Portuguese expeditions thwarted by encounters with powerful and volatile local tribes. The hostilities disrupted their attempts to mine or trade gold and the ownership of claims and land changed hands regularly over the years. Even up to the 1900s, the Portuguese were still actively involved in the slave trade, which did little to improve relations with the locals.

According to what Malcolm learned, Crawley Concession was last mined in 1927 by an Englishman, Cecil Crawley, who died under somewhat suspicious circumstances. Although Malcolm could not find any written account, there were rumours of Crawley's contorted, lifeless body found in the middle of his abandoned mining operation.

Malcolm planned to visit the obstructive planning officer, Mr Ward, at the registry office in Umtali again. He hoped to dig up some of the history of the mine prior to 1927. Perhaps he could establish what had actually happened to Crawley himself. Extracting information out of Mr Ward, though, was like trying to get blood out of a stone. He treated Malcolm's enquiries with an air of suspicion and begrudgingly searched the archives with a distinct lack of enthusiasm.

When Malcolm took over the operation, the main shaft was just 20 metres deep and the two drives followed narrow veins that produced low grade ore. Since then, his exploration deeper into the earth had yielded richer rewards.

He never regretted leaving the family farm and choosing his own path. Robert, his brother, was more suited to the farming way of life. He was the appropriate successor to the family estate when their father passed. Malcolm had always known his future was heading in a different direction.

The two brothers were very different in appearance and personality. Although they were roughly the same height, Malcolm had inherited his good looks and complexion from his father: dark curly hair, green eyes, and handsomely proportioned features. Constant physical work from an early age shaped his body and muscles to a high level of fitness. In his late thirties, he looked healthy and significantly younger.

A drawback to his chosen isolation and mining for gold in remote locations, was little time to socialise and meet women. Occasional trips into the small town of Umtali were completed as quickly as possible to get back to Crawley Concession. Any females he briefly encountered on those errands were either too young, too old, or too married. At this point in his life, he was happy to focus on making a success of his enterprise. He had little desire to start a family. There would be plenty of time for that later.

In comparison, Robert's fair hair and blue eyes had been inherited from his mother who had passed away when the two boys were very young. The large, almost stubborn, jawline and nose could not be blamed on either parent. Although not a stranger to hard labour, Robert's stature was tall and willowy. Robert married his childhood sweetheart Rachael, and they were content with their life on the farm. That was until the war broke out.

Malcolm was well on his way to becoming a wealthy man. The two-storey gold mine had the unique position of being entirely debt-free. Other struggling diggers were not in the same fortunate position. He employed a total of twenty labourers: a relatively small workforce considering the amount of shift work which involved drilling, blasting, lashing and the various roles performed throughout the reduction plant and slimes dams.

In addition to the labourers themselves, he accommodated their wives and children. The mining compound housed around sixty people in total. Two of the miners' wives ran the local school which taught various children between the age of four and fourteen. For three days a week, the clinic was overseen by a qualified nurse. All-in-all, his workforce was content, and staff-related issues seldom occurred.

Malcolm left his office with the assay results in search of Ephraim, the mine captain. Earlier in the day, the mine had received a shipment of timber. As was often the case in the small community of Umtali, any trucks heading out Penhalonga way with consignments would deliver mail to the camps. This morning, along with the timber, Malcolm received the assay results and an urgent telegram to contact David MacGregor regarding Hillside Ranch.

Malcolm always felt uneasy leaving the mine unattended, but his weekly trip into town was due and now he had the additional need to phone David. He muttered to himself again about the lack of a telephone. As soon as he had found the mine captain and instructed him to drill and blast the rockface on the second level, he would make the journey over Christmas Pass.

Malcolm left Samuel his assistant at the General Store on Main Street with a list of required supplies. Despite his fear of venturing underground, Samuel had proved to be a trustworthy and reliable asset. His one true love was Malcolm's British racing-green 1931 Ford AA, 1½ tonne, flat-bed pick-up truck. It was an eye-catching vehicle of rugged beauty. Arched black mud guards stretched elegantly from above the front wheels to form a belt rail below the cab doors. Flanking the chrome Ford emblem and radiator cap atop the black grille, were bulbous chrome headlamps that formed the look of a startled insect. Sturdy, white five-spoked rims contrasted against the black fenders and green bodywork. The double-wheeled rear axle could comfortably accommodate a heavy payload on the solid oak flatbed.

At just sixteen years old, thanks to his mother who taught in the school, Samuel could speak fluent English, Shona, Ndebele, and Tsonga. Not overly blessed with height, he was just tall enough to see over the steering wheel. He had jumped on the spot clapping his hands excitedly when Malcolm decided to teach him how to drive. Even though the Ford had the steering wheel on the 'wrong side', as Samuel pointed out, he picked up the use of the three pedals and four-speed gearbox with relative ease.

He responded to the pitch of the 40 horsepower, 3.3 litre motor. Ever since, he had embraced the self-appointed title of 'head driver'. When not running errands for Malcolm, Samuel could be found cooing over the truck, washing it or critically supervising its servicing. They were yet to find a pair of shoes that fitted Samuel's feet comfortably. It was one of the items on the shopping list today, but in truth Samuel hated wearing shoes and was quite happy to remain bare footed regardless of the weather. From somewhere, he had acquired a black, peaked driver's hat which he pulled down tightly over his unruly curls.

Samuel had a cheerful disposition and was in good physical health, but he had one unfortunate drawback... Malcolm was accustomed to the smell of hardworking men in confined spaces. Mining was tough, physical graft and sweat was a part of everyday life, but Samuel's body odour was the most intensely, pungent aroma Malcolm had ever encountered. When he questioned

Samuel about it, he merrily pointed out that God gave him a natural repellent against mosquitoes. He proudly displayed each unblemished ebony limb completely free of bites as proof.

Malcolm supposed that it would repel not just biting insects but any living creature with a half decent sense of smell! If bottled, his sweat was most likely capable of stripping paint. It took a lot of persuasion, gifts of soap and finally threats of being banned from driving before Samuel reluctantly agreed to bathe. A wash was obligatory prior to a joint road trip. The confines of the cab in the baking October sun would have been unbearable without one. Malcolm was relieved that his companion was freshly scrubbed.

Malcolm crossed the street to the post office to make his calls. The single, squeaking, offset ceiling fan did little to abate the midday heat or dissipate the cloud of smoke emanating from the antique Mr Crank behind the only manned counter. Crank looked well over a hundred and devoid of any bodily fluids required to sustain life, yet a half-finished cigarette protruded permanently from his shrivelled lips. It wiggled uncontrollably as he ushered Malcolm into a small private room to make his phone calls.

His first call was to David MacGregor.

They spoke at length as David gave Malcolm a rundown of what had taken place regarding Arthur Conway and what had subsequently occurred to ensure the land stayed in Elspeth's possession. David elaborated on the handling of the sensitive photographs which incriminated Conway with sexual violence towards young men.

Once the title deeds and money were no longer under threat, David had handed the photos over to Scotland Yard. Conway had disappeared without a trace. His office and town house left no clues as to where he had gone. He was barred from practising law, but this seemed irrelevant since no one could find him. David suspected it would only be a matter of time before he resurfaced.

They discussed the immediate financial needs and bills for the ranch and how Malcolm could access the funds.

David concluded the conversation with, "I must wholeheartedly thank you for handling matters on behalf of my daughter. It would be a good idea to give her a call. My intervention was to resolve a rather unpleasant situation but now the ball is in her court."

After the phone call, Malcolm sat back in his chair with his hands on his head. He contemplated the conversation. It was not convenient to oversee two large ranches a hundred and fifty miles away. Originally, he had offered to help Angus and Robert; keep an eye on their properties until the war was over. Angus was killed in battle and Robert had just arrived back in Scotland. It could be months before he could take up the reins of managing his own farm. There was no telling what Angus's widow, Elspeth, was likely to do.

He was interested in exploring the workings of the *Red Herring* mine on the boundary of Elspeth's property, but he was certainly not interested in the responsibilities of running the ranches. A long-term time commitment outside of his mining interests was not at all attractive.

Regardless, he dialled Elspeth's number. The phone was eventually answered by a breathless woman who had clearly covered a distance to answer the phone. As they talked, Malcolm's perception of Elspeth changed. He was expecting a damsel in distress, but she was clearly confident and proactive. She saw the need to employ a manager for Hillside. The first objective would be to replace the dilapidated boundary fence and section paddocks.

Elspeth had done her homework and realised that predators posed a threat to livestock. Water from the southern stream would need to be pumped into header tanks for the cattle. As they built up their own herd, she planned to rent out some of the land for grazing. The derelict farmhouse would need to be renovated to accommodate the farm manager. Elspeth asked Malcolm to assist in finding a suitable candidate to run the ranch on her behalf then to nominate a builder to renovate the homestead.

They talked further regarding Red Herring before the call ended. In the past, Malcolm had worked with Ashton George, an Australian geologist. He had been trying to comprehend and deal with the complicated series of faults and shifts below the surface of his gold mine. Ashton possessed a rare ability to accurately assess and predict the location of ore bodies. He was instrumental in plotting the direction and depth of the second level currently producing high grade ore. He intended to take him up to inspect the old workings and take some samples. He could spare a week out of his schedule to assess its potential.

Malcolm made several calls to his contacts in Bulawayo. He was well known to the auctioneer, to the Reserve bank manager and the head of the land registry and national archive. He set up meetings with all three. An hour later, Malcolm left the post office to find Samuel. He was desperate to get back to the mine but still needed to see the local planning office. Samuel had procured everything from the list except the pair of shoes for himself. They, apparently, did not have his size in stock. Malcolm checked and signed the invoice and secured the cargo with ropes. The planning office was further up Main Street, opposite the police station.

Mr Ward, the planning officer, often boasted about his twenty-year unblemished record. Supposedly, under his watchful eye, not a single map or plan had been misplaced or stolen. Malcolm and the rest of the community suspected that this marvellous record had something to do with the police station being directly across the road. Perhaps, also, that the moth-eaten archives had no significant monetary value to the average man on the street!

Malcolm had had several dealings with Mr Ward in the past related to obtaining maps, submitting applications, applying for permits and mining claims. He seemed to view Malcolm with an air of suspicion. Information was provided on a strict 'need-to-know-basis'. It was like Malcolm was trying to unearth hidden secrets locked within a magical vault and Mr Ward was the self-appointed gatekeeper preventing it from happening.

Today, Malcolm thought, he would use tactical compliments and flattery to see if he could charm the old wizard... "Good day, Mr Ward. I must say, every time I come into your office, I'm surprised at how clean and tidy it is. You certainly are an asset to our community and a great caretaker of our recorded history. Do my nostrils deceive me or is that the smell of fresh paint in the air?"

It nearly worked. Ward stood up proudly adjusting his waistcoat on his slight frame with a self-satisfied smile before he stopped abruptly, narrowing his beady, little eyes suspiciously. "Mr Hunter, I suspect you are back again hoping for yet another search of the archives into the history of the location of your mine. Am I correct? The last time you were here I searched the chronology and alphabetical listings under 'P' for Penhalonga as well as 'C' for both Concession and Crawley. As I am precisely aware of every item of paper in and out of the archives since you were last in, I can tell you with absolute certainty, there is nothing further for you here and there is no point repeating the search!"

Malcolm slumped his shoulders and shook his head. Pressing Ward further was pointless. He was just about to leave when he turned to Ward with an abstract question. "Mr Ward, in your vast experience, is it possible that records pertaining to the area of Penhalonga and my gold mine could be kept in another archive location?"

Ward thought for a moment, rubbing his chin. The answer could potentially discourage further enquiries from the bothersome Mr Hunter and direct his attention elsewhere. "Only once in the last twenty years have documents been moved from my archive. In 1934 it was thought that a central archive should be set up in Bulawayo. There was a lot of resistance to the idea from within the planning office and from me of course, but until the idea was dropped towards the end of '34, some records were transferred to Bulawayo, yes. Even if what you are looking for was sent there, I would be surprised if you will find them now. That drunkard, Bucket, is worse than useless and certainly not as diligent as I am."

Malcolm returned to his truck, making a mental note to raise the question on his trip to Bulawayo. He was well acquainted with the land registrar and already had a meeting scheduled.

# Chapter 10

## 5TH OCTOBER 1941. ARTWELL FARM – BANCHORY-DEVENICK, ABERDEENSHIRE, SCOTLAND

The acrid aroma of burned bread intensified with a cloud of smoke as Rachael Hunter opened the oven door. Her emotions were in a turmoil this morning. Robert had finally landed in Scotland after taking five days to travel back from Pretoria and was due any minute. Several long years had passed since last seeing her husband. Initially she could have told you how many days and months they had been apart, but as time went by, running the busy farm and looking after her two boys slowly drove her to the point of exhaustion.

Then there was the issue of the land acquisition in Southern Rhodesia. The purchase took the bulk of their life savings. They also had to sell more than half of their land and livestock to cover the cost. All of which she organised in the absence of her husband.

She was furious at the time. After the mad panic of co-ordinating the sales and the bank transfers, she grimly set about taking care of their remaining assets through monotonous necessity. Days blurred together and time drifted by without any real sense of achievement or respite. She felt quite numb to it all. The physical demands had taken their toll on her. Her blonde hair that once cascaded down her back almost to her hips was now streaked with grey. She cut it herself to a manageable shoulder-length that could be tied back in a practical ponytail while performing her chores.

A restless night's sleep had left her feeling ill prepared for Robert's imminent arrival. When she woke, she checked herself in the mirror, something she seldom did these days. Her reflection reminded her she had aged. Her once cat-like piercing blue eyes somehow seemed dull now and edged with crow's feet wrinkles. She applied make-up although she did not know why she bothered. The last time she wore her current green dress was for a trip to church over two years ago. Red lipstick was applied, removed, then reapplied. Her anxiety was obvious as she flapped a kitchen towel to dissipate the smoke.

Jock the thirteen-year-old Jack Russell barked on the veranda, alerting Bruno the three-year-old Alsatian to a stranger approaching. Rachael's stomach turned into knots as she ran to the front door, still clutching her towel. Robert was making his way towards the house along the long dirt driveway. He was still some way out when Jock braked at his feet, finally recognising his owner. Bruno had never met Robert and was set to attack.

Rachael bellowed, "Bruno, NO!"

Bruno had been trained as a guard dog and strangers were not welcome. He launched at Robert's leg but was halted by a walking stick shoved into his gaping mouth.

Rachael shouted again, "Bruno, BACK!"

This time he responded, stopped, and drew back. He looked from Rachael to Robert and back at Rachael in confusion.

"Come here, boy!" Rachael commanded, patting her lap. Bruno turned and ran back to her. She closed him in the house. Introductions to Robert would be made later under supervision. Jock stayed with Robert, delighted at his return.

Robert turned his attention back to Rachael and broke into a run, ignoring the twinges of pain in his leg. Rachael left the porch and ran out to meet him. Both were grinning and crying at the same time. Sobs shook them as they clung to each other. All of Rachael's nerves and apprehension were forgotten as Robert held her face in his hands and tenderly kissed her. Salty lips met with longing and hunger shelved for what seemed an eternity. They walked arm in arm towards the house in silent contentment. Robert dumped his duffel bag and walking stick next to the front door and they stepped hand in hand past the growling Bruno intently towards their bedroom.

They made love with utter abandonment, oblivious to how their bodies had changed since they had last been together. Afterward, Rachael lay spent in Robert's arms while he gently stroked her hair.

Her breathing settled back to a regular rhythm before she said, "I have been very angry with you, Robert."

"I know."

"We need to talk."

"And we will," he agreed before guiding her mouth back up to his for a tender kiss. They made love a second time, slower this time and less urgent but full of tenderness, both equally content to hold and be held. Afterwards they fell asleep holding each other, enjoying the most peaceful slumber that they had experienced since their parting. Before drifting off, Robert pondered over the dilemma of the land in Bulawayo. He desperately needed to get back to the ranch but being reunited with Rachael was the happiest he had been since they parted. Whatever the solution was, he knew he would not leave her again. Sleep easily came with his sense of completeness.

Rachael stirred an hour later and glanced at her watch. A mid-morning nap never featured in her daily routine and her two boys were due back from college in a matter of hours. Robert sensed her alarm and woke up.

"Douglas and Brody are due back from college around lunchtime and I haven't got a thing ready!" she exclaimed, throwing on a pair of farm breeches and a blouse before hurrying off to the kitchen in her slippers. Robert went to his old oak wardrobe at the foot of the bed and selected one of his pairs of overalls. He would take a walk with Jock and inspect the farm. With his extended absence while he fought in Africa, he fully expected the farm to be in urgent need of repair and in a state of neglect. He prepared himself for manual labour and an extensive *to-do list*.

He kissed Rachael before slipping out the back door with Jock. Bruno followed initially at a discreet distance until Robert fed them both a chunk of cured bacon he had taken from the fridge, and it did not take Bruno long before he was walking beside Robert contentedly.

At the tool shed the main door was shut but the building had been recently painted and the hinges greased. The cattle sheds were clean and prepped with fresh hay, salt lick and water. The sheep pens again were as he would have wanted them, well stocked. He noticed the wooden boundary fences had a fresh coat of paint too. The storage barn for winter feed was full dry and secured. Robert shook his head as he walked on; he could find no fault anywhere he looked. He knew how much hard work it would have taken to achieve. The final sheep shed was the building that surprised him the most. It was completely transformed and looked more like a hostel or dormitory. It was locked with a new sturdy door, but through one of the side windows he could see neat rows of beds laid out down the length of the structure. It was impressive but puzzling.

Both of their sons were students at the Aberdeen and North of Scotland College of Agriculture at Robert's insistence. Douglas was now 19, Robert calculated; a year older than Brody; but he was completely out of touch with how they were currently coping with their studies. He had missed out on far too much of his sons' development while he was away. He pictured them both now, Douglas with his shock of brown curly hair, his stubborn chin, and eyes so dark they looked like enlarged pupils. A hyperactive child – always managing to injure himself somehow.

When Brody was born both parents thought there was something wrong with him. He was physically healthy but always so placid, worryingly so after their experience with Douglas. Brody hardly cried or demanded their attention, and when he did hurt himself, it was usually caused by his bigger brother's antics. Robert smiled at the memory and longed to see them both.

When he re-entered the kitchen an hour later with the dogs in tow, his hunger increased tenfold at the smell of fresh bread. It was good to be home, but he needed answers. "What on earth has been going on here at the farm?"

"Why, is there something wrong?" Rachael replied with a grin while setting the modest table with four settings. It would be the first time the family had shared a meal together for several years and Rachael was determined to make sure it was perfect.

Robert leaned forward to select a pickled onion from a bowl on the kitchen table and got his hand slapped, thwarting his attempts. "OW! No, there's nothing wrong. Everything looks incredible. How have you managed to do it, and I see the old sheep shed has been turned into some sort of guest house?"

Rachael smiled. "I will let the boys tell you when they get back. Why don't you go and wash up for lunch, they should be here soon."

Jock barked before both dogs ran off, slipping on the polished veranda floor in their haste to greet the boys. Robert went to the front door and looked out at two young men walking towards the house. The dogs obviously recognised them, but Robert had to wait until they were closer to comprehend the transformation in his children.

Douglas was no longer a skinny little boy with dark curly hair. He was as tall as Robert and broader in the shoulder than his father. It was hard to believe it was the same child, even just at nineteen he was already a powerful-looking young man with fresh stubble on his chin. The dark eyes were extremely familiar, and they looked perfectly set in his handsome face.

Brody was shorter than his brother but still around six foot. He looked like a masculine version of his mother. He was not as broad as his brother in the shoulder, but still looked athletic. His face warmed with kind blue eyes when he smiled. He was a handsome young man and perfectly in proportion, unlike his rather lanky father, but they both shared a head of blond hair.

The boys put down their carrier bags and embraced their father in unison. Robert could not stop the tears from rolling down his cheeks as he held them. When they let go of each other Robert noticed tears in Brody's eyes. Douglas had determinedly held his emotions back. "It's so good to see you both. My, you have changed so much! Look at the pair of you!" Robert was over the moon to be re-united with them all. "Come in, we will talk over lunch. Your mother has been busy preparing it for hours."

The conversation around the table could have been awkward, but it was not. Both sons recognised the happiness they saw in their mother that had been missing for so long. They were genuinely glad to see their father, despite his prolonged absence. Robert was so proud of the young men in front of him. There were still glimpses of the children he knew but what was also apparent was the close bond the two of them shared. They asked about what it was like being at war and Robert replied but saved them from the grim details and the painful memories that still darkened his thoughts. He spoke about sabotaging the mission and the bullet wound, but glossed over the painful loss of Angus, his best friend. Finally, Robert steered the conversation back to their home and addressed his eldest son: "Doug, I have to know how on earth you three have managed to take such impeccable care of the farm?"

Douglas wiped his mouth on his napkin and looked at his younger brother. "Go ahead, Brody, you can explain better than I can."

Brody drained the last of his milk and replied, "It's a bit of a long story really. We initially both found settling in at the college rather difficult, but we stuck at it. Doug and I helped each other through some tough times."

What he meant by that was Douglas struggled with the academic side of his tuition but exceeded at the manual and practical aspects of their training. His build suited the physical work, but more than that, he demonstrated a passion for tending to animals. He seemed to manage his labour assignments with ease. Brody was the other way around. Academically he excelled with the theory of farming and finance. He ended up tutoring Douglas to help improve his grades and Douglas helped Brody get to grips with the physical challenges. While battling their way through their studies, the farm was in desperate need of attention, and it pained them both to see their mother struggle.

Brody continued, "I came up with a proposal and a learning module for the college that could integrate theory and practice on a working farm. Under the right circumstances, a class of resident students could use their time more wisely – work and learn more effectively. I suggested a pilot cohort of twelve resident students to live and work on our farm under tuition from the Aberdeen College lecturers. The outcomes at the end of the semester could be compared against twelve students following the college's existing theory and practice protocols.

"The college was impressed with the scheme, and we ended up with twelve willing hands for an entire term helping on the farm. They were all dead keen to beat the rival students and the final grades were heavily in favour of the pilot project. The college were so impressed they decided to duplicate the learning method and roll it out to similar farms in the region, so now as it stands all current students of the Aberdeen and North of Scotland Agricultural College reside and learn on working farms.

"There is also something else: I approached the faculty with a request to move up a year because I was ahead in my academic studies. With the students taking care of most of the chores on the farm, I could devote more time to study. They accepted and as things stand now, Doug and I will both graduate in December together."

Robert shook his head – amazed. He was silently contemplating what his eighteen-year-old son had achieved. What they had *both* achieved on their own merit. Despite their age, they demonstrated a maturity beyond their years that was truly remarkable and in doing so the farm and the family benefited.

Brody sensed Douglas was being overlooked. "Doug and I *both* tried hard to make sure it worked, Dad. We showed the tutors more efficient methods of building, working with the livestock and machinery. We work well together. We were not able to take all the pressure off Mum, but we did our best."

Robert understood. "I am incredibly proud of both of you. What you have done is nothing short of outstanding."

An idea occurred to Robert, and Douglas gave him an opening. He looked at his father and said, "Tell us about the land you purchased in Southern Rhodesia."

Rachael stiffened and cleared the table while Robert spoke to his boys. He fetched a map and the photographs from his backpack, and they listened in silence until he stopped speaking.

"Two thousand hectares? What's that, Brody, about six square miles?" Doug eventually asked, looking at his brother.

"Closer to eight," Brody replied.

The three of them talked on late into the night, discussing the land from every conceivable angle, terrain, climate, water supply, funds, predators, market, livestock. Rachael eventually went to bed and left them to it.

In the morning Douglas woke his parents with a coffee at 6am. He waited for his mother to wipe the sleep from her eyes before he said, "Ma, Brody and I want to go to Southern Rhodesia to manage the ranch for you and Dad as soon as we graduate. When the war is over, you and Dad can join us."

It was clear from his tone and their body language they had already between them made their decision, but they desperately wanted her blessing.

∾

## 9TH OCTOBER 1941. BULAWAYO, SOUTHERN RHODESIA

The new offices at Queens Park were located two kilometres northeast of Bulawayo city centre, off Reigate Road. Although the original sight of the registry office had been moved to the new government complex, it was easy to locate. It was the only three-storey building in the area and well signposted. Its functional oblong structure and white walls were lined with windows at regular intervals, providing light and air to the civil servants it contained. A square clocktower ascended three storeys clear of the main block from the centre of the eastern facing wall. It flew the solitary Southern Rhodesian flag. The Union Jack was set top left against a light blue background. The green shield and golden pick in the centre symbolising farming and mining; the crest of two thistles and red lion at the top of the shield were taken from Cecil John Rhodes' coat of arms. It fluttered in the light morning breeze as Malcolm parked up. Malcolm considered the flag to be an apt symbol of the young country's resources and potential.

His car turned heads driving through the main town as it always did when it was on show. The 1935 cherry-red two-seater Alfa Romeo convertible Roadster sports car was stunning and the only one of its kind in the country. Its tear-drop fenders and boot made the vehicle look menacingly fast. Under the hood the 6.3 litre straight 8-cylinder engine delivered what the exterior design promised. It was enormously powerful and purred in earnest at the slightest touch of the accelerator.

Malcolm deliberately kept it a secret from Samuel his assistant, hiding it in the locked garage behind Malcolm's cottage. He seldom used it, but it was his only true luxurious indulgence – his pride and joy. Samuel's face was a picture when he watched Malcolm pull out of the mine. He stared in disbelief with his mouth wide open. Now that the secret was out, he would console the poor lad on his return by taking him for a spin, but he certainly would not be allowed to drive it!

Harold Bucket was waiting for Malcolm in his office at the end of the hall on the ground floor. He had lost the senior position of Government Treasurer after being implicated in a bribery scandal over dodgy land acquisitions. His disgruntled *dim-witted* secretary at the time had leaked papers to the press after enduring one too many unwanted gropes and Harold's unwelcomed advances. He was fortunate to still be employed in any capacity, but he remained well connected and had scraped through to his current position by the skin of his teeth and a sizeable charitable donation.

He was now in charge of the important job of shuffling papers in the deeds' office and historical archive. Despite the demotion he still dressed and behaved as he did when he was the treasurer, pompous and self-important. Malcolm brought a bottle of single malt whisky to help loosen Harold's tongue. It was his Achilles heel. Without the benefit of a secretary, he greeted Malcom himself by shaking hands vigorously eyeing the whisky while his flabby jowls wobbled. His balding head beaded with sweat below the shoddy combover and L-plate sideburns. His bloodshot eyes suggested it would not be his first drink of the day.

"Always a pleasure to see you, Mr Hunter, especially bearing gifts," he crooned, grasping the bottle.

"Please call me Malcolm," Malcolm replied, accepting the offered chair.

"Very well! And what can I do you for, Malcolm?"

"It may be a long shot, but I'm interested in the history of my gold mine. I have been through the archives in Umtali with the enigmatic Mr Ward but can't seem to find any background on *Crawley Concession*. That's the name of my outfit. I know the Portuguese have a history of mining in the area, but I'm curious as to what happened to the previous owner. Apparently, he died under suspicious circumstances, and his mine was deserted, but I haven't come across any factual evidence. The last time I saw Ward he said there may be a chance some records were transferred here to Bulawayo in '34. Is there any chance you could perhaps check?"

"Crawley Concession you say," Harold groaned as he shifted his ample rump out of his seat. "Frankly it's surprising you got a thing out of Ward, tight arsed little prick! He firmly believes God himself chose him for his assignment. I will see what I can do. Pour us a scotch, will you?"

Malcolm retrieved two glasses from the drinks tray on the desk and poured a generous shot in Harold's glass and a moderate one for himself. Harold returned a few minutes later bearing a file triumphantly and downed his whisky before collapsing in his seat. The effort of moving several steps clearly tired him out and he dabbed at his perspiration with a handkerchief. "You are in luck! Let's see what we have here," he said, placing his glasses on the end of his nose and paging through the file.

"We have here one death certificate for a Cecil Crawley, previous owner of the mine. Died of a heart attack apparently according to the coroner's report. Nothing further there." He turned over an article cut out of a newspaper, scanned through it, and handed it to Malcolm.

Malcolm read the brief report. Cecil Crawley was found about three days after his death by a truck driver delivering mail to the mines. The driver described the mine as being abandoned without a soul in sight. Mr Crawley appeared to have died with what was described as *a hideous grin on his face*. The article asked for anyone with information to contact the local police station. There was no follow-up article.

Harold was busy reading what looked like an official document. He handed it to Malcolm. It was an application to change the name of the gold mine from *Mahaha Gold Fields* to *Crawley Concession*, signed by Cecil Crawley himself.

"Well now that is interesting," Harold announced, pouring another stiff drink and downing it in one swallow.

"What is?"

"The previous name of the mine – 'Mahaha Gold Fields'."

"Why is that interesting?"

"Do you know what the Mahaha is?"

"Never heard of it."

"The Mahaha is an Inuit legend."

"Inuit as in Eskimo?"

"Yes, one and the same."

"But why on earth would the mine be called that? Not a whole heap of Eskimos running around in the middle of Africa!"

"No, perhaps not, but consider this if you will. The Inuit are originally from Asia but migrated through North America and Canada as far as Greenland. You know already that the Portuguese have been active in Southern Africa for centuries. Very active in Southern Rhodesia, in fact, with the slave trade and filling their pockets with gold. But did you also know that in the 1500s the Portuguese brothers Corte-Real had several voyages of exploration and discovery up the west coast of Africa into the North Atlantic up as far as Greenland? Clearly plausible that they may have encountered the Inuit tribes or Eskimos as you call them and heard of this *Mahaha legend*. It is also highly possible they had a bunch of slaves on board their expedition, harvested from the indigenous tribes in Rhodesia. Perhaps they were so taken by the tale, the Portuguese settlers later named their gold fields after the Mahaha creature. Stranger things have happened!"

"What is the legend exactly?"

"A lot of old poppycock like most legends if you ask me, but the story is this Mahaha demon is supposedly extremely tall and thin, bright blue with long black hair and piercing white eyes. Quite the looker, hey? Oh, and giant fingernails he uses to tickle his victims to death."

"Charming."

"Quite! Apparently, a mischievous bastard with a wicked laugh. His victims often found with a forced smile on their dead lips. Like I said, a load of codswallop."

Malcolm tried to make sense of what he had just heard. Why would Crawley go to the trouble of renaming the mine if his primary concern was harvesting gold? Why was the mine abandoned? It felt like Crawley's death was strangely connected with the bizarre myth. Malcolm was not a superstitious man and did not believe in ghosts or witchcraft, but something stirred, leaving him quite unsettled.

Harold eyed his visitor suspiciously. "Malcolm, I didn't take you for one believing in mumbo jumbo nonsense. Purely a coincidence, just another fanciful legend, dear boy! I have a history major. History is riddled with utter nonsense! Tales, legends, superstitions, and it's all utter crap. Ironically, I have ended up here in charge of records of our most recent history – fools and their exploits."

Malcolm left Harold to the remnants of the bottle, thanking him for his assistance but feeling a little confused.

Malcolm's next two meetings were brief but successful. The bank required a few forms to be filled in. He left with a cheque book allowing him to access capital to pay the overdue bills for Molly's ranch. He made several stops in town, settling accounts before he met with the auctioneers. Jack Turner the owner of the auction house had several business interests, including a construction company Malcolm was relieved to learn about. It was possible for Jack to arrange for a team to renovate the dilapidated farmhouse at Hillside Ranch and would send someone out in the morning to provide an estimate for the costs.

Before collecting Ashton George, the Australian geologist, from the railway station, Malcolm checked in at the local post office. If there was an emergency on his mine in Penhalonga, Ephraim the mine captain was instructed to phone the Bulawayo post office to relay a message to Malcolm. It was therefore necessary for the post office to know his whereabouts. He left word that he would be staying at Cedar Tree Hollow, Robert Hunter's ranch in Insiza, about half an hour's drive from the city.

On the way to the station Malcolm picked up supplies from the general store and butchery, enough to tide them over for a few days. There was barely enough space in the Alfa Romeo's boot for Ashton's backpack and prospecting tools, but it closed in the end with a bit of reshuffling. Ashton generally travelled light with just a spare set of underwear and socks.

After driving over predominately dirt roads surrounded by dry savanna terrain, they pulled up outside Cedar Tree Hollow. It was a newly built, spacious two-storey four-bedroomed granite dwelling. A spectacular thatched roof neatly flowed over the three dormer windows protruding symmetrically from the front facing first floor. The raised veranda railing and front steps were all made from solid cedar wood, and it stretched along the length of the front of the house. A large rectangular chimney extended a few metres above the thatched roof on the right.

"Not a bad shack," Ashton observed, seeing the place for the first time.

The house was completely empty except for two single mattresses Malcolm placed in front of the large fireplace in the lounge. After unpacking the boot, they set off for Red Herring Mine, a walk of around ten miles to the southeast corner of Hillside Ranch. Malcolm led and set a brisk pace as they walked along in silence. His mind kept drifting back to his conversation with Harold Bucket at the archive. He visualised the Mahaha demon in his mind, the tall, thin blue body with long black hair and glowing white eyes. The mental picture made his skin crawl, and he shook his head to dislodge the image.

Ashton kept up with Malcolm's pace easily with his long legs. He was tall and thin with a large eagle-like beak for a nose, never seeming to put on any weight despite his ferocious appetite for meat and beer. He had two or three days of stubble on his jaw and a wide brimmed felt hat covering his forehead and alert eyes. "You alright, mate? You look like some bastard walked across your grave."

"No, all good."

They reached the old mine half an hour later. It consisted of two shafts shuttered with timbers sunk into the rocky ground, surrounded by intermittent shallow pits at random intervals covering an area the size of a football field. Ashton set to work at once, surveying the surrounding area and taking samples with his pick. Malcolm had worked with Ashton before, and he knew it was best to leave him to it. He looked at his watch – they had roughly an hour before they needed to return if they were to avoid walking back in the dark. A coiled rope lay abandoned next to one of the shafts. There was no headgear or tools, just odd piles of rubble, everything else had been removed or stolen.

Ashton returned with a fist size green and white lump of quartz. "I found an outcrop about twenty metres east of here worth checking out. I'll crush and pan this when we get back. Give me a hand with this rope, I want to take a look down this shaft."

Ashton tied the rope around his waist and produced a cap lamp from his backpack. He clipped two sample bags to his belt and held his pick in his left hand. "Let me down nice and slow."

Malcolm wound the rope around his waist and slowly fed it out, bracing his feet a few steps away from the entrance to the shaft. Ashton descended slowly into the darkness as Malcolm strained against the heavy weight. "Stop!" he heard about ten metres in, followed by the sound of the pick impacting on stone and dirt. "Go!" came the instruction a few seconds later and he commenced lowering Ashton further. "Stop!" followed by more pick work and eventually to Malcolm's relief. "OK! All the way up!"

If it was hard work bearing the weight of Ashton on the way down, it was agony bringing him up again. Malcolm pulled with all his might leaning back against the strain and slowly shuffling his feet backwards away from the gaping black hole. Finally, Ashton emerged covered in dust. He got a foothold in one of the timbers and pulled himself out. Malcolm had rubbed the skin raw on the palms of his hands. "Bloody hell, you're heavy! We best make a move to get back before sundown."

The return journey was uneventful, and they both drained a beer before making a cooking fire a short way from the house. They dined on grilled rump steak sadza and tomato relish, which they devoured ravenously after their physical exertion, and washed it down with several beers. Ashton crushed the green quartz rock sample in his pestle and mortar and panned the dust with water by the light of a paraffin lamp, swirling and shaking, rewashing, and repeating the process until he had produced a small tail of yellow metal in the base of the bowl.

"It's a pretty rich sample," he said, handing the pan to Malcolm, "I need to get into that second shaft tomorrow, but my initial suspicion is the dumb bastards had been mining an offshoot of a larger deposit. There is plenty of evidence of the sheering that has taken place by the rocky outcrops. Down the shaft they followed narrow veins of quartz that may have been very rich, but they quickly petered out. The second shaft will add another dimension to the equation, but if my theory is correct and the fault lines are consistent with the sheering on the surface, it may be worth drilling a few pilot holes where I took this quartz sample. You might want to assay those samples for an accurate grading, but I will confirm my findings once I have been down the second shaft."

"Ok, we will head back again tomorrow. Make sure you part with your steak in the morning. You were heavy enough before you ate. We'll head out at sunrise." Malcolm doused the fire, and they went to bed.

Before drifting off to sleep he contemplated the ruin that befell the previous landowners. The owners of Hillside Ranch and Cedar Tree Hollow were long gone. Both had lost absolutely everything in their foolish pursuit of gold. Pieter Potgieter, who owned White Stone Farm on the other side of Hillside Ranch, had also invested heavily in the mining project and he too had lost everything. He still owned his land, but rumour had it that White Stone was currently in a state of disrepair and neglect. Pieter had lost both of his sons in the war, his wife had apparently left him, and his remaining daughter was away at boarding school and never returned home, not even during the holidays. Three families, their homesteads and land destroyed by the failed mine. *Adequately named Red Herring* he thought.

When he finally drifted off to sleep, he was troubled by nightmares of the Mahaha.

# Chapter 11

## 10TH OCTOBER 1941 – CEDAR TREE HOLLOW, ESSEXVALE, BULAWAYO, SOUTHERN RHODESIA

It had seemed like a good idea at the time to crack open a bottle of single malt whisky the night before, but the pounding in Malcolm's head this morning made him regret the decision. They had spent most of the previous day at Red Herring at the edge of Molly's property, sampling the second shaft and surrounding area. Ashton was almost totally convinced his initial theory was correct and the main ore body had been missed. He would have to come back with a drilling rig to sample further below the surface, but the prospects looked very encouraging. Malcolm used his driving gloves to save his hands from further injury as he supported Ashton's weight on the rope up and down the shaft.

On return to Cedar Tree Hollow in the afternoon, Jack Turner's builders showed up and inspected the run-down house at Hillside Ranch. The external structure was found to be solid, and he estimated two to three months to restore the property to its former glory. Malcolm gave him Molly's telephone number in order to pass on the quotation. It was not long after they left when a surprise visitor turned up.

It was difficult to estimate the age of the uniformed officer that stood before Malcolm and Ashton. He was tall, thick set with broad strong shoulders and a barrel of a chest, but most of his face was badly scarred and he wore a black patch over his left eye. The smile looked unconvincing on his disfigured lips as he shook Malcolm's hand with a vice-like grip. He rolled his 'r's in a thick accent as he introduced himself as Henrick Van Royen.

"I'm looking for Robert Hunter. I know I'm in the right place, it's the only Cedar Tree Hollow on the map. Is he here?" Henrick asked.

Malcolm investigated the unblinking steel-like gaze of Henrick's remaining hazel-coloured eye, finding the stranger difficult to fathom. "No, he isn't here. Is there something I can help you with? I'm Malcolm, Robert's brother."

"Nice to meet you, Malcolm. I spent about six months with Robert in Pretoria Hospital. Robert had a bullet wound in his right leg and I, well you can see for yourself how the war left me. Third degree burns from my head to my hips. I used to have nipples!" Henrick burst out laughing at his own joke and it softened the mood slightly.

"Robert told me about his farm and said I should come for a visit."

"I'm afraid he is still in Scotland."

"Ok, that's a shame. I was hoping to ask him for a job. My family have a large sugar cane plantation in the Eastern Cape in South Africa, but my two older brothers and father have got the farm pretty much under control."

"How old are you, Henrick, if you don't mind me asking?"

"Twenty-seven."

"And you have a background in farming?"

"Ya, up until I enlisted farming was all I knew. The Van Royens have been farming for several generations in the Cape. Sugar cane is our main cash crop but we have grown maize and tobacco amongst other things. We also farm sheep and cattle on a smaller scale."

The conversation was interrupted by a van approaching up the driveway. When the vehicle stopped and the driver got out, Malcolm recognised the insignia on the door – it belonged to the local post office. The driver seemed in quite a hurry. "I have an urgent telegram for Mr Malcolm Hunter."

Malcolm snatched the document from the messenger and felt the blood freeze in his veins as he read the typed script.

*Mr Hunter*

*You must return to the mine at once. All work has stopped, and the compound has been abandoned. I will be joining my family as soon as I return the Ford to the mine. I am sorry. Samuel.*

"What is it?" Ashton asked, aware of the sudden change in Malcolm's mood.

"I need to get back to the mine," he replied, handing Ashton the note.

"Don't worry about me. I can make my own way to the station. You had better leave right away," Ashton replied without hesitation.

Malcolm looked at Henrick and said, "Come with me into town. I may have a job for you. I need to make a call before I return to the mine."

# 9TH OCTOBER 1941 LOCHLUICHART, MACMILLAN FARM – EDINBURGH, SCOTLAND

Mary skipped along playfully next to her mother to keep up. The dairy cows had returned to the barn shortly before sundown and were now happily secure and out of the chilly evening breeze. Molly carried a pale of fresh warm milk. She would harvest the rich cream from the top to serve with the apple crumble she had made earlier.

Robert and Rachael Hunter were coming up to visit and due to arrive shortly. It was a four-hour drive for them from Aberdeen via Stirling and Annie, Mary's maid, prepared the spare room with fresh linen and towels. They were the only visitors Molly had entertained since Angus' death but of late she had taken on a more positive outlook on her circumstances. Yes, she was a widow and a single parent, but she was now also the owner of 4000 hectares of prime farmland in Southern Rhodesia. The company of other adults would do her good.

Whatever free time she had, she spent researching the challenges of farming in southern Africa. She learned all she could about Rhodesia, its climate and terrain, its economy and political ties to the United Kingdom. It was a fascinating place with warm to moderate temperatures throughout the year. The towns, rural areas and infrastructure were in a state of rapid development. An interesting arbitrary fact she learned through her reading was that Southern Rhodesia had more than 5000 Italian Prisoners of War (POW) from the Battle of Keren in four concentration camps around the country. The same battle where Angus was killed sabotaging the Italian munition hold.

The POW were being used as a labour force to construct roads, airfields, and an extensive nationwide telephone line installation. The Empire Air Training Scheme (EATS) set up flight training centres for British and Commonwealth pilots to be schooled at multiple locations throughout Southern Rhodesia. The Rhodesian Air Training Group (RATG) was a fast-growing local British asset reporting to EATS. The capital investment and revenue from the initiative bolstered the country's revenue. Even though the world was at war and the global economy was largely in a recession, the youngest and smallest of the commonwealth members was crucial to the war effort and prospered.

Her new mindset helped her to view the future with a growing sense of adventure. When Malcolm Hunter had called her and she spoke out loud for the first time about her ideas and plans for Hillside Ranch, her own words reinforced her resolve. Hillside was now in her daily thoughts, and she had a growing desire to get there. So, when Robert Hunter called and asked to visit, she jumped at the chance. He would have personally set foot on the ground she now owned.

Mary interrupted her thoughts with a question, "Mum, why are we nice to cows?"

Molly knew from experience how Mary's thought process had developed and braced herself. "Well, they are our animals, and we look after them."

"Then why do we eat them?"

"You see, honey, well fed animals produce good quality meat that we sell to keep our farm going, and we eat it ourselves."

Mary was silent for moment before she came back with, "Then why don't we eat Sylvester?"

Molly cringed at the mental image of the grumpy old cat being skinned for the pot. "Because Sylvester is our pet, and besides, he would probably taste awful!"

Fortunately, Mary's attention was distracted by the vehicle that turned into their driveway. Robert and Rachael Hunter arrived. Mary took the milk to the kitchen while Molly greeted her guests. Although there was a significant height difference between the two new visitors, they looked like a nice couple together. Robert was rather tall in his tweed waistcoat and trousers, but he had a broad smile and there was a warmth to his eyes. Rachael had tied her hair back in a bun and she was elegantly dressed in a navy-blue pencil skirt and white blouse. Molly wondered if they had struggled to work out what to wear. It seemed they had dressed for a business meeting rather than a casual visit. She gave them both a hug and showed them into the lounge. Sylvester gave them a frown before re-settling in front of the fire.

Their small talk centred around the farms, their families, and the journey over from Aberdeen. Molly sensed Robert wanted to talk about Angus but was too polite to broach the subject, so she saved him the discomfort by saying, "Robert, you fought alongside my husband, and you were friends. You must miss him too."

"We formed a close friendship during some extreme circumstances. It is difficult to explain what we went through together and harder to accept the fact that he is gone. He was such a character. A good man and a good friend. He frequently spoke of you." Robert sounded close to tears, full of emotion.

"I cannot say it has been easy getting to grips with his passing. He left an empty hole in our hearts and our lives. I was initially furious that he went ahead and bought farmland in Rhodesia without discussing it with me, but I have a better understanding of the circumstances now and I can see the appeal," Molly replied, keeping a lid on her own grief.

"Have you given thought to what you would like to do with the place?"

"Yes, I have given it considerable thought. I plan to employ a farm manager until I can physically get there. Malcolm is looking into that this week. The house needs a lot of work and boundary fences must be redone. Once the property is secure, I will look at renting out some of the land for grazing."

Robert was a little astonished that Molly intended to run the farm. In the back of his mind, he had assumed it would be too much for her and she would get rid of it. "I'm delighted you will move to Rhodesia. We will be neighbours! My two sons graduate from agricultural college at the end of the year. They are a fine pair. Doug and Brody will go over to look after the farm until the war is over, then Rachael and I will join them and start a new chapter in our lives."

The conversation flowed easier with the tension now broken, assisted by a couple of bottles of merlot over dinner. Molly's cottage pie and apple crumble were a big hit with her guests, and even Mary polished hers off rather than chasing it around her plate for an hour. When Robert spoke freely about Angus, their friendship, and experiences, it was therapeutic for both him and Molly. Too many memories had been supressed or passed over. Molly found it refreshing to talk about Angus. She opened up and spoke about their lives together from the first day they met right up until the military envoy delivered his belongings after his passing. She talked about her initial motivation for leaving home, hoping for a life of adventure away from the family tailor shop in Glasgow. She described rediscovering her enthusiasm as she focussed positively on her opportunity in Africa.

Rachael and Mary hit it off and were chatting like chipmunks holding hands as they adjourned to the lounge. "This is Sylvester our grumpy old cat. Mum says we can't eat him because he will taste funny."

Rachael laughed and turned to Robert and said, "We really should have had a daughter."

"But we have two strapping boys!"

"Yes, but we could have done with a little girl too."

Mary beamed with all the attention. Her broad smile made her chubby cheeks chubbier. Her golden plaited hair reaching her waist.

"Time for bed, Mary," came the spoilsport announcement from her mother and the smile evaporated as Mary slinked off to her room.

Rachael had not been overly keen on the debate centred around Rhodesia, but knowing Molly and Mary were going to make the move made her a little more accepting of the idea. She loved her home and was not looking forward to the upheaval of relocating halfway around the world, no matter how wonderful the opportunity was made out to be.

Mary hovered outside the guest bedroom where Rachael and Robert were still sound asleep. She was desperate to introduce Rachael to Flossie, her favourite rag doll, but Molly insisted she wait until they were at least awake. They all slept well after an evening that felt more like a positive family experience than meeting strangers for the first time.

Molly was in the kitchen preparing a breakfast of scrambled egg with rosemary from her herb garden, smoked bacon, and grilled tomato. She tried her best to quietly multitask so as not to disturb the rest of the household, but as she brewed the coffee the phone rang noisily from the lounge. It managed two shrill rings before she could reach it. Nobody could sleep through that racket.

It was Malcolm Hunter. "Hello Molly, I need to be brief. I have an emergency on the mine."

"I'm sorry to hear there's trouble for you, Malcolm."

"I have spent the last few days up at your ranch. A building team will contact you directly with the estimate for renovations to the house. They are a sound crew, and their boss is well known to me. I potentially may have a farm manager for you, but I need you to get a message to Robert. The guy knows him from Pretoria hospital."

"Robert is right here with me. Hold a second, I will put him on."

Robert had heard the phone ring and that it was Malcolm on the line. He hurried down into the lounge wearing pyjamas and uncombed hair. "Hello Malcom, how can I help?"

"Do you know a Henrick Van Royen?"

"You mean 'eye patch' Henrick, the South African from Pretoria Hospital?"

"Yes, apparently, you told him where you would be farming so he came up to see you. He was discharged not long after you. His family run a cane plantation in the Cape but he's looking for a job."

"Of course, I know Henk, yes, I just wasn't expecting him quite so soon. I would certainly vouch for him as a sound bloke, but I have no idea what his farming skills are like. We talked a lot during my stay in hospital, maybe just keep a close eye on him. Rachael and I will be sending Doug and Brody to look after the farm for us. They graduate in December and have both achieved some outstanding work here while I was away."

"That is good news, I look forward to seeing them. Please let Molly know we have found a manager for her. I will touch base with her in a few days, but I need to get going."

# Chapter 12

## CRAWLEY CONCESSION GOLD MINE – PENHALONGA, SOUTHERN RHODESIA

The full beam of the Alfa Romeo illuminated the dirt road as Malcolm finally reached his office. The sun had set more than an hour ago. There was not a single light on anywhere as he looked around the empty mine. The evening air was cool, deathly still and eerily quiet. He kept the headlights on; fortunately they were both still intact.

Malcolm was quite accustomed to high speed but on this occasion when he left Cedar Tree in haste, he collided with an animal. He was almost off the dirt road at the intersection of the main northeast highway when a stray goat shot out in front of him. There was no time to break. The front left fender and bumper impacted with the creature with such force it sent it cartwheeling over the carriageway to land with a meaty thud in the ditch. Malcolm stopped briefly to check the damage to the front of his sports car – the goat was clearly beyond help. There was a large dent the size of a rugby ball in the bodywork and tufts of hair and blood on the bumper and embedded in the grille. Fortunately, there was no further mechanical damage, and the radiator and lights were unaffected. As he reviewed the mess again, he cursed with a shake of the head.

He turned his attention back to the present. There were four generators in total located throughout the development. The one behind his office powered the electrics for the office, Malcolm's home and the perimeter fences. On the first pull of the starter cord, it coughed once before idling rhythmically, instantly lighting up the barren buildings and boundary.

He retrieved a cap lamp and battery pack from the rack in his office, slipped on his mining boots and turned the car's lights off before setting out to investigate the silence. He made his way to the reduction plant behind the noiseless ball mill before heading to the compound. There was not a soul in sight. The settlement too was in complete darkness with no signs of life and no smoke coming from any of the mud huts. It made no sense at all. The operation was a hive of activity when he had left. What could account for it suddenly being abandoned? Samuel's telegram offered no explanation.

The closest village to the compound was an hour's walk along a footpath towards the base of the Penhalonga mountain range. There was no sense making the journey at this time of night, it would have to wait until morning. He would go at first light to speak to the elders of the village to try and get answers, but he was filled with uneasy trepidation as he entered his home and locked the door. He had no appetite but poured himself a stiff whisky. The generator had enough fuel to provide power for half the night. Usually refilling the fuel tanks was a duty undertaken at the change of the night shift, but it would obviously not take place tonight. For the time being the drone of the engine running helped to diminish the sense of isolation.

Malcolm stirred when the generator ran out of fuel. There was no moon, and the night was as black as tar. He had never felt more remote. Sleep finally overcame him but not for long. He awoke to the uneasy sense of a presence in the room. He tried to open his eyes and move, but his entire body felt paralysed. No sound escaped his throat when he tried to speak. Feverish sweat coated his body, drenching the sheets. Still unable to move, his eyes finally opened – forced open, it seemed, to stare in horror at the levitating creature above his bed. Its white pupilless eyes searched deep into Malcolm's soul as his heart pounded against his rib cage. The human form apparition had blue illuminous skin and an enlarged mouth twisted in a devilish grin. When it spoke, the air reeked of rotting flesh, and the voice reverberated through Malcolm's bones. It repeated just one sentence, "Bring me the beating heart of Samson!"

The words were spoken in a tongue Malcolm had never heard before but somehow, he was given the ability to understand. Time seemed to enter another dimension. He could not tell whether he was conscious or not, or how long the visitation lasted. The eyes were terrifying, but in his coma-like state he had no option but to gaze into their hypnotic depths. Malcolm was left completely drained of energy and drenched when slumber finally rescued him.

When he awoke in a panic, he frantically searched the room. There was no evidence of last night's visitation. His pulse thumped through his head and his hands trembled. He shuddered at the vivid recollection of what he had experienced. He ran over the meaningless words that echoed in his head as clear as day, *Bring me the beating heart of Samson.*

He thought back to his meeting with Harold Bucket at the Bulawayo archives and the revelation about the Inuit legend, the Mahaha demon, and the circumstances surrounding Crawley's death. It was too much of a coincidence to ignore. What he had experienced last night was some sort of supernatural phenomenon. He did not like it one bit.

The hastily prepared leather backpack contained a water bottle, dried kudu biltong, and two spare .303 magazine cartridges. Malcolm opted for his lightweight lace-up suede veld skoen shoes for their comfort over long distance. His khaki-coloured shirt and trousers were held up with a brown belt supporting the sheath and metre-long machete. He slung his Lee Enfield rifle with telescopic sights over his shoulder before he left. Discovering the door to his home left wide open made his skin crawl. He was certain he had locked it…

Daybreak licked the buildings with a honey-like glow as he headed out beyond the compound onto the narrow well-used pathway in the direction of the Penhalonga mountain range. As light strengthened the morning chorus of shrikes, doves, weavers and warblers greeted the sun from the flat tops of the mountain acacia and msasa trees that peppered the terrain.

Abruptly the landscape flattened onto a dry open plain about a mile wide. A fawn-grey kudu bull stood well clear of the blond grass, proudly sporting long twisted horns above the herd of smaller reddish-brown impala around him. The kudu followed Malcom's progress with interest while the nervous impala chewed at the grass, the black tips of their ears twitching at the slightest sound.

The path continued through the tree canopy opposite, forking at regular intervals as the ground became more inclined and the vegetation thicker. Malcolm continued following the well-worn walkway, occasionally using his machete to cut away overgrown scrub to allow himself to pass through. The foliage of the denser trees blocked out the morning sun, sheltering the damp soil and undergrowth from the heat. Twice he stopped along this section of path to observe lion tracks that must have been imbedded in the muddy ground after the last rains. The paw prints were clearly visible, ominously huge – almost as wide as Malcolm's outstretched hand.

He was an accurate marksman, but he hunted only out of necessity. Game was shot occasionally to provide a source of protein for his workforce. He ate some of the biltong from his backpack, cured meat from a young kudu bull he had taken down two months ago. A few swallows of water washed away the salty aftertaste before he set off again. The landscape continued to rise before giving way to a large shallow basin. On the crest he had a good view of the sprawling village below. Interlocking footpaths led to a multitude of circular mud huts with thatched roofs. Several rectangular animal pens contained malnourished cattle; the boundaries made from thorny branches to discourage nocturnal predators. A pair of bare breasted women were heading up a path that would intercept with Malcolm. They were oblivious to his presence, carrying clay pots effortlessly on their heads, chatting to each other quietly as they walked.

As soon as they saw Malcolm clutching his machete in one hand and a rifle slung over his shoulder, they dropped their pots and ran back to the safety of the village. A murmur rose from the huts and a crowd began to form as Malcolm entered the outskirts of the settlement. He could feel eyes upon him from the depths of the huts as he passed, occupants shielding themselves from the unwanted intruder.

The grinding of corn, milking of cows and mending of fishing nets all ceased as Malcolm came to a stop in front of the gathered villagers. He stretched out his arms above his head, hoping to reassure the crowd before he addressed them: "I come in peace. I must speak to the elders of your tribe. Who among you is your leader?"

They looked at each other blankly, not understanding the words of the white man, and a pregnant silence followed. Finally, there was movement from a nearby hut and Samuel, Malcolm's assistant, emerged sheepishly. "Mr Hunter, this is the village of my great-grandfather, he is the chief. I will gather him and the elders and translate for you. Most of the tribe do not speak English."

Samuel ran off, returning with four elderly tribesmen, holding hands with one of the ancient individuals. Samuel issued some instructions and six wooden stools soon materialised and were placed in a circle outside the chief's hut. When they were all seated, Malcolm looked at Samuel and asked, "Can you tell me what is going on? Why has the work stopped on the mine? Why has the compound been abandoned?"

Samuel shifted uncomfortably on his stool. "My great-grandfather is Madzinga. He is very old and very wise. It is customary to show respect to the chief of the tribe. It is best you address him as *Baba*. It means *father*, and clap your hands like this."

Samuel clapped his hands together with open palms and said, "Mangwanani Baba, it means *good morning, father.*"

Malcolm imitated Samuel, and the old men clapped their hands in unison in response as a sign of welcome. Samuel then translated Malcolm's questions to Madzinga.

Madzinga hesitated briefly before croaking his dismissive reply: "Your pits in the earth that search for the yellow metal have been cursed. All men, women and children living there have been cursed too, including you." Madzinga pointed at Malcolm while Samuel translated.

"What is the reason for the curse? How can it be broken?"

The chief shook his head and took a while to gather his thoughts. "White men have no understanding of our history and do not believe that evil spirits and the spirits of our ancestors walk among us. The curse cannot be broken."

Malcolm interjected: "I have been visited by the Mahaha."

At the mention of the spirit creature's name, the elders shuddered and rubbed their hands over their heads in a display of grief. The entire village were visibly afraid and murmured amongst themselves.

Madzinga finally spoke. "The Mahaha only visits when he takes. He does not appear to the white man!"

Malcolm persisted. "The Mahaha came to me last night. He spoke to me."

Again, the elders rubbed their heads in anguish when Samuel translated, and the crowd muttered in astonishment.

Malcolm clapped his open palms together and tried to sound more respectful. "Baba, please tell me all you know about the Mahaha."

Madzinga raised his eyes heavenward before returning his stare to the ground in front of him. He spoke reflectively: "Generations ago, men of different colour would come from the east in search of the yellow metal. Many of our men and women were taken as slaves from our village, never to return. The intruders left only the very young, the sick and the old. Infants were stripped from their mothers because the men from the east fed on the swollen breasts of the women. For too long we would hide in the forest to escape being taken or killed. Then one day they suddenly stopped coming and our people were able to settle and prosper once more."

Malcolm tried to imagine what it would be like living in fear. What a dreadful existence.

Madzinga continued, "When I was a young boy, a strange ancient black man came. He said he was a descendant of one of the ancestors taken long ago. He travelled over vast oceans and lands covered in ice to return. He spoke of many things we could not fully understand, and the elders believed he was touched by the spirits. He was outcast, but he stole a young boy as he fled. It was a child of noble birth, my older brother Mbira, destined to be chief. He was a very special child with the mark of the leopard on his back. We searched for Mbira, but not even our best trackers could find signs of where they had gone. It was as if they had vanished.

"For many years our village returned to peace, but on Mbira's sixteenth birthday, his abductor passed on to him the spirit of the Mahaha. We do not know the reason why my brother was chosen or why this mischief was released on our people, but every seven years he returns.

"Seven days before the full moon, his laughter echoes off the mountains. On the night of the full moon, he will unleash his mischief."

"What sort of mischief?" Malcolm demanded.

"He has taken the first-born sons of all villagers on both sides of the mountain. He has at times bullied our livestock, changing the sex of the bulls, leaving only cows that cannot produce or breed. He has stolen young wives from us, never to be seen again. Some of our elders believe he has got the creatures of the forest to do his work. What did the Mahaha say to you?"

"Bring me the beating heart of Samson."

The elders talked amongst themselves before one of them addressed Malcolm directly. "I am Indidzai, and I know of this Samson. He is a male lion that is older than I am. He has killed more men, women, children and livestock than any other predator in our history, but he cannot be killed. I believe the Mahaha has used Samson to do his work in the past. Our witch doctor believes Samson has been given some of the Mahama's power. You are the first white man to have been given a message from him. We must consult Hupenyu our N'anga (witch doctor) on the meaning of what you have told us. Hupenyu will need a gift in order to speak to us about the matter."

Malcolm removed the machete and sheath from his belt and handed it to Indidzai. Both he and Madzinga left to consult the holy one. Samuel looked grieved. He felt bad for abandoning Malcolm along with the rest of the compound, but had had little choice when his great-grandfather visited the mine to warn of the Mahaha's imminent return. Samuel respected his elders and followed the wisdom of their counsel and had returned to the village after sending the telegram to Malcolm in Bulawayo. He tried to avoid Malcolm's gaze.

Malcolm addressed him directly: "Samuel, where are the other labourers from the mine?"

"Some are here in this village; others are scattered over the other settlements on both sides of the mountain," he replied, not meeting Malcolm's eyes.

Madzinga and Indidzai returned a short while later carrying Malcolm's machete and a leather pouch made from a duiker's scrotum, and they handed them both to Malcolm. Samuel joined them to translate. He opened the hairy leather pocket and was about to sniff the powdered contents when Indidzai grabbed his hand. "Poison! It is a gift to you from Hupenyu the N'anga. Hupenyu says you will also need your knife. The powder in the bag is from the bark of a sacred tree not of our world. The N'anga believes the Mahaha has lost faith in the ancient Samson, but the heart of the lion still contains the gift of the Mahaha, the secret to his length of days. Hupenyu says killing Samson will lift the curse."

"How will the poison help me kill Samson?"

"The poison will not kill the beast, but it will blind it. If it cannot see you will have a better chance against him. We will mix a potion with the powder for you to dip your weapons into." Neither Indidzai nor the N'anga knew the origin of the powdered poison but had concrete faith in its power. It was made from the bark of the Manchineel Tree, native to the wetlands of the Americas. Carib Indians had found several uses of the powder as a toxin to ward off the Spanish conquistadores in the 1500s and 1600s. Although it had changed hands and continents over the centuries with multiple owners travelling thousands of miles, the powder still retained its original potency. The small pouch now contained the last of the ground poisonous bark in the witch doctor's possession.

But Malcolm had little faith in the questionable substance. "I don't think it will be much help to my rifle."

Indidzai, on the other hand, had firmly believed in the magic medicine. "You must also dip your bullets in the potion. The poison is very powerful, as is the lion you must hunt. Tanaka my grandson will go with you to help you find Samson. He is our best tracker, and he speaks some of your English words." He turned, anxious to make ready Malcolm's departure.

"I will leave at first light in the morning." Malcom sighed, accepting his fate.

"No! The N'anga says you must leave at once!"

The village was a hive of activity with preparations for the egress of the small impromptu hunting party. Tanaka, Indidzai's grandson, undertook the responsibility of being Malcolm's guide for the potentially perilous mission without complaint. He wore a lightweight dark brown loin cloth and a matching leather headband and little else. A thin strap around his waist carried a hollowed out brown horn about four inches long with a wooden bung for a cork. Malcolm had no idea what it contained but he assumed it was some sort of liquid. Tanaka's only weapon was a long wooden spear with a broad, sharp, leaf-shaped head. The blade had been soaked in the magic potion. The inlaid metal tip was secured to the shaft with neat strips of interwoven hide. He wore no shoes and carried no water.

Tanaka looked to be in his early twenties and in peak physical condition. He was a good foot taller than Malcolm and his bare feet dwarfed Malcolm's shoes when they stood together. Tanaka was a younger replica of his grandfather with chiselled high cheekbones, a wide flat nose, and full lips. His head had been closely shaved and his entire body rippled with honed muscle.

Malcolm felt significantly humbled given his current appearance. The elders insisted that white men gave off a scent of sour milk that would be easily picked up by their prey. To mask his natural body odour, they rubbed fresh cow dung over Malcolm's face and exposed skin. Initially outraged by the concept of being covered in shit, a strange primeval sense of calm and a connection to the land and the tribe began to wash over him.

A week ago, Malcolm was in full control of his destiny. He had not believed in the supernatural or harboured spiritual beliefs. Now he stood at the edge of a rural village, about to hunt a lion of extraordinary reputation at the insistence of a spirit creature that visited and commanded him to do so. His whole world had been turned upside down. For the time being the mine had to be put to the back of his mind. He had no option but to embrace the lateral thinking required to accept what needed to be done. As he checked his rifle magazine and ammunition, he thought how ludicrous it would sound retelling the course of events to anyone else. He was surprised that a part of him looked forward to the wild and unpredictable adventure ahead.

Tanaka pulled Malcolm aside, indicating the brown horn on his thin belt. "The N'anga will be my eyes. When we are away from the village, the spirits will reveal the path to Samson. Come."

He did not wait for Malcolm to respond but set out at a trot, heading towards the distant mountains. Malcolm fell in behind him, determined to keep up. The village had gathered to watch them go. The old mothers and grandmothers ululated; a sound they reserved for mourning and death. The young men and women shouted encouragement and the children laughed, oblivious to the dangers the hunters would face but excited by the occasion.

After about forty minutes of the relentless pace, Malcolm was out of breath and his shirt was damp with perspiration. He was grateful when Tanaka halted suddenly, breathing evenly, showing no signs of fatigue as he reached for the horn on his belt. He opened it and drank deeply of the N'anga's medicine. Malcolm watched as his guide swallowed the rancid smelling fluid. It had a profound effect on his companion. Tanaka fell to his knees, rocking himself back and forth, groaning and muttering. Eventually he rose again and stood upright with glazed eyes and a deadpan expression.

He set off again at a gentler pace, and Malcolm followed. Neither of them uttered a sound. Their direction was driven by a greater force, as they carved their own path through open grassy fields and undulating terrain. They encountered very little game until they were right at the base of the Penhalonga mountain in the late afternoon sun. Up ahead Tanaka had stopped and was crouched at the edge of a treeline. Malcolm saw a wide grassy meadow, like the one he had passed through on the way to the village. A sense of déjà vu washed over him as he scanned to the left of the field and saw what looked like the same kudu bull and impala herd grazing.

Tanaka raised his arm slowly pointing to the trees opposite. At first Malcolm saw nothing of interest. He searched again through the lens of the rifle scope until a twitch of Samson's ear revealed his location. The fearless unblinking golden eyes of the beast stared straight back at Malcolm. Even at a distance the predator was a magnificently intimidating specimen. Malcolm barely breathed as he held the lion's gaze, watching it pant through its open mouth. Its face was scarred from countless battles, yet the eyes burned fiercely.

The large ivory-coloured fangs and teeth were without blemish and menacing, even in their currently unemployed state. The majestic halo of a mane was a plethora of colour from its jet-black roots to the sun-bleached matted tips. Abruptly Samson rose and stood tall in the long grass, before turning to face the grazing herd with his mighty head close to the ground. The movement allowed Malcolm uninterrupted view of the full length of the lion from its flicking tail to the abundant mane and head. He lifted his rifle, aiming for the rib cage slightly behind the front left foreleg, the location of the heart. A millisecond before he pulled the trigger the lion stumbled forward, the weight of his front left paw breaking the surface of the ground into a shallow hollow. The movement shielded his heart from the bullet.

Malcolm did not blink when he pulled the trigger. He saw the bullet strike the front shoulder with a puff of dust on impact. Samson's deafening roar was filled with outrage and fury. The ground shook beneath Malcolm's feet as the mighty beast escaped back into the trees with alarming speed and agility. Tanaka, who had been crouching next to Malcolm in a trance, threw his head back and the wind from his lungs was expelled through clenched teeth with a long hissing. He collapsed and shook violently, exposing the whites of his eyes. Eventually he sat up, seeming to come out of a daze, and his eyes cleared. "The N'anga's spirit has left me. We now follow the blood."

The kudu and impala had bolted. The hunters picked up the prey's blood spore on the other side of the grassy plain and followed it through the trees, ascending the lower mountain slope in a zigzag pattern. There was a lot of blood. Once more up above they heard the mighty roar. The lion seemed to make no attempts to hide its tracks. A third of the way up, they lost the spore on a short granite plateau.

Tanaka circled, scanning the rock and surrounding area several times before returning to Malcolm. "The wounded Samson is now playing with us. Look here." He pointed from the edge of the plateau to a smaller lower rocky shelf across a gully more than thirty feet away. It took a while for Malcolm to work out what he was looking at. The lion had leapt around thirty-six feet to cross the gap. It was an impossible distance to cover in a single leap for any human or feline predator. There was a splatter of blood where Samson must have landed heavily on his injured front leg. Perhaps the cause of the roar they heard moments earlier.

It took another twenty minutes to descend and reroute. After picking up the tracks again, they followed the blood trail to the opening of a cave. The injured devil could be luring them into a trap. Neither of the hunters had any sort of torch. They inched into the darkness as their eyes slowly became accustomed to the lack of light. Every nerve tensed as Malcolm contemplated following a wounded lion into darkness. It was madness. Although the way ahead was high enough to walk upright, tree roots had forced their way through the roof and clawed at skin and clothing like outstretched fingers. Brushing the obstacles aside, they could see the way ahead branched into two distinct black caves. Malcolm hesitated, considering his options. He could leave Tanaka to watch the entrance for any sign of Samson and track his movements while Malcolm returned to the mine to retrieve a set of cap lamps. That could potentially delay the hunt by a full day, and in the interim, they could lose Samson altogether. Heading further into the cave blindly would almost certainly end in their death.

He was still pondering their predicament when a deathly roar came from the entrance of the cave behind them. The wounded lion had somehow exited the rear of the cave and doubled back, trapping the hunters with no means of escape. Tanaka was crouched, observing the floor for prints when the chilling bellow was issued. He instinctively sprang into the air clutching at the dangling roots, climbing like a terrified baboon. His rapid ascent was halted a few metres up when his shaved head impacted painfully against the roof of the cave. He clung on desperately despite his dizzy, throbbing head.

Malcolm shot through the right opening and immediately lost his footing as the ground beneath him gave way. He tumbled end over end down a steep slope with an uneven surface until he came to rest with a thump on a loose floor. He was in utter darkness, and he cursed himself for his clumsiness. He had also lost his rifle. His instinct was to climb back up towards the entrance of the cave, but when he tried, he slid further down the unsteady surface. His wide eyes frantically searched for any shards of light, but he could see nothing. An inhuman stench filled the air around him as he blindly fumbled with his hands over the ground in search of his gun.

He picked up several objects but discarded them. If he had a torch, he would have shone the beam over the base of Samson's den, littered with the discarded decomposing bones of animals and humans. He kicked a human infant's scull as he shuffled forward blindly. It rolled off further down the slope and continued rolling. Malcolm followed the direction of the sound, hoping it would lead to an escape or at least light. Going up was not an option. He tripped again over another long obstacle, and with relief he realised it was his rifle. The scope was missing but the magazine was still in place. With one round already discharged into Samson's front left shoulder, four remained in the magazine. He tried to stay calm as he strained to listen for any further sound. All he heard was his own breathing and the loose ground underfoot. He waited.

His ears started to play tricks on him as his pulse raced. He thought he could hear heavy breathing off to his left, but as he held his own breath to listen it stopped. A second later he heard it again directly in front. On impulse he pointed and fired. The flashing illumination was a visual assault. Did his eyes deceive him or was there a glimpse of Samson? The discharge of the rifle in the confines of the cave left his ears ringing. He forced himself to try and remain calm. Up against a wounded lion with supernatural strength, Malcolm's survival hung in the balance. He closed his sightless eyes and regulated his breathing. A movement close to him triggered his instinct to fire. Tanaka grabbed his forearm. For a chilling moment Malcolm thought it was the jaws of the beast. His guide whispered, "You are lucky I can smell your sour milk skin and cow dung otherwise I would never have found you. Samson is close. Follow me."

Malcolm did not know how Tanaka could navigate his way through the pitch-black cave or where they were heading, but he followed. Their clumsy advancement made enough noise for Samson to easily follow. They rounded a bend and emerged into a giant natural underground amphitheatre shrouded in light from an opening in the cave above them. The extremities and perimeter were still as black as night but at least in the centre they could see. The air was fresher, unlike the den with its mountain of decaying bones.

"Keep your gun ready, he will come for you here. I will wait in the shadows," Tanaka instructed, and Malcolm obeyed, reloading his rifle with his back to the light beam. He circled, scanning the darkness.

The bullet had shattered the lion's front leg below the shoulder, but the poison on the bullet was in too small a quantity to have any effect on the giant beast's eyesight. He crouched in the shadows with his eyes fixed on Malcolm, preparing to pounce. The impact of leaping more than thirty feet across the gully and landing on his injured leg had severed the bone and left it protruding painfully. Blood oozed from the open wound, and he took a moment to lick it. His rasping tongue alerted Tanaka to his location. He zeroed in on the faint sound and hurled his spear from less than fifteen metres away. Even for a trained warrior it was a lucky shot. The broad spear penetrated the soft tissue below the rib cage, slicing through vital organs before coming to rest partially protruding out the other side of the stomach.

Samson bellowed in pain. The blade, heavily coated with the poison, delivered the toxin directly into the beast's bloodstream and its vision instantly turned into a kaleidoscope of colour before failing completely. Pain forced him out of hiding, crazed with lack of sight, tracking his quarry with his acute sense of smell. As he advanced into the light, Malcolm fired the .303 directly into the soft tip of the beast's nose. Samson dropped but rose almost immediately in a fit of rage, surging forward and clawing blindly for his attacker. Malcolm reloaded and fired again, striking the centre of the great feline's chest. With every ounce of remaining rage and strength, Samson lunged. The spear lodged in his stomach cut deeper through kidneys, liver and bowel. A sudden ferocious swipe of the right outstretched paw connected with Malcolm's rifle, sending it into the cave wall. It smashed on impact. Malcolm drew his machete and with both hands forced it into the lion's throat from below as the beast descended on him. The impetus of the attack aided the blade through the carotid artery, severing the vertebrae at the base of the skull. Malcolm was hit with the force of a freight train, the handle of the blade he held dug into his ribs on the right, snapping them like dry twigs. The wind was driven from his lungs as the full weight of the dead lion's head and chest overwhelmed him. He could not breathe. Blood gushed out of the mouth and nose of the beast, flowing freely over Malcolm's trapped face.

It took Tanaka's full strength to heave the lion's head and shoulders sufficiently for Malcolm to wriggle free. He sucked welcomed air into his lungs, but each breath was met with excruciating pain.

Following the violent confrontation, dust drifted lazily in the air, illuminated by the rays of light from above. The slain Samson lay directly in the sun's path, shrouding it in an ethereal glow. In time, Malcolm would regret dispatching the phenomenal creature. He sat panting, regaining his composure.

Tanaka squatted next to Malcolm and placed a hand on his shoulder. "It is not done, my friend."

"It is done! Samson is dead!"

"No. The Mahaha asks for the beating heart of Samson. You must remove it."

Malcolm shook his head, balancing on the machete to get himself upright. He staggered back to the carcass and used the sharp blade to open the belly of the beast, cutting away at the damaged organs until he exposed the heart. Even in the poor light in the cave, it was easy to locate. The organ thumped rhythmically – still very much alive. It continued beating when it was severed from the veins and arteries surrounding it, and Malcolm held it to the light, captivated by its life force.

After leaving Samson's lair bearing the warm, bloody beating heart, Malcolm stood at the cave's entrance and another chill washed over him. He felt a breath on the nape of his neck followed instantly by a familiar stench of rotting flesh. It was the same deathly odour that had assailed him once before in his bed on the mine. Tanaka was transfixed next to him, visibly shaking. The voice in Malcolm's ear commanded him to follow. Again, it was in another language, but Malcolm somehow understood. A blue outstretched hand with talon-like fingernails snatched the lion's heart out of his hand, before the Mahaha stepped ahead of them.

Tanaka's bladder had emptied as soon as the Mahaha materialised. He left the puddle of his own urine and followed behind Malcolm on shaky legs. They descended the lower reaches of the mountain slope and entered a dense forest, heading away from the direction of the village. The Mahaha never looked back at them, but they followed his tall, thin blue body. It glowed like a beacon illuminating the way. Malcolm nursed his painful ribs as he marched, each step a shudder of pain. The demon made swift, silent progress through the trees, the leopard-like black spots on his back clearly visible.

Abruptly the Mahaha bent low and seemed to disappear through the centre of a giant Panke tree. Its enormous trunk looked impenetrable, but a closer inspection revealed a narrow winding opening large enough to squeeze through. Malcolm went in first through the confined passage. It felt as if the tree had swallowed them up and spat them out in a different world. As they emerged through the other side the ground was dry and barren without a blade of grass. Not a single sound from the outside world disturbed the absolute silence. Although there was no apparent luminary, there was sufficient light to make out the simple dwelling directly ahead, a man-made cave of stacked oblong black rocks. The Mahaha sat behind smouldering embers, remnants of a fire. He gestured for them to sit, which they did opposite him.

The strange blue creature momentarily abandoned the pulsating heart and retreated into the cave, returning a minute later. In one hand he carried a carved wooden bowl containing what looked like a mixture of dry herbs, in the other a short blade that could have been carved out of bone or ivory. The Mahaha held the bowl in his lap and placed the heart in it. His upturned face chanted heavenward with unblinking expressionless eyes as he rocked back and forth.

Abruptly the knife he held was thrust into the heart. On contact – blade against throbbing muscle – the Mahaha screamed as if impaled through his own flesh. The piercing cry lasted a matter of seconds but the deafening shrill left Malcolm and Tanaka with their hair standing on end.

The Mahaha began to rock back and forth with a satanic grin, his gaze fixed on Malcolm. The heart had stopped beating and was casually discarded into the fire bed where it sizzled and crackled. The thick red heart blood and herb mixture was lifted to the Mahaha's lips, and he drank noisily on the concoction. It spilled down his chin and throat as he slurped and the Mahaha began to laugh. At first it sounded like a sadistic human chuckle, but as he trembled, gasping for air, it morphed into sounds of the forest. Giddy giggles of hyena gave way to the cries of alarm of vervet monkeys and then the raucous barks of the baboon. The cacophony ended abruptly as the Mahaha's head slumped forward onto his chest.

When it finally spoke, it sounded like a chorus of multiple entities speaking with one voice. Both Malcolm and Tanaka were transfixed by the supernatural spectacle, allowed to understand the words of the ancients declared through the Mahaha's lips, "By doing my bidding the curse has been lifted for seven years until I return."

The Mahaha cocked his head, pointed at Malcolm with an outstretched finger and said, *"Be warned. Your path will be crossed forevermore with many snakes:*

*When the snake strikes, golden hair will be swallowed into the belly of the earth.*

*Beware the one-eyed snake that walks on two legs and swims with the crocodile. He must die twice.*

*When you anger the serpent river god, his vengeance will be floodwater of fire and smoke."*

When it finished speaking the demon grabbed a handful of ash from the fire and blew it through his clenched fist. A mirky haze quickly enveloped their full field of vision. Malcolm and Tanaka together fell instantly into a deathlike induced sleep.

# Chapter 13

## THE PAVILION THEATRE — GLASGOW, SCOTLAND

Michael MacGregor awoke fully clothed on the plush sofa to a pleasant warm and gentle sucking sensation. When he opened his eyes and looked down, he saw Elizabeth Baron's blonde head bobbing up and down with her mouth around the tip of his penis. At the shock of seeing what she was doing, his hands shot out to shove her head aside, but instead of throwing her off his fingers locked into her curly hair and held her there. He closed his eyes, thinking of nothing other than the ecstasy of her attentiveness. Her right hand moved up and down his erect shaft. She skilfully adjusted the speed and grip of each stroke until he flooded into her mouth with pulsating thrusts.

Her left hand gently caressed her clitoris and wet swollen lips leaving her close to her own orgasm. As she swallowed his seed, she imagined it being pumped deep into her expectant womb. The mental image made her come with throbbing pleasure, gasping as the waves washed over her. She abruptly rose, adjusted the waistband of her black satin robe, wiped her mouth on the back of her sleeve and headed for the kitchen to make coffee without saying a word. Michael was left to arrange himself and contemplate his current situation.

He had kept a low-profile following his involvement with Arthur Conway and his subsequent disappearance. Michael's father knew full well his son preferred the company of men, yet he fully expected and insisted on an heir. If Michael was to inherit the family tailor shop and get involved in his father's investments, he would need to marry and have a son. It was a daunting task, one that felt entirely foreign.

Elizabeth had inherited the Pavilion Theatre on Renfield Street in Glasgow from her late husband. She was now one of the wealthiest women in the city and a complete enigma to Michael. He knew she had liaisons and rubbed shoulders with some very influential people, but what Michael knew was just the tip of the iceberg.

Around five years ago Elizabeth had auditioned for a part in a cabaret at the Pavilion. Albert Baron, the then owner of the establishment, sat in the audience captivated by the young twenty-year-old woman on the stage. Her blue eyes seldom left his during her performance, and her seductive smile clutched at his stomach and loins as he watched her move and perform. Her curvaceous figure, ample bosom and shapely legs aroused him, and she stimulated in him a deep hunger – a desire to possess her. He could not care less if she became the star of the show or not, but he wanted her all to himself.

He made his intentions very clear from the start and for a while she enjoyed his advances and affection. He allowed her some success in various pantomimes and productions, but his jealousy flared at her growing fanbase predominately made up of red-blooded men. He hated the way men looked at her and the control she seemed to have over them. His obsession led him into darker fetishes with her. His controlling behaviour left her enduring unquestionable abuse. And then one day something unusual happened.

Elizabeth broke down before him and told him she loved him. She promised to love only him provided they marry. They did and the abuse stopped. He could not contemplate a future without her and so he agreed. Once married, she took control. She learned how to please Albert in ways he never knew existed and she was given full access to his money and assets.

It was not apparent to Albert just how much Elizabeth loathed him. She was using him to her own advantage. While making him feel like the sole recipient of her affections, she discreetly grew her social network and acquaintances. She desperately wanted a child and would have gladly had one with Albert, but it became clear that his seedless grapes held no potential, no matter how many times he emptied them. Once she was certain of being the beneficiary of his estate, she put a sinister plan into action.

Albert's greatest pleasure was to be blindfolded and tied by his hands and feet to their four-poster bed. Elizabeth would then lower herself gently onto his face and he would bury his tongue between her lips while she skilfully pleasured him with her mouth. One night she tied him down with the usual padded cuffs and Albert prepared to receive her hairless lips. But instead of her warm scented flesh, his head was engulfed by a plastic covered pillow as she squatted with her full weight on his chest. She rode his thrashing torso through the panicked suffocation till the end. Afterward she packed away the bonds that tied him down, and when satisfied there was no sign of struggle, she dressed him in his pyjamas and put him to bed.

Using all her acting skills, her call to emergency services was delivered with the right amount of grief and hysteria. There was not the slightest bit of suspicion that the distraught little widow had murdered her husband. She discreetly paid the coroner handsomely to ensure the death certificate stated 'heart attack' as the cause of death. The coroner shortly thereafter vanished, and life moved on.

She was discreet with her new sense of freedom. Her liaisons continued in secret while outwardly she displayed the social graces required to mingle with the rich and the powerful. One of her consorts was the junior member of the Baker Montague and Forbes law firm. Seducing Johnathan Forbes had been as easy as shelling peas. For a supposedly smart man in a well-paid job, he seemed to have the lion's share of his brains lodged firmly in his underwhelming ball bag. Elizabeth performed on him intimate pleasures that his Catholic wife would never entertain. The loose-lipped attorney delivered tantalising detail of the growing fortune belonging to David MacGregor, Michael's father. The shrewd old investor had smartly grown his stock portfolio and wealth under the radar, behind the scenes of his successful tailor shop.

She knew all about Michael MacGregor's sexual persuasion, hook ups and relationships. She even knew that he was instrumental in Arthur Conway's demise. After another late after-party last night, she had asked Michael back to her private quarters to have a meeting. Her apartment was located on the top floor of the theatre. She had never tried to seduce him last night but offered a listening ear once he had overindulged in champagne. He let it slip that his father expected an heir.

In her opinion this morning's antics opened the way for potential liberal dialogue. Elizabeth returned with two cups of piping hot coffee and sat on one of the occasional chairs opposite Michael after handing him a cup.

She avoided any reference to what had just happened between them but simply stated, "Michael, from what you told me last night you are expected to produce a son. I am prepared to offer you that chance. I would like to have a child of my own and I believe you may be a suitable candidate. Of course, I would need to ensure that our mutual child would be suitably looked after in all respects."

"You know of course where my interests truly lie."

"Yes, I do. I'm not naïve, Michael. Some people marry for love but that is not the only reason."

"Are you suggesting a marriage of convenience?"

"To a point, yes. A child deserves to grow up in a stable and loving environment. I am happy to accept your leanings as well as your dutiful explicit discretion. We will maintain the appearance of a married couple socially, and lovingly attend to the needs of our child. Outside of that, and by correlative agreement we may both be allowed to quench our desires."

"It is not how I envisaged my life to be."

Elizabeth could not tell Michael he would be a bloody fool to walk away from his father's wealth. In fact, it was highly likely Michael had no idea what his father was truly worth. Instead, she said, "Life seldom turns out how we expect it to, but a smart union between you and I makes perfect sense."

Michael was swayed to agreeing with Elizabeth. She was smart, beautiful, and eloquent, any man's dream. He may have been less favourable if he knew what she was capable of and that she had already committed murder. He sighed and concluded, "I can see the wisdom in your proposal in theory. Perhaps let's see how well that works out in practice."

Elizabeth smiled sweetly, revealing her perfect white teeth as she sipped her coffee. It was not the first time she had used the skills of her mind and body to get what she wanted, and it would not be the last.

~

# SOUTHAMPTON – ARTHUR CONWAY'S ESCAPE

Arthur Conway lay in his sleeper cab, clutching his leather briefcase that contained his worldly possessions. It was 8pm on the fourth and final day of his rail journey from Edinburgh to Southampton, during which he dared not sleep. He felt more comfortable with the blackness of night alone in his carriage, but the dark rings under his eyes were a clear indication of prolonged anguish. Fortunately, it seemed that the communication between Scotland Yard and English law enforcement had not been quick enough to circulate his photo identity. He had fully expected to be intercepted at any stage during his escape, but he had made it this far undetected and unchallenged.

Following the meeting when David MacGregor revealed he had the photographic evidence of Conway's sexual misconduct, along with proof of embezzling Elspeth MacMillan's land and money, his departure had to be immediate. He was forced to abandon the law practice he had worked so hard to establish and his career was over. Never again would he set foot in a court of law or be seen in public for fear of prosecution. The photographs of the molested young men, once his treasured trophies, were now in the hands of the authorities and he was ruined. At least, *that* part of his life was over.

Immediately after the meeting with MacGregor, he emptied the contents of the hidden safe in his apartment across from his office and headed south. At Edinburgh train station he made a call from a public phone to Otto Rendenbach and put his flight into motion. His disappearance would never have been possible without the preparation put into place while working as a junior solicitor at the Baker Montague and Forbes law firm. He had learned early on in his career he had a gift at spotting opportunities to syphon funds from his employer's and his clients' accounts. The challenge was where to put the money and how to access it.

The solution presented itself and was easier to put into action than he had imagined. The only item in his possession that originally belonged to his deceased mother was her Swiss passport. There was no particular reason why he had kept it – perhaps deep down he knew it may have future value. He cared little for the memory of his mother and thought of her with not the slightest hint of emotion. Memories of what she looked like had long since faded or been forced from his memory.

One evening while checking his ledgers, he noticed his mother's Swiss passport sitting in the bottom of his safe. He picked it up and as he held it, he thought about how many of the company clients had bank accounts in Switzerland. Some of the accounts used alias names and several of those accounts contained large sums of money. Handling deposits and transfers was a regular part of Arthur's workload. He studied the brown Swiss passport with the embossed white cross in intimate detail and discovered that there were no apparent watermarks or security features. This he verified by making a few phone calls. Surely it could be easily duplicated.

On further investigation Conway discovered that it was relatively easy to open Swiss bank accounts, but the accounts he wanted needed to be under an entirely different identity for what he intended. On further consideration, if he could produce a fake Swiss birth certificate, he may be able to apply for an authentic Swiss passport. So after 'borrowing' a client's Swiss birth certificate, he duplicated it but in the name of Conrad Amman, Amman being his mother's maiden name. He did not even need to attend a meeting at the Swiss embassy to apply for his passport. He filled in the application and his passport arrived in the post less than a month later.

What followed was a delightfully intricate level of deception that gave him an enormous sense of satisfaction. He opened Swiss bank accounts in his own name 'Arthur Conway' but had several corporate accounts traced back to a fictional alias. He embezzled money from his employer at every opportunity. Some of the deposits and transfers were traceable with a bit of digging but they would amount to around £50,000 in total. However, his most concerted activities were channelled through his range of trading accounts in the name of Conrad Amman, none of which were directly traceable to him. So, when he was finally caught and fired, he gladly returned the £50,000 he was accused of, but the £250,000 squirreled away in the network of accounts belonging to Conrad Amman was untouched.

While still employed by Baker Montague and Forbes, Conway travelled to Zürich as Conrad Amman on his new Swiss passport to test the water. Accessing his accounts was delightfully easy. It also became evident that appearing to the bank in person and being a Swiss national, made additional services available, all at the highest level of secrecy.

When Arthur Conway started his own law firm in Edinburgh, he occasionally topped up some of his Swiss accounts, but the activity was minimal. In hindsight he should have transferred more. At least now that he was forced to flee his home and his business, he had an escape plan, a clear destination, and a means of survival.

The phone call Conway made from Edinburgh train station before he left was to one of his previous clients, Otto Rendenbach. Otto ran a small private aviation company out of Calshot on the coast near Southampton. Off the books, Otto ferried anything to anywhere within the range of his small fleet of planes. His cargo included laundered money, criminals, guns, and explosives, for the right price pretty much anything he could fit into one of his aircrafts. Otto was forced to ditch a plane in the Irish Sea in the middle of a storm. The insurance company contested the claim and filed a lawsuit against Otto, claiming he was transporting illegal substances. If the allegations were proven in the court room, Otto would have lost his aviation licence and his livelihood. When Arthur Conway accepted the case and established that the cargo was opium destined for a high court judge in Dublin, he legitimately argued that the case fell under the jurisdiction of the Irish court. In the end the court surprisingly reached a verdict in favour of Otto's claim. He retained his licence and received a settlement from the insurance company. As a token of thanks, Otto delivered a consignment of opium free of charge to the grateful blurry eyed judge and Conway was paid handsomely for his troubles.

When Conway considered his escape options to Zürich, none made more sense than flying there with Otto Rendenbach. The world was at war, Germany was marching through France and there was constant threat of attack on Britain. Conventional travel by road, sea and rail was simply out of the question.

His phone call to the short, stout German had been brief: "Otto, I need to get to Zürich urgently. It is a matter of life or death."

Conway hired a black cab for the final leg of his trip from Southampton railway station to Otto's warehouse and hangar. He relaxed a little as the taxi pulled up outside the barrier of a large fenced-off area. The beam of the lights illuminated the perimeter fence and gate bearing a weathered sign advertising *Calshot Private Air Hire – O Rendenbach*. Two large corrugated iron warehouses were silhouetted against the night sky, sitting silently in the middle of a grassy field. It was not long before a short balding man in dirty khaki overalls appeared before the gates. Conway paid the taxi driver and greeted Otto with a firm handshake, clutching his briefcase.

They walked in silence until Otto led them to a side door of the closest hangar. He closed the door behind them before he flipped a switch. A series of modern fluorescent lights began to flicker in turn in the high iron ceiling, eventually throwing light to every corner of the immaculate concrete floor. As Conway's eyes grew accustomed to the brightness, he noticed two small aircraft parked neatly in the centre of the building. On the opposite wall, tools of every description were neatly arranged on hooks or shelves in their appointed place alongside two large six-foot steel lockable toolboxes.

The hangar was meticulously clean. The faint smell of fuel and oil seemed to complement the visually well-organised scene. Conway was impressed but had business to attend to. "Nice operation, Otto. I'm hoping you are going to tell me you have worked out how to get me to Zürich as quickly as possible."

Otto was almost completely bald and a good foot and a half shorter than Conway. His piercing blue eyes softened as he smiled. He pulled a grubby mutton cloth out of his back pocket and wiped his hands before walking up to the closest of the two planes.

He tapped the fuselage lovingly and replied, "I have just finished modifications to this little beauty. She is refuelled and ready to go. We leave in one hour."

Conway glanced over the strange looking two-seater aircraft. He had never flown in his life and was a little apprehensive that the odd craft could get him to his destination in one piece.

Otto read the expression on Conway's face. "Don't worry, Arthur! She will get you there."

Conway did not share his enthusiasm. Otto looked proudly upon his Albatross AL102W. Its two open cockpits were aligned along the fuselage directly behind the single Argus inverted V8 237HP engine. There was little protection against the ferocious wind and elements. The entire craft was a little over nine metres long with a wingspan of just over thirteen. The strut-based lower wing completed the biplane design and sat on top of two torpedo-shaped floatation devices, allowing the craft to land on water. Apart from the small glass windshields in front of the cockpits, the entire plane had been recently painted matt black.

Otto led Conway to a small corrugated square office at the back of the hangar. It was large enough to house a collapsable metal desk and two chairs. A map of the English Channel and northern Europe was spread across the tabletop held in place with metal valves, tappets, and discarded engine parts. Otto traced the route they would take. "Zürich is too far for a non-stop flight for the Albatross. I have arranged for us to refuel here." Otto pointed to Port Morny on the French northern coastline. "It's a two-hour flight to Morny Deauville. The stopover is less than an hour before a four-hour flight to Zürich. We will be landing on Lake Zürich near Bäch."

"We're landing on the actual lake. Have you done this successfully before?"

"Oh yes! We land on the sea at the mouth of Port Deauville to refuel, and we land on Lake Zürich at Bäch long enough to refuel and get you onto dry land. With flight time and refuelling, be prepared for a seven-hour transit. You will need to change into these." Otto pointed to a woollen-lined leather flight jacket, trousers, and matching helmet and goggles. "I'm afraid the cockpit will be a tight squeeze for your briefcase and a change of clothes, but there is no storage space anywhere else on the plane. Any spare compartment I have used for auxiliary fuel tanks, including the landing gear pontoons. Let's pray we don't catch a stray bullet although the fireball would be quite spectacular!"

As Conway struggled into the heavy flight suit, he couldn't help but recollect that Otto had already ditched a plane in the Irish Sea. His escape route had been decided. It seemed he had no option but to put his life in the hands of this crazy little German. His sleep-deprived state made the whole concept of his disappearance feel like some sort of bizarre dream. He already craved a good meal and a warm bed.

When Conway returned to the Albatross still clutching his briefcase and suit under his arm, Otto was running through his pre-flight checks and fiddling with the propeller. "Arthur, you sit in the second cockpit from the front. Strap yourself in and make yourself as comfortable as possible. We have no intercom once we are airborne. Any urgent messages write on this." He handed a notepad and pen to Conway.

Conway placed his change of clothes on the small cockpit seat, fastened his seatbelts and wedged his briefcase between his knees. Otto spun the propellor and the hangar was instantly filled with the deafening roar of the powerful motor. The Albatross clumsily lurched forward the second Otto was in position in the front cockpit and headed out into the black night. Otto had fitted reserve fuel tanks in the pontoons as a backup in case there were issues touching down off the French coast. Small spring-loaded wheels were mounted on the base of the pontoons, but Otto had not had the luxury of time to carry out a practice take-off with the craft fully laden with fuel. The fuel-filled pontoons seemed far too heavy for the small aeroplane. Nevertheless, Otto clenched his jaw and opened the throttle as he taxied onto the runway. The engine screamed in defiance and the body of the plane vibrated violently. Conway instantly regretting his exit plan, but it was too late to back out now.

He was flung back into his seat as the Albatross gathered momentum along the runway. Otto pulled back on the joystick and heard the tail of the pontoons contact with the tarmac. As he turned his head a spray of sparks from both pontoons trailed the plane on either side like a firework display. If he did not get the Albatross off the runway soon, it would be too late.

Otto closed his eyes and pulled back on the tiller. The little plane grunted, and defied gravity, leaving the runway and sluggishly rose into the night sky. He dared not look at Conway. He was quite certain his companion had not enjoyed the white knuckled take-off, but he had a two-hour flight time on the first leg of the journey to calm his nerves.

Conway's screams during take-off were drowned out by the deafening roar of the engine and the force of the wind. Otto ignored him frantically drumming on the fuselage, and it eventually stopped. Conway dipped his head to escape the assault from the wind and eventually dropped off to sleep exhausted. Otto had omitted to mention that their scheduled refuelling at Port Morny Deauville was not guaranteed. Although his contact had confirmed he was still functioning out of the warehouse and hangar at the port's entrance, there was an increasing German presence. Villas, hotels and even the local casino had been commandeered by the German forces. It was one of the reasons Otto had hastily fitted reserve fuel tanks into the pontoons of the Albatross' landing gear. They were due to arrive at Port Morny around midnight. Otto would have to make the judgement call when they got there, and they may have to take their chances and fly on with the fuel they had on board. Conway would have objected to taking such a gamble, so Otto deliberately omitted those details.

*Savonnerie Morny* (Morny Soap Factory), was the largest landmark at the entrance of Port Morny Deauville. The production plant occupied three full blocks. The oversized elucidated advertising billboard had a red background and the company name emblazoned in bright yellow capital font. Otto had used it as a landmark on previous night flight crossings to France. David Dubois' Trafic et Commerce warehouse sat directly in front of the soap factory at the mouth of the port. David was Otto's contact who would refuel the Albatross. It was a little after midnight when the lights of the French coast came into view – the soap factory billboard thankfully still well lit. The plane was two miles west of the target and Otto banked to line her up on the port entrance. It was possible to navigate by moon and stars flying in total blackout on a flight path Otto could do with his eyes closed, but losing altitude and approaching the harbour just above the ocean still made the experienced pilot's palms sweat.

As Otto was about to reduce speed and prepare to touch down, a German army truck rounded the corner and parked outside the entrance of David Dubois' warehouse. Soldiers poured out of the back and immediately opened fire. The sound of the shots was drowned out by the noise of the aeroplane engine but the flashes from the muzzles were clearly visible. Otto tugged at the joystick to increase altitude and accelerated. The Albatross startled the soldiers as it raced overhead, and a few of them fired blindly at the racing shadow. Otto had a fleeting glimpse of David Dubois lying face down in front of his premises in a growing pool of his own blood. Fortunately, none of the bullets impacted with the little plane and they continued their journey unmolested.

Otto scribbled a quick message on a pad and handed it to the white-faced Conway behind him; it read: "Close call! Plan B it is then – thank God for reserve fuel tanks!"

An hour after their close encounter with the German soldiers on the French coast, Otto was forced to engineer the mid-air manual switch to the auxiliary fuel tanks. He gained altitude to perform the manoeuvre. He had anticipated a potential airlock in the fuel transfer and fitted a manual hand pump to ensure effective flow. He opened the fuel transfer valve and squeezed the hand pump until the oval rubber was stiff and firm in his hand – adequate fuel flow, hopefully! For a few seconds the Albatross coughed and spluttered before returning to its steady rhythm.

Their flight plan took them equidistant between Paris and Orleans on a bearing southeast over Dijon and into Switzerland at Basel, finally to intercept with Zürich on the same heading. Otto intended to fly as low as possible for the duration of their flight over occupied France to make their advance as inconspicuous as possible. They raced on through the night over terrain peppered with trenches, barbed wire and smouldering craters.

Burned out houses and villages with tendrils of smoke lazily drifting on the cold night air were reminders of the rapid and relentless German advancement on the ground. Otto observed the carnage with remote indifference. Despite his German heritage, he looked at the scenes below with neither pride on the German conquests nor compassion for the French victims, and focussed on the immediate job at hand as he always did, in this case the safe delivery of Arthur Conway to his destination.

After crossing over into Switzerland Otto relaxed a little and gained altitude to allow a greater range of sight. He had flown to Switzerland several times but had never landed a plane on Lake Zürich. The idea in theory was easy enough, but approaching the landing zone was riddled with potential hazards, particularly a night landing without lights. He also had the fuel to think of.

Again, in theory, they had enough to reach their destination, but the makeshift auxiliary tanks were not monitored by the plane's fuel gauge. They deviated little from their flight plan but still could not be certain of their dwindling reserves or have the luxury to circle the lake several times to ensure the safest approach.

It was now four hours and twenty minutes since crossing the French coastline but there was no sign of Lake Zürich or a body of water large enough to land the plane. He banked the Albatross into a slow anticlockwise turn while he rechecked his bearings and scanned below for clues as to where they were. The scenery looked unfamiliar.

Up ahead he could see what looked like a large village on fire bellowing dense clouds of smoke into the night. He cautiously circled the area. Below was not a scene of burned-out houses but an industrial town working through the night – smelting furnaces were the cause of black smog. He recognised the area as Winterthur, a town twenty miles north of Zürich. He immediately banked right to alter his flight path due south. After another ten minutes, he began to recognise the landmarks and terrain surrounding the outskirts of Zürich. He grinned triumphantly when he picked out the smaller Lake Greifensee, northeast of Lake Zürich. Its inky black surface shone in the moonlight, resembling a careless abandoned oil spill. Otto knew with all certainty he was on the right track and minutes away from his destination.

From high altitude, Lake Zürich could be described as an oxbow-shaped body of water, but to Otto, it always reminded him of a broad smile. Tonight, the perimeter of the shimmering grin was framed by sporadic lighting concentrated around Zürich itself and to a lesser extent the smaller towns and settlements linked by the tarred and cobbled Seestrasse framing the perimeter.

He flew over Zürich and kept the aircraft twenty metres above the surface of the water. His intended landing spot was located on the western bank almost exactly halfway down the length of the lake at the remote village of Bäch.

The newly deceased David Dubois, who was last seen lying in a pool of his own blood, had put Otto in touch with the local fisherman at Bäch where Otto was to land. Kelby Fischer was a third-generation fisherman that lived on the shore of the little village and apparently had a jetty long enough to accommodate the Albatross once it had landed. David had organised for the fisherman to ensure sufficient supplies to refuel. Otto was to pay cash on arrival. If the landing and refuelling was successful, Kelby Fischer would make more money than he would have ever seen. For a village with a population of less than four hundred, for the humble fisherman it was an opportunity of a lifetime.

Kelby was instructed to line his jetty with a series of lanterns. The two most prominent lanterns were to be extinguished and relit at the sight of the approaching aeroplane. The signal was to confirm the location and that it was safe to land. Otto checked his watch. He was thirty-four minutes behind schedule, but when he reduced speed and altitude and zeroed in on the brightly lit pier, the two foremost lanterns went out in succession and were promptly relit. Otto smiled and looked forward to meeting the fisherman. He was even more keen to refuel and get back home.

The Albatross, almost entirely devoid of its heavy load of fuel, touched down onto the smooth surface of the lake as light as a feather and taxied gently up to the wooden jetty where two men dressed in wellies and full length hooded waterproofs waited to receive them.

The plane was tethered while the two occupants disembarked and stretched their stiff and weary limbs. Kelby stepped up to Otto wearing an expression of distrust on his weather-beaten, bearded face and offered his hand.

Otto removed his flight goggles and helmet, revealing bloodshot eyes surrounded by a pinkish halo of clean skin, the rest of his face was soiled almost black from the exhaust fumes of the engine and dirt collected during their nocturnal adventure. He smiled broadly and accepted the hand and spoke in German: "You must be Kelby Fischer, yes? Otto Rendenbach. Pleasure to meet you, my friend! You have the fuel?"

Kelby nodded, still looking at the motley pair suspiciously. Otto opened his flight jacket and produced an envelope containing a substantial pile of cash. He removed roughly half of the notes and offered them to Kelby. "Half now, the other half once my little bird has been refuelled and I'm ready to leave."

Kelby accepted the cash willingly. Although he tried to mask his excitement, the efforts to refuel the plane doubled and both men worked frantically at the hand fuel pumps under Otto's direction.

Conway stood on the jetty, a little bewildered. He looked like a forlorn castaway clutching his briefcase to his chest. Otto came to him eventually and slapped his shoulder. The unexpected contact nearly sent Arthur into the water, but Otto grabbed him by both shoulders and said, "Some journey, Mr Conway, eh? Safely delivered to Switzerland as requested. I have arranged a ride for you into Zürich with Mr Fischer here. From there you are on your own. Is everything ok, Mr Conway?"

If Conway had the strength and energy to quibble with Rendenbach over the risks he had taken, being shot at, and exposed to the ferocious chilling elements and fumes he would have done, but he was spent. The trauma of the last few days had also played havoc with his constitution. He nodded, opened his briefcase, and handed Otto a brown envelope full of cash. Otto did not count it but stuffed it into his jacket pocket and immediately returned his attention to the plane.

Conway stripped off his flight suit and stuffed it in the cockpit that had been his sanctuary for the duration of the journey. He was suddenly overcome by stomach cramps and before he could don his crumpled suit, he ran in his underwear and socks to the edge of the wooden pier and hurriedly prepared to squat. In this new chapter of his life on Swiss soil, Conway's first deposit was not cash.

Once the refuelling was complete, Otto handed over the remaining payment to the delighted Kelby. He was now in far better spirits having completed his task and in possession of a hefty payout. He walked up to Conway who had now managed to dress and said, "My son will drop you in Zürich now."

# Chapter 14

## 'LOCHLUICHART' — MACMILLAN FARM — EDINBURGH, SCOTLAND

For the last two days the bitter Arctic wind had brought with it sheets of unrelenting rain and sleet. It hammered mercilessly against the windows, rattling them in the panes. Molly and Mary were tucked up in Molly's king-sized bed, huddled close under the covers. Mary had her feet resting on her hot water bottle, listening intently as her mother read out loud another passage from Rudyard Kipling's *Jungle Book*.

Rather than send Mary off to sleep, the stories excited her, and her rapt attention absorbed every word while she created images in her mind. They had read the book together so many times that Mary memorised the passages associated with the pictures word for word. She often corrected Molly as she deliberately deviated from the script to test Mary's attention. Reading together at night before bed was a regular event, they both enjoyed. It was seldom that Mary slept in her mother's bed, but occasionally, such as cold wintery nights, it was a warm indulgent treat for them both. Story time was a precious shared experience.

With each passing day Molly was increasingly absorbed with matters relating to Hillside Ranch in Southern Rhodesia. Since employing Henrick Van Royen as her on-site manager, she had a weekly meeting with him. This morning was their third such telephone meeting since his employment, and work was well underway securing the perimeter with new fencing. Henk, as he liked to be called, had received consignments of creosote wooden poles from the Inyanga highlands and bales of barbed wire from Salisbury. A team of twelve labourers were working on the project under his supervision and apart from a few minor hiccups, they were making steady progress.

This morning, she was informed of an exciting development. Henk would usually have to travel into Bulawayo for their phone meetings, but plans were underway for the installation of power and telephone lines on the national grid and Insiza was the next phase of the development. It meant soon the ranch would have its own electricity supply and telephone. The local authorities were using labour from their POW camps. It seemed ironic that the Italian enemy her late husband Angus had fought against were now involved in building the infrastructure that would make their lives easier.

Molly kissed her daughter on the temple and as she often did, asked Mary questions about what they had just read. It always surprised Molly just how much Mary retained from the stories. She knew all the characters by name and understood the plots and twists. She never tired of the books and listened intently to every word. Tonight, Mary was in a playful mood. Molly turned to her and asked, "So what is the name of the bear in the book, Mary?"

"His name is Bhageera."

"No, that's the name of the black panther; Baloo is the bear."

"No, Baloo is the name of the python."

"No, Mary, the snake is called Kaa. What about the child, the little boy in the story, what's his name?"

Mary was quietly thinking for a while before confidently answering, "Michael. His name is Michael!"

Molly looked at Mary with a puzzled expression and saw the mischievous grin on her daughter's face. Molly launched a tickle attack on the unsuspecting child who let out shrieks of laughter, and as she wriggled free, she sat up and said to her mother, "Next time you read me a story ask me some harder questions, ok?"

Mary turned over and fell asleep within seconds. Molly marvelled at how quickly her daughter was growing up. Her beautiful thick blonde hair reached to the small of her back when it was plaited. She seemed to get taller as every week went by, but it was not just the physical growth that was surprising, she was developing an enquiring mind and a wicked sense of humour. She seemed infected with the same enthusiasm and interest in Africa as her mother.

Molly herself was an avid reader, but these days all she read about was South Africa or Southern Rhodesia. She picked up her current book and continued reading. It was written by Percy Hone, published in 1909, called *Southern Rhodesia*. According to the book the name 'Rhodesia' itself was first used in the 1880s. An exploration arm of the British government – the British South African Company led by Cecil John Rhodes – had acquired valuable mineral concessions for the territories below the Zambezi River. It opened a huge potential for mining gold and other minerals but also opportunities for agriculture on fertile virgin soil. Yet according to the book, in a census carried out in 1907, apart from the estimated six million indigenous people and local tribes there were fewer than 15,000 settlers in an area of land roughly the size of the United Kingdom.

No matter how much potential there was in the productive minerally rich soil, the land seemed to fight back. In 1901 a large consignment of cattle was imported from England, entering the country from the east; 98% of the herd perished through African Coast Fever. In 1907 the year of the census, 3550 animal predators were culled for attacking farmed livestock. The largest culprits being lion and leopard. The statistics did not include the widespread incalculable damage to crops by elephant, baboon, wild pig, and other animals. Molly made a mental note to discuss the scale of threat with Henk at their next telephone meeting.

She thought about Malcolm Hunter and his injuries sustained during the hunt for the infamous Samsom. He had nearly lost his life! Malcolm was vague and dismissive regarding the details. All he said was it had been necessary to kill a rogue lion that terrorised the workers on the mine. He had spent three days recovering from a collapsed lung and broken ribs in hospital. Every time she asked anything about the incident, he brushed it off and changed the subject. He seemed different and more aloof. She tried to envisage what it would be like confronting a lethal predator as he did, but even her active imagination would surely fall short of the reality.

Molly noted that the book referred to the indigenous people as 'Kaffirs'. Although Kaffir labour was fundamental to the success of farming and mining enterprises, they were portrayed as inferior to the white settlers they worked for. They were trainable to some degree, but it suggested they were less intelligent, uneducated, lacking hygiene and competence. She picked up a similar sentiment echoed in her conversations with Henk. She wondered how the labourers themselves felt about that lowly perception of them.

The ongoing war was now the only obstacle holding her back from moving to Rhodesia. She had already discussed selling off the bulk of her farmland in Scotland to Liam Fitzgerald, her Irish neighbour. As Angus had pointed out in his letter, Fitzgerald had been after the land for quite some time. Molly made it clear that as soon as the war was over, she would set a reasonable market-related price and he would be given first option to buy. They had an unwritten agreement in principle. All that needed to happen was the bloody war had to end.

Molly kept accurate ledgers of the accounts for Hillside Ranch. There was currently plenty of money in her account with the Reserve Bank of Southern Rhodesia, but like all good thrifty Scotswomen, she had to have every penny accounted for. The priority was securing the boundary fences, then separating the internal paddocks into useful grazing ground and pumping water up to the northern fields. Henk had at least made a start and she was dying to see the ranch with her own eyes. The renovations on the main house were nearly complete. Once finished she would consider whether to build a homestead as her late husband had intended, or construct a more modest home for her farm manager. She had plenty to keep her occupied with for the time being. She was not under any illusion that Rhodesia was an exotic fairy tale location. It was wild, perhaps even brutal, but it fascinated her, and she was itching to get there.

Molly was shortly expecting the arrival of two books she had ordered for Mary. *Wild Animals* by James Gilchrist Lawson and *Jungle Animals* by Frank Bucks. She hoped to feed Mary's curiosity and interest in Africa. After all, it would eventually be her home.

# ARTWELL FARM – BANCHORY-DEVENICK, ABERDEENSHIRE, SCOTLAND

A total of seven de Havilland Albatross cargo aeroplanes were built in 1938 and were operated by Imperial Airways. The lightweight ply-balsa-ply fuselage and wings were powered by four V-12 supercharged air-cooled motors. With a fuel capacity of five hundred gallons, each plane had the largest range of any airborne vessel in the sky. When the world went to war for the second time, the Royal Air Force utilised the aircraft extensively, exposing its vulnerable and temperamental nature. One aircraft snapped in half on the runway during loading, another burst into flames in mid-air due to an on-board fuel leak, and three disintegrated on landing. The decision was made to remove them from service and the remaining two planes were pensioned off to an ex-fighter pilot William Haig.

William served with the RAF until his medical discharge for single-sided deafness. His plane had exploded moments after he ejected, leaving him with an impairment unfit for service. He turned down the position of flight instructor for the British and Commonwealth Air Training Group based in Southern Rhodesia. In his opinion, being robbed of his passion of combat flight, teaching pimply faced youths the ropes appealed to him not in the slightest. Instead, he purchased the remaining two decommissioned RAF Havilland Albatross planes and set up his private airline charter company. To begin with he felt a bit like a racing driver that had been told he could only drive a bus forevermore, but he soon settled into piloting the cumbersome sluggish airships and lost himself in the sense of freedom he experienced in the sky. Since the RAF had washed their hands of them, they were still left with the dilemma of how-to courier vital time-sensitive documents and cargo. William Haig was thus contracted to fulfil that vital role and his two planes were currently stationed at RAF Dyce Aberdeen Airport at the beckoned call of the planes' previous owners.

Robert Hunter, his old school buddy, had contacted him shortly after his return to Scotland. He would presently be flying Douglas and Brody, Robert's two sons, to Southern Rhodesia where they would run the family farm Cedar Tree Hollow in Insiza, Bulawayo.

He was sat in the Hunters' living room, very much aware of the conflicting emotion of everyone present. The family had enjoyed several weeks of being united again, but Rachael had no choice but to let her boys go. She could barely keep back her tears at the thought of them leaving. The excitement of the two young men, on the other hand, was almost tangible. Robert was thrilled for the opportunity his boys had ahead of them, but like Rachael a part of him wished that the family could stay together. Living as a unit again was a tonic after his military duties and hospital recovery.

Douglas and Brody would need to travel light. It was one of the conditions stipulated by William Haig. Both were allowed just one backpack. Robert made the necessary arrangements for his boys to access adequate funds once they arrived. Getting them there was by no means without risk. The war raged on, and their journey would take five or six days with as many stopovers.

William was dressed in khaki flight overalls and brown leather ankle-length boots. His shortly cropped military-style haircut suited his facial features. He looked at least a decade younger than his forty-four years. There was no grey in his jet-black hair and confident brown eyes smouldered in his ruggedly handsome face.

He spoke with a calm assurance, ignoring the slight tension in the room. "I will tell you what I can about the flight plan, but I am carrying some sensitive information so I cannot be specific about the details or dates and times of departure and arrival, or the exact location of the airports. The whole trip is likely to take five or six days. The uncertainty of the exact duration of the transit time depends on what happens when we arrive in London. There may be a slight delay waiting for some intel I need to courier to Cairo. Once we have left London it will be exactly five days – London-Austria, Austria-Greece, Greece-Cairo, Egypt, Cairo-Uganda, and Uganda-Southern Rhodesia. There is a military airfield five kilometres from Bulawayo. We will be able to get Doug and Brody into town and from there they will be on their own."

The boys nodded their agreement. They had gone through the outline of the flight several times with William and their father. William was repeating it mostly for Rachael's benefit.

William added, "During the day, my plane will be concealed in an airport hangar. Take-off and landing will be done at night. Cruising altitude is around 20,000 feet. I have flown this route several times and all destination airports have protocols in place to maximize safety for take-off and landing. There can never be absolute security when the world is at war, but I can tell you that all reasonable measures have been taken and to date I have flown without incident or direct personal threat. I am in constant communication with all stopover destinations prior to departure and arrival, and I will be informed if there is anything untoward developing and have time to re-route if necessary."

Robert asked William to telegram Malcolm Hunter before they left Uganda on the last leg of their journey to Bulawayo. Malcolm would meet the boys in Bulawayo and take them out to the farm. Rachael listened in silence. She was heartbroken that the imminent departure of her sons meant they would not be there for Christmas. She did not like the lengthy trek they were undertaking or the fact that she had no idea when she would see them again.

When Robert had negotiated with William to take Douglas and Brody, it was necessary to get permission from their college for their premature departure. They had both completed their exams and assessments, so their graduation was a certainty, but they would miss the ceremony. In view of the circumstances the college had been extremely understanding. Robert also put his farm forward for the next intake of students in the coming year. It meant that up to sixteen students had access to hands-on training on the farm, and Robert was guaranteed enough free labour to ensure the farm continued to run smoothly. It was all thanks to the foundations laid by his two sons in setting up the initiative. He had every confidence in them to make a success of managing the farmland in Bulawayo. The boys had their hearts set on going and Rachael had no say in the matter to make them stay. She would miss them terribly.

∾

# CRAWLEY CONCESSION GOLD MINE – PENHALONGA, SOUTHERN RHODESIA

Malcolm completed his inspection of the underground drives with satisfaction. The blasting on level two revealed a continuation of the gold enriched ore body. Eighteen tonnes of rock and rubble was ready to hoist to the surface to make its way through the elaborate

crushing process before being fed into the reduction plant. Fresh
rail tracks were laid to access the rock face, and timber shuttering
was in place supporting vulnerable areas of the drive. It was his
first trip underground since the lion hunt and his ribs ached with
the physical effort. He climbed into the hoist and looked forward
to being back on the surface.

At the close of the bizarre meeting with the Mahaha, Malcolm
and Tanaka had fallen into a deep sleep. When they awoke, the
Mahaha's camp was abandoned, and Malcolm was in excruciating
pain, struggling to breathe. He had fainted halfway back to the
village and Tanaka made a litter from cut branches to help drag
the unconscious Malcom the rest of the way. Once at the village
Madzinga set four members of the tribe, including Samuel and
Tanaka, to carry Malcolm back home. Malcolm recalled nothing
of the journey or the helter-skelter trip to Umtali Hospital with
Samuel driving the Ford and Tanaka's wide-eyed white-knuckle
ride on the back with Malcolm, Tanaka's first ever journey on
motorised transport.

Malcolm spent three days in hospital recovering from surgery
and treatment to reinflate a collapsed lung. He also had three
broken ribs. Work on the mine recommenced following the return
of the workforce and families who'd dispersed under threat. The
Mahaha had been appeased with the slaughter of Samson the lion.
Tanaka ensured the village heard every embellished detail of their
heroic confrontation and both hunters now enjoyed an elevated
status. While Malcolm recovered in hospital, Ephraim, the mine
captain, supervised the reorganisation of shifts and got the mine
back up and running again. Malcolm was now affectionately known
by the village and his workforce as *Muvimi* (*Hunter* in Shona).

Quite often at night Malcolm would be troubled with nightmares of the hunt. The lion's fierce golden penetrating eyes, its raw power and the taste of the predator's blood choking him as he suffocated under its mighty weight. He was plagued too by the Mahaha. It was such a surreal encounter that he struggled to make sense of it awake, never mind asleep. The three-fold prophecy dominated his thoughts:

*"When the snake strikes, golden hair will be swallowed into the belly of the earth."* Malcolm dreamed of a young girl or young woman with golden hair. In his dream she was at times riding a horse. On other occasions she walked carefree through an open grassy field, but in both sequences a large, fanged snake struck at her or the horse, sending her plummeting into a black hole in the earth. In all scenarios her face was indistinct, and it was no one he had ever met. He was never sure whether she survived or not.

*"Beware the one-eyed snake that walks on two legs and swims with the crocodile. He must die twice."* In his dreams a man with an eye patch fell from a ledge into a crocodile-infested gully where he was certain to be eaten alive. How could anyone survive that fate? The only person he knew with an eye patch was Henk. Surely it could not be him. Was any of it remotely real or true?

*"When you anger the serpent river god, his vengeance will be floodwater of fire and smoke."* Those visions puzzled Malcolm the most because they were always different. At times he saw an enormous snake swimming in a swollen raging river. It seemed to be breathing fire and smoke. Other times he saw smouldering debris and dead bodies floating away on the current.

He had not been back to Samuel's village since the lion hunt, but he decided he was well enough to make the trip. He needed to consult Hupenyu the witch doctor on the meaning of the visions.

It was early afternoon when Malcolm and Samuel arrived at the outskirts of Madzinga's village. The murmur from the gathered crowd seemed to be one of excitement. Without fail, every member of the tribe had to place a hand on Malcolm. Samuel whispered that it was a sign of adoration. Even the little children got in on the act and darted in to touch him before speeding away in a cloud of dust, shrieking with delight. Madzinga emerged and brought calm to the assembly. He led Malcolm to his hut, and they sat on wooden stools while one of Madzinga's wives brought a pitcher of warm millet beer and clay cups.

Malcolm clapped his hands respectfully in the traditional greeting and said, "I see you, Baba (father)."

Madzinga responded with, "I see you, Muvimi."

They exchanged pleasantries in the usual custom with Samuel translating before Malcolm announced, "I would like to speak to Hupenyu. I have questions for the N'anga about the Mahaha. I ask your permission to meet with the holy one in private." Malcolm opened his backpack and revealed an array of gifts for the village: packs of fresh kudu meat, cured kudu hide, a nylon fishing net, rope and two sharp hunting blades.

Madzinga accepted the generous gifts, all except the kudu hide. It surprised Malcolm what the chief said next, "Hupenyu has been expecting you. Take the kudu skin as a gift. Tanaka will show you the way."

Tanaka materialised from among the crowd looking the same as when Malcolm had last seen him, minus the long spear. They greeted each other like old friends. Tanaka had insisted on staying by Malcolm's bedside until he regained consciousness after his operation. He led Malcolm over the raised centre of the village and descended an area where the mud huts petered out. The N'anga lived a short way from the hub of the village. When the ground flattened out, they followed a worn path framed by granite boulders until they stood in front of a neatly thatched dwelling. There were multiple wooden stakes bearing weather-bleached skulls of wild animals. Some of the poles were lined with snakeskin, the most prominent being the unmistakable shadowy patterned python. At the entrance to the hut the ground was polished to a shine and two leopard skin rugs led to the open doorway. Tanaka showed Malcolm to a carved wooden seat and left respectfully without another word.

Malcolm thought the surroundings were an appropriate environment for a mystic. What he had not anticipated was Hupenyu. He fully expected an antique man with bones in his nose or hair, carrying some sort of magical staff full of trinkets and charms.

Hupenyu glided silently out of the darkened inner sanctuary of her hut. She was completely naked and walked with confident, unashamed grace. Her age was impossible to fathom but she appeared to be in perfect physical condition, and sexual maturity. Her skin was unblemished and the colour of ebony. Her short, cropped hair accentuated her noble head. She had high cheekbones, a neatly formed nose and full voluptuous lips. It was her eyes that were most remarkable of all, brilliant azure blue. She stood across from Malcolm as he marvelled at her radiant beauty.

Her breasts were full, shapely, and pert. Her nipples were darker still and became erect as Malcolm gazed over them. Her hairless legs were strong and long, leading up to wider curvaceous hips. Her womanhood was bare, with neat full lips guarding her opening. Malcolm forced himself to return his attention to her striking eye. She assessed him with a quizzical tilt of her head.

"I see you, Muvimi," she spoke in mildly accented English as she sat cross legged on one of the leopard skins opposite him.

"I see you, Hupenyu," he replied, intrigued at the sound of her voice and her fluent English. He got up and handed her the kudu skin. She accepted the humble gift with a nod and Malcolm returned to his stool.

"Your bravery and courage have rid us of a mighty demon that plagues our people. For that I thank you. You are not here to talk about the hunt, are you, Muvimi? I knew you would come, and I looked forward to your arrival. I too have a gift for you." She retreated into her hut and returned with a bracelet. Without asking him for his consent she took his right hand and placed it above her breasts as she squatted in front of him. She tied the interwoven bands and braids over his wrist never taking her eyes off his. Malcolm was intoxicated and felt his breath catch in his throat. Afterward, she returned to her leopard skin.

Malcolm examined the gift as she spoke. "This charm will protect you and ward off evil. It is made from the hair of Samson's mane along with whiskers of leopard and cheetah. It is bound with the gall bladder of the adder, mamba, and cobra from the forest. It is a powerful charm, and you must never take it off. Keep it!"

"Thank you, Hupenyu. The Mahaha told me snakes will fill my path in the future. I am uncertain about all the words he spoke to me. It is why I have come to see you." Malcolm was now also curious to learn more of Hupenyu herself, but he did not have to ask. She seemed to already know what he was thinking.

She smiled at him, revealing perfectly white teeth. "Mr Hunter, you must see deeper with your eyes of understanding. I can take many forms."

As Malcom looked on in astonishment, she transformed into a haggard, toothless crone with shrivelled duds and mottled sagging skin covering gnarled arthritic limbs. Malcolm nearly fell off his stool. She then instantaneously changed into the ancient male equivalent, the epitome of what Malcolm expected in the first place, complete with bones in his hair and pierced nose. Finally, she turned back to the graceful young woman she was originally. He was speechless.

"Do you see, Mr Hunter? I have been in my current form since before your great-grandfather was born. I can stay this way because I have been chosen by the spirits and am untouched by the hands of any man. If my body is pure, I can be as the day the spirits chose me, but if I were to couple with another, my lifeforce and connection to the spirit realm would end and I would fade just as every other mortal. That is what you wanted to ask, was it not? Not just the words of the Mahaha. You now want to know me. Forget me, Mr Hunter."

Malcolm shuffled uncomfortably under her scrutiny.

She continued, "What you must understand is there are good and evil spirits just as there are good and bad in men. I am the bridge between man and spirit. Entities like the Mahaha are extremely rare and very powerful. Denying their existence does not dissolve their power or make them unreal. Predicting the future comes at great cost to the chosen body of the spirit. Not all mediums possess such power. The Mahaha is one of the most powerful I have encountered. His prophecy too is as much a blessing as it is a curse.

"My spirit was with you when you left for the hunt. I witnessed you enter the cave and watched as you cut out the heart of Samson. I saw you enter the den of the Mahaha and looked on as he pierced the beating heart. I heard the prophecy uttered to you. The Mahaha blew the magic dust not only to put you to sleep but to sever my contact with you. He sensed me there. I too fell into a deep sleep when he blew the powder. When I woke, I was weak. Blood poured from my nose and mouth and my herbs and medicine slowly brought me back to health.

"What I can tell you about the prophecy is this: It will happen as the Mahaha has foreseen. They will not happen at the same time, but they will happen within your lifetime in order of the way they were told. I cannot tell you who the prophecy relates to. The charm I have given you will protect you from mischief, but it can also give you strength when the time comes if you put faith in my words and my power.

"To press me further on the meaning of the prophecies will be to ask of me more than I can give. It would be a journey into the spirit realm where return is uncertain. Do you understand, Mr Hunter?"

Malcolm had not received the clarification he was after, but he felt a certain kinship or connection with the N'anga. He believed her. He said nothing, just sighed and nodded. Africa had already proved to be a land full of secrets and intrigue. Although he did not understand it all, his perspective was broadened beyond anything he could ever have imagined.

Hupenyu stood and walked over to Malcolm and took his hand. "There is one more thing I must tell you. You must leave this place. You must leave this village, these mountains and your mine. Trouble has found you here and the Mahaha will return. He has the power to take all that is yours. This place is connected to him. Leave and seek your future elsewhere away from the Mahaha's reach. You must go now, Muvimi."

She tenderly held his face and kissed him. Her tongue gently probed the inside of his mouth, and he held her close to him. He felt giddy when she pulled away. He knew that she intended it to be their first and last kiss.

# Chapter 15

## GLASGOW, SCOTLAND — MACGREGOR RESIDENCE

Elizabeth Baron was not surprised when she received the invitation or summons to attend a meeting at David MacGregor's private home. Her engagement to Michael had been a low-key affair held in one of the small reception rooms at the Pavilion Theatre. None of Michael's family had attended the occasion following strict instructions from David MacGregor. She was not intimidated by David, she had control over his son and once she produced an heir, she would be well on her way to accessing the MacGregors' wealth.

She was shown into the hallway by Veronica, David's wife, who extended the politest business-like greeting she could muster with a forced smile. Veronica was wearing a new black dress but looked worn out and haggard, Elizabeth thought. She was thin. Her straight grey hair seemed to match the colour of her lifeless eyes. The price of a lifetime of care and support to her husband and two children perhaps. Elizabeth handed Veronica her mustard yellow camel wrap woollen coat and admired her own reflection in the full-length hallway mirror. Elizabeth wore a short-sleeved navy-blue suit. It was square in the shoulder and masterfully fitted to reveal her curves. The skirt stopped just below the knee showing off her shapely legs and navy-blue heeled pumps with a neat bow. She had chosen this suit because David MacGregor, one of the best tailors in the whole of Scotland, had hand made it for her personally.

When she was shown into David's office, she smiled to herself. Men with small penises always surrounded themselves with extravagant, expensive toys. She looked at the oversized desk that dwarfed David. He did not bother to stand as she entered. It annoyed her but she let it slip.

"I see the suit fits you well," he uttered, showing no real sign of admiration or genuine interest. Elizabeth knew he was more interested in his craftsmanship rather than the glorious body underneath. Her mind shifted briefly to a mental image of a coupling of Veronica and David in the throes of passion. David's pants were around his ankles. He wore his crisp white shirt, dark waistcoat, tie, and glasses and delivered his strokes in the missionary position to the accommodating emotionless Veronica. She imagined both glad for it to be over to return to the important tasks of polishing silver or reading the Financial Times.

He continued, "I won't keep you long as I am sure you are busy. I have taken the liberty of drawing up a set of documents for you to sign before your wedding."

Elizabeth threw her head back and laughed. "I will not be signing anything you put in front of me, Mr MacGregor, or should I call you *Daddy?*"

David offered her a seat and slid a set of documents over to her. Elizabeth paged through. The lawyer's jargon was lengthy, but the overall message was abundantly clear. If she signed the agreement, once wed she would have no claim to the MacGregor family trust or have any financial ties.

David got out of his chair and walked to his safe and retrieved a set of four coloured files. He kept the brown file and returned the rest. He spoke calmly: "You have been an interesting person to get to know. I can understand why you would agree to marry my son and produce a child, but you are under the illusion that you will sweep in and lay your hands on what I have worked for my whole life. That is not going to happen, and I will tell you why."

David opened the folder and removed a set of reports. He separated them and pushed them across the desk to her. It was a set of autopsy reports carried out on her deceased husband Albert Baron, both prepared by the same pathologist on the same day but both reports were entirely different.

The first report bore the official date stamp of the local coroner. It concluded the cause of death as Myocardial Infarction – heart attack. The second unstamped and unofficial report for the deceased stated the cause of death to be Positional Asphyxiation – suffocation.

Elizabeth stared at the two reports, feeling the blood drain from her face. She cursed herself at leaving the pathologist Abell Clamp alive. He was so close to his retirement, the substantial pay-out she gave him was sufficient for him and his family to disappear without a trace and live happily ever after. Somehow David MacGregor had got to him, and that daft bastard Clamp had kept both reports in his possession as insurance. Elizabeth was speechless.

David continued, "When you and Michael considered your nuptials, I took an active interest in your background. I thought seducing the junior lawyer from Baker Montague and Forbs was a little much. Johnathan has been in a fair bit of bother as a result, but he was smart enough to reveal what you were interested in: my financial portfolio. I dug a little deeper into your sudden rise to glory and inheriting the theatre from your late husband, despite having only been married to him for a short time. His death was of obvious interest. I eventually tracked down the pathologist that wrote the official report. I'm surprised you left loose ends. When he was sufficiently encouraged to talk, he produced these."

Elizabeth had to think quick on her feet, but the wind had been knocked out of her. She had underestimated David MacGregor.

"I will outline some of the details of the documents I have prepared." David walked around the desk and sat on the edge next to Elizabeth and picked up the substantial folder of legal documents. "The enclosed contains explicit regulations relating to your marriage to my son. If you produce a male heir, the trust fund will provide adequately for him financially. It will be administered by me. In the event of my death, it will be managed by my law firm and surviving family. In the event of the untimely death of my son and you have not produced a male heir, the contents of the autopsy reports will be processed through the proper channels. You will have outlived your usefulness, and I will turn my back on you. You see, Elizabeth, I am prepared to be a reasonable and generous ally, but cross me and you may as well deal directly with the devil himself."

Without seeing an immediate way-out Elizabeth abruptly stood and snarled in David's face, "I don't need your money or your bent bloody son!"

She went to leave but before she got to the door David removed his spectacles and wiped them on his handkerchief before he calmly said, "Sit down, Elizabeth. If you walk out that door now the autopsy reports will immediately be handed over to the authorities. Come, my dear, you have papers to sign."

# WHITE STONE FARM — INSIZA, BULAWAYO, SOUTHERN RHODESIA

Pieter Potgieter sat in a drunken haze on his veranda watching a dust devil swirling across his barren land. His head throbbed from prolonged excess, an attempt to quash the scars of loss and ruin. He had dispensed with the formalities of bathing quite some time ago, immune to the musky alcohol sweats and the stench that emanated from his body. A cloud of flies that lazily fed off his greasy hair and filthy clothes were his only companions. His bare feet and untrimmed toenails were caked with dirt. Mampoer Peach Brandy was his only source of nourishment for the last few months. Self-abuse had reduced the once able body to skin and bone. He looked significantly older than his fifty years.

The last two years had been a succession of crushing blows for Piet. He was the last remaining landowner of the trio of investors in the Red Herring Gold Mine venture on Hillside Ranch. The other two, once his friends and neighbours, were long gone. He had no idea where they were now, and he did not care. Piet had been easily led. The promise of wealth and easy money greatly appealed to him, but in the process, he foolishly neglected his land.

None of the three farmers that invested were experienced miners, and between them they eventually lost everything. When the mine finally went bust, Piet could not even afford to pay his depleted workforce. In retaliation, the disgruntled labourers ransacked Piet's home before going in search of alternative employment. The fields that in years gone by had yielded acre after acre of golden maize were now bare and lifeless. He was informed that both of his sons had been killed in the war. Piet had hung on to the hope that when his boys returned, they would get the farm back on track. When they were both taken from him, something inside him snapped. His daughter Victoria, his only remaining child, was away at boarding school. When she found out that her mother had finally left her drunken husband, Victoria had no interest in returning to the derelict farm, so even during her school holidays she stayed away. She chose rather to visit friends. Piet never really saw eye to eye with her and she despised her father. At sixteen years of age, she was fiercely independent.

What Victoria did not know was that her mother never left at all. Six months ago, Piet in a drunken rage had shoved her. He had not intended to kill her, but as she fell her head struck the wrought iron fire grate in the lounge and she never regained consciousness. Unsure what to do, Piet left her where she had fallen for four days until the smell of her decomposing body forced him to dispose of her. She did not have the luxury of a burial.

When Piet was a toddler, his father had caught two baby crocodiles in the Zambezi River and introduced them to the small dam in front of the farmhouse. The little snappers were given godlike names of *Goliath* and *Zeus*. Over the years the crocodiles fed on the catfish in the pool and continued to grow. Occasionally they were thrown carcasses of baboon or pig, animals shot for crop protection. Goliath now at around forty-five years old had grown into an eighteen-foot-long beast. Along the way, driven by hunger, he had killed and devoured Zeus, his brother. So, when Goliath was fed the corpse of Piet's wife, he managed to dispose of her without too much trouble.

Piet's father had handed down the secret family recipe for distilling the potent peach brandy. It was with regret Piet noticed he was now down to his very last bottle. He was too far gone to brew another batch. The once abundant plantation that provided the fruit for the distillery at the rear of the farm was thinned out by drought and neglect. What little fruit that remained lay rotting on the ground. Piet had nothing left to live for. He drained the remaining scalding liquor and staggered to the edge of the shrunken water hole. It seemed fitting that Goliath should dispose of him in the same manner as his wife. He collapsed in the stinking mud, resigning himself to his fate, and passed out. What Piet neglected to notice was that Goliath had left over a month ago. The lifeless dried-up puddle with its stagnant putrid mud had finally driven Goliath to search for an alternative home.

∾

## CEDAR TREE HOLLOW RANCH — INSIZA, BULAWAYO

Douglas and Brody Hunter had arrived at their new residence a fortnight ago with an overwhelming sense of freedom, the lengthy plane ride from Aberdeen soon forgotten. Within days they had furnished their home with necessities from the various local suppliers in town and had procured a breeding pair of Vlaamperd horses. Douglas insisted on the pitch-black stallion whom he named *Ace*. His steed was just over 16 hands at the withers with strong, long legs and a thick glossy mane and tail. In a little over a week horse and rider were an inseparable unit.

Brody had a slightly shorter chocolate brown mare. She was far more placid than Ace but had intelligent eyes and inquisitive ears. Brody named her *Mona*. Both horses were fundamental to carrying out their daily tasks which currently centred around replacing the boundary fence. The enormity of the task dawned on them as they consulted the scaled down aerial map of their 2000 hectares from the ridge at the back of the farmhouse. Brody being the more academic of the two calculated the length of the perimeter to be nearly eight square miles! He estimated it could take two weeks just to cover the area on horseback, longer if they were to stop and make estimates on materials required to repair the run-down sections. On the day of their arrival, Henrick Van Royen, the manager of Hillside Ranch next door, took the two boys to show them the work he had started on the border between the two farms. It gave them an idea of what was involved.

Today Douglas was continuing the inspection alone, expecting to be out until dark. Although they were yet to encounter predators or wild animals directly, they prepared for the inevitable. His new shotgun nestled securely in its sheath alongside the saddle bags which contained a notebook and pen and supplies for the day. He took Ace out at a canter towards the southeast corner of the boundary adjacent to White Stone Farm. It was the worst section he had come across so far, badly maintained and needing to be fully redone. It would be a massive undertaking.

For both boys, each day was an exciting adventure that left them happily exhausted at the end of the day. Their farm had fertile soil that stretched as far as the eye could see. The northern section was full of flat-topped acacia. For the last two nights they could hear the black faced vervet monkeys shrieking in the tops of the trees, most likely being hunted by leopard. The African climate was warm and dry. For Doug as he rode, the air seemed to carry on it a special scent of its own.

For the last month Goliath had hauled his immense body in search of food and shelter. In water he could rely on his powerful tail to propel him like a deadly torpedo to attack and kill. On dry land, however, he was slow and cumbersome. He could move quickly if need be but only for a short duration. He was not fast enough out of water to catch a rabbit or deer. During the heat of the day, he sought out shade in the undergrowth or ditches at the side of the road. His only meal so far was a decaying dead goat that had been hit by a car and lay decomposing in one such ditch. Fortunately, the other scavengers had not discovered it. It was less than what he needed but it gave him the energy to continue his quest. His colossal head was the width of a beer barrel, and he lumbered on, weaving his way through an open field in the baking sun. His acute sense of smell could not pick up any indication of anything worth eating, or the much-needed sweet fragrance of fresh water. He trundled on, panting through his toothy humourless grin.

He spooked a black mamba in the grass that hissed and slithered off at an incredible rate, far too fast for Goliath's stubby legs to give chase. He followed the direction of the snake as the ground began to incline. He struggled over the rocky surface to the top of a small hill. On the crest the air carried with it a new scent: water! He was faster down the other side, spurred on by the momentum of his great bulk and the strengthening aroma feeding his weary legs with new endeavour. A body of water came into view.

Victoria Potgieter had just led her team to victory in the interschools girls' hockey tournament. Her bruised shins were a testament to how hard she tried during her matches. When she held the trophy in celebration, she noticed the proud parents looking on and clapping. It reinforced her loneliness and the absence of her own family. Vicky was closest to her mother, but since she'd left out of the blue six months ago, she had not heard a single word from her. It did not surprise her in the least that she had finally left her drunken husband or the run-down farm, but as the months slipped by without any contact from her, Vicky went through a very difficult time. She felt angry, abandoned and truly alone.

Victoria never spoke of her family, the loss of her two brothers whom she had looked up to, or the disappearance of her mother, or her alcoholic father and dilapidated home. Victoria chose her own path. As she came to the end of her high school education, with no financial backing for university, she planned to enrol as an apprentice training in veterinary science in Salisbury. That way she could study, have hands-on training and support herself on her humble wages. She certainly would not ask her father for financial help. Even if he had the means to assist, he would not part with a penny for her. As it was, he was too busy drinking what little they had left. He seemed to be content working his way through the cases of Mampoer Peach Brandy distilled on their farm in years gone by. She could still remember the smell of her father's sweat the last time she had seen him, unshaved and unwashed. The stench was an assaulting combination of sickly sweet and sour at the same time. She hated him.

Yet once the hockey tournament had finished, instead of heading off to Salisbury as planned she took the bus from Thornhill High School in Gwelo and headed back to White Stone Farm to say a final farewell to her father. Perhaps he had knowledge of where her mother was.

Her personal belongings had already been forwarded to Salisbury. She carried with her just her school backpack and a bottle of water. She was still dressed in her hockey gear with her short bottle green sports skirt and white polo shirt. Her knee length hockey socks were gathered around her ankles above her white plimsoles. Several fresh bruises were clearly visible on her shapely tanned legs. She looked almost identical to her mother when she was sixteen, blonde hair cut in a bob. Green eyes dominated her pretty face. Passers-by would have considered her presence and attire out of place walking along the dirt road that led to the farmsteads.

A thought suddenly occurred to her: if she was to say goodbye to her home, her father and the Insiza region, she should visit her favourite place one more time. *Mermaids Pool* as she had named it was nestled in a shallow saddle surrounded by trees. It was a body of crystal-clear water with a surface area twice the size of a hockey field, fed exclusively by an underground spring. To her knowledge it had never dried out, even through years of drought. The gently sloping southerly entrance to the pool was a picturesque piece of paradise. It even had fine white sand like a private beach retreat. The opposite end of the pool was deeper with underwater stone shelves that allowed you to stand or sit in the cool water. The northerly perimeter was framed with solid rock. Over the years a stream had eroded a narrow walkway from the top down to the water's edge.

The pool was located on the boundary between the Potgieter's White Stone Farm and Cedar Tree Hollow. She left the dirt road, heading for her favourite place. It did not take her long to reach the crest of the saddle and her first view of Mermaids Pool. It looked so serene and inviting. From her vantage point she could also see her rundown homestead in the distance. The prominent white rocky outcrop of calcite near the old peach plantation was visible from her elevation; it was how the farm got its name.

By following the dilapidated boundary of White Stone Ranch, Douglas could see firsthand years of neglect. Wooden poles that once bore the weight of the barbed wire fencing were in places absent all together. Rusted wire hung in disarray. Where posts were still standing, they were riddled with termite holes and wood rot. He contemplated running a fence erection team and disposal team simultaneously – something had to be done with the rusty wire. If left in place, it could pose a hazard to livestock. He would feed the information back to Brody to work out a budget and timeframe for the task. Nearly four miles of boundary line in this section alone would need to be completely redone. He thought about paying his neighbour Piet Potgieter a visit – maybe they could come to an agreement of shared cost for the replaced fencing.

Although the topography up until now was mostly open field and gentle undulations, towards the southern corner boundary the terrain became more inclined and rockier. Ace walked steadily on until horse and rider stood on the edge of a flat granite plateau overlooking a hidden body of water below. Douglas had no idea the pool existed. He was just about to retrieve the map from his saddle bag to double check when a movement in the water caught his eye.

He looked more closely and noticed a young girl standing knee deep on a shelf in the water. She was topless, wearing only a short green skirt. As he looked at her, she noticed the horse and rider on the ridge and waved, apparently unashamed by her semi-naked state. Doug dismounted, tied Ace's reins to a tree on the ridge and negotiated a worn path that descended to the pool below.

When Doug reached the water's edge, he immediately felt foolish for bringing his shotgun. He placed it on the bank and felt slightly at a loss as to what to say or do. The girl in the pool made no attempt to cover herself. He found it difficult to tear his eyes off her pale unblemished chest and dark pink, erect nipples. He was completely off guard and had a lump in his throat.

She broke the silence, fully aware of the direction of his gaze. "Hi, I'm Vicky."

Douglas shuffled uncomfortably and investigated her pretty face, noticing in detail her green eyes, damp blonde hair, and the array of freckles over her neat little nose and cheeks. She tilted her head as she smiled, encouraging him to communicate.

"Doug," he said, a little higher pitched than he would have liked then cleared his throat and added, "I'm Douglas Hunter, I have just recently taken over the ranch."

Victoria bent down, washing the cool water over her arms. The movement allowed Douglas to watch her pert breasts move and change shape as she dipped into the water, so he almost missed what she said next: "I'm Victoria Potgieter. I live, or rather lived next door to you. Welcome to *Mermaids Pool*. It's right on the boundary of our two properties."

Doug's brain was incapable of rational thought or conversation. His body seemed to have sensed the moment when it could take over of its own accord. It manifested its control with a throbbing sensation in his loins.

Vicky smiled knowingly and chuckled. She dropped her skirt, rolled it into a ball and threw it onto the bank at Doug's feet. She allowed him a fleeting glance of her entire naked body before she dived headfirst into the water. She surfaced closer to the shore and stood up. She noticed the prominent bulge in Doug's trousers which he immediately tried boyishly to cover with his hands.

"You don't say much, do you, Doug?" Vicky teased. She asked more formally, "Would you like to join me for a swim, Douglas Hunter?" She treaded water, watching him, then she swam backwards to her original perch. She stood up again allowing him to view her glistening body and the triangle of hair at the base of her smooth flat belly. Doug abandoned the efforts to hide his erection and disrobed clumsily, first his boots, then his shirt and finally his trousers.

Victoria let out a little purr in her throat, barely audible. Douglas had broad strong shoulders and a chiselled physique. His erection was proud and thick as he entered the pond. The water was pleasantly cool, but he hardly noticed, he had such an overpowering urge to hold the beautiful girl who had captivated him from the moment he saw her. He was entirely under her spell.

When they stood together facing each other knee deep in the water Victoria took control. She pressed her full body up against him as he bent to kiss her. She gasped at the feel of his steel-like arms wrapped around her pulling her tighter. They kissed, clumsily at first but soon their lips worked together, their tongues exploring and probing. Vicky guided them a little deeper into the water where Doug could stand, and her weightless body had the freedom to float. Still holding her arms around his neck, she wrapped her legs around him allowing him access to her.

They became one as Vicky guided him into her inner depths. Doug gasped at the almost scalding warmth compared to the cool water of the pool. Vicky whispered "Slowly" in Doug's ear and he listened and stood rigid. Vicky moved gently up and down his stiff shaft until she started to pulse around him. She quickened her downward thrusts until they both climaxed together, transported to a world of ecstasy until the final shudders subsided.

When Vicky detangled her arms and legs from Doug's body and took a step back, Doug suddenly felt vulnerable and exposed. He turned and swam back to the ledge. There was a turmoil of emotion going through his young head. He felt like he had entered the water a boy but come out a man. He desperately wanted to hold her again and experience the exquisite pleasure they had shared just a moment ago. They had barely completed a conversation but had shared the most intimate of moments. He watched her standing on the rocky shelf, smiling at him cheekily. She now had rosy cheeks and a certain glow.

As he stood to address her, in the corner of his eye he noticed a shadow move below the surface of the pool.

Victoria had removed all her clothes apart from her short green skirt and discarded them on the beach along with her backpack before entering the water. She swam breaststroke unhurriedly on the surface through the warmer shallows out into the deeper water where it was cooler.

She had just reached a rocky shelf on the opposite side of the pool where she could stand when Goliath descended onto the beach. He caught his breath, panting with exertion and the oppressive heat. He took in the scent of the clothing with little interest before entering the pool. The sun had beaten down on his scaly armour and the cold water was a welcome respite. He lay in the shallows, adjusting to the temperature before he ventured out further. From the surface he had a clear view across the water. His eyes fixed on Victoria on the other side of the water hole. He took a deep breath and silently submerged.

He had no trouble navigating, visibility was good. His powerful tail eased him gently forward as he negotiated the underwater sanctuary. The rocky floor had a solid steep gradient leading up to the shelf where his prey now stood. He positioned himself ready to strike. A second target suddenly entered the pool and joined the first. He patiently waited as he observed their coupling. There was greater chance of a successful kill targeting one or the other but not both together. The instincts of a predator unchanged for millions of years kept the hunter focussed and alert. He did not have to wait long. Soon the original target was back on the shelf. He launched into the attack; his powerful tail propelled him up the rocky slope. His prey did not stand a chance…

Before Douglas could utter a word, the water next to Victoria erupted, a grotesque monster with gaping jaws seized her. The leviathan devil's gigantic head engulfed her in a crushing grip from the base of her neck to her hips. Both arms were pinned as the air was squeezed out of her crushed lungs in a gurgling terrified scream. The momentum of the attack took Goliath and Victoria over the shelf and into the deep water on the other side. It was all over in a matter of seconds. Doug looked on in frozen horror. The ripples subsided, leaving no evidence of the violence moments before.

Doug shook himself and grabbed his shotgun. He could do nothing except pace back and forth along the bank. There was no sign of the creature or Victoria. He stood there naked, trembling, and he started to sob. He shouted her name and paced the edge of the pool.

Victoria was dead within seconds. The terror of the strike, the crushing force of the jaws and the inability to breathe resulted in a quick kill. Goliath never relinquished his grip as he submerged to the depths of the pool. Once his prey stopped moving, he unhurriedly carried his prize back towards the shallows. There he released her, took hold of a limb, and started his death roll.

Douglas was still naked and holding his gun when he heard sounds of splashing coming from the other side of the pool. His immediate thought was *Vicky is alive!* She had somehow managed to break free and swum to the shore. He sprinted barefooted in the direction of the shallows. In his haste he did not feel the ground beneath him or the thorns that tore mercilessly at his exposed skin.

"Victoria, I'm coming!" he yelled, scrambling onto the beach and then suddenly stopped in his tracks as he came face to face with Goliath lying next to Victoria's torso. The crocodile was chewing on one of her detached legs just ten paces away.

Goliath was quite accustomed to having humans watch him eat so he paid Douglas little attention. Victoria lay on her back with her mouth and eyes open in the same manner Douglas last saw her. The puncture marks from the initial bite were deep gashes. In the short time it had taken Doug to reach her, Goliath had removed and consumed all but one of her limbs.

Douglas raised the shotgun and fired at the barrel-like head. The impact shifted the beast a metre in the water. He dropped the leg and submerged out of sight. In the distance Doug heard another gunshot clearly audible. It came from the direction of White Stone Farm. He paid it little attention. The lifechanging rollercoaster of emotions of the last hour took their toll. He bent over and vomited copiously the bile from his stomach.

For the first time in a long while Piet Potgieter was aware of the stench around him. He awoke with the sun beating down on his face. The dried clay mud burned on his skin. He was confused. Goliath had let him live. He barely had the strength to haul his drunken body upright. He staggered back to the porch where he saw the empty bottles littering the floor and steps. He shuffled inside, squinting as his eyes grew accustomed to the darker interior. His hands shook as he fumbled with the keys to his gun cabinet. It was one of the only possessions left untouched when his house was ransacked. He carried his shotgun out onto the veranda. When he placed it in his mouth, he could not quite reach with his hands to fire the weapon. He staggered about aimlessly before he slumped into a deck chair. With the butt resting on the porch floor, he replaced the barrel back in his mouth and used his big toe to pull the trigger.

# Chapter 16

## BULAWAYO — ST MARY'S CATHEDRAL

The funeral for Pieter and Victoria Potgieter was a poorly attended functional affair held on a day when the rest of the world had no interest in paying their respects. The local vicar, Reverend Mathew Gregory, conducted the ceremony in the cool high-ceilinged sanctum of the Bulawayo St Mary's Cathedral. There were no relatives present. Apart from Mr and Mrs Mills, the owners of the central hardware store, the only other people present were Douglas, Brody, Malcolm, and Henk.

Victoria had worked for the Mills family during her school holidays to earn pocket money. They took Vicky under their wing and observed with sadness the decline of the Potgieter family. Piet still had unpaid accounts with the store, but the childless couple loved the ray of sunshine Victoria brought with her, so it was for her sake not Piet's they attended. The local police had retrieved Victoria's remains along with the bloated Goliath found floating belly up in Mermaids Pool, his stomach swollen with the half-digested meal in his stomach. The single shot from Douglas's gun had wreaked enough havoc on the armour-plated head to ensure eventual death.

It was little consolation to Douglas. In the whole scheme of things, he had spent hardly any time at all with Victoria, but he still felt robbed and traumatised by the series of events. From the highest level of euphoria to the darkest terror and revulsion. He did not tell a soul of what he and Vicky had shared moments before her brutal attack, not even Brody or the police. In his version of the event, he spotted her swimming in the pool moments before the attack. It was somehow easier to process than the reality. As the days went by, he was more distant and aloof. It was therefore a surprise when he announced to Brody that he would be attending the funeral.

The same mortuary wagon taking Victoria and Goliath into town was loaded with the dead body of Piet. His emaciated corpse was missing the upper two-thirds of his skull and brains that were left plastered on the walls and floor of his porch.

Brody was extremely concerned about Douglas, his moods and distance. It was so unlike him. In desperation Brody spoke to Henrick but he was equally stumped. He suggested getting Malcolm to have a word with him. When Malcolm received the telegram from Brody he immediately left for Bulawayo and arrived the morning of the funeral. But there was no time before the ceremony for him to pull Doug aside for a talk.

After the short sermon the small gathering left the church and stood outside in the afternoon sun in a sombre mood. Malcolm, Henk and Brody looked at Douglas, hoping he might enlighten them as to why he took Vicky's death so personally. He said nothing.

Henrick broke the silence: "Doug, are you just annoyed you didn't have enough time to give her one?"

Douglas shot out his arms with such speed it took the others by complete surprise. His vicelike grip twisted Henk's shirt at the throat so violently Henk's remaining eye bulged and his scarred face turned bright red, but when Henk saw the pain in Douglas's eyes, he suddenly understood why he had struck a nerve. Instead of retaliating, Henk pulled Douglas towards him and wrapped him in a bear hug.

He whispered in Doug's ear, "It's ok, little brother, I'm here for you."

Douglas held onto Henk and began to sob. Through his tears he lamented, "I held her moments before…" He could not bring himself to finish the sentence.

Malcolm and Brody exchanged confused glances until the penny dropped for them too. There was no need to press Douglas further for an explanation. Something had obviously happened between Doug and Vicky before the attack.

Malcolm tapped Douglas affectionately on the shoulder and stated the obvious, "I think we can all do with a drink."

The *Cape to Cairo* public house was a short walk from St Mary's Cathedral. The four of them sat in the shade of the outdoor veranda with ice-cold beer quenching their dry throats.

Brody broke the silence: "I have come up with a fencing solution that works out cheaper than wooden poles – cement."

"Cement? Those cast concrete posts are nearly twice the price of creosote," Doug replied, grateful for something to discuss rather than internalising his emotions.

"Not if we make them ourselves. The other day I read an article about the POW camp in Gatooma. The perimeter was a two-metre-high barbed wire fence. When I studied the photographs, the concrete columns were manufactured with holes to thread the barbed wire through. It is such a simple design but rather clever because they are strong, can be erected quickly, require little maintenance and last far longer than wood."

Malcolm asked, "What about the cost? You said you could make them cheaper than wooden poles. Explain that."

Brody shifted in his chair. "Premiere Portland Cement mine their lime on site and make their own powdered cement less than ten kilometres away. I had a chat with them, and they can supply the raw materials in bulk for us to make our own posts. I got Moses to build a wooden mould and we have already made our first samples. Apart from a few minor modifications, we are there."

Douglas thought he spotted a flaw in Brody's plan. "You do realise of course that we need a shit load of posts, that means a large workforce. That doesn't sound like a cheap alternative to me."

"Well, we currently have twenty-four male labourers working on the fencing project. They have come from all over the country and have a makeshift settlement a few miles north of our boundary. The wives are currently not doing anything, I mean not actually employed. I was thinking we could give them permission to build a village within our borders and employ the women to manufacture the concrete posts. From what I hear the average African female can work just as hard as the men, if not harder. By giving them an area of land to call home and a chance to earn money, we will benefit from staff with a sense of loyalty, and we will have ourselves cheap labour." Brody finished and looked around the table from one to the other waiting for a reaction.

Malcolm spoke first: "Was there no compound there before?"

Brody shook his head.

Malcolm continued, "What Brody is proposing makes real sense. I can tell you from personal experience that it is vital to the smooth running of your operation to ensure your workers are adequately provided for. My mine has a settlement with a school and a clinic. We have very little staff turnover and relatively few incidents with our workforce. My mine is somewhat unique that way when compared to how other mines operate in the area, they generally have no end of trouble."

Douglas thought about the mammoth tasks and challenges ahead. They would all require his mental focus.

He sighed and sat forward. "I haven't been myself lately and I haven't been much help to you, Brody. We have a lot to do and there's no time to sit around and mope. We are going to have several projects running at the same time. I will split the team working on the boundary fence tomorrow to release labour to get started on the internal paddocks. Shumba is currently the team leader for the fencing crew. We will meet with him first thing in the morning to propose the compound idea. He seems to be the spokesman for the workers. Brody, can you rework the numbers on the concrete posts to make sure it is viable and cost effective?"

Henrick's admiration for the two young lads had grown in the relatively short time he had known them. At just nineteen and twenty the two brothers were embarking on running what could potentially be one of the largest cattle ranches in the country.

He turned from Doug to Brody and offered some advice: "There are a few things I can tell you about boundary fences, boys – they are primarily built to keep your livestock in and mark your territory, but it is virtually impossible to keep wild animals and predators out. Antelope migrate and fences don't stop them. An adult Kudu can jump a fence two metres high without breaking a sweat, nearly double that height when spooked. Impala and smaller game will go through the gaps and sometimes under. Wild pig, porcupine and badger will burrow. Monkeys and baboons will do all the above. As for lions and leopards, they prey on pretty much everything I have already mentioned as well as everything else I haven't, so you won't stop them coming in either.

"With a little luck you will not have a herd of hungry or pissed off elephant trying to get through your lovely fences because they will snap the concrete posts like dry twigs. They have a keen sense of smell and will push down a fence to get to fruit trees, especially the marula tree. I have seen a few of them on your farm. I would advise you to cut down any fruit tree within a kilometre of your boundary fences.

"Once you have livestock in your paddocks, you are going to need to be vigilant and have them under surveillance 24/7. Carry out a regular reconnaissance of your boundaries. Predators will target your livestock at night, so armed nightwatchmen will be sensible. That's the best advice I can give you."

~

## CEDAR TREE HOLLOW – INSIZA, BULAWAYO

The workforce did not need much convincing about the idea of a settlement within the boundary of Cedar Tree Hollow. The designated area became a hive of activity with the construction of mud huts with thatched roofs. With no real limitations on space, the blank canvas was transformed into a kraal of twenty-four huts in a large circle facing a central community area. It was evident the sense of pride the workers felt towards their new home. The wood from the felled fruit trees was used in the construction of the huts along with eucalyptus and blue gum.

Moses demonstrated his carpentry skills in making chairs and tables out of the available timber. It was difficult to assess his age. Like his biblical namesake, he had a crop of snow-white hair on his head and beard, yet his ebony skin was youthful and without blemish or wrinkle.

An enclosure made from thorn branches contained the small herd of goats and on completion of the construction work, one was slaughtered for the celebratory feast. A fresh batch of millet beer was brewed for the occasion. Doug and Brody joined the villagers politely sipping the sour dough warm alcoholic concoction with less enthusiasm than the others.

Moses fashioned improved moulds for the concrete posts. The female labourers soon found their rhythm in working with the cement, ferrying water containers and bags balanced easily on their heads. Babies strapped to their backs did not seem to hinder their productivity. The energy and enthusiasm for the task was clear to see. Their new compound had given them all a sense of belonging.

~

# RED HERRING GOLD MINE – INSIZA, BULAWAYO

It was with a degree of reluctance that Malcolm Hunter decided to sell his Crawley Concession gold mine in Penhalonga. It was a smoothly run, profitable concern but given the advice from Hupenyu the witch doctor he felt he had little choice in the matter. It was not a decision he took lightly, but he believed it was the course of wisdom. He had developed a newfound respect for the spirit forces at work and their influence on the people that lived in this unique land. Although he did not fully understand or could explain how he felt, his decision was influenced by his first-hand personal experiences.

A shrewd investor would snap up the gold mine, it would simply be a matter of time. He notified Harold Bucket from the Bulawayo national archive who was still well connected in financial circles and for the moment Malcolm just had to wait.

Ashton George, the Australian geologist, had taken extensive samples of the Red Herring gold mine on Molly's ranch and the assay results were positive, so Malcolm switched his attention to the new location. About half of his workforce from Crawley Concession relocated to Bulawayo, including Samuel his assistant, Ephraim the mine captain, and Tanaka, Malcolm's guide for the lion hunt.

Malcolm and Henk worked together on the layout of a compound to house the farm and mine workers. The settlement accommodated eighty to a hundred residents in total and included a school and clinic.

Malcom was reminded of Hupenyu the witch doctor every time he looked at the string bracelet on his wrist. It was apparently a gift to safeguard him. He thought of their bizarre meeting, their one and only kiss. He knew with all certainty he could never have her, and the realisation left him feeling empty. To help defuse his emotional turmoil he forced himself to recall her manifestation as the old man and the ancient crone Hupenyu had morphed into. It did not really help. His nights were often plagued with visions of her, or the extraordinary lion hunt, or the bizarre Mahaha. Hupenyu had confirmed that the puzzling threefold prophesy would come true. No matter how much he considered the sketchy framework, he had no idea who it related to:

*When the snake strikes, golden hair will be swallowed into the belly of the earth.*

*Beware the one-eyed snake that walks on two legs and swims with the crocodile. He must die twice.*

*When you anger the serpent river god, his vengeance will be floodwater of fire and smoke.*

On a positive note, the telephone and power lines were now installed throughout the Insiza district. Cedar Tree Hollow and Hillside Ranch now had their own phones installed. Electric power to the new mining site was a distinct advantage. Malcolm forced himself to focus on his new direction.

~

## ZURICH, SWITZERLAND – ARTHUR CONWAY'S GOOD FORTUNE

Arthur Conway travelling under the name of Conrad Amman with his Swiss passport could not have had a smoother transition to life in Zurich. Within a matter of days, he had landed himself a job as an accounts manager at Wehrli Bank. To his astonishment he quickly learned that the bank handled accounts for Nazi Germany and personal accounts for members of the Third Reich including Adolf Hitler himself. It was not just cash deposits of Reichsmarks the bank handled either, there were vaults containing art and artefacts plundered during the German advance through Europe, and gold harvested from the prisoners of war, mostly

Jews. Whilst tiptoeing the delicate political tightrope of supposed neutrality, the Swiss banks were wallowing in a financial drunken orgy with Germany.

One of the personal accounts under Conway's control belonged to Hitler's right hand man, Hermann Göring, and it became the key to a lifechanging fortune. Arthur was just simply in the right place at the right time and was perfectly capable of dealing with the opportunity that presented itself. A consignment of German Reichsmark and valuables arrived by military escort from Göring's personal estate in Schorfheide, Germany.

Conway personally supervised the receipt of money and items, stamped the official deposit slip, and loaded the delivery into its designated vaults. It was only after the German entourage had left that he spotted a monumental error. The handwritten cash deposit slip added up to RM9,600,000, but the total had been transposed as RM 6,900,000.

He noticed how the quality of the written entries deteriorated towards the end of the paperwork. What Conway had no way of knowing was that Hermann Göring was personally preparing the documentation in another morphine-induced haze. As the drug coursed through his veins, Hermann's blurred mind drifted between the numbers on the page in front of him and a far more fulfilling recollection of his last sexual encounter with his young secretary Helga: 69 was his favourite position.

Conway doctored the deposit slip entries to tie in with the total of 6.9 million and just like that he became the grateful recipient of the difference – RM 2,700,000. He split the remaining cash into several smaller deposits through his network of accounts and resigned from his job the same day. That evening after a large gin and tonic, he contemplated his good fortune. Since being in

Switzerland, he had kept a low profile and his carnal desires under lock and key, the suppression of which had steadily eaten away at him. In another man's hands the vast sum would have been sufficient to live comfortably. But to Conway it was his means for revenge, the means to unleash hell on the unforgiven. The vast fortune gave him immense power and he felt almost immortal. Tonight's celebrations would include brutalising another young male and restarting his new photo album, perhaps of his very first trophy kill.

He would deal with Michael MacGregor, the bastard that humiliated him at the Thistle Hotel and who took the photos that ultimately ended his career in Edinburgh. Then he would deal with David MacGregor, Michael's father – the brains of the outfit. Finally, he would get his hands on the land that was rightfully his, Molly MacMillan's assets and the ranch in Southern Rhodesia.

He raised a toast to Göring: "Thank you, Hermann, you daft German fucker."

~

## PAVILION THEATRE – EDINBURGH, SCOTLAND

The wedding of Michael MacGregor and Elizabeth Baron went ahead despite her having to sign the prenuptial agreement forced upon her by Michael's father. Elizabeth would find a way around it; she was certain of that. The key to the family fortune still lay in producing an heir. In theory it was simple enough, it just involved somehow engineering pregnancy from her homosexual husband.

After the reception, she kept Michael waiting for over an hour as she changed out of her wedding dress into an outfit she had chosen for their consummation. When she finally called him through to the bedroom, he was greeted with a sight he was certainly not expecting. Instead of sexy lingerie, Elizabeth wore a men's style three-piece navy-blue suit, a white cotton shirt and a blue silk tie. Her beautiful blonde hair was scraped back and hidden below a black woollen fedora hat. She wore a stick-on black moustache that looked comically out of place on her otherwise pretty features. Michael burst out laughing and applauded her efforts to look masculine. As she turned to walk towards the bed, the back area of her trousers around her buttocks had been carefully cut away to reveal her perfect ostrich egg-like cheeks. She wore no underwear.

She lay on her back on the bed and spread her legs in the air exposing herself to him, "Take me in the rear until you are ready, then fill my womb with your seed."

There was a momentary hesitation, but strangely Michael did not need to be asked twice...

Conway re-entered the country in the same manner he had left. An off the grid flight courtesy of Otto Rendenbach's two-seater Albatross. Whilst in Zurich, Arthur received two regular English newspapers, the Scotsman, and the Daily Mail. It was the wedding notice of Michael and Elizabeth that pricked his attention. It was published twenty-eight days before the happy event, plenty of time for Arthur to concoct his plan. He flew in a few days before the wedding and found it relatively easy to enter the theatre where the reception was being held. There was no apparent need for security. How wrong they were...

While the reception was in full swing Conway made his way up to Elizabeth's apartment on the top floor and waited. Again, no security, not even a locked door. He milled around the art deco rooms with casual disinterest, killing time. Finally, the newlyweds returned, chatting casually, unaware of the danger they were in. Arthur was forced to spend another agonising hour behind the heavy floor-to-ceiling blackout curtains in the bedroom while Elizabeth painstakingly slipped into her nuptial garb. His weapon of choice was a razor-sharp six-inch blade – a fired pistol would have attracted unwanted attention, and he needed a quick kill and a clean getaway. His clothes, like his leather gloves and balaclava, were black. The only part of him exposed was his hate-filled eyes.

He waited until Michael withdrew from Elizabeth's rear and plunged into her expectant womb to deliver his seed before he struck. Michael was still pumping when the blade slid effortlessly between his ribs and into his heart.

At the sight of the masked assassin, Elizabeth screamed and instinctively struck out her right hand into Conway's face. Arthur had not expected resistance from her. Elizabeth's fingers dug into Conway's temple and her thumb and inch-long nail slipped under his eyelid and penetrated the left eye. Arthur's head was filled with neon light before the excruciating pain hit him. He left the knife lodged in Michael's back and retreated from the room, clutching his face. Elizabeth was pinned under the dead weight of her motionless husband.

Duncan Funeral Directors of Edinburgh prepared Michael MacGregor's coffin with a purple silk lining as requested by the family. The golden handles contrasted against the dark hardwood body. The only other coffin in that day belonged to Patrick McDonald, an ex-policeman who had recently passed away in his late eighties. Patrick's family had requested an embossed golden lining and so the two coffins were not easily mistaken. Fortunately, it was a relatively slow day for the parlour. But with both members of staff off sick, the funeral director was frantically racing around preparing the caskets himself. In his haste he somehow managed to switch the name tags.

The first part of Conway's plan had been successful. Michael's death gave him immense satisfaction. The loss of sight to his left eye was a small price to pay for finally dishing out his vengeance. He should have been more careful, but he wore a black eyepatch to cover the grotesque opaque sightless weeping eye. Every time he fitted the patch, he thought about how wonderful it had felt sending the sharp blade into the heart of his enemy. He viewed his new facial adornment as a badge of honour.

The next step was to take advantage of the collective mourning group of MacMillan and MacGregor family members at Michael's funeral. He had paid handsomely for the manufacture of the explosive timing device in Switzerland. A local watchmaker had engineered a timed detonator from a standard bedside alarm clock. The makeshift bomb was another reason for the clandestine re-entry into the country.

He kept close watch over the funeral parlour waiting for his chance to enter. The placement of the bomb in Michael's coffin was crucial to his plan. He observed the funeral director exit the front of the premises to prepare the hearse out back. With the absence of all other staff, Conway entered the open unmanned reception area and slipped into the back room that contained the two coffins. He peeled back the gold lining of the coffin bearing Michael MacGregor's name tag and inserted the time bomb, careful to leave the lining in its original neat state.

As advertised, the funeral for Michael MacGregor would take place at 2pm at Barony and St James Church on Albany Street. Arthur had already chosen his vantage point, half a block away from the graveyard. His pulse raced at the thought of the entire family being wiped out in one hit. He tried to imagine the scene of mutilated bodies and the screams of the dying. The arrangement of the explosives and shrapnel was powerful enough to shred any living soul within twenty metres of the blast radius. Rusty nuts and bolts would wreak havoc on the flesh of the victims. He left the funeral parlour undetected.

When the director re-entered, he made a final check of the inventory list and realised his mistake of switching the labels. He shook his head as he corrected the error. If his staff had made the same mistake they would have been in all manner of trouble. Fortunately, they were not there to witness it. He had no idea that correcting the simple error would save the lives of the MacMillans and MacGregors and seal the fate of whoever attended Patrick McDonald's ceremony.

David MacGregor watched his son's coffin lowered into the earth
to its final resting place. He had cried himself dry over the days
leading up to the funeral. His shoulders sagged and he looked
like he had aged several years in just a week. Naturally he blamed
himself for Michael's death. Afterall it was on his insistence
that he involved Michael in setting Conway up in the first place.
Several times he reminded Michael to be vigilant, fully expecting
some form of retaliation when Arthur resurface but he had not
anticipated brutal murder.

Conway had not been seen since the incident at the theatre.
The police launched a man hunt and closely monitored the airports
train stations and exit routes out of the city. So far there was no
sign of him. The hospitals, outpatients', clinics, doctors' surgeries,
and even veterinary centres were checked for any male patients
treated for left eye injuries. There were a few reports but none of
them turned out to be Arthur Conway.

The sombre gathering around the graveside at Michael's
funeral were close family, little Mary and Molly MacMillan,
Michael's parents David and Victoria, Uncle Hamish, and
Elizabeth the widow. Conway was sat in the back of a taxicab
half a block away. He wanted to be closer but there was a strong
police presence in and around the church and graveyard. David
MacGregor was convinced Arthur Conway was not done yet and
the police agreed. Conway was, however, close enough to at least
hear the bomb explode. He waited, checking his watch frequently,
any minute now...

The explosion eventually came. Not from Michael's coffin
or the graveyard within earshot of Arthur's vantage point, but
four blocks south at St Catherine's Cathedral, the funeral of the
deceased ex-policeman Patrick McDonald. In view of the volume

of police officers showing their respects to their ex-colleague and the death toll from the blast, Arthur Conway instantly became the most wanted man in the United Kingdom.

The envelope of cash for Otto Rendenbach would be substantially thicker this time around. Not only had he help orchestrate getting Conway in and out of the United Kingdom undetected, but he had also arranged for Arthur's emergency treatment to his damaged eye. Friends of friends the little German was acquainted with, people who were untraceable and happy to use their expertise and be paid handsomely for their silence. There was also the taxicab in which Conway now sat, doctored by Otto himself, with a hidden compartment large enough to conceal a man.

Arthur had failed to rid the earth of the remaining MacGregors and MacMillans on his radar this time round, but he had overstayed his welcome. It was time to embrace the uncomfortable cramped recess for the long ride down to Southampton and Otto's airfield. Arthur wondered if his reception in Zurich would be any warmer than the UK. Surely someone at the Wehrli Bank would have cottoned on to how he had managed to embezzle RM 2,700,000 from under their noses?

It was impossible to console Mary after the death of her uncle. She loved Michael immensely. She lay on her mother's bed face down sobbing into the pillow. Molly thought it best to let her cry out her grief rather than hold it in. She stroked Mary's golden blonde hair and the back of her black dress.

As Molly sat in silence, she contemplated the brutality of her brother's murder. Arthur Conway was again at large and had somehow managed to escape off the face of the earth. If he was that hellbent on revenge, none of the MacMillans or MacGregors were safe. She had to protect Molly. She left her daughter to retrieve Angus' old double-barrelled shot gun from the gun cabinet and placed it under her bed. She poured a handful of shotgun cartridges into the bedside drawer. Molly desperately wanted to leave immediately and take Mary to Southern Rhodesia, as far away from Arthur Conway as possible. What hatred would move a man to take someone's life? It made her shudder.

She thought of her dearly departed Angus who was taken from her on the battlefield in Keren. How many lives had *he* taken? Surely it was different and more acceptable taking another man's life fighting for the freedom of others, but how could you live with such memories?

She wondered how different her life would have been if Angus had never joined the army in the first place. They would still be together as a family unit. She suddenly felt very much alone and was overcome with grief. That night as she lay in bed cuddled up to her daughter, she promised herself that she would follow through with Angus' dream to resettle in Southern Rhodesia. She would take Mary to Africa, and they would start their new life together, a fresh start with an exciting future. *When would this wretched war end?*

# Chapter 17

Out of the two ships waiting to enter Cape Town harbour, the Roxburgh Castle belonging to Union Shipping Line, was by far the inferior. After several weeks at sea the restless, confined passengers were forced to wait a further two days before they could disembark. With its distinguished cargo the HMS Vanguard had the priority to port first.

The regal fortress, nearly 250 metres in length, was the ultimate warcraft and unique in many ways. It was the only English vessel with triple-16 inch turrets. After several modifications its 400 tonnes of fuel gave it a range of more than 8000 nautical miles. First-hand experience gained from the British fleet in conflict on the high seas had influenced the design of the extensive armour plating. Even at its most vulnerable, the five-inch steel decking protection could withstand the impact of a 1000-pound armour-piercing bomb released from 14,000 feet. On a trial run the twin three-blade propellors 14 foot in diameter achieved 30 knots, but they were rendered inadequate and were replaced by a five-blade system to reduce vibration through the impenetrable hull during operation. Yet with all the delays tinkering with the design and the modifications, it had never fired a round in anger. The war had ended before the one-of-a-kind masterpiece was ready for action.

When Jan Smuts, the president of The Union of South Africa, extended an invitation to the Royal Family to visit, the HMS Vanguard was redesigned yet again. This time with the view to transporting the four members of the British monarchy along with 2000 supporting staff officers and crew safely across the seas. In preparation for arrival, every square inch of it from the top deck to the engine room was swept, cleaned and polished by the attentive crew. The majestic vessel was escorted into Cape Town Bay surrounded by three smaller South African frigates to a welcoming procession full of pomp and ceremony.

Viewing the spectacle were the anxious passengers of the humble Roxburgh Castle. After their rather dull and uneventful journey, the rails on deck were crammed with men, women and children eager to see the parade and the long-awaited shoreline. Witnessing the momentous arrival of the very first Royal Family visit to South Africa added to their excitement.

Four of the voyagers had added reason for their impatience. With the war now finally over, Molly and Mary MacMillan, Robert and Rachael Hunter were en route to their new homes and farmland in Southern Rhodesia. Once docked, they would make their way inland by rail.

Mary's elation to see Africa with her own eyes for the first time was almost tangible. She looked up into the blue sky, soaking up the warmth of the morning sun on her pretty face. When Molly looked at her, she could barely believe her little girl was only thirteen. With beautiful blonde hair almost golden in appearance, her little Mary could have passed for an eighteen-year-old. Physically she had already matured. It did not escape Molly's attention that men found her attractive. She was still just a child, and Molly was quite forthright in warding off admirers. Mary possessed an innocence appropriate to her age.

From her regular reading she had a well-rounded general knowledge, particularly when it came to Africa. Birds and wildlife were her favourite topic. Although not yet having set foot on African soil, she seemed akin with Africa's spirit. She could tell you the Latin names of a host of creatures and birds in Southern Africa, as well as their diet and habitat.

She also possessed a natural gift for drawing. Her pencil and pastel work duplicated illustrations from books with stunning detail. They were both restricted to one travel case each – a container of belongings and personal effects would arrive at their new home a month later – but Mary's drawing pad and pencils were essential to this leg of the journey. She planned to sketch along the way.

Molly had sold their remaining farmland, sheds and barns in Scotland to Fitzgerald their Irish neighbour. She retained the main homestead and two and a half acres of land, neatly fenced off. Annie, Molly's assistant and nanny to Mary, was allowed to live in the main house with Sylvester and tend to the garden for a modest monthly retainer. If Annie was attentive to the established herb and vegetable garden it could produce enough to sustain her and turn a small profit.

Over the last five years leading up to the end of the war, Molly had managed Hillside Ranch from afar as best she could. Henk had proved to be a trustworthy manager, heavy handed with staff at times but reliable and honest. It was difficult to oversee all aspects of her enterprise from a distance and she was excited about seeing it for the first time with her own eyes. The immense task of the perimeter fence was complete. Henk had built himself a cottage away from the main farmhouse and preparations were underway for their arrival.

Despite the last two consecutive years of drought, the underground water supply was holding up. The modest cattle herd was growing even with the ever-present threat of predators and disease. The ranch was a constant financial drain and it worried Molly, but last year was the first time it had turned over a welcomed profit. Henk worked on growing their own cattle herd and assured her that calving season this year would be twice as productive as last year, but that was still seven months away. He sectioned off several paddocks and sublet some for grazing. The capital from the sale of land in Scotland would be put to good use in further expanding their operation.

On the voyage over Molly read *The War History of Southern Rhodesia*, published by the military historian J F McDonald. The book was more than just a collection of data, facts and figures. It contained personal accounts of men and women of Rhodesia and their first-hand experiences in combat during the war. In some ways it helped her to deal with the loss of her own husband Angus. It felt like a shared experience with those who had fought. For such a young country, Southern Rhodesia's contribution in support of Great Britan was quite remarkable. By the end of the war more than 10,000 European men and woman had served in some capacity alongside British and Allied Troops. They were posted in Britain, the Mediterranean and East Africa, serving in the army, navy or air force. It was an astonishing statistic, especially since the number of European settlers in 1939 was just 39,000. A further 15,000 African males from the local tribes were drafted to fight alongside them or to work as labourers building the airfields and aerodromes. The various flight training schools throughout the country trained more than 8,000 British and Allied pilots. Apart from the manpower investment, Southern Rhodesia was the second largest supplier of chrome and asbestos to Great Britian. The economy of the small country had boomed during a time of international conflict and global recession. It was a fascinating read.

Malcolm Hunter's mining operation was now in full production, and from what Molly could gather it was turning over a tidy profit. When Malcolm first commenced the operation, he worked along with Henk to build a compound large enough to accommodate both farm and mine labourers and their families, but the constant fighting and conflict between them eventually lead to split settlements. The move did not have the desired effect and trouble continued, although she did not understand the reasons why.

Molly looked forward to meeting Malcolm Hunter. His assistance over the years was invaluable, but for some reason since the lion hunt incident in Penhalonga he was not quite the same towards her. He was more reserved and shut off. She still looked forward to meeting him all the same.

Arthur Conway had not posed a direct threat to the MacMillans and MacGregors again after the murder of Michael, her brother. The botched sabotage of Michael's coffin resulted in an explosion that had caused the death of twenty officers attending retired Chief Constable Patrick MacDonald's funeral. Nearly twice that number were badly injured or maimed in the incident. The frantic search for 'the most wanted man in the UK' by Scotland Yard and Interpol in Switzerland and the rest of Europe continued but without success. Conway added to a growing list of crimes. In Zurich he was linked to the brutalised bodies of two young men. Each murder victim had the interlocking Mars Symbol carved into his torso. It was believed that it was Conway's new calling card, a tattoo he bore on the calf of his leg. There was also the case of the embezzled German Reichsmarks from Wehrli Bank.

Arthur Conway continued to evade capture. He was always one step ahead of the authorities who inevitably arrived to abandoned apartments where their quarry had evaded them. In Switzerland, north of Zurich, police received an anonymous tip-off that the fugitive had been spotted entering an apartment in Koschenruti. Conway himself provided the lead and the booby-trapped flat claimed another two police officers.

Their investigations took Interpol as far as Morocco where another young male had been murdered and left with Conway's carved Mars tattoo. That was over a year ago and then the trail went cold. With the lack of any sightings of Conway or clues, they could not discount the latest murder to be the work of a copycat killer.

Try as he may, David MacGregor with his extensive resources and private investigators could not add any further pieces to the puzzle. It frustrated him. He was obsessed with bringing Conway to justice and knew it was only a matter of time before he resurfaced.

Conway was never far away from Molly's thoughts, too. It was one of the reasons why she was so eager for her and Mary to move to Southern Rhodesia. For her mentally it distanced them from his threat, and she viewed Hillside Ranch as their own private sanctuary, but was there anything stopping him from following them to Africa?

Alongside Molly and Mary MacMillan were Robert and Rachael Hunter. They had sold their farm in Aberdeen, so it was all or nothing for them at their new ranch, Cedar Tree Hollow in Insiza. Fortunately, their two sons Douglas and Brody were running the farm successfully. They had overcome any challenges presented and somehow made a profit year on year. The production of their cement posts was so successful, that even after their boundary lines were complete, they received orders from farmers and businesses in Matabeleland and production continued. Their market garden originally set up to supply the farm itself with vegetables expanded. A newly opened farm shop sold directly to the public as well as supply produce to a few grocery stores in Bulawayo.

Robert still walked with a cane. The bullet wound he sustained in Keren when Angus lost his life had left him with a permanent limp. As the war dragged on, he became more restless and impatient. His sons doing so well was a two-edged sword. Of course, he was incredibly proud of them, but their success was achieved largely without his input and therefore he felt less necessary. He was unsure what roles they would each play once they were reunited, but as the long sea voyage ended, he quashed his misgivings and stoked the growing embers of excitement. He was a proud father of two exceptional boys, and the love of his life Rachael was by his side. Compared to the stuffy confines of their cabin, on deck the occasional waft of smoke from the ship's funnels was not offensive on the otherwise crisp fresh air. The future was bright. He hugged Rachael and kissed her tenderly on the cheek.

Both of Rachael's sons were in their prime and had thrown their heart and soul into making the family farm a success. Neither were married, yet it did not seem to bother them. Rachael could not wait to see them again. She was apprehensive about the move and objected to selling their family farm and home. She looked out at the bay in front, surrounded by the imposing flat topped mountain range that to her symbolised the vastness of the challenges ahead. Robert hoped his positivity and enthusiasm would rub off on her.

## INVICTUS MINE – HILLSIDE RANCH, INSIZA, BULAWAYO

Originally the rock samples taken from the old workings of Red Herring mine were granite and quartz, rich in copper and gold. Diamond drilling carried out by Ashton George the Australian geologist had revealed a greenstone basalt belt below the surface running twelve metres at its widest. The structure of the reef warranted an open cast operation. Intermittent quartz veins ran through the green belt, boosting the yellow metal yield. With the initial excavation down to twenty metres, the greenstone belt widened like a cooking pot, flanked with fibrous green tremolite and black chlorite schist. It then narrowed like the funnel of a tornado, descending until the rich tail was less than eight inches in diameter before disappearing altogether. Ashton was called upon once more to unravel the secrets of the earth. After further sampling and drilling he presented Malcolm with his findings. The tail they followed was cut off by an underground fault.

Ashton proposed the location of the first underground shaft and after five days of drilling, blasting and lashing the waste rock, they intercepted another rich reef of the same greenstone. The geologist's predictions were correct, and the mine prospered once more.

For Malcolm the two operations were entirely different. His old mine Crawley Concession in Penhalonga was a smoothly run, predictable, trouble-free enterprise. He had little difficulty with his workforce, that is up until the arrival of the Mahaha. Five years had passed since those paranormal events occurred, yet nothing had taken place that could be the outworking of the three-fold prophecy:

*When the snake strikes at golden hair, she will be swallowed into the belly of the earth.*

*Beware of the one-eyed snake that walks on two legs and swims with the crocodile. He must die twice.*

*When the river serpent becomes enraged, it will bring vengeance with fire and flood.*

On Hupenyu, the witch doctor's, advice, he left the area. He still wore the bracelet she gave him to ward off evil spirits and to protect him from animals and snakes in the wild.

Ironically, his new mine, renamed *Invictus,* was riddled with snakes. Bites were regular and most were fatal. Several species of cobra ventured into the open cast mine hunting for vermin, and encounters with the workforce were inevitable. But additional attacks transpired between the compound and the mine. Lazy arrow-headed puff adders with their perfectly evolved straw yellow and reddish-brown camouflage blended in with the pathways they infested while patiently waiting for prey. They struck at the bare feet and ankles of miners on their way to and from work, their cytotoxic venom inevitably causing death. Feisty black mambas if disturbed rose two-thirds of their body length to deliver deadly neurotoxic venom to the face or chest of their victim.

Whatever precaution Malcolm put in place, it made little difference to the volume of bites and fatalities. Workers were advised to wear gumboots and overalls to and from work, but it was impossible to enforce the directive with three eight-hour shifts seven days a week keeping the wheels turning. Protective clothing was oppressive in the African heat and discarded as soon as possible. They were willing to run the gauntlet in freedom even at the risk of attack. Malcolm, however, had never been bitten: perhaps Hupenyu's protective bracelet was working after all.

The initial compound built to accommodate the mining and farming staff brought nothing but conflict. Malcolm could not understand why the community did not gel, but even after the workforces were split, the trouble did not settle. At least half of the employees Malcolm brought with him were Shona from Penhalonga, the others he sourced locally were Ndebele. The two tribes constantly squabbled. Malcolm limited their access to and consumption of alcohol as it invariably was the catalyst for confrontation. Growing trends made locally brewed alcoholic drinks significantly stronger than their traditional millet beer more readily available, so Skokiaan, Nipa, and Kuchasu were banned.

A hoist driver operating the early morning shift arrived for duty with more Skokiaan than blood in his veins after a heavy session the night before. He sent four miners to their death at the bottom of the newly opened shaft. Security was tightened at the change of every shift. Anyone that missed work because of being intoxicated was fired and ordered to leave. Malcolm scheduled a meeting at the land registry and national archive. He hoped to pick Harold Bucket's brains on local tribal history to better understand the consistent derision.

The new owner of Crawley Concession, an anonymous European investor, appointed his German manager Huns to manage the operation. A short, stocky, cagey little man with a powerful handshake and sharp blue eyes Malcolm only met once. After inspecting the mine for the first time, Huns rang Malcolm a week later to complete the purchase. The funds were wired to Malcolm from a Swiss bank account. A few months later Malcolm heard that the German had built an airstrip for his rare two-seater MK IX Spitfire closed-cockpit plane, clearly not short for cash.

With his hands full at Invictus, Malcolm left Hillside Ranch to Henk who managed with an iron first. Molly was in for a big shock, Malcolm thought. Although he respected her strength and determination, he felt the Scottish lass may not be quite ready for Africa. The raw beauty, stunning scenery and moderate weather all year round made Southern Rhodesia unique and spectacular, but it was equally wild, rough and unforgiving. For Malcolm his personal experiences so far had left him believing it was also deeply spiritual.

When Piet Potgieter took his life with his own rifle, Malcolm purchased White Stone Farm at auction. With capital released from the sale of Crawley Concession, he acquired it as a convenient base from which to run Invictus. The dilapidated farmhouse was completely renovated. Goliath's rancid waterhole was excavated to create a tranquil pond with a fountain water feature. Malcolm knew the unutilised hectares of fallow farmland would increase in value of their own accord. With the war over, thousands of settlers opted to relocate to Southern Rhodesia. Some had spent time in POW camps or trained as pilots in the combat flying schools throughout the country, others had simply heard tales of the special little country crying out to be developed and worked.

Malcolm's brother Robert himself was currently on his way over. Perhaps there were further family joint ventures to consider. Robert's sons Douglas and Brody had already proved they could successfully run the nearby farm at Cedar Tree Hollow. For the moment, Malcolm was content with a comfortable home close to the mine.

He left Invictus in his Alfa Romeo, enjoying the freedom of the open top and responsive throttle. A bottle of single malt whisky sat on the seat next to him, a gift for Harold Bucket.

As Malcolm entered the stuffy office, Harold attempted to be engrossed in his significantly unimportant paperwork. Despite the heat, he still wore a beige three-piece suit. The buttons on his waistcoat strained under the bulk of his excessive weight. He stood with a grunt to offer Malcolm a hand. "So how are you finding your new diggings? Enough of the bright metal for you? Kaffirs giving you any grief?"

Malcolm produced the bottle of whisky which Harold looked at lustfully, like a pubescent boy seeing actual naked breasts for the first time. He didn't wait for an invitation; he produced a set of glass tumblers from his drawer, one clearly already used, and poured a dram in each glass.

Malcolm replied, "There are constant issues between our workers. I brought a few Shona with me from my previous mine, good reliable experienced miners. I never had half as much trouble with them as I do now. They constantly clash with the local Ndebele. It's bad enough when they are sober but my god when they are pissed, they are impossible. Is it just a tribal thing, do you think?"

Harold drained his glass and refilled it with a stronger measure before sitting back in his chair to summon his wisdom. "You must understand, Mr Hunter, the white man has been in this country for a relatively short time. The last time I saw you, you were keen to understand the history of your gold mine in Penhalonga. *The Mahaha Goldfields*. I was able to assist as I recall. Perhaps you should be more concerned with more recent events in the country's history?" Harold drained his glass once more and refilled it almost to the top.

With fewer visitors these days, Harold had less opportunity to show off his extensive knowledge of local affairs, but Malcolm's meeting and the whisky opened the recesses of his mind. "You see, even before Cecil John Rhodes secured the mineral rights for the British South African Company under the royal charter of Her Majesty the Queen in 1890, the local Buntu tribes were harassed and frequently raided by the Ndebele or Matabele – descendants of the Nguni from further south. If you ask the Shona and the Ndebele about their version of history, it is likely to be full of tales of one's dominance over the other, but the truth is they have fought amongst themselves for thousands of years.

"The King of the Matabele in the 1890s, Lobengula, united his people and is believed to have had over 100,000 warriors at his disposal at any one time. As such, he dominated this area, authorising frequent raids on weaker opposition tribes and villages, stealing their cattle and so forth. At times the encounters were brutal, mothers and children were not spared, and entire villages razed to the ground. When the European settlers arrived, all the black tribes collectively had a new enemy – the white man.

"As the settlers grew in number so did the Police wing of the British South African Company, at that time to a little over 700. Although Lobengula grew increasingly suspicious of the white man and regretted granting the mineral rights, he was forced to accept the growing white population and police presence. He instructed his Impis (regiments) NOT to provoke attacks on the white settlers under fear of death. They obeyed of course until the police intervened with a local tribal matter.

"At Fort Victoria a Mashona chief named Gomara insulted the Matabele king and failed to pay accolades to Lobengula's kingship and chose rather to fall under the protection of the local police. Lobengula instructed his Impis to make an example of Gomara, which they did by raiding and burning his villages. The police felt obliged to intervene and engaged the Matabele, killing at least 40 of the raiding party. Lobengula was furious. Two weeks later Lobengula mobilised 3500 of his Impis and attacked a 700-strong British South African Police (BSAP) column at the Shangani River. Despite being grossly outnumbered they were in possession of Maxim machine guns that cut through wave after wave of the Matabele assault. It was reported around 1500 of the Impis were slaughtered.

"A week later just fifty kilometres north of here around 6000 Impis attacked a BSAP column, and another 2500 Matabele were felled thanks to the Maxims. Lobengula was pursued right here to Bulawayo where he lived. He was driven out and his settlement was burned to the ground. There were several other skirmishes as the Matabele fled, but when Lobengula himself died of poor health – smallpox or dysentery – in 1894, the impetus of the Matabele rebellion petered out."

Harold, clearly parched after speaking at length, refilled his glass and drained the contents without a hint of the scalding liquor showing on his clammy, puce-coloured face. Malcolm took a sip of his own whisky, reflecting on his lion hunt. Tanaka was an imposing figure, broad and tall in his loin cloth and intimidating with his warrior spear. Malcolm tried to imagine what an advancing wave of 6000 Matabele warriors would look like armed with their weapons and shields. It was something he found difficult to comprehend.

He was still a little puzzled and asked, "Was there further conflict between the local tribes and the British settlers?"

"Yes," said Harold, taking a deep breath. "A second uprising not long after that, in 1896 if I am not mistaken. This time the plot was a little more sinister. Ultimately the Shona and Matabele would join forces to drive the white man out of their country for good. Do you know what a 'Mlimo' is, Mr Hunter?"

"No, I don't."

Harold belched. In the confines of the office, it stank of stale alcohol and rotting meat. Malcolm nearly retched. For Harold it was such a regular enough event that his expulsion could be celebrated or scorned without bother either way.

Harold released the buttons on his waistcoat and let out a prolonged sigh. He clearly felt at home chatting to Mr Hunter, so much so he pushed his chair back and with a groan crossed his legs and rested his feet on the corner of his desk. He felt a bit jealous of Malcolm in a way, the young buck with good looks and a determination to succeed – a future. Plus of course he brought welcomed gifts and asked interesting questions. He relaxed, preparing himself for a coherent recital of the second Matabele war.

Malcolm listened as Harold described the uprising against the European settlers incited by the *Mlimo* (Matabele spiritual leader). The Mlimo blamed the consecutive droughts, plagues of locusts and pestilence killing their herds of cattle on the growing presence of the white man on their land. He proposed an all-out attack on 29th March 1896 following the ceremony of the *Big Dance*. With divine intervention he promised that the white man's weapons would be ineffective and powerless against the masses of Matabele warriors. The attack was well timed, since at the beginning of the year the British South Africa Company had sent most of its troops led by L S Jameson to fight against the South African Republic in the Transvaal.

Prematurely, some overzealous Matabele warriors started assaulting farms, settlements and mines on 20th of March, slaughtering men, women and children. More and more Impis took up the battle cry and within days there were thousands marauding through Matabeleland. The Shona tribes to the north joined in with the slaughter and within a week 300 European settlers were killed countrywide. Outlying survivors took flight to Bulawayo and Salisbury. In Bulawayo around 1000 settlers were barricaded in, surrounded by 10,000 Matabele warriors, yet no concerted offensive was forthcoming. Perhaps the Matabele still feared the deadly maxim guns so effective against them in their first rebellion. Fortunately for the trapped settlers, their phone lines were left intact, and they were able to call for reinforcements that eventually provided relief two months later.

Although the Mlimo was assassinated, it was uncertain whether they had killed the right figurehead or whether the BSAC fully understood the hierarchy of the Matabele spiritual leaders.

In Mashonaland the rebellion again was heavily influenced and incited by the spiritual leaders, but the uprising was eventually brought under control by reinforcements from the Cape Colony. The BSAC regained control of the Shona and Matabele (Ndebele) tribes, but for Malcolm the historic events were more of a clear demonstration of their collective objection to the white settler's presence and less about internal tribal rivalry. The fact that those historic events had taken place just over fifty years ago, still in living memory of the older generation, made Malcom firmly believe more rebellion would follow.

Added to Malcolm's experience with Hupenyu the witch doctor, the Mahaha demon and Samson the extraordinary lion, the confrontations were further evidence that the indigenous people were heavily guided by and influenced by a deep spirituality.

# Chapter 18

## HILLSIDE RANCH, INSIZA, BULAWAYO, SOUTHERN RHODESIA

It would be a matter of time before Molly and Mary MacMillan finally arrived from Scotland to take up residence in the main house, so Henk set about building himself a home north of the main Hillside Ranch house. The dwelling itself, including the lounge chimney, was made from waste stone acquired from Invictus mine. It was finished with a thatched roof, the grass cut from the fields of the ranch, combed, and neatly trimmed. The front door opened onto a veranda that led to a small garden containing a braai (barbecue) area. Occasional blue gum and msasa trees were enclosed by a planted bougainvillea hedge.

It was a two bedroomed cottage with an open plan living area with a large fireplace. He was a simple man with simple tastes. When Doug and Brody Hunter saw it for the first time after its completion, they were impressed. When he still lived in the main house, his daylight hours were spent attending to the needs of the farm. It was demanding physical work and he lived by the philosophy *early to bed, early to rise*. On returning from work, he would often soak in a hot bath, washing off the sweat and grime from the day, and enjoy a generous dinner and a glass of brandy before going to bed. Occasionally he invited Doug and Brody over for a bit of company or he would visit them on their farm next door. On the rare occasion after swapping too many stories around the fire and downing one too many brandies, he would stay over in their spare room. But since his cottage was finished it felt like his own space and he always enjoyed returning to it.

His new quarters was considerably smaller than the main house but that made it feel cosy. Moses the carpenter genius that worked for the Hunters had made the frames of two large sofas. They were big enough to seat three fully grown adults comfortably. The cushions were manufactured from cured leather cow hide and densely stuffed with sheep's wool. He chose granite floor tiling throughout. Occasional sheep skin and cow hide throws broke up the solid grey floor area. The result was a tasteful, comfortable space – home.

A king-size bed took pride of place in his bedroom surrounded by a dressing table and double mahogany freestanding cupboards with full length mirrored doors. There was little time for cleaning in his busy routine, so he employed the services of a young girl from the farm compound. Lulama was a timid unassuming young soul, not quite seventeen. Next to Henk she looked like a small child. Her dark inquisitive eyes, large flared nostrils and full lips were not out of the ordinary, but her top front teeth grew forward and straight out, almost horizontal to the floor. They rested on her bottom lip and her combined facial features gave the impression she was permanently trying to decipher the origin of an unpleasant smell. She had sucked her thumb incessantly as an insecure youth, a habit she still subconsciously continued when she slept. Henk once remarked to the Hunter boys, "Ya, she cleans well but my Christ with those teeth she could eat an apple through a tennis racket."

Henk's little pad was spotless thanks to Lulama. In the evening, she prepared basic ingredients for master Henk to make himself a dinner of sorts. Any leftovers she was welcome to take home the next day. They seldom spent more than a few minutes in each other's company. Henk would issue instructions for her cleaning duties and when he returned to an empty cottage, it had always been done.

One evening Henk hobbled home earlier than usual with an injury to find Lulama polishing the lounge floor. While supervising fence repairs a tense strand of barbed wire had snapped and cut a gash deep into his lower calf, difficult to reach. When she saw Henk in pain she automatically went to his aid.

Against Henk's protests and expletives, she cleaned and stitched his wound. She poured him a large brandy and put him to bed. It had been an eternity since Henk felt any form of tenderness and he reached out for her. His clumsy and rough advances were not met with resistance. Afterward, Lulama returned home as she usually did.

The next day Henk went about his duties but found a reason to return home while Lulama was still there. After she dressed his injury, he took hold of her again, but more gently than before. Lulama left afterwards without a word, returning the next morning as she always did. Henk, after his physical injuries, burns and disfigurement, had resigned himself to the fact that he would never experience love or female companionship again. He knew what he did with Lulama was wrong. It was not love that he felt, but it was good to be able to hold someone.

Henk and Lulama spent more time together. He made sure he came home when she was still there. Lulama's role changed. At first, she tolerated Henk's unwanted attention, but then she started to embrace it, and learned how to please him. Then how to be pleased in return. She occasionally spent the night in Henk's arms after they had shared his bed, and the status of master and servant blurred for both. Whatever it was, it became significantly more complicated when Lulama fell pregnant.

Initially she tried to hide her condition from everyone, especially her family, but three months into her pregnancy Henk noticed the change in her abdomen and breasts. He talked to her about an abortion, but she refused and attempted to claw his remaining eye out at the mere suggestion.

Henk was now in a real predicament. He could not legally marry Lulama in a European court of law or church. There were the social implications to think of. Privileged whites just did not marry underprivileged blacks. Although Henk could not care less what everyone else thought of him, he still had to tread carefully. It could potentially impact on running the farm and keeping the farm trading accounts open. The more he investigated the dilemma, the more concerned he became, and time was not on his side. Lulama was already growing before his eyes with his baby in her womb. At that point Henk did not care for the unborn child, he simply wanted to choose the path of least resistance. He had grown fond of her company but was focussed more on the pleasures of their coupling rather than the potential result or responsibility.

In the end Henk was forced to approach Lulama's father and request her hand in marriage in the local Ndebele custom. It was an awkward meeting. Akhumzi was a shrewd old soul and Lulama was his youngest and only unmarried child. After fathering seven children and producing only one son he had a lifetime of experience in negotiations with the wedding protocol. He also understood the unique complexities of the situation at hand. He knew that his youngest daughter was with child, and that the young tribesmen of the village never paid her the slightest bit of attention. The only man that was ever near her was her employer, the ugly, disfigured, white, one-eyed devil. So, when Henk called for an urgent meeting, he knew exactly what it was about.

According to the traditional custom the wedding ceremony would take place in three parts. First, there was the *Lobola* (bride price), an agreed payment in livestock or an equivalent alternative value. Second, the *Bukhasi*, the bride-to-be would spend a week sheltered away with experienced older women teaching her what was expected of a good wife. Finally, their marriage was sealed when the newly-weds produced their first child.

Wise Akhumzi did not want to be stuck with aging unwanted dependants and stupid master Henk was doing him a favour and possibly Lulama's only hope. Lulama had prepared Henk for the procedure and the two men met outside Akhumzi's mud hut. Henk really did not want to be there bargaining with the old kaffir at all. The discussion needed to be over as quickly as possible.

He addressed Akhumzi directly, dispensing with the usual customary greeting and polite salutations: "I want to marry your daughter Lulama according to your custom, and I will give you a cow – lobola."

Akhumzi let the disrespectful manner of his future son-in-law slide. He scratched at his grey beard thoughtfully as if searching his soul for a response. "You will give me two cows and £5 and my little angel is yours."

Henk's temper was easily ignited but he kept it under control. "I accept, but for two cows and £5 Lulama will continue to have her own hut in your village and can stay there whenever I choose. Her child will be accepted and welcomed as one of your own."

Akhumzi faked his most ingratiating smiled and shook Henk's hand. "I accept… my son." But in his own mind he was thinking if the coloured half caste little turd is too much trouble, accidents happen so easily in the bush. The meeting ended as abruptly as it had started. On the walk back to his cottage Henk was scheming how to supply two cattle from Molly's herd without raising suspicion. He would have to put their loss down to rinderpest. He still had to part with £5!

Six months later Lulama produced a healthy toffee-coloured little cherub. He was a contented infant that did little more than eat, sleep and shit. Henk was indifferent to Felix, the name he chose without much consideration or interest. During the day Felix was strapped to Lulama's back as she tended to the chores of the house, humming or singing to the baby as he slept. She was for the first time in her life truly happy.

She accepted their separate living arrangements without question, quite content to be alone with her son and to have him all to herself. Henk provided for them in a financial sense, but that was about the length of his involvement. Even when Lulama's body had fully recovered from her pregnancy and returned almost to its original untouched state, he seemed to show no interest. He would leave for work before she arrived and would return from work well after she left.

Henk had gone to see Malcolm to arrange shared transport of supplies to the farm and mine. On the way back still a good thirty minutes from home, Blitz his grey stallion encountered a cobra on the path ahead. During their time together as horse and rider they had many such encounters, and the wise horse stood his ground without whining and Henk sat perfectly still. But the Mozambique spitting cobra without warning raised half the length of its body, spread its hood and released its venom from two metres away with deadly accuracy. It happened in an instant. The toxic spray was not aimed at the horse, but the rider, and it struck Henk in a fine mist directly across his patch and remaining good eye. Instantly he was aware of an intense, acidic, excruciating burn. The snake disengaged and slithered off undeterred. Henk leaned forward and said to Blitz, "Gaan huis toe (go home)."

On the long walk back, Henk lay across the horse's neck and withers, not trusting himself to sit upright. His eye was swollen shut and when he forced it open the pain intensified along with vertigo and nausea. He nearly passed out several times but finally Blitz stopped. He reached the stable adjacent to his cottage, but Henk had no strength or coordination to dismount. He rolled off the back of Blitz and crashed to the ground with a painful thud. Lulama heard him cry out.

With Felix asleep and strapped to her back, she raced once more to Henk's aid. She heaved his massive frame upright and led him as he staggered and swayed into the cottage and onto his bed. His good eye was weeping and oozing watery blood. As a child Lulama had watched her father treat the eyes of cattle and goats that suffered the same fate after encountering the spitting cobra. Each time he would bathe the swollen eyes with cold water and salted water repeatedly to flush the poison out. On the second day he prepared a concoction of goat's milk and wild honey, and forced the liquid into the swollen eyes. He repeated the treatment for three days. On the fourth day the swelling was largely gone. Only once in the many treatments her father administered had an animal lost its sight. Lulama figured this big white ox must be strong enough to fight the poison and recover.

When Henk and Lulama communicated it was a mixture of English Afrikaans and Ndebele. She explained what she was doing and set about attending to him. For medicinal purposes she also administered enough brandy to allow Henk to sleep. Day and night she attended to him. The only time she left his side was to prepare food and attend to Felix.

Felix had never spent so much time with the ugly giant, but he watched with interest as his mother fussed over Henk. His vocabulary was growing, a mixture of the languages he heard around him. On the fourth day Henk could open his eye for small intervals and was pleased that although his vision was blurred, he was not totally blind. When he bent down though, a thousand needles felt like they were forcing the eye out, so he continued to rest.

After a week he was able to move about and spend most of the day out of bed. During that whole time, he never mentioned the constant presence of the child or the fact that Lulama had tended to him tirelessly, even feeding and bathing him. Her ministrations had not been entirely lost on Henk. During his recovery he expected to tire of the constant presence of Felix, but he was incredibly well behaved and already seemed to have his own sense of humour. He often heard Lulama laugh at something Felix had said or done. As they sat at the small dining room table in silence, eating a meal of sadza and relish, Henk broke the silence by placing his hand on Lulama's arm and said, "Thank you."

She did not reply but smiled and nodded her head in acknowledgement. Felix, who was sitting on his mother's lap observing the gesture, stretched out his little coffee-coloured arm and rubbed Henk's hand and tried to mimic the monster's deep voice, "T h a n k y o u!"

Lulama sat dead still trying not to laugh. Henk froze. Wide eyed, Felix looked from his mother to Henk in rapid succession. Finally, Henk threw his head back and roared with laughter. Felix got such a fright he nearly soiled himself, but when Lulama dissolved with uncontrollable laughter, Felix joined in himself. For several minutes Henk laughed, thumping the table, but eventually calm returned. At this point Felix confidently shot out his arm again to rub Henk's hand with a more comically dramatized, "T h a n k y o u!" It set them all off again until they were clutching their stomachs, wheezing and crying with laughter.

That night they all slept in Henk's large bed. The following morning Henk informed Lulama what time he would be home. He showed her the second bedroom and said, "This room is for Felix now."

Over the months that followed they settled into a routine of sorts. Felix got used to his new room and sleeping on his own. In the evenings Henk talked and played with the boy, carving animals, and toys out of wood. The white devil monster and the little half-caste kid played and laughed tirelessly. They relished each other's company. Outside of the four walls Lulama was still simply the cleaner, but inside they were a contented unit. Henk still had to give some thought as to how he would explain his 'arrangement' to his boss Molly MacMillan who would be arriving in less than a week. Would she be understanding and liberal enough to accept his circumstances? Only time would tell.

~

## GLASGOW, SCOTLAND – MACGREGOR'S PERFECT CUT TAILOR SHOP

The MacGregor's *Perfect Cut* tailor shop was located on the corner of Argyle and Maxwell Street opposite Clyde's Confectionery and Coffee Shop in the heart of Glasgow, a short walk from the Central Station. David's great-grandfather had shrewdly purchased the store in that location to benefit from the footfall of the regular travellers and commuters utilising the train services. The property increased substantially in value over the years simply because of where it was situated.

The glass floor-to-ceiling shopfront displayed mannequins parading exquisitely crafted, high quality, fashionable suits. Two luxurious sofas offered customers ample seating before the main reception desk. To the right a set of screened changing booths shared their space with neat shelves of coloured fine cotton and tweed. The screened off rear hid the organised engine room with its sewing machines and orders in various stages of manufacture. David MacGregor had modernised his equipment over the years. He followed with interest the genius of Isaac Singer who had produced the first electric sewing machine in 1889. His clever tweaks and attention to detail had revolutionised the industry. The latest innovation, a new electric foot pedal Singer was late – it should have been delivered yesterday.

Several times throughout the day he walked through to reception where Veronica his wife manned the till to see if his order had arrived. He paced anxiously like an expectant father in a maternity ward, only to return to his duties with a sigh, disappointed and empty handed.

Since the death of Michael his son, and with his concerted efforts uncovering nothing as to the whereabouts of his assassin, David had thrown himself into his work. At night he would lock himself away in his study, poring over his files, intel and reports associated with the murderous deviant Arthur bloody Conway.

In Switzerland his investigators had established that Conway was travelling on a passport bearing the name Conrad Amman. The embezzled RM 2.7 million belonging to Hermann Göring from Werlhi Bank in Zurich led to an investigation into all accounts associated with Arthur Conway and Conrad Amman, but in all cases, the accounts had already been drained and the trail led them in circles. Around the same time, a week apart, two young men were found murdered in their apartments after being sodomised and tortured. Both were left with the interlocking male sex symbol carved into the bodies. David drew Interpol's attention to the photograph of the same symbol tattooed on Arthur Conway's calf. He suggested Conway was leaving a calling card. It was hard to prove. In each case there were no eyewitnesses or evidence linking the deceased to him. There were more missing persons in Switzerland, young men of the same age and description, but the police were left with no clues, not even a body. They just disappeared.

In Geneva, a man matching Conway's description withdrew CHF 80,000 (Swiss Francs) and CHF 60,000 from separate banks. In both instances he presented authentic passports, matched the signatures, and passed the security protocols to withdraw the funds. Both passports used in the fraud were recovered from a flat in Geneva with no trace of the money or Conway.

An anonymous report of a sighting of the wanted fugitive at an apartment in Koschenruti turned out to be a booby-trapped flat – the tip-off came from Conway himself. Another two dead officers were added to his list of victims. He was playing with the law and running rings around them. Finally, the death of the young man with the identical double male sex symbol carved in his chest in Morocco took Interpol on another wild goose chase, but there was no evidence it was Arthur Conway. A copycat killer perhaps.

Veronica summoned David from the back of the shop. When he walked into the reception area, he was surprised to see Hamish his older brother wearing a suit, waiting patiently on one of the sofas while Veronica handled a transaction at the cash register. A large cardboard box sat on the counter next to her bearing the label *Singer Manufacturing Company – Le Vergne Tennessee USA*.

A sole occupant was seated in the shadows at the furthest of the four small tables from the entrance of Clyde's Confectionery and Coffee Shop. He sipped a half decent espresso as he casually paged through the morning paper. His presence would not be noticed by a casual glance from passersby on the street, but his chosen position afforded full view of the Perfect Cut tailor shop across the street. The man wore a black suit and waistcoat over a crisp white linen shirt. His well cut and oiled black hair blended with his fully manicured beard and moustache. Tortoiseshell spectacles were perched on the end of his nose. They were not there to aid his vision, but to detract from his unreadably fathomless dark eyes. Only one eye functioned. The other was a glass replica made by a French ocularist in Geneva.

The glass facial prosthesis was heavier than the newly fashionable acrylic eye replicas in production, but Arthur Conway found it to be the closest resemblance in shape and colour to his good eye. In the cold it would weep, but he tolerated the inconvenience for its realistic finish.

Clever disguises and cunning had kept him free of capture. Fundamental to the effectiveness of his plans were high quality fake documents and passports acquired through his contact Otto Rendenbach. The resourceful little German had come to his aid on multiple occasions. To date Arthur had managed to enter and leave countries in and around Europe one step ahead of Interpol. His coffers were topped up by two bank thefts in Geneva where his meticulous planning had allowed him to walk up to the counter and claim large withdrawals and walk away without suspicion. On one occasion he fled to Morocco where Rendenbach was temporarily stationed.

After refusing to buckle under Nazi pressure to anti-Jew legislation, Sultan Mohammed V, the ruler of Morocco, was assisting high powered Jewish citizens to flee the country. Otto had run errands for the Sultan previously and Rendenbach was employed to use his aircrafts to carry the human cargo to safety.

He did not participate in the rescue efforts through a deep-seated moral obligation, but rather for the substantial financial rewards. When the net was too close for Conway's liking in Europe, Otto flew him to Casablanca, Morocco where Arthur was advised to 'lay low'. He had only been there three days when Conway's lust for violence drove him to abuse and murder a young male in his mid-twenties. Otto was furious. Instead of being paid to ferry the intended Jewish cargo, he had to get Conway out and clear of the authorities. He flew him into Gibraltar, Southern Spain, where Arthur was left stewing for two weeks before he could receive a new passport to continue travelling under the radar.

As Arthur sat studying the tailor shop over the top of his newspaper, he pondered his own current good fortune. Yesterday while Perfect Cut reception was unoccupied, he had intercepted a delivery driver with a parcel intended for David MacGregor. His surveillance had been to access when and where to deliver a special parcel of his own. Conway had learned a great deal about explosives while he was on the run. The bomb intended for the MacGregors and the MacMillans was incredibly effective – just in the wrong coffin! The booby-trapped apartment in Switzerland had worked a treat. He used a pressure switch under the internal floor mat of the front door to detonate several charges loaded with nuts, bolts and C4 explosives. The victims were unrecognisable, and an open casket funeral for them would not have been an option.

He had waited long enough to exact his revenge on David MacGregor, the man responsible for his initial fall from grace that had ended his lucrative law practice in Edinburgh. His son Michael had paid the price for his involvement in David's operation. And following today's successful annihilation, Conway could redirect his efforts to the remaining MacMillans, especially his half-brother's widow Elspeth. With every penny he stole or solicited, with every drop of blood he shed, and with every life he snuffed out, Arthur's lust for vengeance grew. He had decided long ago that if he was to be outlawed, then an outlaw he would be.

The one phrase he repeated over and over to himself was, "The unforgiven will fall."

It made perfect sense to target the tailor shop. With a bit of ingenuity, he could take out a few of the MacGregors at a time. He liked the theatrics of a bomb – the noise, devastation, mayhem and death – but it was not something he wanted to read about in the paper. He originally considered hiring assassins or snipers, but there was little fulfilment as far as he was concerned in just reading about it in the news. He wanted not only to orchestrate it, but to see it unfold before his very eyes, or rather eye.

The precise nature of sourcing, constructing and transporting an explosive device was only part of the equation. With the end of the war, access into and out of the UK was significantly easier but he was still a wanted fugitive and travel of any sort required meticulous planning. At Dover in the south of England he infiltrated returning troops from Calais, tasked with ferrying the remains of the fallen back to British soil. His forged papers gave him authority to commandeer a vehicle and transport deceased Scottish soldiers to the Redford Barracks in Edinburgh, which he achieved without being challenged.

The pre-arranged collection of the explosives and trigger devices took place in Edinburgh. He posed as a taxi driver and drove two passengers to Glasgow, again without being interfered with. For the last three days he had staked out David's tailor shop from multiple vantage points but returned twice to Clyde's coffee shop as it afforded him the best vantage point of the reception area. Last night, once in possession of David's intercepted parcel, he removed the sewing machine and assembled the explosives in its place with a trigger wire attached to the external wooden case. When the lid was next removed, the bomb would detonate almost instantly. He had the forethought to deliver a letter to Hamish MacGregor, supposedly typed by David, his brother. It read, "Please meet me at my tailor shop at 1pm tomorrow. Wear a suit and don't be late. David."

Hamish was the muscle and David's sidekick at the meeting that had ruined his career. He deserved to die with his brother in the blast. Conway thought it fitting that the brute underwent the discomfort of squeezing himself into a suit for his own funeral. He observed Hamish arrive punctually as requested. The paid delivery boy would arrive with the bomb at precisely 1:03pm. To his relief it happened just so. The excitement pulsed through his veins and quickened his breathing. His glass eye was watering, but he barely noticed.

David gave Hamish a nod, wondering why he was there, but his priority at that moment was his delayed package on the counter. He used a letter opener to slit the tape securing the cardboard box. The rounded wooden lid of the sewing machine had a convenient handle in the centre. David hauled out the heavy box and ran his fingers over the varnished surface, heightening his anticipation. He did not look around at Hamish as he flipped open the metal catches to open the case. "What brings you here, Hamish?"

Hamish was puzzled: he had been summoned by his brother as he had been countless times in the past. "You told me to be here by one and to wear a bloody suit!"

There was an audible 'click' in the room.

Hamish screamed, "David! No!"

He was too far away to influence David's and Victoria's fate. Instinctively he dived into the sofa which toppled over him like a cocoon. The explosion turned the tailor shop into a fire ball. Shrapnel and debris shattered the glass front with a boom that shook the street and blew out the windows of the coffee shop and surrounding stores. Arthur Conway clutched his briefcase and joined the other pedestrians fleeing in terror.

# Chapter 19

## THE PAVILION THEATRE – GLASGOW, SCOTLAND

The full-dress rehearsal of the *Errand into the Maze* ballet was drawing to a close in front of a virtually empty auditorium. Ahead of the opening night, Elizabeth and Vincent MacGregor sat four rows back watching the final scene gracefully played out to the symphony from the live orchestra. Unlike Vincent, who sat wide eyed on the edge of his seat, soaking up the visual and auditory bombardment with ecstasy, Elizabeth's mind was elsewhere. She had pulled a lot of strings to get the performance of Martha Graham's production at her theatre. It was scheduled to run for two weeks, and every night was sold out. She was in negotiations with the production crew to extend their stay to open additional showings, but even without the proposed extension, the gross profit earned was a new record for the Pavilion.

She recalled her earlier meeting with David MacGregor's law firm. His premature death had put an end to her plan of getting her hands on his fortune and the old bastard's will confirmed that. His daughter naturally inherited everything and in doing so it put David's wealth beyond her reach. She looked at her son with a mixture of emotions. He was supposed to have been the tool to exact an inheritance without bounds, but with David now gone her scheming and manipulation would amount to nought. At least her bizarre coupling with Michael, her husband, had resulted in a boy! The shortest bloody marriage in history. His seed was still being sewn when he was murdered in front of her, on top of her! She shook her head.

Vincent noticed and asked, "What's wrong, Mummy?"

"Nothing, my son, everything is ok." She stroked his head as he returned his attention to the stage. Everything was very far from ok if she told him the truth. David had been generous enough to provide for her son financially to ensure he had a good education. It was a ludicrous concept that Vincent should go through university only to choose a dead-end career in tailoring, all for David's obsession with tradition and the MacGregor name. How bloody absurd!

The ballet ended abruptly. Vincent shot out of his seat, clapping enthusiastically. He was far too young to understand the message behind the performance. *Errand into the Maze* was based on Ariadne and the Minotaur from Greek mythology exploring their inner demons and fear of sexual intimacy. He was, however, transfixed by the drama from start to finish.

Elizabeth sighed. "You are probably going to be as bent as your father, aren't you, my love?"

Still clapping, Vincent looked sideways at her and replied, "I'm not bent, Mummy, look how tall I am when I stand up!"

# KIRKCALDY, SCOTLAND

Hamish and Becky were sat in companionable silence on the rocky spur, looking out at the tumbling grey clouds gliding above the turbulent sea. The tip of the long surf-casting fishing rod wedged in the rock, nodded to the ebb and flow of the current. Their two loyal Alsatians Bonnie and Clyde lay nearby, ignoring the gusts of wind that tugged at their furry coats.

Hamish preferred to be outdoors in the fresh air. Since inheriting their new home after David's murder, they had sold up Becky's butcher shop and moved to Kirkcaldy. A sanctuary for healing the wounds to mind, body and soul was how they viewed their new three bedroomed house. Hamish had no idea his brother was such a wealthy man. The generous inheritance set them up for life.

Where they were currently sat, Hamish and David had fished together when they were kids, before their lives were complicated with responsibility, before the wars and the bad men that afflicted their lives. Hamish fought daily against his failure to save his family from harm. He wished he could spend a few hours in a room with Arthur Conway. He was still out there somewhere and still a threat to Molly and Mary, still a threat to himself and his lovely Becky. He looked at her and she was still as beautiful as the day he first saw her. Her long blonde hair cascaded down her back. She looked back at him with her pretty blue eyes and smiled. She interlocked her arm with his and drew him closer.

Hamish was dressed in his waterproof chest-high waders and a thick polo neck grey jumper. His attire hid his many physical scars, but his face reflected the genuine love he felt for Becky. She wore denim overalls and wellington boots. The dark blue uniform seemed to enhance the depth of her eyes.

She knew full well how deeply her man thought and how much he blamed himself for the loss of his family members. She decided to shift his attention. "So tell me, my love, what are we hoping to catch for our supper tonight?"

"Well, this section of shoreline," he said, indicating the alcove around them, "is predominately a rocky ridge with deep pools at high tide. It's a good spot to pick up mackerel that patrol the shoreline. To catch them I would use brightly coloured foil feathers, but I'm not after mackerel today. I'm using mackerel fillets to catch the predators that feed on them: giant sea bass. It's one of the best eating fish in my opinion. I once caught a ten pounder with David at this very spot when we were lads. Bass are extremely quick; they have to be in order to catch the mackerel who themselves are fast swimmers."

"Speaking of fast swimmers, I have something to tell you." She paused long enough to ensure his full attention and added, "Well one of yours made it… I'm pregnant."

~

# CEDAR TREE HOLLOW – INSIZA BULAWAYO

Brody's scientific and mathematical approach to farming was key to ensuring the steady growth of their herd year on year. His journals and diaries kept statistical analysis of every aspect of their cattle from conception to slaughter. The small dairy herd consisted of twelve brown and white mottled Scottish Ayrshire cows serviced by one bull. The beef herd were hybrid Mashona Sanga cows mixed with an imported breed of short horn English North Devon. During the breeding season the two large bulls could service forty cows each in sixty days, but to speed up the rate of production Brody imported bull semen from Damara Stud located in western Bechuanaland. The precious liquid was harvested and flown to a landing strip near the Mphoengs Tribal Trust land on the Ramaquabane River, where Brody himself collected it and drove it directly back to the farm. The semen was administered within forty-eight hours to ensure its effectiveness. It took on average fifteen minutes to inseminate one cow. Doug and Brody working around the clock could manage one hundred and eighty cows between them in just twenty-four hours.

The simple breeze block office constructed behind the main house contained wall mounted calendars monitoring the lives of heifers and steers that were slaughtered between thirty and forty-two months. Calves were weaned at one month. The slaughter ledger recorded steer and heifer weights between 400 and 600 kilograms. Truckloads of cattle were consigned to the Shackleton Abattoir in Bulawayo for processing. To achieve the target weight, supplementary feed of maize, sunflower heads, peanut cake, and molasses were added to their diet. The herd branded with an overlapping 'CT' was growing its resistance to Nagana and East Coast Fever, as were the Hillside Ranch stock of hybrid Sanga and Aberdeen Angus.

For Brody each day was a combination of mental and physical challenges that required a good eight hours of sleep to revitalise him for the next day. Doug, on the other hand, frequently spent the night hunting the many predators that breached their boundary and threatened their cattle. Uncle Malcolm had relinquished

Tanaka from all other duties to accompany Douglas on his nocturnal vigils. The two of them would often be out until the early hours, returning with fresh kills, predominately leopard and lion. Since witnessing the brutal death of Victoria Potgieter, Doug was determined to deal with the threat of predators directly. He often slept just a few hours each night as a result. If he attempted a full eight, he tossed and turned, worrying about the herd. It was better for him to be actively involved in hunting.

It was 5:30am and Douglas was stood in the kitchen drinking a strong cup of coffee with a spoon of sweetened condensed milk. It was how he started his morning after his meagre sleep. Tanaka suddenly knocked and opened the back door. "There is trouble at the compound. An elephant pushed through the northern boundary last night. Several huts have been destroyed and one of the workers has been trampled, you must come."

Doug ran to his gun cabinet and retrieved his bolt action .404 Jeffery and ammunition belt. It was the highest calibre rifle he possessed in his arsenal. The small magazine accommodated three of the powerful rimless rounds and a fourth could be loaded in the barrel. It was the weapon of choice for big game, but Doug had never hunted elephant. He would find out soon enough if it was powerful enough to bring down such a mighty beast. For Tanaka he chose the .303 Lee Enfield. The ten-round magazine was full of soft nose brass cartridges. Tanaka's spear would have to sit this hunt out, a little more than a toothpick in relation to the size and power of what they would be up against.

With Tanaka taking the lead they set off on foot in the direction of the compound. The sun was beginning to rise as they entered the settlement to the sound of women wailing. A crowd circled a disembowelled and trampled corpse covered in a blanket.

293

Tanaka exchanged a few words with the chief before relaying the news to Douglas: "He says the dead one is Jacob, he thrust a spear into the elephant, and it turned on him. It is an old male with tusks this long." He gestured with both arms fully extended.

"Great," said Doug, "so we are after a wounded bull. What could possibly go wrong?"

They left the bereaved party behind and set off into the direction of the rising sun. The spoor was easy enough to follow on the bare dusty earth, the fifty-centimetre diameter footprints suggested the old male padded away at a run. According to the chief, the elephant had a two-hour head start.

At least the cloudless sky ensured no rain would wash away the bull's tracks. There was very little blood until they found the spear handle snapped off at the base of a tree. The spear head was obviously still buried somewhere in the tough old grey hide. The space between the elephant's tracks narrowed as it slowed and changed its bearing north. Doug surmised it was heading back in the direction it had entered the ranch. It had stopped to feed, suggesting it could not be in too much pain. Raw gashes were left where it had stripped bark off a msasa tree.

Tanaka never slowed his pace for more than two hours until they crossed a small stream where the elephant stopped to drink. Wet footprints were still visible on the opposite bank. The old bull could not be too far ahead. They listened as a tree snapped nearby; it was obviously feeding again just up ahead. Both hunters readied their rifles and proceeded in cautious silence. Doug signalled Tanaka to flank the elephant's location to the left. It was important for them to always remain in line of sight during the hunt and downwind. As they advanced, the top of a large acacia tree shook violently as the massive bull harvested the sweet seeds from its umbrella-like canopy. It let out a low rumble of satisfaction as he stuffed a cluster of twigs, leaves and branches into its mouth. The colossal grey mound became visible through the waist-high blond grass. It stood like a solid serene granite boulder three and a half metres at the shoulder at least. From Doug's position the elephant stood side on facing Tanaka's direction. Douglas's heart raced from the exertion of the pursuit and the adrenaline that pumped through his veins. Although he had never hunted elephant before, he had read enough books on the subject to know the limited success of a side on head shot, but the wide tree trunk prevented any shot to the heart or lungs. He nodded over to Tanaka to ready himself and aimed the Jeffery on the elephant's skull at the entrance of the ear canal.

The gunshot shattered the tranquil silence and the bullet slammed into the elephant just an inch off target. Instantly the bull shook its heavy head, let out a trumpet of rage and charged forward towards Tanaka. Through its blind fury it focussed his attention and bore down on the hunter with remarkable speed. Doug reloaded and fired again at the swinging head. Tanaka was firing and reloading in quick succession, but none of the penetrating rounds seemed to alter the impetus of the charge. Doug reloaded and aimed behind the left foreleg and fired again. The .404 round pierced the beast's enraged heart and it fell with a pounding thump at Tanaka's feet, ploughing its ivory tusks into the earth amid a thick cloud of dust.

Tanaka stood transfixed, staring at the motionless mass with his heart pounding loudly in his chest. He had fired eight of his ten rounds into the elephant without it seeming to faulter. He was seconds away from being trampled when Doug's third shot luckily reached its target. With hunters' remorse, they stood in silence, taking in the motionless expanse of what was at least eleven tonnes of sheer power moments earlier. Tanaka had stood his ground for the duration of the charge, but his legs now turned to jelly, and he had to sit down. The spear head protruded from folds of skin below the right hip. The wound was not fatal but had caused enough pain to anger the bull in the compound.

Douglas ran his hand over one of the magnificent tusks. The exposed length of it was well over a metre, stained yellow from the sun and the juices of the mighty trees it had felled, stripped and consumed. A further third length of ivory was buried in the gigantic skull. Tanaka placed a shaky hand on the bull's head and muttered a short prayer.

Finally, Doug spoke: "I would like you to come back with a team to cut out the tusks. I'm going to get James Shackleton to send a team over to remove the hide and butcher the carcass. There is enough meat here to keep the village in protein for years. We need to work fast – scavengers will have already picked up the scent of the kill. I want as much of the old bull to be utilized as possible. Thank you, Shamwari (friend), for your help today. It is the most incredible creature we have brought down so far, a real shame its life has ended, but we had little choice in the matter."

# Chapter 20

## CAPE TOWN, SOUTH AFRICA

Walking through the streets of Cape Town for Molly and Mary was an insight into ethnic and cultural diversity. The white folk were from all corners of the earth speaking English, Afrikaans, Dutch, German and a variety of languages they had never heard before. The dress code was equally varied, from fashionable suits to overalls and everything in between. Such variety in the coloured people too, every shade of brown and black from the deepest ebony to tortilla. Molly had read about the rich array of tribes in the country, but to witness it with her own eyes was incredible.

A cloudless blue sky did little to brighten the palpable tension that hung in the air. Police on horseback martialled the streets, no doubt there to enforce the 'Whites Only' and 'No Blacks Allowed' signs displayed outside shops, restaurants and establishments. It was shocking to see the enforced segregation and it did little to abate the uncomfortable atmosphere. Jan Smuts, the president of the Union of South Africa, had invited the Royal Family to visit. The cavalcade earlier in the day had been welcomed by rows of supporters waving British flags as the stately vehicles and entourage passed, but there were clashes with police from protestors. Pro-supporters of the National Party caused a fair bit of disruption, reflecting growing unrest in the political arena, opposition that would eventually lead to the downfall of Jan Smuts' regime.

Racial tension had been escalating in the country for decades. With the recent evolution of the agricultural industry and the introduction of tractors, combines and equipment, farms once short of local manual labour were now repelling black employees and dispatching them to *settlements*. During the last war there was an influx of black labour into the city's private sector, but growing pressure to repel and exclude anyone that was not white from areas and districts in and around Cape Town intensified. It puzzled Molly that the colour of one's skin could be so looked down upon. Was there more to it than that? Would it be the same or worse in Southern Rhodesia, their new home?

By the expression on Mary's face, she was equally perplexed and uncomfortable, so once they had worked out how to get to the train station for the next leg of their journey there was no objection when Molly suggested returning to the hotel.

After four days of confinement and the endless clickety-clack, time had entered another dimension. As interesting as the scenery was, there was only so much time you could spend staring out of the passenger window to pass the time. Molly read every newspaper and magazine available and finished her novel *The Hucksters* by Fredrick Wakeman. She was bored stiff. It was another hour at least before they finally arrived at Bulawayo station. Her impatience was reflected on the faces of others around her, including Robert and Rachael Hunter. Over the last few days, they had exhausted their diverse topics of conversation, one of which was the rather bizarre letter Molly had received, an anonymous proposal to buy her ranch. She read it so many times she had memorised the words.

*For the attention of Elspeth MacMillan*

*I intend to purchase from you the land in Southern Rhodesia registered as Hillside Ranch. In doing so I propose a non-negotiable £4/acre. Enclosed you will find Agreement of Sale documents. Your signature is required on all pages demarked with an 'x'. Sign and return to the address indicated within four weeks of receipt and a transfer will be made to your Royal Bank of Scotland Account. I am in possession of your account details and the precise acreage of the land in question. It would be in your best interests to accept.*

She showed the documents to Robert and Rachael Hunter who were as astonished as she was. There was no name indicated on any of the correspondence as to who the proposal came from. The letter was typed, and the documents were couriered, but without an address of the sender. The return address was a post box in Marseille, France. Molly took the liberty of phoning to find out who it was registered to but according to the French post office the post box did not exist. It was all a little odd. The wording of the letter was chosen to intimidate and threaten. She instinctively expected Arthur Conway had something to do with it, given his attempts to get his hands on the ranch when Angus her husband was killed, but why attempt to purchase the land for less than a quarter of its value? She had received that letter nearly three months ago in the middle of selling off her land in Scotland and preparing for their relocation. There had been no further contact or correspondence on the matter. David, her father, had a copy of the letter and was conducting further investigations of his own.

Molly mused how different the four-day trip was through Mary's eyes. Everything about the train journey was an adventure that heightened her senses. She was awake before dawn listening to the clatter of the approaching tea and coffee trolley. The second the waiter knocked on the sleeper cabin door she would be out of her narrow top bunk to greet him with a cheery Ndebele, "Salibonani (good morning)."

She found romance in the sights, sounds and smells around her. The carriages were like giant living creatures that groaned, creaked and shook as they clumsily clattered along the track. During the day she was never bored. She would spend hours staring out of the window at the ever-changing landscape, sketching scenes and marvelling at the expanse of the open plains. Several times the train slowed down to wait for the line to clear of wild animals. On one occasion, a herd of elephants were crossing the track and a large bull stubbornly refused to budge. The driver inched forward to intimidate him without success. Eventually it was only a long shrill blow of the steam whistle that sent him trumpeting off in disgust. Mary watched the entire scene with head and shoulders squeezed out of the carriage window.

Herds of impala were plentiful, twice as many as the top-heavy wildebeest and zebra. Sightings of giraffe and ostrich were less common but the diversity in nature was awesome, far more exciting in real life than seeing them captured on pages in books. Only once at dusk did she spot a lone leopard underneath a large baobab tree. She had a good mind to ask the driver to stop so she could take in the majestic splendour of the beautiful creature and sketch it. She would have done if her mother had not objected to the notion.

When they travelled through a heavy thunderstorm, she stared wide eyed at the fork lightning that electrified the sky. The rain instantly transformed the smell of the air. Africa was so alive and fascinating. She frequently interacted with the other passengers up and down the carriages, and for them she was a ray of sunshine on the long trip.

Meals served in the restaurant car were a highlight. Each one of the waiters warmed to Mary's friendly nature. It soon became the norm for them to teach Mary a new Ndebele word each day. She learned the names of all the staff including Henry the miserable fat conductor who usually performed his duties with casual indifference. But even he would interact with Mary and occasionally have a laugh. If she was sketching when he walked past, he would stop and watch her and marvel at her talent.

At night when the window shutters were pulled closed and the only illumination came from the dimmed passage lights, she would drift off to sleep, imagining the nocturnal creatures active on the plains outside. She slept soundly through the jolts of the uneven track and the whistle of the train on her narrow top bunk, looking forward to the adventures of the next day.

This morning was her last breakfast, and she was served by her favourite waiter Sixpence. She had never met another human being named after an English coin. The gap in his front teeth made his smile that much more memorable. She informed Sixpence sadly that it was her last breakfast and he insisted on giving her an extra helping of smoked bacon. As she ate, she thought about some of the poor settlements they had passed along the journey with mud huts and thatched roofs. She never imagined a train journey could be so much fun, but along with the disappointment of it coming to an end, she would finally get to see their new home!

The only passenger of the Scottish quartet not underwhelmed by Bulawayo train station was Robert Hunter. He had made this trip once before with his good friend Angus MacMillan, which had set the wheels in motion for a life changing journey in many respects. On that occasion they had viewed and purchased adjacent land. With the war finally over Rob could realise his dream of working the land with his sons. How much would Douglas and Brody have changed since he last saw them? How he wished Angus could have been there with them now. He felt for Molly as he watched her gather her things and prepare to disembark to start her new life without her husband. He was excited to see his boys and get off the train.

The engine hissed a tired burst of steam like a heavy sigh as the passengers started to leave. The station consisted of a small ticket office large enough to accommodate two occupants at a squeeze. The dusty parking area beyond the concrete siding was designated by a blue gum pole fence where a few vehicles and a carriage shared the facility with a handful of tethered horses. On the platform a scattering of individuals made up a sparse welcoming committee. A pensive group of four stood to one side, watching the passengers step down.

Douglas and Brody Hunter were dressed in similar khaki attire with riding boots and cowboy hats. Malcolm, freshly shaven, wore blue jeans, a white long-sleeved shirt rolled up at the sleeves, a suede brown waistcoat and comfortable veldschoens. His unruly curly hair had been combed back. All three were tanned to a dark brown with regular exposure to African sun. It made the fourth member of the group stand out like a sore thumb: Mathew Baker, the MacGregor family solicitor from the Baker Montague and Forbes law firm had flown in from Scotland to see Molly MacMillan. He looked old and pale in his expensive black suit and black tie, holding his leather briefcase, trying to compose himself for the necessary meeting. His demeanour had rubbed off on the others – the joy of meeting or reuniting somehow sullied by their companion's unenviable task.

Mary stepped off the train first carrying her suitcase and a bag over her shoulder. At the first sight of her, Brody gasped out loud. She wore a plain white dress and matching plimsoles. The sun caught her hair, making it shine like pure gold. To him she omitted an aura of beauty and innocence so powerful that he barely noticed his parents climb down behind her. Molly was the last of the four out.

Malcolm saw Molly for the first time with her shock of auburn hair and pale skin and his heart was squeezed with a mixture of joy and sadness. Her smile beamed as their eyes met. Malcolm looked exactly how he sounded on the phone, tall, dark and handsome. She tried to fathom the emotion on his face. They had never met before but spoke often on the phone over the years. It felt only natural for her to drop her suitcase and run to embrace him like an old friend. Malcolm held her and stroked her hair, hoping to empower her somehow for what she was about to hear.

Rachael and Robert hugged their boys in turn with tears of joy, immensely proud of the rugged men that stood before them. They introduced Mary, who smiled and shook their hands confidently with a surprisingly strong grip. She seemed not to notice Brody blush. For him, it was love at first sight.

Molly finally turned her attention to the pale, pensive, well-dressed stranger. She did not know who he was.

He stretched out his hand to Molly. "Mrs MacMillan, I am Mathew Baker, your family solicitor. There are important matters that we need to discuss in private and I'm afraid it really cannot wait."

"What is it? As you can see, I have just stepped off the train after a rather long trip."

"It really needs to be discussed in private immediately. I'm sorry."

Mathew's stern manner and insistence was starting to annoy her. "What on earth is this about? I've only just bloody well arrived?"

"It concerns your family, Mrs MacMillan. We attempted to reach you in Cape Town when you arrived but failed to do so. I have flown from Scotland to handle matters with you directly."

Molly was about to blow. She grabbed Mathew by the lapels of his suit and shook him. "Stop talking in bloody riddles, for god's sake, what is it?"

Mathew sighed, "I'm sorry to have to tell you that your parents David and Veronica are no longer with us. There was an attack – Arthur Conway."

Molly released Mathew and leaned on Mary's arm for support before she fainted. Malcolm caught her before she hit the ground.

∽

For three days Molly locked herself away from the world, alone in her room trying to process her grief. Mathew Baker stayed in the guest bedroom. He would remain as long as necessary until Molly was ready to handle the important files he had brought with him from David's safe, along with his last will and testament. Mary felt very alone. She had lost her uncle Michael and now her grandparents. It was a lot to deal with at such a young age. Malcom spent as much time with her that the demands of running the mine would allow. He tried to imagine what she was going through in a foreign country, not knowing anyone. He found her to be incredibly mature for a young girl of her age.

All four of the Hunters visited daily. Rachael brought over a cottage pie for dinner. Doug and Brody were there for support, neither knowing quite what to do or say to help Mary with her unique losses. They were all terribly kind and supportive and it was what Mary needed, but Henk made the most positive impact on Mary's healing. The day after they arrived, he pitched up with the Ford farm truck towing a horsebox trailer. In the back was the most beautiful creature Mary had ever seen: a young chestnut-coloured mare. From the back of the truck, Henk offloaded a brand-new leather saddle, bridle, horse feed, and grooming kit.

Henk slipped easily into the role of instructor and taught Mary how to ride. She chose the name *Honey* for her new horse and the two of them instantly bonded. Honey's placid nature was just the tonic Mary needed. Her daily instruction included how to saddle up, fit the bridle, clean the stable and groom her new friend. Felix was a little jealous of how much time his father spent with 'Igolide inwele' (golden hair) his name for Mary.

On the morning of the fourth day, Molly emerged from her bedroom wearing a khaki-coloured jumpsuit, ready to face the world. She looked very pale, and her eyes were puffy and bloodshot. Apart from dealing with the tragic loss of both parents, what bothered her greatly was that the funeral had gone ahead without her able to say goodbye to them. Conway had struck again just as David her father had predicted, but the brutality of his attack and the way her parents were taken from her was savagery beyond words.

Uncle Hamish had miraculously survived the blast. Mathew explained that a large sofa had shielded him from most of the blast and shrapnel. When the medics found him, he had lost a lot of blood from puncture wounds to his arms, legs and torso, but no vital organs were badly injured. He would be scarred for life, but alive. He attended the funeral along with Elizabeth, Michael's widow and her four-year-old son Vincent Michael MacGregor.

Molly spent half the morning with Mary, watching her ride under Henk's supervision. She seemed quite at home on her mount and beamed with pleasure. It was the best thing Henk could have done for her. It helped her to focus on something other than the processing of her own grief. Molly needed to talk with Henk to get up to speed with matters relating to her ranch and cattle, but she could not put off her meeting with Mathew Baker any longer. From what he had outlined, it would likely take several days to get through.

She looked around her at everything she owned and none of it seemed real. How many days, months and years had she spent longing to set foot on Hillside Ranch soil. She barely noticed the cloudless sky or the rambling acres each way she looked. It was all hers, thanks to her late husband Angus, and his dream to farm with her. She had cried herself dry and felt like an empty husk, but somehow, she would need to find the strength to go on.

Mathew was seated at the dining room table dressed in a pail grey pinstriped suit that David MacGregor himself had tailored. Molly was all too familiar with her father's craftmanship. Just seeing his work before her reinforced her loss. Mathew had a pile of files on the table in front of him and his black briefcase next to his chair.

He stood as she entered the room and embraced her. "We have a lot to get through, my dear, but take as much time as you need."

She sat opposite Mathew, who perched his silver-framed reading glasses on the end of his nose as he consulted the notes in front of him.

He sighed, forced a smile, and began: "The financial matters relating to David's last will and testament are rather complex. I met with your father just two weeks before he passed to make some amendments and to prepare a legal framework for his instructions to be carried out to the letter. He was an incredibly shrewd and forward-thinking individual. With the threat of Arthur Conway constantly hanging over his head, and making little progress in locating him despite his concerted efforts, he prepared for the worst.

"The life assurance policies I set up for him and Veronica a decade ago were reviewed and increased to £500,000 each and you were named as the beneficiary, being his only remaining child. I am currently processing the claim on your behalf. It will be months yet before the funds are released but there is no reason why it will not be honoured. Once it is through, I will notify you to arrange a transfer to the bank of your choice."

Molly was speechless. Her father was a third-generation tailor. How on earth could he have been worth so much?

"As you can see, he has left you a sizeable sum that will adequately take care of you and Mary for the rest of your lives, but you will soon learn there is much more. Your father was incredibly proud of his family name and his tailor shop. He intended to pass it down to Michael, but sadly he is no longer with us. It will now be signed over to Vincent Michael MacGregor on his eighteenth birthday. There is not a lot left of the shop after the blast but the rebuild is being dealt with through the family trust which I will discuss in more detail later. Elizabeth, Michael's widow, although not benefitting directly from a lump sum inheritance, will receive a monthly payment to cover the needs of Vincent until he turns eighteen. It is generous enough for them both to live on comfortably, although Elizabeth herself has many financial interests of her own. She was not your father's favourite person and for good reason. Should Vincent wish to attend university, the trust fund will cover the costs. He will also inherit your father's home which has been fully paid off. As for what will happen to the running of the MacGregor tailor shop until Vincent is of age remains to be seen, but I have someone in mind that could take up the reins. That's not a part of your father's will but I will see what I can do."

Molly boiled the kettle to make a pot of tea. She had no idea her father had access to so much money. The notion of a *trust fund* was beyond her comprehension.

Mathew cleared his throat consulted his notes and continued, "To his brother Hamish, David left one of his Scottish investment properties, a three-bedroom cottage on an acre of land on the coast near Kirkcaldy along with a lump sum of £30,000.

"That leaves the remaining eleven investments, all of which are now yours, Molly. At current market value they total around

£170,000. In addition to that, your father has shares in the stock market, some of the trading accounts he looked after himself and some I administered on his behalf. The last time we met, David handed the remaining trading accounts over to me to manage. The family trust fund is based on the liquid assets and stocks which are currently valued just under £700,000." He took his glasses off and sat back in his chair with his arms folded, studying the bewildered expression on Molly's face.

After a long pause he added, "Your father was a very wealthy man, a perfectionist tailor, but so much more than that. Over the last four years his financial planning and forethought saw his investments and capital increase fourfold. He was certainly one of the smartest investors I have represented. He taught me a thing or two about the stock market."

The wealth of money and assets she was to inherit was extraordinary, but she would have traded every penny to have her father back. She put her head in her hands and found a reserve of unspent tears.

Mathew stood and patted Molly on the shoulder. "Take your time, Molly. We will leave it there for now." He left the house to get some air.

Molly thought about her relationship with her father as a child and as an adult. The life of the tailor fitted him down to a tee. Although a rather quiet and controlled man, he was a stickler for timing and discipline. He was a perfectionist and took pleasure in crafting high quality clothing. Respect and honour for the family name *MacGregor* was significantly important to him. When Molly exercised her need for independence and adventure away from the family shop, David did not hold her back.

She thought how stifled she felt when she lost Angus, her husband, widowed at such a young age, running her own farm while attending to the needs of her daughter. Once she had set her mind to move to Southern Rhodesia to realise Angus' dream, she had wished her life away until she was able to get there. Since arriving, her world once more had been turned upside down. Was this the adventure she sought? She was not even sure what adventure she wanted anymore, and yet in the last hour she had just discovered that she was a millionaire, thanks to her father.

He gave her the freedom to fly and did not hold her back. He never pushed or pressured her into a life she did not want. He let her go. At the first sign of trouble who did she call? She called her father, and within days he dealt with that conniving greedy lawyer, retrieved Angus' missing letter and saved the very land she now stood on. Without his involvement she could have lost everything. The family had paid dearly for acting on her behalf, first Michael her brother and now both her parents. Arthur Conway was not done, and she needed to be strong enough to deal with that threat head-on.

Molly regretted not getting to know her father better when she had the chance. He cared deeply about his family and did everything in his power to help and protect them. He kept his investments quiet all the while trying to ensure they had a secure future. She forced herself to be stronger and called Mathew in to continue their meeting.

When Mathew sat down, he opened his briefcase and withdrew four coloured files and placed them in front of him. "These files were retrieved from your father's study, and I was instructed to hand them over to you in the event of his death." He pushed the files over to Molly.

"I have read the contents of each file in turn as per your father's instruction and prepared a brief list of contents of each. I thought it might help you prioritise the order in which you wish to read them. The label on the pink file shows subject matter pertaining to you and your mother Veronica.

"The brown file is exclusively relating to your brother Michael, his life and relationships including the most recent, Elizabeth Baron. The black file is a record of financial investments including the title deeds for the eleven properties that will be transferred into your name. It lists all the active accounts trading on the stock exchange and his bank accounts. His personal accounts and those of the tailor shop are also there. There is a lot of red tape in getting money out of his personal accounts but once it has cleared it will amount to £250,000. There was another £40,000 in cash in his safe. I brought that with me, and I will sign it over to you before I leave.

"The details of the two private investigators your father used on a regular basis I have attached to the cover of the red folder. It is the largest collection of documents and reports of which Arthur Conway is the main focus. David's organisation and filing throughout is based on date order, 'most current first'. There are several weeks if not months of reading in the four folders but they are now yours. I must warn you, some of it is heavy reading. I knew your father well but was quite surprised at some of the content. As your father's solicitor, I have a duty to carry out his instructions. I'm trying to do this to the best of my ability and look after your interests at the same time. Please forgive me if I go too fast or come across as blunt and uncaring. There is so much I need to get done before I return to Scotland. Please be rest assured that I will continue to support you in any capacity as I have done your father over the years."

Although Molly had just been told that she was now an incredibly wealthy woman, the extent of her inheritance somehow made the loss of her parents feel even more significant.

Mathew ploughed on: "By comparison, your mother's will, and accounts are very straightforward. Her bank account was primarily used to cover the typical expenses involved in running a family home. At the time of her death the balance was £48. That will be transferred to you. She has asked for all her worldly possessions and clothing to be donated to charity, everything apart from these." Mathew opened his briefcase and retrieved a flat blue velvet necklace holder and a silver pill box. Mary opened the velvet container to find an antique pearl necklace. The lid of the pill box was inlaid with mother-of-pearl in the design of a single rose. Molly thought it was an odd item to inherit.

That night Molly sat on her bed with the four coloured folders. She paged through the contents of the pink file. In date order it began with her birth certificate, school reports and achievements from her youth and ended with a copy of her title deeds for Hillside Ranch. There was a copy of the letter Angus had written to her, along with a copy of his death certificate.

The section pertaining to her mother was jaw dropping. The file contained medical reports relating to Veronica's diagnosis and treatment for depression. It apparently was triggered by the birth of Molly's brother Michael. There were letters from Veronica addressed to David, apologising for having an affair around that time. Over the years leading up to Molly's birth, the letters from her doctor and specialists relayed the success and failure of different barbiturate medication trials. She was on prescription drugs right up until the day she died. How could Molly not have known any of this?

The next morning the meeting between Mathew and Molly continued. Mathew explained the content of each set of documents Molly was required to sign. The process took most of the day.

Finally, Mathew removed his glasses and rubbed his eyes. "That about does it as far as your parents are concerned. The final task we need to plough through is YOUR will. I have assumed you would want to leave everything to Mary, so I have taken the liberty of preparing this for you."

He handed over another thick folder to Molly and between them they secured Mary's future in the event of Molly's untimely death. Mathew stayed almost a week in total but by the time he left to return to Scotland, he was satisfied that at least in a legal sense he had achieved everything he had set out to do.

Shortly before sunset Molly summoned Henk to the main house for a meeting. When he arrived, she offered him a seat at the dining room table and sat down opposite him and said, "Henk, I have every reason to believe that a man named Arthur Conway poses an imminent threat to our safety. By *our* I mean Mary and I, but by association you and everyone and everything on this ranch. Tomorrow, after we have taken Mr Baker to the station, you and I need to put our heads together and work on security measures. We do not have a limited budget, but I believe we do have *limited time*."

# Chapter 21

## HILLSIDE RANCH, INSIZA, BULAWAYO

The priority for Hillside Ranch shifted to implement precautionary measures to deal with the threat of imminent danger. The arms dealer in Bulawayo was delighted to assist in turning the ranch into a well-stocked armoury. The gun cabinets installed in the study were loaded with single and double barrelled twelve-gauge shot guns. When Molly handled the weapons on display at Baron's Gun n' Accessories, she favoured the Winchester .95 for its quick lever action reload mechanism. The box ammunition magazine was located under the barrel in front of the trigger. Henk advised against it for it weighed nearly four kilograms. Molly's response was, "Well I will just have to get stronger then, won't I! I like the feel of this weapon."

She had to admit it was heavy but, in her hands, it felt well balanced, and her decision was final. For Mary she selected a lightweight Winchester 1906 .22 calibre pump action. Molly's choice of handguns included Walther PP and the smaller Walther PPK with a variety of holsters to allow the side arms to be worn under the arm, belted around the waist, or concealed on the shin.

A shooting range was set up away from the house. Mary wanted it to be further from the stable so as not to spook the horses; however, Henk pointed out that their mounts needed to get used to the sound of gunfire. Once sufficiently experienced with discharging handgun and rifle from a static standing position, tuition would switch to achieving the same from horseback.

Mary's daily schedule became a varied and disciplined routine. Molly hired a tutor to deal with Mary's private academic lessons which lasted from 8-12 daily, thus eliminating her risk and exposure attending a conventional school in Bulawayo. The afternoon was dedicated to horse riding and target practice.

Peter Baron, the owner of the gun shop in Bulawayo, put Molly in touch with James Shackleton. All four of his sons, each born a year apart, had served in some capacity in the war and miraculously survived unscathed. James ran a large abattoir in town and struggled to find enough work to keep his offspring gainfully employed when the war ended. It was proposed they be considered for security detail. They were proficient with handling weapons, and their military experience would be handy.

A meeting was set up for the four Shackleton lads who pitched up at Hillside Ranch late in the afternoon as Henk's rifle range tutorage ended. Henk knew their father well as he handled the contract slaughtering for the ranch. He was a broad shouldered, solidly built, balding giant in his mid-fifties. His dark complexion and features were more menacing than handsome. His overall presence left Henk hoping never to have to brawl with the old butcher, so he had high hopes for his sons. As they emerged from their vehicle and assembled in a straight line, standing to attention in front of Henk, several things became instantly apparent.

They were James Shackleton's children without a doubt. The same almost neanderthal pronounced forehead and high cheekbones, mirrored in each of them like loaves of bread made from the same dented bread tin. Although the boys were born a year apart, remarkably each sibling seemed slightly shorter down the line. Mrs Shackleton with her unshakable faith had named them after biblical characters in alphabetical order from oldest to youngest. Aaron was twenty-four, followed by Barnabus, Caleb and Daniel.

As he walked down the assembled line of identically-dressed brothers in blue overalls and gum boots, he studied their faces. It was like looking at the result of an ever-receding gene pool. Aaron had the sharpest looking eyes, for example, but by the time he reached Daniel the expression was vacant, like no one was home. He tried to imagine an assembly of twenty-six of them had the breeding programme finally reached the end of the alphabet. It was too comical to keep to himself, so he said, "Christ, I'm glad your mamma stopped at 'D'. If her production line reached 'Z' little *Zachariah* would be capable of little more than sitting in a pool of his own shit, blowing spit bubbles."

There was a stifled smirk on Aaron's face, but he said nothing. Daniel would not have his mamma insulted so he blurted out, "Ya? Well, you're fuckin' ugly and your wife's a kaffir!" The words were barely out of his mouth when Henk backhanded him in the face so hard Daniel was knocked out cold and lay motionless in the dirt. The other three remained in line without paying Daniel any notice. Perhaps during their upbringing, they were accustomed to harsh physical discipline.

Molly moved as if to attend to the unconscious boy, but Henk raised a hand to suggest otherwise. He was not done testing the remaining trio.

"I bet even before she reached 'M' Mummy Shackleton would have to sleep suspended upside down with her legs strapped together to stop your little half-wit brothers slipping out of her bucket fanny too soon. Before she reached 'P' she would probably have the good sense to throw away the baby and keep the afterbirth. Why not just have the one and be done with it, or why the fuck breed at all? Do any of you pricks have another smart remark?"

They shook their head in unison.

Henk pointed to Daniel and instructed, "Right, throw that gobby little shite back in the truck and get back here so I can see what you are made of."

Before the sun went down Henk had established that the three remaining brothers were accurate marksmen. By 8pm they had survived whatever gruelling physical challenge he put them through. When they finally collapsed onto Molly's veranda, they were drenched in their own sweat. Henk addressed them once they caught their breath: "Aaron, you, Barnabas and Caleb, meet me back here at 5:30 tomorrow morning to start your training. Tell your father I have no need of Daniel; in fact, if he ever sets foot on this farm again, I will bury him myself."

Molly witnessed how Henk had handled the potential new recruits. Her initial reaction was to intervene, put her foot down and object to his tactics, but he was preparing their home to face a threat from a cold-blooded killer capable of anything. She hardened herself to the acceptance of what needed to be done. Henk was right to ensure that anyone employed to oversee their security needed to be vetted and put through their paces.

Further to their meeting yesterday evening, Molly discussed with Henk the details pertaining to the orchestrated murder of her family members by Arthur Conway. From her father's red journal which she pored over long into the night, she produced the few photographs in her possession. They included photocopies of the pictures Conway had used for his Swiss passport in the name of Conrad Amman, and the two more recent shots from the fake identity documents used on the bank robberies in Geneva. A notorious murderer and criminal was not likely to have his photos taken willy nilly, so it was all they had to go on. Molly herself had never seen Conway in person. Out of her surviving family, Hamish had spent the most time in Conway's company, the day he assisted David in getting her issue with the title deeds for Hillside Ranch resolved. Elizabeth had had a partial fleeting glimpse of Arthur's face the night Michael was murdered.

She knew that he was tall and had Caucasian features and was missing his left eye, but the passport photos from Geneva showed a man with two eyes. She learned from her father's file that it was possible for a false eye to be fitted. One of his investigators was looking into the shortlist of acrylic and glass eye producers in Europe to try and find an address linked to Conway.

A small entry in the journal suggested a person of interest known to Conway was Otto Rendenbach. He was traced to an airport hangar near Southampton where he was registered as 'Calshot Private Air Hire'. On inspection they found it abandoned. Conway had managed to get in and out of the country at least on one occasion by means of Rendenbach's private plane. Through the registry of light aircraft in the UK, they traced an Albatross AL102W previously owned by Otto. The plane had been modified to accommodate reserve fuel tanks. The increased range could get the pilot and one other passenger as far as Zurich if need be. The aircraft was designed to land on water which meant Lake Zurich could have been used as a landing zone. Wehrli Bank where the RM 2,700 000 were embezzled from the Third Reich was in Zurich, the same location where two dead bodies were discovered with Conway's calling card. After the robberies in Geneva and the booby-trapped apartment in Koschenruti, there was no further activity until the bombing of the tailor shop.

It infuriated Molly that the police again had no clue where he was and not even a single eyewitness linking Arthur Conway to the scene of the tailor shop. He may not have even been in the country.

Before Henk returned home for the night, Molly asked him, "What do you think of the Shackletons then? Do you think they are cut out for the job?"

Henk sighed; he was still pondering the reference the half-witted Daniel had made to his 'kaffir wife'. If Daniel had heard about it, it meant the town would be rife with gossip. He still had not discussed his situation with Molly.

He stood up stretched and replied, "I put them through their paces this evening, they are fit enough, and they can shoot straight, but I will keep an eye on them over the next few days. If they are capable enough, I want them to organise a rota, each to man a team conducting surveillance over an eight-hour shift. In theory 24-hour security. I will grill the farm labourers to establish how many of them can shoot and be trusted with firearms. We can provide security stations to cover the main house and gate, but it is impossible to man the perimeter of the fences if an attack was initiated from out there. We will concentrate on securing the homestead first and work our way out into the paddocks and perimeter. I have your gelding arriving tomorrow morning so we can get your riding lessons underway. Tomorrow afternoon we will do more work on the firing range."

"Thank you for your help today, Henk, I really appreciate it." Molly paused, aware there was something on Henk's mind. She continued, "Is there anything you wish to discuss?"

"Things are a little complicated in my house. Lulama is… she is my wife under Ndebele law and Felix is my son. It is not something I want to shout from the rooftops because such a union is frowned upon in the local community. There is no provision for us to be married in the local church and there will be plenty of gossip now that everyone in town knows. I have kept it to myself and kept to myself, but I need to let you know that I'm likely to be the topic of conversation as a result when I go into town. It hasn't been an issue up until now, but it may present some trouble in the future."

Mary contemplated Henk's predicament, knowing that it was difficult for him to talk about it. She placed her hand on his forearm and said, "Yes, I did sort of put two and two together. They are obviously welcome here as a part of our ranch and will be thought of as an extension of our family. I'm going to be relying heavily on you and I would like nothing better than for every one of us to be safe and secure and not feel threatened. Through necessity I am preparing myself for a potential attack from a ruthless man. The ranch has been your home for several years now and you have done a good job in my absence. If there is anything you or your little family need just let me know. Simply by being near Mary and I, you and your family are also at risk. We will ensure security measures for all that live here including your household. That stands regardless of whatever anyone says or thinks of you in town."

"Thank you, Mrs MacGregor, it means a lot." With that, Henk turned and left for home.

Over the next six months Hillside Ranch was a hive of activity with every possible trade represented in a bid to transform a homestead into a fortress. A team of builders erected two identical gatehouses on either side of the entrance to the property joined by a wrought iron retractable gate on wheels. The entry point would be manned constantly by at least one armed security member. From inside the guard house, windows afforded a clear view of the entrance as well as the external stone wall under construction along the boundary facing the main road. No one was allowed onto the property without a prearranged appointment.

Electricians wired up external security lights around the main house, cottage, stable and outbuildings. Streetlights fashioned as old lanterns were erected at regular intervals to illuminate the long driveway. Carpenters attached wooden shutters to the external walls outside all windows. When closed and bolted, individual shutters could be opened from the interior to provide line of sight for defence. Both front and back access points were replaced by solid mukwa timber doors, three inches thick.

The gun room now contained enough munition for a small army. Rows of cabinets contained .303, .308 and .404 rifles along with shotguns and handguns. Floor to ceiling shelving stocked rounds, ammunition, and spare magazines. A clipboard recorded the infantry and weapons issued to the security unit and rounds used on training exercises.

One of the old long wooden barns was converted into a well-lit indoor pistol firing range. Targets could be set at any distance from twenty to eighty metres. The rear wall was packed to the roof with rows of sandbags to absorb the discharged bullets. Hillside Ranch's trading account was the largest Baron Gun 'n Accessories ever had on its books.

Robert Hunter was employed to assist in the training of the security unit. His military experience was useful. He had spent six months in hospital with Henk recovering from a bullet wound to his leg and the two of them got on well together. Between them they daily trained the initial twenty recruits from the compounds and whittled them down to a twelve-strong crack shot unit. Each day was filled with drills and instruction on disassembly and reassembly of each firearm, target practice and physical fitness.

It was Robert's idea to officially recognise the recruit's *graduation* on completion of the fast-track training programme. Henk initially laughed at the idea, but Rob explained that it would be good for morale for the unit to have an identity, a sense of belonging and a clear purpose. So, a makeshift ceremony was set up on the lawn in front of the main house where Molly, Mary, Henk and Robert stood in front of the parading security unit. The twelve new recruits and the Shackleton boys stood proudly to attention.

Robert stood on the steps and delivered his motivational speech which Henk translated into Ndebele and Shona. "Today each of you stand before me no longer as an individual but as a band of brothers, no longer just a man but as a unit of warriors, a special force to fight for freedom from our enemy. As you carry out your duties, hold your heads proud of defending this home and the homes of your wives and children. May the good Lord empower your eyes to be far seeing like the eagle, your ears finely tuned like the bat-eared fox, and may he grant you the nerve to shoot straight when called upon to do so. I now salute you, my brothers, and name you *Buffalo Security Ranges of Hillside Ranch.* Please step forward to receive your new uniform."

Each new recruit did so in turn with a beaming smile to the applause of the small party on the veranda. Robert shook their hand before passing them their khaki fatigues, brown boots and beret.

Once they were back in line, Henk turned to Robert and said, "Christ, man, your sermon was so moving, I've got a tear rolling down my leg." To the assembled guards he turned and growled, "And if I catch one of you bastards asleep on the job, I will cut your bloody balls off! Now get back to your training."

A few of the recruits instinctively shot a hand out to cover their genitals, imagining the loss of their favourite tools. After the ceremony even Henk had to admit that their collective enthusiasm and commitment improved.

Robert tried to keep the smugness out of his voice when he said to Henk, "You see a bit of recognition goes a long way. Even if it warms their efforts by a few degrees, it was worth it."

"Ya," he replied, "but I will keep my blade sharp because if I do actually catch them asleep on duty, I will absolutely cut their balls off."

# Chapter 22

## HILLSIDE RANCH, INSIZA, BULAWAYO

The unaccustomed freedom from the tense atmosphere at Hillside was a welcomed respite on her exhilarating ride with Brody through the Hunters' land this morning. Molly had finally relented to the ongoing requests for Mary to be allowed out on her own. Molly quite liked the young lad, but trusted no one when it came to being in the company of her daughter. It did not go unnoticed the effect Mary had on men in general, and Brody was no exception. He blushed outrageously and became tongue tied around her. That was not what bothered Molly exactly, it was the change in *Mary's* behaviour in Brody's company. Her cheeks coloured and she teased the boy relentlessly, enjoying every minute of his apparent discomfort. The security team today managed by Caleb Shackleton were manning the gate and perimeter. Mary took her .22 calibre pump action rifle with her as well as the Walther PPK holstered under her left arm. Brody carried his double barrel shotgun scabbard on his saddle, but they enjoyed the ride without threat. Her curfew was 1pm sharp. Henk and Molly were due to return at the same time from their trip into Bulawayo to get supplies.

Mary kept to the deadline and was back at one as instructed. Honey stood enjoying the relief from saddle and tackle as Mary brushed her down with the curry comb. The placid mare responded to Mary's gentle touch with half closed eyes soaking up the well-earned grooming. Mary's sleeveless white blouse was tucked into her fawn-coloured jodhpurs which in turn were tucked into her brown leather calf-length riding boots. Her skin, once porcelain-like in Scotland, was now tanned and almost the same colour of her mount. She was lost in her own thoughts recounting her morning. Brody eventually relaxed and conversation between them flowed more easily, that is up until the point when he tried to kiss her.

They had galloped through an open field, a race which Brody apparently allowed her to win before they dismounted beneath a tree near the shallow end of Mermaids Pool. Mary was sketching an Impala ram drinking from the edge of the water when Brody lent in to kiss her. She instinctively slapped his cheek rather hard, then grabbed the bewildered boy by the shoulders and kissed him in return hard enough to split his bottom lip. After that brief awkward moment, they both remounted their horses and rode back to the ranch in silence. Side by side they rode, almost touching, both feeling a sensation in their stomach, a growing longing somewhere between pleasure and pain. Mary briefly squeezed Brody's hand before riding off home. She was smiling to herself, recalling his handsome tanned face, blue eyes and shy smile, paying little attention to the approaching vehicle coming up the dirt driveway. It was only when the driver's door slammed that she was brought back to reality. She expected to see her mother and Henk, but instead there was a bearded man she did not recognise. Her first thought was *gangster*. His black suit and hat matched his black car, whatever it was.

He walked towards her. "And who might you be?" he asked.

"I might be Grace Kelly, but I'm not," she replied tartly in high spirits. She could tell straight away the stranger did not take kindly to her attempt at humour.

She followed up with a demurer, "Is there something I can help you with?"

"I'm looking for Elspeth MacMillan."

"She's not here… but she will be back any minute." She added the last bit because Arthur Conway walked towards her and now towered menacingly over her. All visits to the ranch were by appointment only. No one mentioned anything about a visit today. If that's the case, then *why has security let this man through?* There was a coldness to the stranger's expressionless eyes.

"That must make you Mary MacMillan," Conway surmised.

The statement was uttered with barely veiled contempt. Mary said nothing in response, just nodded and took a step backwards praying that the man in front of her was not Arthur Conway. He advanced and suddenly backhanded Mary across the face with such force she went sprawling into the gravel. Her head was filled with blackness peppered with shards of light. When she came-to, she was on her back on the floor of the stable. Her cheek throbbed with pain and blood ran down her neck and blouse. She was struggling to breathe and to her horror discovered that her attacker was on top of her, tearing at her trousers. She heard them rip.

Aurthur Conway had come to see Elspeth MacMillan. After all he had done to her family it was outright arrogance to walk straight up to her front door. The pathetic security guard at the gate had fallen for Arthur's little trick. He had pulled up next to the entrance with a flat tyre and asked the only armed guard, Caleb

Shackleton, for assistance. Conway gave him a £5 note for his trouble and simply slit his throat as he tightened the last wheel nut. After which he threw the buffoon's body in the ditch, opened the wrought iron gate, and drove his black Chevrolet Fleetmaster right on up to the front door. He had packed plenty of fire power onto the back seat but as he looked around the abandoned farmhouse there was no apparent security to challenge him further. Such was his ego he was quite prepared to single handedly take on whatever Elspeth had in the way of defence. Then he spotted Mary in the stable.

The MacMillan woman had refused to sell her ranch, a rejection he fully expected. His below market rate offer was intentional, simply a part of his plan to get her attention, but it was not just the ranch he was after. He wanted the MacMillans and the MacGregors to suffer before they were expunged. His strategy today was to intimidate, but ultimately, he intended to destroy.

Finding Elspeth's little bitch unprotected was a golden opportunity he would not let slip by.

"I'm going to enjoy this a lot more than you will," he muttered through gritted teeth as he reached down to unzip his trousers.

Mary's legs were forced open, her jodhpurs torn, and her bare flesh exposed. It was not her body that excited him, but the prospect of inflicting pain. Once ruined, he would take great pleasure in strangling the life out of the little sprog. The thought of her face turning purple as she struggled for air aroused him. Her long blonde hair was tangled with straw from the stable floor. Her hands clawed powerlessly at his face. Conway had already removed Mary's holstered Walther PPK and thrown it out of harm's way. As he shifted his weight to prepare for her invasion, the slight respite gave Mary the briefest of moments to move. Her outstretched hand closed around the shaft of something heavy in the straw. Arthur had his prey trapped and she had nowhere to go. He prepared himself for entry as the pitchfork handle smashed into his temple. Mary swung the weapon with all her might. Conway collapsed sideways, giving her the chance to wriggle herself free.

She jumped onto Honey bareback, grabbed the mane with both hands and aimed her towards the door. Horse and rider were soon clear of the entrance, and Mary coaxed her mount into a gallop. Conway shook his head to clear his vision and gathered himself, leaning on the stable door for support. He unholstered his pistol, drew it, and aimed at the fleeing target.

Mary clung on to Honey as tightly as she could. She heard the crack of shots fired and felt a bullet brush her hair as it passed. Honey was spurred on with greater effort and they were soon out of range. Mary sobbed as she rode. She had not considered a direction or destination, just simply escape from the brutal, senseless attack.

Conway had no means of pursuit over rough terrain and the shots he fired may have attracted attention, so he got back in his car and left. The dust had barely settled when Molly and Henk returned to an empty house. A flock of sheep being herded down the access road to the ranch delayed their return by a matter of minutes.

Molly's cheeks flushed in frustration to find both Mary and her horse missing. That would be the first and last time Mary was allowed out with that Brody. She phoned through to Cedar Tree to give him a piece of her mind and to demand her daughter's immediate return. Henk was fuming to have found the gatehouse unmanned, the gate open and the house without a single security guard to be seen. He went off to investigate.

Several times Mary glanced back to ensure she was not being pursued but had not noticed the blood running down Honey's hind leg. When she was certain she was safe, Mary slowed the exhausted horse to a gentler pace on the worn path they followed. Their flight from danger had taken them south and Mary recognised the area of the old workings near Malcom's mine. Honey winced. As she slowed, she felt the full pain of the bullet wound in her hindquarters. The adrenaline of their escape had masked the impact of the projectile and the initial injury. She began to limp. The two old mine shafts covered with timber shutters were sectioned off with a metre-high wire fence bearing the warning sign *DANGER – KEEP OUT.*

Although the mid-afternoon sun dispensed abundant heat, horse and rider were both shivering. Mary's cheek throbbed painfully and ached as she touched the swollen bruise. She contemplated her appearance, bloodied with torn clothing. She needed help but she could not ride into Malcolm's mine in her current state. Neither could she return home in case her assailant was still waiting for her. It was then she noticed Honey's discomfort and prepared to dismount.

Out of the corner of her eye Mary saw a sliver of earth strike. The ground at the side of the path next to Honey's front leg suddenly sprung to life, a loud hiss followed by a flash of brown. Honey reared, whining in terror. Momentarily transfixed, the puff adder was lifted clear of the ground as its inch-long fangs delivered its toxic venom into the soft tissue of the horse's foreleg. With a flick of its hoof, Honey sent the snake cartwheeling into the long grass. Panic-stricken, she bolted sideways and cleared the fence. Mary was unprepared for the sudden manoeuvre and was flung clear of Honey's back. For a moment she was aware of flying towards the wooden shutters of the mine shaft, then the agony of impact followed by nothing...

The hysterical Honey, now free of her rider, cleared the fence once more and raced in terror to distance herself from the scene of the attack, the scalding hot pain forcing its way up her foreleg and the throbbing stiffness in her rear. Up ahead the two-metre-high barbed wire perimeter fence of Invictus Mine came into view. In her crazed state she approached the barrier intent on clearing it rather than skirting around. As she prepared to jump, her good foreleg slipped and snapped with a loud crack. The impetus of her charge propelled her into the barbed fence, snapping the uprights and strands of wire. The barbs clung to her hide like a metallic thornbush. The more she thrashed about the more tangled she became.

Two mine workers close to the scene were in full view of the insane horse. Both were mesmerized and stared in horrid fascination. Eventually one of them ran off to find Malcolm.

~

## INVICTUS MINE, INSIZA, BULAWAYO

Tanaka maintained his traditional dress code regardless of the season. He looked out of place in the small mine office with his brown loin cloth and woven leather headband, sitting on the chair opposite Malcom's desk. He had just returned from another nocturnal vigil with Douglas Hunter. In the early hours of the morning, they had finally shot the rogue leopard that was terrorising the local farms, killing livestock. For three nights they had lain in ambush in a makeshift hide. Their bait – a tethered live goat doused in blood. Malcolm was listening to Tanaka's colourful recital of the kill when the phone rang. It was Molly and she was frantic.

"Ok, calm down, Molly. There's probably a perfectly good reason why Mary is late." Malcolm immediately regretted trying to placate a mother's instinct for danger.

Molly continued, "No, I will not bloody well calm down! There are tyre tracks on the driveway from an unknown vehicle, the gate was wide open, and Henk found Caleb Shackleton dead in the ditch with his throat slit."

Malcolm's blood turned cold. At that point a worker ran into Malcolm's office and reported the horse tangled in the fence. He informed Molly and told her he would ring her back once he had checked it out.

Malcolm retrieved his rifle and Tanaka followed as they were guided to Honey's location. When they arrived, it did not take Malcolm long to realise the mare was beyond help. It lay panting in a cocoon of wire, frothing from her mouth and nostrils. Tanaka circled the trapped animal. Apart from the obvious shattered foreleg, he pointed out the weeping puncture wound from the snake bite, and with concern, the bullet wound in her rump. Malcolm stroked her cheek gently talking soothingly to her. He cleared the gathered workers, loaded his rifle, and put the poor beast out of her misery.

As if by an unwritten code between them, Malcolm and Tanaka immediately set off at a trot following the spoor. Tanaka went ahead, studying the ground following the churned earth from

Honey's racing hooves and the occasional droplets of blood. It did not take them long to find the scene of the snake attack, and more troublingly the shattered cover to the abandoned mineshaft. Malcolm felt the blood drain from his face and the hair on his forearms stand on end. It was the first part of the prophecy...

*When the snake strikes golden hair will be swallowed into the belly of the earth.*

Tanaka was with Malcolm the day they had encountered the Mahaha following the hunt of Samson the lion. He was present when the blue demon uttered the prophetic words. By the harrowed look on Malcolm's face, Tanaka knew something was wrong. Then the penny dropped, and he gasped. Both men stood motionless, contemplating the significance of what had just taken place. Then the reality of Mary's demise returned to both in full force.

Malcolm gathered himself before issuing instructions to his trusted companion. "Shamwari (friend), go to the mine and get Samuel to bring the truck and Ephraim, the mine captain. Bring headlamps and rope, thirty metres." Malcolm then considered retrieving the dead body and added, "Bring blankets."

Malcolm shook his head. What would be better: phoning Molly back to tell her Mary was dead or pitching up at the ranch with the corpse wrapped in blankets on the back of his truck? First things first, retrieve the child's body.

Without a torch the entrance to the mine shaft was just a gaping black hole. Malcolm knew from personal experience it descended just over twenty metres. He did not look forward to finding the twisted and broken body of Molly's child. He cursed himself for not making a more robust cover. The timber boards must have shattered on impact and descended with Mary as she fell.

When Samuel arrived, they tied the rope to the bumper of the truck and secured the other end around Malcolm's waist. He refused to let anyone else down to collect Mary. Once his helmet was in place and battery pack secured to his belt, Malcolm turned on his headlamp and looked down into the open shaft. The strength of the beam was not strong enough to reach the bottom, but it did not need to be. To his astonishment Mary was hanging like a rag doll against the wall of the shaft a third of the way down. A network of roots no thicker than Malcolm's index finger had forged their way out of the earth in that section of the shaft. It looked almost as if the roots embraced the falling child to save her from certain death. She was lucky to have landed where she did and there was a chance she could still be alive.

When Malcolm reached the motionless child, he was elated to find she was warm to the touch and had the faintest of pulse in her neck. The roots gradually relinquished their grip and Malcolm cradled Mary as gently as he could on the rough ascent back to the world.

# BULAWAYO GENERAL HOSPITAL

After three days in a coma Mary came-to with a pounding headache. Her eyes were shut but, in the distance, she could hear the familiar voice of her mother arguing, "I'm telling you it is Arthur bloody Conway! The same man responsible for the murder of the rest of my family. Here's his picture. What are you going to do about it? Look at the state my daughter is in. She has been like that for three bloody days. She is lucky to be alive, but the doctors are not sure if she will ever wake up."

A male voice replied, "I understand you are upset, Mrs MacMillan. I will circulate the photo amongst our police force immediately and contact border patrol to see if anyone matching his description has passed through. Please notify me when Mary wakes up. Her eyewitness account will be useful. I will also get in touch with Interpol right away."

"Thank you, commissioner," her mother replied and Mary could hear her footsteps get louder as she returned to her bedside.

Mary slowly opened her eyes. "Mum…"

Molly gently took her hand. "Oh my darling, I have been worried sick. How are you, sweetheart?" She pressed the emergency buzzer next to Mary's bed to call the nurse. "Don't try and sit up until the doctor has checked you over."

The doctor and nurse entered the room together. They checked Mary's vital signs, temperature, and pupil dilation with a pen torch. The doctor then directed the nurse to give Mary a sedative. He looked at Mary and said to her, "You may not feel like it right now, young lady, but considering what you have been through you are very lucky indeed. A few nasty cuts and bruises, but no broken bones otherwise. I don't see any reason why you shouldn't make a full recovery. The X-rays showed no skull fracture, but head trauma injuries must be monitored. I would like you to remain in hospital for a few more days to ensure there is no brain haemorrhage. What that means, Mary, is that if the brain has been injured it can bleed. I have given you something to help with the pain, but it is likely to make you feel sleepy. Complete bedrest, OK? And no visitors." He looked over at Molly as he said the last bit.

After the doctor and nurse left, Molly smiled at Mary. "I'm going to bring you a few things, fruit, and juice. I will fetch your art pencils and paper if you feel up to sketching, and a few books to read. When you feel a bit stronger, we can talk about what happened, ok? Please make sure you get plenty of rest, my love."

Mary nodded, shut her eyes and slept.

## HILLSIDE RANCH, INSIZA, BULAWAYO

After a further week in hospital the doctor was satisfied that Mary was well enough to return home. She was distraught when she learned Honey had been put down, but there was no chance she could survive the injuries she had sustained. Mary stood at the entrance of her empty stable, weeping, partly because the vacant space reinforced the loss of her beloved horse, but also it was the scene of her attack, Conway's attempted rape. Molly held her as she recounted what she remembered about the incident.

They both turned to watch a truck and trailer pull up in front of the house. It was Brody. Mary ran across and embraced him. It was the first time they had seen each other since their horse ride the morning of her assault.

Brody reluctantly broke the embrace and said, "There is someone I would like you to meet."

He opened the horse box to reveal a chestnut mare the spitting image of Honey. The only difference was the white diamond between her intelligent eyes.

"Oh, Brody, she's absolutely beautiful," Mary exclaimed and hugged Brody again and planted a kiss on his cheek. Molly cleared her throat to remind the two of them she was still present.

After leaving Hillside Ranch, Arthur Conway headed back to Bechuanaland. Before he reached Plumtree border patrol, he pulled over and attached the self-adhesive stickers to the doors of his Chev. The signs read 'Francistown Mining Supplies'. He slipped out of his suit and put on a dirty pair of overalls. His stick-on beard and moustache were replaced by a grey wig to cover his short dark hair. When he looked at himself in the mirror, he looked exactly like his fake passport photo. Lastly, he changed the registration plate and set off once again.

The border post gave him no trouble, but he was furious with himself for being outsmarted by a teenage girl. His failure brought him down a peg or two. Pitching up at the farm on his own without back-up was a mistake brought about by his own arrogance. Along the way back he came up with a more sensible and calculated approach to ensure success. The next time he set foot on Hillside soil he would have back-up. Failure was not an option...

## HILLSIDE RANCH, INSIZA, BULAWAYO

The three security guards who had abandoned their posts the day Mary was attacked were relieved of their duties, but before they were allowed to go, they were assembled with the rest of their old unit including the remaining two Shackleton brothers for their exit interview. After being stripped of their uniform, they were tied naked over a stack of gum poles. A few lashes of Henk's sjambok (whip made from hippopotamus hide) loosened their hesitant tongues.

It turned out that when Henk and Molly left for town, the guards thought it prudent to use their unsupervised time to play a game of 'Tsoro' (Mancala-based board game). They were close enough to the main house to hear the shots fired by Arthur Conway, but instead of rushing to Mary's defence, they ran away in terror and hid in the compound where Henk later found them.

After the truth was established, Henk turned to the remaining security team and looking from one to the other and said, "Their stupidity cost the lives of one of the Shackletons and allowed the attack of Miss Mary MacMillan, whom we have sworn to protect. Mrs MacMillan pays your wages that puts food on the table for your families. I have never seen cowardice like it. You have now lost your jobs but worse than that you have lost the respect of your comrades. They will decide the severity of your punishment." He walked over to Barnabas Shackleton and handed him the sjambok.

A bundle of mutton cloth was wedged between the teeth of the three former employees. One by one they took up the whip and thrashed the exposed skin on their backs, buttocks and legs. Eventually the shrill cries at every stroke dwindled into soft whimpers. By the time the discipline had been administered, the tortured trio lay motionless with ribbons of skin hanging from their bruised, bleeding bodies. Their families were then allowed to collect them before leaving the ranch in disgrace with the worldly possessions they could carry.

# Chapter 23

T aking shelter in the abandoned warehouse was no escape from the blistering heat. Looking up at the wrought iron roof was like facing an over grill set on high. Periodic bursts of automatic gunfire drifted in on the occasional warm breeze. The location was chosen not for its hell-like climate or uninteresting landscape, but rather for its isolation.

Two 3-ton Bedford QL 4x4 trucks were parked to one end of the enclosure, both mechanically sound and sufficiently fuelled in their long-range tanks to achieve a 1200 km round trip. Their sand-coloured exterior was scarred and marked from previous missions, but new bottle-green tarpaulins covered the wooden benches that would seat the assembled task force. The originally thirty-one mercenaries were whittled down to twenty-seven. Three perished during training exercises with live ammunition and one was shot in the face by Arthur Conway this morning for insubordination. When you are dealing with a band of bloodthirsty, ruthless trained killers, it is best to be clear on who is in charge. It would be one less gun-wielding member of his unit, but it was worth the sacrifice.

It had not been an idle six months since his encounter with Elspeth MacMillan's daughter. Conway had drafted recruits from Southern Rhodesia, Portuguese Mozambique, Bechuanaland, and South Africa. With the war over, there were plenty of volunteers to get their hands dirty for cash if you knew where to look. He paid out cash incentives once he had checked their credentials and approved their employment, but four times their sign-up bonus would be paid on completion of their mission.

He studied the layout of the map in front of him. Hillside Farm boundary and position of the main house and outbuildings were roughly drawn based on Conway's recollection of his last visit. A dirt road led to the main farm entrance, and a second ran parallel to the northern perimeter. His plan on arrival was to deploy one of the trucks to the north to head through the farm compound towards the main house. The second vehicle would enter through the main gate, with the split forces scheduled to rendezvous simultaneously at the main homestead. The instructions were simple: Take Mary MacMillan hostage and leave Elspeth alive and unharmed. Everyone else was fair game for eradication. It did not matter if they were part of the security detail, or an unarmed labourer. Skin colour, gender and age were entirely irrelevant. If it lived and breathed on Hillside soil, it must simply be dispatched. As for outbuildings, everything must burn.

Mary captured alive opened an opportunity for Arthur to use her as leverage to get Elspeth to sign over her land. If necessary, he would send her daughter back piece by piece. Should Elspeth be eliminated, Mary would most likely inherit everything. He would then impose plan 'B' to free her of the burden of ownership and once achieved, take great pleasure in disposing of the little rat. There were no guarantees with his trigger-happy mob, but if the worst came to the worst and both Mary and Elspeth were eliminated, it was not a total disaster. With the land, livestock and building destroyed, he could pick up the property through a third party at auction for a fraction of its original value.

Arhtur's plan was a win-win situation regardless, far more sensible than his first single-handed gung-ho attempt. He had limited time to instil absolute discipline with his rough and ready entourage, but the level of mayhem he would unleash excited him. It had not escaped Conway's attention that Otto Rendenbach over the years had tired of getting him out of a tight spot, but it was the final throw of the dice that would involve reliance on Otto once again for an escape route.

Otto was extremely well connected with a network that could provide high quality fake passports, birth certificates and identification documents. With Arthur on the run, wanted for multiple murders and thefts, he relied heavily on the little German. It was one of the reasons why Arthur had agreed to finance the purchase of the Crawley Concession gold mine in Penhalonga. Huns Schroder was Otto's new identity. Arthur had only discovered the connection between Malcolm Hunter and Elspeth MacMillan after the purchase was finalised. Malcolm's brother Robert was with Angus MacMillan the day he was killed. Malcolm now worked Invictus Mine, on Elspeth's Hillside Ranch. He also owned White Stone Farm nearby. Not that it mattered much in the whole scheme of things as to the outworking of Arthur's plans, but Malcolm had to be factored in as a potential support to the MacMillans.

Robert Hunter and his two sons on the adjacent farm Cedar Tree Hollow were also allies with Elspeth. That, too, Conway had planned for. The task force for their upcoming mission numbered 28, including himself. Over the years Arthur had evaded the smartest of Scotland Yard Interpol and law enforcement the world over, so the local authorities posed no more impediment to his plans than a potential roadblock or barricade. There was sufficient fire power to deal with their pathetic resistance.

He reflected on his life. His father had been a well-to-do landowner, a family man and a farmer. His whore mother died giving birth to what would have been Arthur's brother, but the newborn was so weak it died along with his mother. The lustful drunk's seed was too weak to produce a healthy sibling. Arthur was forced to grow up in an orphanage. He had put himself through law school and eventually set up his own law firm. His biological father became one of his clients and Arthur used his position to extort as much money as possible from the old fool. When his father was killed during a German air raid, Angus MacMillan inherited everything, and Arthur nothing.

When David MacGregor intervened on Arthur's plans to get his hands on Angus' estate in Southern Rhodesia, David had ended Conway's career. Since then, he had been on the run. He had adapted to his new lifestyle, learning how to survive and plan his revenge. Michael MacGregor and his father David had been dispatched by Arthur personally. Nothing would stand in his way for the completion of ridding the world of MacMillan and MacGregor.

Arthur's second-in-command was a member of the far-right wing movement of the National Party in favour of overthrowing Jan Smuts, the president of South Africa. When Conway approached Clause Schoeman, he proved to be a valuable find. After raiding a military hold, he succeeded in securing arms and ammunition that included two fully operational flame throwers and light weight Doron Plate fibre glass laminate bulletproof vesting.

A crew of four were mounting Vickers Machine Guns to the Bedford trucks, bolting the tripods of the 20kg monstrosities to the roofs. The rear canopies were altered to allow the installation of a wooden platform and strapping to accommodate a team of three to operate the weapon in transit if necessary and to deal with a potential unwelcoming reception at their destination. Next to the tripod a bracket was welded to house the 250-round canvas belts to feed the automatic firing action capable of 450-rounds per minute. The front bumpers of both trucks were reinforced with sections of steel railway sleepers.

A second team of four attended to securing the flame throwers for transit over rough terrain and loading the sundries of wire cutters, rolls of wire, shovels, spare fuel and first aid kits.

Clause supervised the preparations of the hit squad, dressed in black, fully kitted with a range of rifles and automatic weapons. Each carried meagre rations and water for their ten-hour journey to Insiza. Assembled in their battle fatigues, they were an imposing mob. Conway's final briefing reiterated the priorities of the mission. Mary was to be taken alive, and Elspeth left unharmed, everyone else and everything else must die and burn.

To launch their midnight attack on Hillside, they mounted up and rolled out at 1:30 pm; each driver had a passenger kitted out with maps and schedules. Conway took the lead vehicle and Clause brought up the rear. First scheduled stop would be thirty minutes before Plumtree border patrol to set up the Vickers gun crew and to review the modus operandi for dealing with resistance.

# PLUMTREE BORDER POST, SOUTHERN RHODESIA

Enias Chibangwa was sat at his desk, excavating his nostrils, staring into space, contemplating the tough decision of whether to have a wank before or after his dinner of sadza and gravy. Christ, the Plum Tree border post was dull! The most exciting thing that had happened today was watching two chacma baboons fighting over the apple core he had thrown into the bin earlier. The sun had just set, and his colleague Boniface saw to the all-important job of lowering the barrier to officially close the border between Bechuanaland and Southern Rhodesia.

The annoying little prick only ever talked about how fantastic his new wife's tits were. Enias had to agree they were quite spectacular and decided they would be the focal point of his after-dinner stimulation. The last vehicle had passed through three hours ago and his paperwork and admin were complete for the day. It seemed pointless to man the border after dark but at least he was being paid for his shift and did not have to tolerate a night of his wife snoring like a walrus in his ear.

In the distance he heard a vehicle approaching. He glanced out the window to see Boniface stub out his cigarette and look in the direction of two sets of approaching headlights. As they drew closer, he could see the outline of trucks, but the sound of the engines was all wrong. They should be slowing down for the barrier not speeding up. He could see Boniface's mild curiosity quickly morph into panic. The lead vehicle opened fire, turning the earth around the railing into a cloud of dust. Boniface twitched repeatedly as tracer rounds tore through him. He fell to the ground seconds before the lead truck smashed through the barrier.

Enias instinctively hit the deck as bullets flew through the windows and doors, imbedding themselves in the plaster and brickwork. Fortunately, the convoy did not stop. He lay motionless listening to the fading growl of their engines. Finally, once they were out of range, he stood up and dialled the number for Bulawayo Central Police Station.

## HILLSIDE RANCH, INSIZA, BULAWAYO

Molly hung up the phone and shouted to Mary, "Get Henk. That was the police commissioner. Two armed trucks broke through Plum Tree border and are heading this way. My guess, it's Arthur Conway! I will ring Malcolm and the Hunters."

## BULAWAYO TOWN CENTRE

Behind the makeshift barricade of barbed wire and wooden poles across the Plum Tree Road, two Land Rovers sheltered a dozen officers armed with police issue rifles and hand pistols. It was the best the police commissioner could come up with in the short time it took the approaching trucks to travel the 100 km of road from the border. He did not have to wait long before two vehicles travelling side by side at speed came into view. At five hundred metres out, he gave the signal to open fire. The random shots were immediately answered by high velocity rapid fire from heavy artillery. The Land Rovers were little protection as the bullets tore through the aluminium chassis like a knife through butter and slammed into the row of defenders one by one.

The two Bedford trucks stopped just short of the barricade without relinquishing their barrage of heavy fire. On cue, two soldiers stepped forward and threw phosphorus grenades that exploded on impact with the Land Rovers, rendering them useless. With the barrier neutralised, the machine gun fire ceased. The soldiers remounted as the lorries nudged the roadblock aside. There was no further resistance to their advance through the empty Bulawayo streets. Next stop – Hillside Ranch.

∿

## HILLSIDE RANCH, INSIZA, BULAWAYO

At midnight the occupants of Hillside Ranch heard the exchange of fire at the gatehouse where Barnabas Shackleton and his team of six armed guards provided the first line of defence. The rapid fire from the machine gun overpowered everything. When the shooting stopped, a loud explosion was followed by the sound of a large vehicle approaching. The entrance was breached within seconds. Henk slung his .308 over his shoulder and holstered his handgun at his waist before he ran back to his cottage to fetch Lulama and Felix.

As he sprinted towards his home the sky towards the compound glowed ominously. He could hear the faint rapid pop

pop pop of automatic gunfire. He burst through his front door and found Lulama and Felix huddled together in the middle of the floor, clutching each other. On the way in he did not notice the wooden shutters were wired shut.

Lulama looked up at him wide eyed. "There have been men outside our house!"

The front door was suddenly slammed shut and something heavy dragged across it. Henk cursed himself for designing the door to open outwards. He loaded his rifle and fired at the door twice and heard a thud as a body hit the ground. As he ran from room to room, he noticed all the shutters were closed. When he looked out the back kitchen window, a flamethrower gushed a steady bright flame directly into the dry thatch. Three soldiers were aligned outside, armed with AK-47 assault rifles and they opened fire. He ducked below the ledge as bullets shattered the glass and wooden frame, showering Henk with shards and splinters. Through the open window he heard the intensifying roar as the dry roof turned into a blaze.

Henk crouched as he ran back into the lounge where smoke was already seeping through the ceiling. He dropped his rifle, drew his pistol and tucked Felix under his arm. He charged at the front door and barged it with his shoulder with all the strength he could muster. The hinges snapped under the weight, and his momentum sent him and Felix over the metal barrel barricade. He dropped Felix as they fell through the door. Henk shot up, firing his pistol at the row of mercenaries facing him. Felix had just made it to his feet when two bullets struck him in the chest, sending him reeling backwards towards the burning cottage. A string of bullets thudded into Henk in a diagonal line from his thigh up to his neck and halted his advance. As he lay in the dirt, he watched his motionless child just out of reach. At the same time the lounge ceiling collapsed noisily, drowning out the screams of Lulama in her fiery hell.

In the main house, Douglas, Brody, and Tanaka held off the frontal attack from the lounge. Mattresses were propped over the main windows as a buffer against grenades and shrapnel. The trio fired through gaps to the side of the shutters.

After dealing with the compound and setting it ablaze, the second truck entered the main gate to reinforce the assault. They suffered no casualties whilst callously dispatching unarmed, defenceless men, women and children. They parked up next to the lead vehicle, disembarked and opened fire.

Molly, Mary and Malcolm guarded the rear kitchen. The solid wooden door had already been fired at, but nothing had penetrated the solid structure so far. The shutters over the windows allowed restricted view of the movement outside and partial openings to shoot through.

Molly's heavy Winchester .95 aimed through a gap in the kitchen window dispatched the attackers in her line of sight. The dining room table had been turned on its side as a barrier in case the kitchen door was somehow compromised. Mary crouched behind it, holding her .22 pump action rifle. Floods of tears rolled down her cheeks as she watched the growing flames from the stable. All the horses were locked inside. Malcolm was close to the back door, listening to the scuffles and muffled conversation, trying to figure out the next phase of attack. A sudden loud explosion from a breach grenade blew the door off and knocked Malcolm unconscious. As the smoke cleared, three soldiers were led into the kitchen by Arthur Conway.

Molly instantly recognised him despite his helmet and combat gear. She shot him in the middle of his chest, reloaded and fired a second round into the same location. He fell backwards onto the floor. No one could survive that velocity bullet in the centre of his chest. A second soldier immediately behind was shot between the eyes by Mary. The third fired at Molly hitting her once in the chest and once in her upper arm. Mary screamed. Rough hands pulled her up off her feet by her hair. Conway's body and Mary were dragged out of the kitchen into the moonlit night.

In the front of the house Brody, Douglas and Tanaka had repelled any attempts to breach the house and dead bodies littered the lawn. A hand grenade was rolled onto the veranda by the front door but before it could explode, Brody unlocked the door, picked it up and hurled it at the closest truck. It landed in the back and ignited the fuel tank when it detonated. The blast took out another two assailants in the process.

The attack ended as abruptly as it had started. They heard the engine of the remaining truck fire up. Doug saw three mercenaries mount the rear before it left. Brody ran through to the kitchen to find a groggy Malcolm kneeling over Molly. She had lost a lot of blood.

He looked up at Brody and said, "They've taken Mary. You come with me. Doug, phone through to your parents and tell them to get Molly to hospital. Once they arrive, you and Tanaka follow me in the Ford. They will be heading for the Plum Tree border, it's the shortest route out of the country."

Molly was conscious. She grabbed Malcolm's arm and croaked, "I got him, Malcolm. I shot him twice in the chest! I killed the bastard..."

The barn containing the farm's petrol and diesel supply near the firing range was ablaze. As the roof collapsed, the fuel tanks exploded, sending burning fragment of timber and debris into the dry grass. Within minutes an uncontrollable fire swept through the paddocks and fields. The trapped panicked cattle barged the fences in an effort to flee. Some broke through the barrier and stampeded in a bid for freedom, but many were not so lucky. Crazed lit beasts ran in all directions like demented fiery demons until they collapsed. Nothing could be done to help them.

The southerly breeze steered the fire through the fields away from the homestead. By the time Malcolm and Brody were ready to leave, the assailants had a ten-minute head start. Brody sat in the passenger seat with his rifle and ammunition in the footwell. There was no time to pay respects to the bodies of Henk and Felix who still lay where they had fallen next to the smouldering remains of the cottage and Lulama's smouldering grave.

Malcolm and Brody left Doug preparing the Ford for departure and sped past the main gate scattered with the corpses of their security team. There would be plenty of time to grieve later. He floored the accelerator of the Roadster on the main road leading to Bulawayo, shifting through the gears. Brody had never travelled at such a speed before. He watched the speedometer surpass the 180 km/hour mark with ease and still the car lurched forward like a greyhound not yet at its full potential. He was more accustomed to the sedate pace of the Ford. The howl of the engine and the force of the wind assaulted his face and ears. He looked over at Malcolm. His eyes were calm and focussed behind his goggles. His gloved hands gripped the steering wheel, masterfully altering course through the corners with the slightest of hand movements.

On the other side of Bulawayo, a team of emergency workers and police were reeling after another assault from the passing Bedford and its lethal Vickers machine gun. All four of the State Land Rovers and Ambulances had been immobilized. The dazed survivors milled around their freshly fallen comrades. There was no point in stopping but it was clear that Arthur Conway had been here a short time ago and it confirmed his direction was the Bechuanaland Border.

Once back on the open road, Malcolm pushed his sports car to its limits. It was not long before the red taillights of a vehicle up ahead came into view. With the border post closed there was seldom traffic on the road at that time of night. It was 2:30 am and the full moon radiated its glow over the surrounds. Even so, when Malcolm slowed the Alfa and turned off the headlights, it took a while to adjust to the darkness. They followed the reflecting tarred road that stretched ahead like an endless silvery snake. Malcolm kept his distance.

Mary was sat wedged between Arthur Conway and Clause Schoeman. Her tears ran down her cheeks and soaked the hessian bag over her head. She recalled seeing her mother go down after being shot at least twice. Was she still alive? Her wrists were bound before her head was covered. As she was being tied up, she recalled the driver resuscitating Arthur Conway. His chest was exposed to reveal the shattered fibreglass bulletproof vest with one round embedded in it and a puncture mark just below the weakened surface. Her mother had shot him twice in the chest. The trauma to the rib cage had stopped Conway's heart. After removing the breast plate Clause used his knife to dig out a bullet lodged in the body of Conway's sternum. He dressed the wound before performing cardiopulmonary resuscitation. Unfortunately for the rest of the world, Arthur came back to life through a fit of coughs and splutters.

He sat next to Mary, nursing his chest. It was an effort to breathe. The dumb bastards had shot Elspeth MacMillan but at least they had managed to extract the snivelling little wench who sobbed incessantly next to him. As he washed down a pair of painkillers, he forced his mind to focus on how much fun he would have breaking Mary in. She would eventually see the good sense to sign over her inheritance to its rightful owner; perhaps he could extract more than just the ranch.

Of the original 28-strong force, only five remained. Arthur Conway, Clause Schoeman and three veterans in the back of the Bedford. Arthur had no intention of farming once Hillside was in his possession. He cared only for the increasing value of the land itself. Taking ownership was purely exacting justice and a matter of principle. He did not like Africa one bit. Apart from the bloody heat, it was full of uncivilized black tribes that constantly fought amongst themselves and hated the English. Once he was rid of the MacMillans, he would follow through with his plans of relocating to his new property in Odense, Denmark.

Harry Truman, the President of the United Status, had recently outlined the post-war economic recovery programme for Western Europe. The Marshall Plan pledged $13 billion in financial aid. Denmark's allocation was the highest per capita in Europe. Arthur quickly acquired property in the worst bombed areas of Odense and already had plans underway to get his hands on as much of the charitable free funding available. It would be the foundation from which to rebuild his empire. He spoke fluent German – and Danish, like most Scandinavian languages, had German roots. He would rather capitalise on the opportunity in Europe than fry in this god forsaken, uncultured hell hole.

Brody knelt on the passenger seat with his rifle aimed at the truck ahead as Malcolm inched forward, narrowing the gap between the Alfa and the Bedford. He could not risk pot shots at the vehicle in front for fear of injuring Mary. If he pulled the trigger, he needed to be deadly accurate. At 50 metres out Malcolm switched his headlights onto full beam. With the soldiers stunned in the bright light, Brody began to shoot. He released three rounds into the rear of Bedford in quick succession before return fire struck the front of the Alpha. The Vickers machine gun was useless to repel an attack from the rear, but a single volley of automatic rounds ripped into Malcolm's car, smashing the headlights and windscreen. Malcolm slowed the Alfa while Brody reseated himself. He was certain he had hit all three. Two of them had fallen without resurfacing.

Perhaps the third was wounded. They allowed the truck to pull ahead out of range and followed from a distance.

After another 10 km of tailing at a sedate pace, Malcolm knew they were in trouble. Neither of them had been hit but the temperature gauge of the Alfa had steadily climbed, and they were forced to pull over. Steam hissed out of the front grille where two bullets had ruptured the radiator.

Malcolm kicked a tyre in frustration. "We will have to wait for Doug and Tanaka. Let's hope they are not too far behind."

It was a long twenty minutes with little conversation, both men fearing the worst for Mary and powerless to do anything but wait. When Doug eventually pulled up, they both scaled the tailgate into the back almost before it had fully stopped. Malcolm tapped on the roof to get them going.

Fifteen minutes later they reached Plum Tree Border post. They were greeted by a rather jumpy Enias Chibangwa, rightly unnerved by the earlier shooting. He pointed his rifle at the approaching Ford and ordered it to halt. Malcolm and Brody stood in the back of the truck with their hands raised. Behind Enias, six reinforcement guards were stationed where Boniface had been gunned down.

After Malcolm had reassured Enias that they were no threat, he was surprised to find out that no vehicles had approached the border from any direction in the last hour.

Brody thought for a moment. "I think I know where they have gone. The only other route out of the country is through the Mphoengs Tribal Trust Land. I have travelled that road before. We import bull semen from Damara Stud in Bechuanaland. We collect it from an airstrip on the other side of Ramaquabane River. Not many people know about the airstrip. It isn't on the map. My guess is they plan to fly their way out. The reserve is about 240 kilometres away. The dirt roads aren't great, but I know the way. We passed the turn off about half a kilometre back. Doug, let me drive."

Before they could pull off, Enias ran back over to the Ford. "Mr Hunter, we have received a telephone call from your brother at Bulawayo Hospital. He says Mrs MacMillan is out of surgery. She is stable but in the intensive care unit."

Once they reached the Mphoengs turn off, Douglas and Tanaka stood in the back of the Ford holding onto the railing behind the cab. It was more comfortable to stand and use their legs like shock absorbers to counter the undulations of the uneven gravel surface than to sit and be jolted about on their backsides. Brody pushed the vehicle as fast as he dared, but they could not average more than 60 km/h.

Around them the dry bush was relatively tranquil. The road ahead was peppered with elephant dung in various stages of decay, from freshly steaming dark mounds to paler, flattened, dried stains. During their four-hour trip their advance was slowed by the large grey herbivores ambling along the road. Twice they came across buffalo, but large herds of impala were plentiful. Worryingly though, there was no sign of a vehicle that had passed recently, and no dust lingered in the air. After sunrise visibility improved and Brody turned off the main beam. At 7am they came across a kudu that had very recently been hit by a vehicle. It was dead and fresh blood dripped from its nostrils. A few minutes later they found the Bedford.

Initially they held back, expecting a trap. But when Douglas went on ahead to inspect it, he found three dead soldiers in the back; two had facial gunshot wounds and the other, an injury to the kidney area. The cab was abandoned. The front grille was dented, and clumps of kudu hair clung to the metal. Doug tapped the petrol tank – empty.

He returned to the Ford. "They've gone ahead on foot. Tanaka, come with me."

Tanaka set off at his usual tracking pace armed with his spear and knobkerrie, with Doug hot on his heals with his .404 slung over his shoulder. He maintained his pace for a good twenty minutes, studying the ground. Brody and Malcolm followed a few paces behind. Tanaka suddenly raised his clenched fist, signalling the party to halt. He pointed at the dusty path at a damp patch where someone had recently spat. Up ahead the pathway inclined and split. Both headed in a direction following the flow of the Ramaquabane river. Tanaka signalled that he and Doug would follow the lower of the two paths away from the footprints. He would attempt to get ahead of their quarry.

Malcolm and Brody readied their rifles and followed the used track. As the path elevation became more inclined and thicker with vegetation, the rushing flow of the river below masked all other sound. Brody took the lead. He rounded a narrow corner and a few metres ahead he saw Arthur Conway leading Mary by the bonds on her hands. The last remaining soldier brought up the rear of the group. He was pulling himself up a steep section of the gauge when Brody dropped to his knee and fired a single round.

The shot was clearly audible above the turbulent water and Conway turned. He saw Clause lying on the path, bleeding from a wound to his buttocks. Brody fired again, striking the soldier under his chin. Arthur returned fire from his drawn pistol as Brody and Malcolm dived for cover. Arthur's lungs were burning, and his chest pounded with each breath. From the crest of the gorge, it would be a short downhill run to the bridge leading to the airstrip, Otto Rendenbach, and freedom.

They continued their pursuit. Brody stopped and pointed out to Malcolm where Tanaka had advanced. He was slightly ahead of them, closing the gap between him and Conway as the paths slowly converged.

Brody put his hands together and bellowed, "Mary!"

She instantly froze. Arthur turned and aimed at Brody exposed in the middle of the path. Before he could fire, Tanaka hurled his knobkerrie that looped end over end in its ungainly flight before it connected sharply with the back of Conway's head. Arthur's glass eye dislodged and rattled on the ground as he collapsed. Mary ran down the path into Brody's open arms.

Malcolm closed the gap as Arthur lay staring up into the morning sky. He fired a single round into Conway's exposed chest. The bullet shattered spine vertebrae as it passed through. With his boot he nudged Arthur off the side of the path. Initially he slowly rolled in an ungainly tangle of paralysed limbs, but he increased his momentum until the final free fall sent him splashing into the water below.

From the shallow opposite bank, Malcom watched four crocodiles enter the water and swim lazily across the surface to where Arthur Conway floated on his back. One of the beasts sunk its jaws into his outstretched arm and immediately started its death roll spin. As bone, tendon and muscle were severed from his body, a demonic inhuman scream emitted briefly before his head was pulled underwater. It reemerged to be greeted by a second hungry mouth engulfing his skull. A violent shake of the leviathan's powerful neck plucked the head from the torso. The crocodile treaded water as it chewed and crunched down on its meal. The water boiled crimson red as the feeding frenzy freed the corpse of its limbs. As the crocodiles returned to the opposite bank, remnants of Arthur Conway's torso and blood were carried away on the current.

Malcolm picked up the glass eye and hurled it like a pebble into the water. As he watched the small inanimate object hit the river with barely a splash, he uttered the second part of the Mahaha's prophesy for no one else's benefit but his own: *"Beware the one-eyed snake that walks on two legs and swims with the crocodile. He must die twice."*

A cargo plane had taken off from somewhere nearby and flew low over the gorge, witnessing the spectacle.

Otto Rendenbach paced nervously back and forth below the monstrous C-47 cargo plane. Arthur was late. The unmistakable sound of gunfire stopped him in his tracks. He then made a series of decisions based on his own self-preservation. He had already carried out his pre-flight checks twice. He was only just over 5'6", but alone on the otherwise abandoned runway next to the camouflaged aeroplane with a length of 20 metres and a wingspan of 29, he looked like a lost insect. The aircraft itself should be manned by a minimum of three but he set in motion his single-handed flight.

Before settling into the cockpit, he offloaded a crate of Arthur Conway's worldly possessions and a briefcase belonging to his employer. Arthur was welcome to it if he survived, and so was anyone else that stumbled across it. He warmed the two radial Pratt and Witney 1200 horsepower twin engines and taxied down the runway.

The sluggish bird lifted off the uneven surface with shuddering groans as it started its ascent. Otto banked over the river in time to see Arthur Conway being consumed. He smiled and nodded to himself as if acknowledging a fitting end to a unique man that was neither friend nor foe. He tilted his wings up and down in a final farewell salute.

# Chapter 24

## CRAWLEY CONCESSION GOLD MINE – PENHALONGA, EASTERN HIGHLANDS, SOUTHERN RHODESIA – OCTOBER 1948

A storm was brewing. Through the cockpit canopy the single occupant had a spectacular view of boiling cumulonimbus clouds forming above the Eastern Highlands' mountain range. Strong winds, lightning and thundershowers were not the sort of weather to be flying in. It did not trouble the pilot; he was scheduled to land long before the heavens opened and unleashed the forecast deluge.

Otto Rendenbach nosed the Spitfire forward with an enormous sense of wellbeing. For the last six months he had not had to pander to the whims of the vengeful Arthur Conway. Countless times over the years he had been beckoned to ferry that man around Europe and Africa with a string of demands. He shook his head, recalling how frequently he had put his own life on the line in the process. Sure, he had benefited financially in every case, but to be rid of him filled the little German with elated freedom.

He thought about the gold bullion locked away in the secret safe underneath his lounge floor. Even without the profit share that would have gone to Conway, Otto was made for life. With the strong box now full, he had enough money to live wherever he wanted without working another day in his life. He could sell the mine and be done with the responsibility of managing his black workforce, done with the endless noise, mud and toil. He had not missed the mine one bit over the last two days. Otto was on his way back from Cape Town where he had viewed his future forever home, ten acres of vineyard overlooking an alcove on the coast. The homestead with its own airstrip and hangar, perfectly suited his needs. His offer had been accepted, he just needed to transfer the funds.

There was not a breath of wind as he banked to line up with Crawley Concession landing strip. The long dirt track was free of animals as he throttled back and touched down. Suddenly, directly ahead a creature materialised. A menacing blue human-form, tall and thin with long black hair. Its eyes glowed and it grinned as it hunched, staring at the approaching plane, unfazed by the impending collision. Otto could not swerve or slow down, so he braced for impact.

There was no thump when the aircraft passed through the Mahaha, but for a split-second Otto felt an acute tightness in the centre of his chest like an electric current passing through him. At the same time his ears were filled with raucous laughter, and his vision was full of blue dancing light. He came to a halt, breathless, clutching at his chest. He craned his head left and right for a view behind, expecting to see whatever it was lying in the dirt. There was nothing: the air strip was as clear as it had been before he prepared to land.

He looked down at his shaking hands and shook his head. "Otto, you are losing your marbles!"

As he approached the mine on foot, instead of the expected rhythmic clatter of the ball mill there was an ominous silence. It had been the usual hive of bustling activity when he left, but now there was not a soul to be seen. The conveyor belts were motionless, still laden with ore. The reduction plant was unmanned and deserted, as was the compound when he inspected it. He shook his head and returned to his house, confused. The first thing he did on entering was remove the rug in the centre of his lounge and unlock his safe. His rows of neatly stacked gold bars were as he had left them. He let out a huge sigh of relief and relocked the safe and covered it.

That night he lay awake in his bed, contemplating his options. Was it worth the effort to try and find his missing workforce? He decided that in the morning he would refuel his plane, take the gold and just abandon the mine. Shortly before midnight he eventually drifted off to sleep, but not for long.

Otto awoke, paralysed and covered in sweat. He could not blink, speak or move. He stared directly into the glowing pupilless white eyes of a blue human-like apparition levitating above his bed. The creature grinned ominously. When it spoke, the air became saturated with the smell of rotting flesh. It spoke a language Otto had never heard before, yet somehow, he was able to understand it.

*"I have come for my yellow metal you have pulled from the earth. I will return in seven years for more. Continue digging to continue living. Heed the words of the Mahaha."*

Time took on another dimension. Otto was unsure how long the visitation lasted. The words were repeated again and again for what seemed like an eternity. It was the same creature he had encountered earlier on the runway. Finally, it left, and Otto slipped into a deathlike sleep.

He woke with a splitting headache and searched about him frantically for his visitor. Had it been a nightmare? He recalled the strange words etched in his brain and, in a panic, threw aside the rug and opened the safe. It was empty...

## 23RD APRIL 1954 – HILLSIDE RANCH, INSIZA, BULAWAYO, SOUTHERN RHODESIA

Malcolm Hunter was sat on the balcony in his tailored black suit, paging through the latest batch of British newspapers. They were nearly two weeks old. A series of articles had been published under what the press budded, 'The Hillside Massacre'. The accounts were well written and an accurate insight into what had transpired that fateful night. He looked out over the trickle of well-dressed guests, some already seated on the neat rows of chairs set out on the manicured lawn.

Molly had spent two weeks in hospital recovering from her gunshot wounds before she and Mary moved into White Stone Farm with Malcolm. Hillside Ranch underwent radical redevelopment following the attack led by Arthur Conway. Although the main house had suffered superficial damage, most of the outbuildings were burned to the ground. A stone memorial was erected outside the original homestead. It bore the engraved names of all that perished. It included Henk, Lulama, Felix, the three Shackleton boys, and the men, women and children slaughtered in the compound, sixty-five in total. The old site of the compound was left as it was the night of the assault. The new settlement made from bricks and mortar and asbestos roofs was built to the east of the old location. It included a clinic and a school. The new workforce and their families never visited the old village. They believed it was haunted by the restless spirits of those that had passed. It was said that at night you could hear the cries of the dead reliving their torment.

Henk's cottage was restored to its former glory, with stone from Invictus mine and a thatched roof. The mantelpiece above the fireplace contained three identical brass urns personalised with the names of the deceased. The furniture in each room was remade to replicate its original state, right down to the sheepskin and cow hide scatter rugs. A plaque to the left of the front door read, "This house will forever be the home of Henk, Lulama and Felix tragically taken from us 23rd April 1948. May their souls rest in peace." Along with the refurbished main house it served as guest accommodation for visitors to Hillside Ranch.

As a tribute to her late husband Angus MacMillan, Molly had designed the new main double storey, six-bedroomed ranch house overlooking a stocked trout lake. Every bedroom upstairs enjoyed unobstructed views of the rambling acres down to the lower stream. Two separate lounges with matching large cowhide sofas were decorated with scatter cushions of the MacMillan and MacGregor tartans. They were separated by a spacious snooker room and bar. Above the stone fireplaces hung a tapestry of the Battle of Falkirk which had once taken pride of place in David MacGregor's study in Glasgow.

Molly's body healed a lot quicker than her mind. Her life had been a series of tragic losses. First Angus, then her brother Michael, both parents, Henk, his family, and most of the men, women and children from the compound. Even now, six years on, the series of tragedies troubled her thoughts.

Over the years since that fateful night she and Malcolm had drawn closer, initially as friends and eventually as lovers. There were parts of Malcom that still seemed locked away from her, but he became her dependable rock. Without him, she would never have got through the tragic events that befell her. Initially, she held back from emotional attachment to another man, loyal to the memory of her late husband, but over time Malcolm filled a void that was missing in her life. It took Malcolm a long time to let Molly into his heart, but his love for her grew from the smallest of embers into a steady flame. His life was enriched by her company and today as a symbol of their commitment to each other, they would be joined together as husband and wife.

Molly stared at her reflection in the mirror and adjusted the straps of her embroidered wedding dress to accommodate her enlarged breasts. She checked her side profile in the mirror and patted her stomach proudly. She wondered how Mary would take the news that she would have a baby brother or sister. And how would Malcolm react? She would tell them both after the wedding.

Molly initially refused to talk to local and international press following the assault on Hillside Ranch, but followed the articles released in 1948 outlining Arthur Conway's involvement in 95 murders. An abandoned crate and briefcase belonging to him was discovered on an airstrip in Bechuanaland near the Southern Rhodesian border. After being studied by local authorities it became the property of Scotland Yard. It helped to fill in the blanks of Arthur Conway's whereabouts over the years as he evaded international law enforcement.

Conway's trophy file included photographs of his four victims in Switzerland, two the authorities knew about and the burial locations of two more missing persons. The graphic photos were considered too shocking to be released to the press. There were pictures of the victim in Morocco, at the time thought to be carried out by a copy-cat killer. Most importantly, there were account codes to access Arthur's secret bank accounts. Once seized by the state, Mathew, the family solicitor from the Baker Montague and Forbes law firm, coordinated the distribution of the seized capital to the families of Conway's victims. After receiving the life assurance payout from her parents' policies, Molly waived the right to compensation from the Conway fund, but she helped to dispense the payouts to the local villagers affected by the attack. It was a lengthy process since most of them did not possess bank accounts.

The briefcase case also confirmed large payouts to Otto Rendenbach who Interpol were after but knew very little about. It turned out that he was running Malcolm's old Crawley Concession gold mine. Malcolm had kept a copy of the article published in the

Rhodesian Mining Journal in 1948 when Otto was found dead next to his aeroplane. The death was suspicious in that the mine had been completely abandoned and Otto was believed to have had a heart attack, but the article described his face as 'contorted into a sadistic grin'. None of the locals would comment on anything to do with the incident. Molly worked out that Otto's death was exactly seven years since Malcolm hunted down the infamous lion known as Samson. When she questioned Malcolm about it, he just brushed it off.

Two months ago, on the advice of her doctor and psychologist, Molly had finally agreed to meet with the British reporters from The Scotsman and The Daily Mirror to tell her story. The medical specialists suggested it would be good for her mental health to achieve a sense of closure with the events that took place on the 23rd of April 1948. The most recent series of articles entitled 'The Hillside Massacre' were based on first-hand accounts from herself, Malcolm, Mary, Tanaka, Brody, and Douglas. She had since been approached by an author who was interested in writing about her life story. She had not yet decided on whether to go ahead with the idea or not.

Mary stood in front of the full-length mirror while her maid adjusted the lace bodice to allow more room for her swollen breasts. Her elegantly fitted wedding gown hugged her curves. A knee length slit allowed her tanned legs to walk freely unhindered by the flowing dress tail. She stood sideways to inspect the profile of her belly. It could pass as reasonably flat if she pulled it in. By her calculation she was three months pregnant. She patted the little bump proudly, wishing she could have told her mother the happy news already, but she would wait until after the wedding.

She was not surprised that she was with child. Since she and Brody had lost their virginity together under the umbrella of the acacia tree next to Mermaids Pool four months ago, they had been together regularly. They both had an insatiable desire for each other, and it was a miracle they had managed to wait as long as they did. Once their carnal desires had been unleashed, it was an impossible flame to extinguish. Brody was the epitome of her perfect man. He was strong, handsome, smart, kind, gentle, funny, tender, and patient. Their lovemaking had evolved from its initial clumsy, needy, urgent thrusts to a tidal wave of coaxed pleasure that slowly grew to heights and depths that surpassed her wildest expectations. She felt her nipples harden just at the thought of having him inside her.

Since that dreadful night so long ago when the farm was attacked and she was taken hostage, Brody had become the most important person in her life. She loved her mother dearly, but Molly was so deeply scarred by her tragic losses that she sometimes became reclusive and lost in her own world. Malcolm was their level-headed, dependable male presence. Mary hoped that their wedding today would be a positive way forward for both Malcolm and her mother. Malcolm had opened his home to them while Hillside was being refurbished and the new homestead built. She had watched on as Malcolm and her mother's relationship changed over the years. They were both clearly fond of each other, but it was nothing like the passion she shared with Brody.

It was not just the physical act of love that Mary looked forward to. Instead of stolen moments and sneaking off in secret, they would be free to hold each other. Brody would be there at night when the demons came to haunt her sleep, just as he had been by her side in one way or another since the night she was abducted. He was the first person to hold her when she was rescued.

That day as he hugged her, he whispered in her ear, "I will look after you and defend you with the last drop of my blood. I love you."

The night of the dreadful attack the ranch was left in ruins. The awful culling of the innocent workforce and their families was too dreadful to comprehend, but Brody supervised the clearing up of the fallen men, women and children. The fire that had destroyed the huts spread to the dry fields where the cattle grazed. Their herd scattered in panic, some trapped and burned alive in the blaze, others stampeded through paddocks and boundaries. Again, Brody supervised the clean-up operation and the rounding up of escaped cattle.

On completion of her schooling, Molly suggested Mary attend art school in the UK, but the thought of being away from Brody for several years made it an impossible option to even contemplate. The only time she and Brody had had a disagreement was discussing where they would live once married. Space was not the issue, but the location was.

Brody and Douglas had built Cedar Tree Hollow together from day one. That blank canvas had been transformed into a profitable concern through their combined blood, sweat and tears. When Brody asked for Mary's hand in marriage, Molly had offered him the position of manager of Hillside Ranch. He would have access to limitless funds, but the trouble was, he would be an employee. For Brody it was not an attractive proposition. Mary had assumed he would just simply live in the brand-new homestead with her, Malcolm and Molly and live happily ever after. But it was not that simple: to Brody, ownership and space meant everything. They debated building a separate *manager's house*.

Hillside Ranch was not short on land, but negotiations broke down when Brody suggested that the solution once married was for Mary to live with him at Cedar Tree next door. The three-day stand-off culminated in Molly redesigning the homestead to have a self-contained three bedroomed wing where Mary and Brody would live, and Brody being given 20% equity in Hillside Ranch.

Ahead of their honeymoon in Scotland, two crates of Mary's oil paintings were carefully packed and dispatched to Edinburgh National Gallery where they were to be displayed at an exhibition during their visit. The owner of the gallery had bought one of Mary's pieces whilst on holiday in Salisbury and drove out to Hillside to personally meet the talented artist.

Mary looked out of her bedroom window at the gathering of guests on the lawn below. Today the double wedding symbolised new beginnings for them all.

Robert and Rachael Hunter were seated in the front row on the right, smartly dressed for the big occasion. They spent most of their time these days working together at White Stone farm. They grew Bana grass and maize crops that provided stock feed for Cedar Tree Hollow. Robert intended to make Malcolm an offer on the property. After today Malcolm would live with Molly here at Hillside Ranch, so it was perfect timing he thought.

Robert looked across at Rachael with a cheeky grin and put his arm around her. "It's good to see you so happy."

"I am happy, "she replied, "I'm happy that Brody has found a good woman. Since that dreadful nonsense in '48, our farm has truly become our home. It took me a long time to adjust to the move over here, but I must agree now it was a good idea to do it. Brody will be leaving home but he isn't going far, is he, just next door in fact. I just wish Douglas could find someone like Mary. She is such a lovely girl, and so talented."

"She is, yes. Between them they are going to produce good looking kids, won't they, *Granny Rachael?*"

"Don't say that, it reminds me how old I am."

"I will still fancy you when you're a gran, honey."

Hamish and Becky sat together with their twin boys Archie and William in the second row on the left. The two little devils had a shock of ginger hair and were covered in freckles.

Hamish leaned over to tick them off. "Hey! You two put your caps back on, otherwise you will fry like vampires in this bloody heat."

Becky groaned as she shifted in her seat to tuck William's shirt back in. Although she still had three months to go with her pregnancy, she was already huge.

"The next one had better be a girl," she said. The flight over from Scotland was hell. The excited kids had barely slept a wink and fought or played virtually the entire way. Hamish had slept through most of the hardship. She was already wishing she was back at home.

Douglas and Brody were in the car park, greeting guests and directing them through to the front garden. They were both dressed in matching black suits. Doug tugged at the tight collar underneath his bowtie to relieve his itchy neck.

A shiny, black, chauffeur-driven Bentley VI pulled up and out of the back a handsome middle-aged Caucasian man stepped out, but it was his companion Douglas could not keep his eyes off. She looked half the man's age. Her tightly fitted navy velvet dress hugged her curvaceous figure, emphasising her breasts. Her olive skin was flawless. Plaited jet-black hair reached down to the small of her back. Her dark brown eyes seemed to smoulder in her beautiful face, and when she smiled her perfect white teeth were framed by full ruby red lips. The couple walked up to Doug and Brody and introduced themselves.

The man offered his hand and said, "Greetings! I am Andrew Coil, and this is my daughter Isabelle. I hope you don't mind but we have come in place of Harold Bucket. It's probably not a bad thing to be honest because his *plus one* would have been a wheelbarrow and a keg of whiskey. I'm not in the country for long. I was hoping to have a word with Malcolm Hunter."

Isabelle offered her gloved hand to Doug who took hold of it and gently kissed it. Her smile was the most beautiful thing he had ever seen. Brody ushered them off in the direction of the front lawn, and looked at his brother who was watching Isabelle's jostling buttocks as she walked away.

Doug looked at Brody and said, "What?"

Brody punched his shoulder and replied, "Close your mouth, you're drooling."

Malcolm met Andrew and Isabelle Coil on the lawn and showed them to their seats.

Before he sat down, Andrew turned to Malcolm and said, "I wish to speak to you later, Mr Hunter. I have been tasked to design what will be the largest manmade lake in the world here in Southern Rhodesia on the Zambezi River. I'm hoping you might put me in touch with a colleague of yours, Ashton George, the geologist."

After they were seated, Malcolm stood at the back of the rows of seats and a strange sensation washed over him. He felt a tug and when he looked down there was a naked black child holding his hand. She looked about three years old, but her blue eyes were strikingly familiar.

She looked up at Malcolm and whispered, "Nyoka (snake)."

Then her voice changed to that of Hupenyu the witch doctor. She pointed in the direction of Andrew Coil and said, "*When you anger the serpent river god, his vengeance will be floodwater of fire and smoke.*"

Malcolm stared at Andrew Coil in a new light, with his skin tingling. At a turning point in his life, the day of his wedding to Molly, a complete stranger had entered his world. A man somehow connected to the final chapter of the Mahaha's prophecy. Hupenyu saw fit to reinforce a warning. He looked back at the little girl by his side, but she was gone…